The McClane Apocalypse
Book Seven

Kate Morris
Ranger Publishing 2017

Ranger Publishing
Copyright © 2017 by Ranger Publishing

Ranger Publishing can bring authors to your live event. For more information or to book an event, contact Ranger Publishing @gmail.com or contact the author directly through KateMorrisauthor.com or authorkatemorris@gmail.com

Cover design by Ebook Launch.com

Manufactured in the United States of America
Library of Congress Cataloging-in-Publication Data is on file
ISBN 13: 978-1545449776
ISBN 10: 1545449775

Dedication

To my McClane fans who have supported the series from the beginning. Thank you so much for all the fan letters, emails, and Facebook messages. Your kind words and support have kept me going through some difficult times the last few years and encouraged me to continue on with this series.

As always, please continue to support our troops and visit RangerUp.com. Buy a cool t-shirt, be the envy of your friends, and spread the message. Twenty-two a day is still too many.

Thanks,

Kate

Chapter One
Sam

Life in Dave's compound is much different than it was with the McClane family. She was placed in a women's barracks, or so that's what Dave's wife explained them to be. It is more like a long bunkhouse with many twin-size beds, two showers that don't always run very hot water, and a single toilet room. Gunny's family housed their dairy farm laborers in the bunkhouse. Those people are long gone, likely out there somewhere with their own families. Or at least Sam hopes they have reunited with their loved ones. The building is constructed of painted white cement blocks with a matching interior. She'd like to paint the walls with murals of lovely shades, but at least the building is cozy and warm, especially with the cold winter settling in. There are two girls much younger than her, orphans who were taken in by Dave's group living in the bunkhouse. Also cohabitating in the building are around twenty women older than her, widows of the apocalypse, or women who were taken in from the sex camp who were freed. There is also a girl her age, Courtney, with whom she'd become fast friends. Her parents had also been killed by violent marauders in the beginning. She'd traveled with a small group far from her home in Virginia until they were also attacked. That's when Dave's group came upon the survivors. The others had gone their own way, but Courtney had decided to stay on with Dave's people. Sam is certainly glad she did since it is safer than being on the road. She is very thankful for the newfound friendship. It helps to soften the ache of homesickness she feels when she allows herself to dwell on her McClane family.

Dave's wife, Connie, has also helped her along. She is very sweet, mild-mannered and doesn't put up with much from her raucous husband. They are rather humorous to watch. She is usually pretty busy with her own children, though. They have three; two boys and a girl. They are all much younger than Sam, as well, but she tries to help Connie with them when she can. She has her own set of chores that she must attend to each day that requires much of her time.

Although she misses her McClane family, having her uncle back in her life has been the biggest blessing. They have been working day and night trying to establish their own medical clinic that she'll help him run, along with Dave's Army medic and a nurse they rescued from the sex camp. She's also been studying and learning a lot from the nurse. Gunny's large farm is completely secure and just outside the town of Hendersonville. They have converted one of the equipment sheds into a men's barracks, complete with newly finished plumbing and heat. There is a house nearby that they are trying to fix up into a medical clinic. Some of Gunny's, or Henry as she now calls him, men have been hanging drywall and plywood and building interior walls to make individual patient rooms. Dave seems less worried about allowing people from town so close to their farm than the men in her family always were. Grandpa's farm was always a secret, but Henry's compound is less remote than the McClane farm, and he said that everyone already knew about it and about Henry's family. His farm is an impenetrable fortress in Sam's opinion. She feels safe, and that's not something to take lightly, as she knows so well.

She rises before dawn, unable to sleep and anxious to be up and moving. Dave and a few of his men are meeting with some of the McClane group to head north to Fort Knox. It makes her uneasy. She is unsure and distrustful of Robert McClane and his motives. She wanted so badly to tell Dave of her feelings, but she doesn't know him that well yet. So, instead, she is going out to feed the horses, of which they have many more on Henry's farm. They also have many more people living on his farm, so it makes sense to have a bigger herd of livestock. Sam pulls on black jeans, an orange sweater and her black coat. Lug sole boots are last. The weather has been dry but cold lately. She can't wait for spring.

"Where ya' headed?" Courtney asks from her bed near Sam's, startling her.

"Out to feed the horses," Sam whispers so as not to awaken the other sleeping women and children. She has her own twin bed, but many are still sleeping on roll-away cots that Henry explained they found in a hotel in Nashville. They are working every day on runs to acquire more bedding, beds and linens.

"Wait up," her new friend whispers in return. "I'll come with you."

Sam bides her time organizing her space and making sure everything is neat and tidy while her friend pulls on clothing and shoes. Courtney hadn't come to Henry's farm with much, according to her. She and her group had been robbed many times while she was with them, leaving her with so little. Dave's wife has taken it upon herself to become the den mother to all of the young women and orphans on the farm. She and Dave live in the main house with Henry, but the other soldiers and their families either live in bunk housing like Sam or in small cabins they've built over the years. Connie makes sure they all have what they need, including clothing and toiletries. Or she makes her husband get it for them while he and his men are out on runs for supplies. Sam hadn't needed anything from the new group because she'd brought everything she owned from the farm. She even has her art supplies tucked securely away under her bed, but she hasn't felt motivated to draw anything yet. There hasn't been inspiration in her new surroundings. The first few nights, she'd wept quietly in her bunk. She was terribly homesick for the family and heartbroken because of him. But she has learned that time does heal one's wounds. She just wishes that she didn't have them to begin with.

"Ready," Courtney whispers and taps her shoulder.

They leave the building, closing the door behind them quietly so the other women can sleep. The work on Dave's compound is no less time-consuming and tiring than on the McClane farm. Everyone needs their rest, and most crash at night like they are going into a coma. She is finally sleeping a few hours at a time but not usually the whole night. There was a big adjustment period that she went through the first few nights. It hasn't really sunk in yet. The sounds, the strange bed and sleeping quarters, the different people, none of it helps her sleep. At night, the biggest problem is being left alone with her own thoughts, which haunt her like apparitions from her past. They do nothing to calm her spirit to prepare for deep sleep. Most nights, she lies awake for hours.

She and Courtney walk to the horse barn, which is a former single story building with a dirt and sawdust floor where hay was stored. They keep the hay in the loft of the old bank barn now and the horses in the open barn. They don't have stalls, but there is a gate at the end to keep them locked in for the night. Like the McClane farm, they only keep pregnant mares or injured horses in the barn. It reminds her of the farm where she took riding lessons when she was younger. It's more of an indoor riding arena than a hay or horse barn anyway and is built like Grandpa's equipment shed. At one end are two, small stalls where they allow the pregnant mares to give birth. It keeps them safer than allowing them to do so in the field where other horses could interfere.

When they arrive at the barn, Sam scoops oats into a wheelbarrow while Courtney grabs a clean set of leg wraps for a gelding with a bowed tendon. Sam is fairly sure he'll never be ridden again. That type of injury is not usually something most horses can fully recover from, especially at his age. At best, he'll only be able to handle the weight of someone small or a child and definitely not at a pace faster than a walk. She overheard Dave discussing it with his men that maybe they should donate the horse to town for meat. She's glad it never came to that at the McClane farm.

"Got my wraps for Buddy," Courtney declares. "I'll meet you out there."

4

"'Kay," Sam answers with a smile.

The sun is just rising as she pours the last scoop into the cart and pushes it toward the horse pen. She doesn't get far before one of Dave's men, a sentry that Dave keeps on the barn at all times, meets up with her and insists on taking it.

"I've got this, ma'am," he says.

Sam offers a grim smile and nods. "Sure."

His men are all mannerly, kind and sometimes a little too helpful. She hardly does any work on the farm because as soon as she tries to lift a finger, she is met with this.

"Thanks…," she pauses, trying to remember his name.

"Perry, ma'am," he answers for her and tips his tattered military cap.

"Right, sorry," she apologizes.

"No problem, miss," he says with a wink and resumes pushing the wheelbarrow again.

"Are you off to catch some sleep now?" she asks, making small talk with him.

"Nah, I'm on for the rest of the day," he answers.

"Why?" she asks. "I thought you guys took turns on watch duty."

"Yes, ma'am," he says. "We normally do, but with Sergeant Winters being gone, we gotta' stay on shift."

"Right, makes sense," she concurs. This is something that is troubling her very greatly. Dave and his men are meeting up with Cory, John and Kelly, who agreed to escort Hannah's father to Fort Knox, check out the place. They have all promised to return to their prospective farms posthaste, and Sam hopes it is true. The original agreement with Grandpa was that Kelly wouldn't leave the farm, but he also didn't feel comfortable leaving the decision to John alone as to whether or not to get involved in Robert's plans. She's very worried about all of them, but she knows that Hannah must be out her mind. And Sam is also worried about Dave, too. He is a very kind, good man who has so many people relying on him. She certainly doesn't want anything to happen to him or his men while they are on the road. She knows firsthand how dangerous it can be out there.

"Don't worry, miss," he says, trying to allay her concerns that must be so visible on her face.

"Sure, that's simple," she says in a joking tone. She gets a smile in return from the stocky soldier. She's pretty sure he was a part of Dave's team in the Army. There are so many more people roaming around on this farm that it's been a struggle getting to know and remember each one.

Perry leaves the wheelbarrow near the gate in the barn for her and tips his hat and leaves. She spreads the crimped oats in a long, black rubber trough for the horses, who finally realize that she is there bearing breakfast. They nicker and whinny to her in greeting. There are only five horses in the arena, so they don't fight and kick at each other. If there were more, it might turn into an all-out food war. She joins Courtney in the stall at the back of the barn where she is rewrapping the gelding's legs.

"Six months ago, I didn't know squat about horses," Courtney confesses.

"Really? You're a natural with them," Sam praises.

"I've learned a lot from Gunny. He's a great trainer. Loves farming."

Sam hasn't had much of a chance to get to know Henry yet, but he seems very nice. The fact that he's letting her and her uncle live on his farm doesn't hurt in her estimation of him. Everyone calls him Gunny because he used to be the machine gunner in some military unit. He's a lot like Kelly and Cory, big and imposing. But she suspects he's a lot deeper than they give him credit for being.

"Yeah, he seems very patient," Sam replies.

They finish their chores and head out to the dairy barn. Gunny's family farm used to be a huge dairy operation. They had a few horses for entertainment, but it was mostly a dairy farm. When Dave and his men came, they increased the herd of horses substantially. They still run quite a few head of cattle, mostly because of the demand. They trade dairy products with the townspeople in

Hendersonville for supplies. Dave's group is a lot less generous and more business-like with their town than the McClanes, who primarily act as good stewards of the town of Pleasant View. Dave doesn't put up with much from the townspeople, according to her uncle. If they want something from his group, he demands a barter. If they can't give anything, then they are expected to work off their trade in labor. Uncle Scott also told her that the people respect him and Gunny, who acts as Dave's right-hand man. Everyone knows that the farm belongs to Henry, and they admire him for sharing in the bounty of their toils at the farm with them, even if they have to trade for it. They don't share food with the townspeople other than the overflow of dairy goods. Each family in town is expected to grow gardens and hunt for their own food. Her uncle explained that there are just too many families living on the farm to share in the food stores.

They are up to twenty-three horses, and none of them are used for entertainment anymore. His horses pull plows, take people on patrols, and work as farm equipment when the implements aren't running. They don't quite have all the unusual setups that Grandpa initiated on the farm with the equipment, but they do have other inventions that have aided in their survival. She knows that John and Derek are hoping for a visit when they return from Fort Knox so that they can discover and exchange ideas with Dave and Henry. Cory, being the most mechanically minded, will no doubt come, too. As far as Sam is concerned, having Dave's group as allies will probably be a very vital asset in the McClane family's future.

There are already six people milking cows in the dairy barn when they arrive, so they walk to the chicken pen where Sam releases them for the day. The birds cram through the small door, their feathers flapping and shedding in their haste to be the first ones to the morning meal of grubs and bugs. Some things don't change on a farm, even if one's address does.

After they have collected the eggs into the baskets and boxes near the coop, she and Courtney turn and head to the main house where the eggs will be washed and stored. There is a 'mess hall,' which she at first thought was an untidy hallway and had mistakenly figured that people just dropped their coats and hats on the floor. Dave had chuckled at her and rubbed the top of her head. It had made her homesick for John's attention. Then he explained that the mess hall was where everyone joined for meals. Feeding so many families is an ordeal of epic proportions. The mess hall is a building that the men built when they first arrived on Henry's farm. It can hold many tables and chairs and families, which it does for most meals. There are picnic tables and long, rustic tables and benches that the men made from wood harvested on the farm. Occasionally the men in Dave's group, his inner circle of soldiers, will dine in the main house so that they can hold meetings. But most of the time they all eat together when it is at all possible due to work and sentry schedules. Sam can smell the aromas of breakfast being prepared in the mess hall. It makes her mouth water and her heart sick as she misses Hannah and Sue.

"Good morning, ladies," Henry says as he looks up from his coffee at the kitchen table and quickly stands. As far as creature comforts go, Dave's compound is a lot more stocked up on certain items than the McClane farm. With so many more soldiers to go on runs, they have quite the stockpile. A few other soldiers are sitting with him, and they all rise to greet Courtney and her. Sam just nods and waves before leaving. She trusts Henry and Dave. She's not sure about the rest of them, although she knows that Dave would never allow predators into his compound. Most of them, she's learning, are men from his unit.

Courtney stays and chats with them. Sam suspects that she has a crush on the one man with dark skin and hazel eyes and a muscular build. His face lights up every time he sees Courtney, and he has a magnificent, broad, and brilliantly white smile. But he usually tries to hide it. Sam is pretty sure he is just shy, especially around her new friend. He is a very imposing figure, and she overheard one of the men teasing him about being quite the lethal killer. He'd given his friends a dirty look when he'd noticed that Sam had entered the room. Apparently, he doesn't want his more sinister side to be exposed to the women, especially not Sam who could take negative intel back to Courtney. His secret's safe with her, though. Everyone has something they want to keep concealed from the ones they love. He is sweet and kind, but she can't remember his name, either. Lieutenant Stevens, perhaps. Dave's compound is a lot like Grandpa's farm with all of the military men and their crazy nicknames for one another. As soon as she has someone's name memorized, they go and call each other something else like AIT Barbie, or Flash-Bang, or Alley-Cat. She's still not sure how someone would catch the nickname Alley-Cat in the first place. She's pretty sure a lot of the call signs are negative and insulting. It's going to take some time getting to know everyone.

"Miss Patterson, wait up," Henry calls, tugging on his coat as he exits the home behind her.

His house is nice, quaint, not as big as Grandpa's. But it is a typical, white four-bedroom, two bath older farm house. It's cozy. The touches his mother must've placed in the home are still present, like the doilies on the oak coffee tables, the nick-knacks and candlesticks on the fireplace, family photos in silver frames.

"Did you need to speak with me?" she asks. Sam wants to help out in the mess hall. Like the McClane family, Dave's group has a lot of little kids that need attention and looking after. Some of the soldiers have wives and children of their own. She is on her way to help set up the buffet tables, which is how they serve all meals.

"Um, yes, ma'am," Henry answers, shoving his hands deep into his coat pockets. His breath comes out in white vapor clouds in the cold morning air. "Are you settling in all right?"

"Yes, fine," she answers. It's the truth. She has settled in. she just wishes that she hadn't had to because she misses her home and family.

"Do you need anything?" he asks. "Clothing? Warmer underclothes or anything?"

"No, I'm good. I've got everything I need," she replies with a nod and a half grin. The smile is fake. She finds that if she offers it, even if it doesn't come from a genuine place, it still comes off as sincere. If she had everything she needed, she'd still be living at the

McClane farm. But she does have everything she needs to survive. At least, for now, she does.

"Yes, ma'am," he says and then adds, "Just let me know if you require anything else. I've got an in with the guy that runs this place."

He winks for good measure. This time Sam does grin crookedly.

"Sure. Thanks," she answers and walks away.

He's a nice guy. It seems like most of Dave's men are decent and trustworthy. She's just not the kind of person who can trust people anymore, even if they seem harmless.

She keeps busy the rest of the morning in the mess hall setting up the buffet with some of the other women and teenagers while waiting for her uncle to awaken. He's been burning the midnight oil studying diseases, especially plagues and poxes. He reminds her a lot of Reagan, who she desperately misses. It's like a hole has been punched into her chest, and she's waiting around for someone to magically fill it in again, to erase the hollow feeling she has there now. That place where her love for Simon used to dwell.

Chapter Two
Cory

They've been driving a short time, haven't come across any roaming vandals, which is unusual for them, and are traveling in the Hummer behind Dave's pick-up truck full of men. Cory is fairly confident of their returning to the farm unharmed being a nearly one hundred percent probability. Dave's team has a fifty cal mounted on the bed of the pick-up truck like the technical they encountered many times in the Middle East as Dave described it with a laugh. It helps the odds. Plus, four more men are in the deuce and a half bringing up the rear.

Reagan's father has been sleeping in the back of the Hummer most of the trip so far. They brought along enough sleeping bags and supplies for camping out in the woods somewhere if it comes to that. Her father still seems too weak and frail to even make a trip to their small town, but he felt it was necessary to meet up with his men, which is a whole hell of a lot farther than their town.

His brother is driving while John rides shotgun and he rides in the back.

"Hey!" John calls out. "Pull over… yeah, up there, bro. At the convenience store."

Kelly maneuvers the vehicle while John radios the truck to let them know of the stop.

"Need help?" his brother asks.

"Nah, I got this," John answers with a wink.

John jumps out of the Hummer, and Cory follows to stretch his legs but more importantly to keep watch. Kelly stays behind the wheel but has his window rolled down in case something happens, and Robert is still dead out in the hatch.

"What the hell's he doin'?" Dave asks as he approaches on foot. "Gotta take a piss or something?"

"Not sure," Kelly answers.

A moment later, John emerges from the store again and jogs to them. He tosses a bag of hard candy to Cory, who nods appreciatively, and hands Dave a twelve pack of beer. He pulls two cans of baby formula from his pack to show them.

"You went on a fuckin' beer and formula run?" Dave inquires. "This is startin' to feel all too goddamn familiar."

Everyone laughs. The way Dave delivers his words with a slow, hanging drawl is a crack up to Cory. His sarcasm is dry, and he uses the f-word rather prolifically.

"No, looking for something for the little woman," John explains.

"Piss warm beer?" Dave asks as he removes his ball cap, pulls his long ponytail back into the cap again, and replaces it to his head.

John chuckles and says, "No, she has this affinity for Skittles candy, my friend."

"Candy," Dave replies drolly.

"Sugar junky," John says sheepishly.

"And she's pregnant," Kelly puts in.

"Oh, well, why didn't you fuckin' say so?" Dave jests. "It all makes sense now."

Some of the other men laugh and jeer in a moment of mutual male camaraderie. Dave tosses beer to his men and offers one to John, who refuses. So do Cory and Kelly. He's not a big fan of beer, especially warm, four-year-old beer.

"My wife wanted damn pickles. Pickles!" Dave says loudly above the melee. "Where the hell was I supposed to get pickles?"

"Did you find some?" Kelly asks with a lingering grin.

"Hell yes, I did!" Dave replies with a grave expression. "I'm not a total fuckin' idiot, man."

Everyone laughs again. Dave grins crookedly. He is not a big man like himself and Kelly but more lean, shorter, and lanky as hell. There isn't an ounce of fat on him, and Cory's pretty sure he could give him a good run of it in a fistfight.

One of Dave's men asks, "Did you get your woman the Skittles, bro?"

"No, gonna have to keep lookin'," John answers.

"We'll all keep an eye out. Don't want you to get your balls busted when you go home," Dave says, punches his fist to John's and turns to go.

They pile into the vehicles again to resume their journey. Two cans of formula for their newly orphaned and adopted baby on the farm isn't going to go very far. They are hoping to find cases or even a damn pallet of the stuff. Daniel is already small; he needs formula or a lactating wet nurse, of which nobody can find. Talia volunteered, of course, to nurse him when she delivers her own baby, but that is a long way off. The kid needs sustenance now. Cory worries the little guy won't make it. They all do, and it pisses him off. Anything that messes with kids, even fate, angers the men on the farm. He knows Doc is feeling the full burden of this situation on his shoulders.

The road is cluttered with abandoned vehicles, and a light snow must've fallen last night in this area. Cory hopes they don't get into shitty weather the farther north they go. It was bad enough last winter when he was on his own in Ohio and Pennsylvania. Usually, Tennessee doesn't have the harsh winters that the more northern states suffer. He's glad Doc's farm wasn't established in Pittsburgh or Cleveland. He's not looking forward to bad weather on top of everything else that could be waiting for them up north at Knox.

He's thought a lot about Robert and his plans. Cory's not sure what to think of this potential civil war. He sure as hell doesn't feel any allegiance to Robert McClane, but he does bear a fierce loyalty to Doc and his family. They took him and his brother and sister in without the faintest hesitation. Doc also took in Huntley, Sam and Simon without question. He knows this for sure. He was able to sit in on some of those meetings. He owes Herb McClane everything. However, he doesn't want to fight for his son. Robert seems power hungry, even if he doesn't want anyone to see through his claims of not wanting to run the country. Cory believes that about as much as he believed that Sheriff Jay didn't want to run his new town that ended up being a flop.

He's relieved that Jay Hernandez and his people are gone. It took them a few days to pack everything and get a caravan moving south, but at least they're gone and nobody has to worry about them anymore. Cory had been a part of the secret detail that had ensured that Jay's group had moved on. He and Derek took two of Dave's men, including his sniper, and followed them for about thirty miles. It was important to insist they leave the area. He knew how hard the decision was, but Cory also understood that it needed to be done, which is why he also volunteered to make sure they followed through with their agreement and left. Jay was a terrible judge of character who'd allowed jerkoffs into his town who had almost killed some of the McClane family and his own people. Cory worries that Jay will end up getting his people killed, but he also isn't going to lose sleep over it, either. He has his own family to look after. He's hoping he can take over the responsibility someday of also considering himself to be the sole proprietor of Paige's care.

"Up ahead," John says over his shoulder. "Stay frosty."

Cory sits up straighter and leans forward slightly in his seat. He sees what John and his brother caught sight of before he did since he was daydreaming about Paige, something he does with too much frequency. She's a huge distraction, and one he thought he'd never encounter in this lifetime.

There are cars and trucks left on the sides of the road, a few in the middle of the freeway and some flipped over onto their sides and roofs. That isn't the disturbing part. That's normal to see. There are also dead bodies. This is the part that isn't as common.

14

"Damn," Kelly remarks as they veer around the bodies and follow Dave's truck, which is being driven by one of his men.

"What the hell is going on around here?" Cory asks quietly as he notices fresh, red blood near some of the bodies. Sometimes they'll encounter dead bodies, but they are usually in a state of late decomposition. If they were murdered, as most of them usually are, the blood around them is dark brown or even just a black stain on the concrete or other surfaces. This is clearly fresh.

"Looks like a battle took place," John observes.

His brother slows to a snail's pace as does the truck in front of them. "I don't think these people were the victors."

"No," John agrees.

"Wonder what happened?" Cory asks rhetorically.

Kelly ponders, "Fighting for food maybe."

Perhaps his brother is right. In the middle of the street is a lot of debris and a few empty coolers. The people seem to have been unarmed, but maybe the others who killed them took their weapons when they defeated them. It sends an unbidden chill up his spine.

"Few days ago at best," John notes. "This happened fairly recently if I were to guess."

"Yeah, they haven't been here long," Cory agrees. "Covered in snow but not rotted or gnawed on by wild animals yet."

Dave calls them on their radio and says they'll take another route. Dave knew they would occasionally be stopping to scout out baby formula, so they'd planned on arriving at their destination by tomorrow morning since it is not far. They may be taking a longer path to get there. Cory would like to return to the farm as soon as possible, so this pisses him off. However, they don't need to engage a group in a battle while they aren't on their home turf, especially if it is a large group of people.

As they veer around bodies and vehicles, Cory sees in a ditch a woman who has clearly been raped by whoever assaulted and killed this group. It turns his stomach. There is extensive bruising around her neck. Someone has strangled her and left her for dead in a ditch with the bottom half of her body exposed. John sees her, as well, because he groans with disgust. If this were another time, another day and the two of them were just on a supply run, their plans would change, and they'd hunt down the bastards who did this. Then they'd take the intel back to the farm and gather the other soldiers to take them out. Today, for now, these bastards have earned a reprieve. But if he knows John as well as he thinks he does, his friend and mentor is also contemplating a return to this site in a few days to do some tracking.

They trudge along on a back road that hasn't seen maintenance in years and has the ruts to prove it as Cory wipes down his rifle with a well-oiled rag from his pack. He snacks on the hard caramel candies that John lifted at the convenience store. He'll take the rest of the bag home to the kids. This trip is dragging ass. They stop twice more to remove debris and fallen trees from the road. They should've been able to make it to Knox in three hours or less, but this is going to be an all-day excursion. Travel is never fast anymore. Moving around on horseback is sometimes faster. Dave's truck makes a left at the next intersection, and they continue on at a snail's pace.

"What the hell happened here?" Kelly asks as he slows to a stop.

Cory looks out his window at their surroundings. Trees have been knocked over into the road, their branches scattered like toothpicks from a fallen box.

"Trouble?" Kelly asks.

"Not sure," John replies.

Cory isn't sure, either. As he glances around, he can see other trees in the woods near them that have had their tops knocked off and are laying on the ground.

"High wind storm or a trap?" John asks.

Cory's brother nods, "Maybe a bad storm. Hope it's not a trap. We don't have time for this shit."

Cory adds, "This is gonna take a while to get around all the shit in the road."

"What's going on?" Robert asks wearily from the back.

His wife promptly replies, "Nothing, dear. Just some trees in the road. Rest, Robert."

She reaches over the seat to pull his blanket up higher onto his thin shoulder. He nods and is out again within seconds.

The rest of them get out of the vehicle.

"Stay here," Cory tells her before following his brother to Dave's truck.

"Do what you do best, you rangy, raggedy-assed bastards!" Dave calls out to his men with great affection. "Move out!"

They lightning speed separate, and Dave is sending groups of men to scout the surrounding area for trouble. Cory waits with his team for orders from Kelly or John. They don't give a command, so he continues to stand guard at the front of their vehicle scanning the area carefully. He notices that his brother's posture is tenser than his own. Cory wonders if it is because he senses danger or if the situation itself has him on edge. He's noticed lately that anytime he has to leave the farm, Kelly seems more and more uncomfortable. Cory doesn't blame him. His brother has a wife and kid back home. It would make Cory nervous leaving them, too.

"All clear," comes across Dave's radio in intermittent calls.

"Must've been a storm ran through here, sir," one of his men says to him when he rejoins the group.

"Yeah, saw what's left of a few homes on that ridge over yonder," another with a particularly strong, southern accent remarks as he points west of them. He is as well-conditioned to the fast perimeter check at a brisk pace as Cory would've been. He isn't winded, nor does he seem tired even though it was a wide check. "They're either burnt to the ground or leveled flat like kindling. No human coulda' done that."

"Yes, sir," the first one confirms as the others come in from their routes. "Tornado for sure."

"Lucky it missed us," Dave admits. "Let's clear this road and get movin' again."

"You heard him, boys," the one with the southern accent commands. "Asses and elbows, people!"

Dave turns to them and says, "If those asshats from the road back there get in our path, we'll be mowing them down."

"Hooah," John says and bumps his friend's fist.

Kelly nods and adds, "Yeah, we don't have time for shit like that. We've gotta get back to our farms."

"Planting season will be on us soon," Cory says.

Dave chuckles and says, "Hell yes, it will be. We're all a bunch of farmers now."

"Farmers who shoot people on occasion," John jokes, earning another fist bump from Dave.

"I see, you're carrying an M4, Doctor Death," Dave remarks.

"Yeah, picked it up in Arkansas when we stopped to find Kelly's family," John explains, unslinging and flipping the short rifle over to show his friend.

"You like that better than the 16?" their friend inquires.

"Sometimes," John answers honestly. "Still keep the Kimber on my side, though. For those reach out and touch someone close quarters kind of situations."

"Yeah?" Dave says. "I've got a .44 cal for that."

He whips it out and turns it sideways so they can get a look.

"Subtle," John jokes.

"Now there's a pistol," Cory remarks with respect. The wood grips are inlaid with what looks like rosewood swirls, metal that is probably real silver and gold. He's a little jealous.

"She does have a bark," Dave says with a lopsided grin. "I call her 'Betty'."

"Betty's one mean bitch," Cory jokes.

Dave laughs and says, "Betty was my mom's name."

"Oh, shit!" Cory says. "Sorry, man."

"No, my mom was a mean bitch, too. That's why I call my girl here that," Dave expands, causing uproarious laughter from everyone.

His brother, ever the pragmatic one, says, "Good stopping power, though. Practical choice. Six shooter, though. I prefer a fifteen round mag."

Dave chuffs and says, "That's 'cuz you can't hit shit, old man."

"Hey, my eyesight ain't what it used to be."

They all have a chuckle as Dave's men continue to clear the area. He leaves the men to their gun talk and jogs over to help Dave's men. He hauls branches away while two of Dave's men use a chainsaw and cut up a large felled tree resting at an awkward slant across the road. A retching sound catches his attention, and he pauses in his work to go investigate. A few feet into the woods he spies Robert and his wife. The man is bent over and vomiting into the weeds while Lucy rubs his back. He sounds awful. Cory wonders if this trip was a bad idea. He has wondered the same thing many times since the first mention of it, but not because he was worried about Robert's health. Leaving the farm so weakly fortified makes him anxious. The Professor stayed behind with Derek and Doc, and a few of Dave's men are supposed to come by and check on the place, but Cory hopes this all goes smoothly so that they can return as soon as possible.

Knowing Simon is keeping an eye on Paige, which he no doubt is doing, makes him feel a little better. He'd just rather do the job himself. He still wakes up with nightmares in the middle of the night as his mind recalls the shooting and tortures his subconscious with the vivid images. He can still see her being shot and crying out. She'd taken a bullet for his brother. When he'd first met Paige, Cory never would've thought her capable of being selfless. Now he knows her so well, so intimately. He also knows he's in love with her. He knows that she's in love with him, too. She just doesn't want to admit it. That's fine. He is a patient man, somewhat. She'll come around. And if she really doesn't love him, he'll find a way to convince her that she does.

After they remove the rest of the debris, they get moving again after Kelly helps Robert back into the Hummer. Cory is pretty sure Reagan's dad isn't going to make it, but he holds his tongue. The dude looks like he has one foot in the grave.

"You doing all right back there, sir?" Kelly asks.

Cory is surprised at his brother's show of respect. He knows his brother is not fond of Robert. Most of the people on the farm are not.

"Yes, fine, thank you. Just a little motion sick," Robert replies.

Cory doesn't believe him in the least. Her father falls asleep again within moments, and his wife dozes beside Cory against the window. They aren't much for road trip companionship, not that he requires any from either of them.

A short distance up the road, they run into a family in what appears to be a broken-down RV. It is parked in the middle of the road at a slant, flanked by abandoned vehicles on either side. Their choice is going to be to push it out of the way or drive down into the muddy berm, which is steep and they could possibly get stuck. The hood is up, the side panels open, and people are standing around it, including women and children.

"Looks like they could use our help," John says what they are thinking.

"Yeah," Kelly remarks and pulls up beside Dave in the road about fifty yards from the stranded motorists. They make a plan to offer aid if they are friendly. Cory volunteers to approach them with John and Dave at his side. Kelly will provide cover along with the rest of Dave's men.

"Having trouble, folks?" John calls out as they approach within twenty feet.

A man in his late forties says, "Yes, I think it's the radiator."

"We might be able to help out with that," Dave says in a quieter tone as they come within ten feet.

"Good, we'll take your supplies and your guns and food," a young man says as he rounds the other side of the RV with a shotgun raised to his shoulder.

Chapter Three
Paige

The weather isn't as miserable cold as it has been, so she dons a warm coat and hat and heads outside. She has been cooped up for so long and laid up for weeks with her wound that the idea of one more day of resting on the sofa seems like a cruel form of torture.

"Where do you think you're going?" Sue asks as they pass in the yard.

"Um, don't know. Anywhere."

Sue chuckles and says, "Tired of being stuck in the house?"

"Oh, yes," Paige answers on a full exhale.

"I'll walk with you," her friend offers.

"You don't have to," Paige is quick to answer. "I know you're busy with the kids and all that."

Sue rolls her eyes and says, "I could use a break, too."

Paige smiles with understanding. "I bet you could."

They stroll over toward the chicken coop, which now has a small addition attached and constructed from the salvaged wood pile in the horse barn. This is strictly for nesting hens and new mothers thanks to Cory's construction skills and her architectural design. He even cut out the profile of a hen with her two peeps from a leftover piece of plywood. He commissioned the little kids to paint the artwork. There are definitely some interesting color choices in the feathers. Then he tacked it onto the small addition. His ingenuity never ceases to surprise her.

"How have you been feeling?" Sue asks her as they walk toward the horse fence where a few are frolicking in the rare snippet of sunshine peeking through the clouds.

"Better. Still a little weak but a lot better than I was," Paige answers honestly.

"Good. We were all worried," Sue answers and then slyly adds, "Some more than others."

"Well, I feel bad that everyone was worried," she answers noncommittally. She doesn't even want to speculate what Sue seems to be implying. She has meticulously avoided Cory since her accident. Everyone has been staying close to the farm since it happened. They've only gone to town strictly for clinic days and nothing else. John and Kelly held a meeting and gave their opinions that the town needed to work on the wall by themselves until spring. The family just can't afford the expenditure of gas running back and forth all the time. Soon they'll be out of gas completely, and without another dependable source, they won't be making any more trips to town. The CNG program for the vehicles hasn't been completely foolproof, and they are still working on it daily. Her brother has even been contributing ideas on how to get it up and running. Taking Robert McClane north to his base is using a lot of their final reserves.

"I think Cory seemed particularly glad you were recovering," Sue repeats the implication as they lean against the horse fence and watch a mother in the smaller paddock with her new baby. He's all spindly legs and tiny nickers. He jumps and frolics and loses his balance. Then he rights himself and looks around accusatorily as if he's sure someone pushed him. Then it's right back to the bucking and play.

"Yes, I'm sure he was," Paige deflects. "I did try to protect his brother. I think he feels obligated to look after me now or something."

"Maybe it's more than that," Sue guesses.

Paige is growing anxious. Their relationship, or lack of a relationship, is not something she wants to discuss, not with anyone on the farm. They are sworn to secrecy, a secret she insisted on and intends to keep.

"How is Reagan doing? Still sick?" Paige asks, diverting the conversation away from herself.

Sue rolls her eyes and shakes her head, "Oh, jeez, yes. It's so bad. I was a little sick when I was pregnant, but nothing like her. It's weird. I would've thought she'd be sick earlier in her pregnancy. She's almost four months. Weird."

"Well, it's Reagan, so it's probably normal."

Sue shares a laugh with her.

Paige sobers and adds, "Maybe she was sick and was hiding it from us. I feel bad for her, though. That must be miserable. I haven't seen her today."

"She's in the barn with Gretchen and Lucas. I guess she's going to work with them on their riding skills. I don't think they have a whole lot of experience."

"That makes three of us," Paige jokes and looks toward the horse barn in time to see Reagan leading two horses from it while Gretchen and Lucas follow closely behind. "Oh, yeah. There she is now. That seems dangerous. Should she be handling the horses?"

"She doesn't put up with much."

"From who? John?" Paige jokes, getting a loud laugh from Sue.

"I think she'll be fine," Sue explains. "As long as she doesn't ride. Grandpa already said she shouldn't."

"Right. She could be thrown or kicked or something," Paige says with a groan. "I hate the horses."

"Cory said you've ridden with him a few times. Must not be too bad," Sue probes again.

"It's more of a means to an end sort of situation. It's better than walking to visit with Talia. And it also beats having to drive a horse over there by myself. With my luck, I'd still end up walking back if you know what I mean."

Sue smiles and asks, "Speaking of pregnant, how's she doing?"

Paige smiles brightly, "Better. A lot better. I got to visit with her yesterday."

"Yeah, I saw Chet dropped her off with his four-wheeler," she remarks.

In the riding paddock, Reagan shanks on the reins of one of the horses she is handling. It makes Paige smile. Sue was right about her sister. She doesn't take much sass from the horses, even though she loves them. Paige grimaces. She hopes she doesn't have to ride them anymore. They are fun to watch, lovely and majestic, just not for her.

"I guess Grandpa let her off bed rest for now then, huh?" Sue asks her.

"Yes, he said as long as she doesn't have any more false labor, then she can get up and around but not a lot. That's why Chet brought her over instead of walking on her own."

"Good. I want her to deliver a healthy baby," Sue comments as her soft brown eyes drift off into the distance as if remembering something unpleasant. Paige knows she lost a baby a few years ago and feels sorry for her friend.

"I hope she doesn't have problems like that girl did the other night. Mia was young, younger than Talia," Paige says.

"That doesn't really mean Talia would have problems just because she's a little older. She's hardly in danger because of her age. She's young, too. It's just that pregnancy and birth are just dangerous now. Our doctors don't have the same access to medical science and equipment like they used to."

"At least we have doctors!"

Sue nods. "True. I sometimes wonder about the women out there, women who might be like you were when you were on the road traveling with your friends or people who are moving from area to area looking for help or a place to stay. What do those women do?"

"Hopefully not get pregnant," Paige comments.

"True, but that isn't always an option or possible."

"Abstinence would go a long way. That's what we did. Of course, we weren't exactly looking for a romantic connection with anyone."

"Not even with your friend Gavin?"

"No, we were all three just friends," she explains to Sue.

"Must've got lonely out there," Sue says.

"Um, no, not really. We had each other. It was more of a situation of survival. Romance was the last thing on our minds. I think Gavin was sleeping with a woman in that group we were traveling with through Ohio. He never said, but Talia and I speculated."

Sue smiles and nods knowingly. "But not you?"

"No way," Paige says with honesty. "First, it wasn't exactly like we felt desirable in any way. We barely even had a place to shower or wash up most of the time. It was rough. And secondly, I wasn't looking for companionship with anyone."

"Yeah, that's too bad. Hey, but look at you now. You have the opportunity and running water now," Sue teases with a nudge of her elbow against Paige's arm.

"I just want to hold Simon and myself together. I can't ever lose him again."

"But you're safe and have a roof over your head. A lot of the younger men in town have made their interest known."

Paige snorts. "Yeah, right."

"If not the men in town, then who? Is there something going on with you and Cory?" Sue asks out of the blue, causing Paige's cheeks to burn.

"What? No way. That's… silly. Hey, if you don't mind, I'm gonna walk over to the shed and see what my brother is up to. He might need some help," she blurts before Sue can continue with her interrogation and her knowing, brown-eyed stare.

Sue chuckles and smiles. Paige has seen pictures of Grams hanging all over the farmhouse. She believes that Sue resembles her. The older woman had that same, keen insight in her eyes. She makes a hasty retreat and heads for the med shed. By the time she reaches the building, she is out of breath. This weakness and lack of stamina is getting old. Reagan keeps telling her not to overdo it, but this is ridiculous. She just wants her energy and strength back. She wants to go running again. Even walking at a faster pace than snail would be nice. Doc says the same thing: take it easy, rest, baby steps, it'll come back on its own without pushing it. Her frustration is off the charts. But she'd do it all over again, even if it meant giving her life for Kelly. He is a good man, a great husband and the best father.

"What's up, bro?" she asks her brother as she approaches the back of the shed where he is working. He appears to be grinding herbs in a marble mortise and pestle.

Simon turns to greet her with a half frown. He has been very irritable lately. Actually, irritable would be nice. He's been awful and somber and grouchy. Cory asked him the other day if he was on his period. Paige laughed. Simon shot his best friend a nasty glare and stalked off.

"Just working," he explains and turns back to his table.

Not to be put off so easily, she pulls out a stool and sits beside him. He continues to grind away without talking.

"Worried about the guys?" she asks and plucks a stem of herbs. The leaves smell woody and slightly peppery.

"Sage," he answers her unasked question about the herb. "And, no, I'm not worried."

She replaces the herb bundle to the table.

"Yes," he says, amending his first assessment. "I'm a little worried, but not about the guys so much as the motivation behind Robert's agenda."

"Agreed," she says with a furrow of her brow. "I don't want them walking into danger."

"They won't," Simon reassures her. "They aren't stupid. They'll check the place out before they just go steamrolling in there."

"Right," she returns with a small bit of doubt. Being the daughter of a senator and having learned a lot from her father about politicians, she is distrustful of Robert. She picks up another bundle of herbs tied with twine. It doesn't smell good like the other.

"Saw Palmetto," he answers. "It's pretty exciting actually. We were able to get a start from Dave's medic. He wants to add his own greenhouse, too, on the farm... over there."

The derision in his tone when he speaks of Dave's farm is unmistakable. She knows the source of his anger. Sam is gone. She lives...over there now.

"Great!" she says, trying to be enthusiastic. She knows next to nothing about the herbs. "What's it for?"

"Oh, um. It's good for older men. Helps to shrink the prostate and helps the urinary tract."

"Really? That's the thing we're worried about? Old dudes having to get up in the middle of the night to pee?"

He turns and actually grins at her. It's the first time she's seen this from her handsome, nerdy, little brother in a long time, at least since Samantha left.

"It's important. We'll use the harvested berries, make a powder. The only problem is that the tree doesn't like shade, so it'll have to be in the greenhouse year round. "

"What else are you working on?" she asks, poking her nose closer to his small, marble bowl. It has a delightful smell.

"Lavender. Going to mix it in with some calendula oil and use beeswax to make a salve."

"And what's that going to do?"

"The mixture will be good for healing wounds, good for the skin, antimicrobial."

"Cool," she replies. "Thank God you and Sue know how to grow all this."

He chuffs and says, "No, I don't so much. Sue is the key person in the herb greenhouse. She is the one keeping it all thriving. If it were left up to me, they'd probably all be shriveled and scorched. I just learn what I can from books and Dr. McClane."

"You sure spend a lot of time out here."

He shrugs, "I just try to help."

Paige doesn't point out that he was spending most of the day holed up in the shed or the greenhouse when Sam was still living on the farm, as well. She suspects it was to avoid her. Now she suspects it is just to keep his mind occupied.

"Speaking of books, I know the librarian is hoping we'll start going on runs to collect books. A lot of them were ruined, even quite a big section of the children's library."

"Yeah, we could probably take a few trips. Chet came out to hang with me in the milking parlor yesterday when he brought Talia over. We talked about taking a quick run somewhere."

"While the guys are gone?"

"I don't think it'd be a big deal. We wouldn't have to go far. Most small towns have at least a decent sized library. Besides, we owe our town librarian a lot more than most people."

"You got that right. I owe Mrs. Browning some blood, literally."

Simon chuckles and says, "I don't think you'll be in shape to give any of it back for some time. Herb said the other day he retested you and your blood was only up to a seven-point-six. You have a long way to go to get to a twelve."

"Too many numbers for me," she replies glibly. "Doesn't matter. I'm feeling a lot better."

"No, you're still really run down and tired. You can try to hide it, but I notice more than you think."

Paige doesn't like the way this sounds. She sure as hell doesn't want him to notice anything regarding herself and Cory. She decides to change the subject, "Daniel seems to be growing already. Like a little string bean."

"Yeah, he's a fighter. Got some lungs on him."

Paige chuckles and nods. "Oh, yes, he's a real screecher when he wants to be. Is that normal? I mean, good grief. I hear him downstairs in Hannah and Kelly's room all the way up in my room some nights. What a pair of lungs. Maybe he'll be an Olympic swimmer someday."

"Or a professional yodeler," he jokes and then frowns.

She expected him to find their teasing funny. Perhaps he is distressed because they both know there will likely never be another Olympics, not in their lifetimes. It used to be something they enjoyed together. They'd always watch the Olympics, summer or winter with their mother. They were total addicts and could name all of the U.S. team for just about any sport. She always loved the track and field events. Simon liked hockey, and their mother was an avid fan of the ice-skating events.

"What is it?"

He shakes his head before answering, "I just don't know. Everyone is getting so attached to him. The little dude might not make it, Paige. Don't get too attached to him, all right? I was in a meeting with Reagan and Herb yesterday about him. He's not doing that great. Herb said he should be gaining more weight by now. I guess they gain pretty fast at this stage. He's not. We just don't have the formula we need for him or a lactating mother."

She hangs her head and nods. "He's a preemie. Maybe that's why he isn't growing very fast."

"They already factored that in. Dr. Wallace said he should be gaining better, too."

He never refers to Sam's Uncle Scott by his first name. It must bother Simon even to reference her uncle by anything other than a formal title and his last name only. Perhaps her brother sees her uncle as the man who took her away.

Her brother continues while plucking leaves from a woody stem, "He said he'll check around their town to see if any of the newer mothers are still lactating and if they could afford to pump for Daniel. Moving him or giving him over to someone else's care is out of the question. Doc isn't willing to do so. I think he's afraid that Daniel won't make it if he isn't keeping twenty-four-seven watch over him. I think he feels responsible for this. It wasn't his fault."

"Yeah. It sucks. It's not fair that his mom died like that. He'll never even know her. But you're right. It wasn't Herb's fault. Or yours or Reagan's, either. It just happened. She was weak. That would've been Talia or me if we'd gotten pregnant on the road. I doubt we could've endured childbirth."

"No kidding. I'm just glad nothing like that happened. Hopefully, the guys will find more formula somewhere."

"I'm sure they will," she reassures her brother. "If there's one thing I know about them, it's that they are very good at foraging for what the family needs."

"Yeah, I used to go with Cory a lot by ourselves before you arrived," he tells her. "We got pretty good at supply trips. The older guys had us doing a lot of the short runs so they could work on stuff here on the farm. It was fun…unless it wasn't."

She smiles. She knows exactly what he means. Situations can escalate in a heartbeat out on a run. She knows this firsthand, especially from their run to Nashville where she and Cory had a problem with those jerks at the college and she fell through the floor and almost died. She's thankful that Cory is so strong.

"What's going on with you and Cory?" he asks, surprising her. His eyes meet hers.

"Um, what…what do you mean?"

"It seems like you two are getting a little too close. Is that true?"

She scoffs loudly with a fair amount of over-exaggeration and replies, "What? That's crazy, Simon. We can barely tolerate each other."

He turns back to his plants but says, "I don't know about that. He seems very interested in you. I don't like it."

She attempts a laugh, but it mostly comes off sounding nervous to her ears. It's not a good cover. "No, I don't think so. He's dating that woman in town or one of the neighbors or both for all I know."

"He's not seeing either of them anymore," he remarks and hits her with a knowing stare and adds, "And you know that."

She pretends to be sidetrack by the plants and says, "Hm."

"Stay away from him," Simon warns in a threatening, low tone.

"Hey, that's a bit presumptive of you. Plus, I don't like you talking to me like that. You aren't my father. We both know he's gone now."

"I'm responsible for your safety and well-being, Paige. You're my sister," he says, hitting her with another hard stare. "You are my responsibility. I'm your brother, damn it."

"Easy," she says with apprehension. He never swears, so she knows he is upset. "Simon, calm down. Stop with the machismo. I took care of myself on the road for a long time. You're my brother, but I don't like you thinking you have full reign over my every move."

"But I do," he says with a matter-of-fact cockiness that starts her temper rising.

"Good Lord. Now you sound like Cory. Don't be a jerk."

She hops down from her stool with irritation, feels her internal stitches pull uncomfortably, swears under her breath and stalks from the room in a huff. She has to get away from him. She also has to stay away from Sue. Two times in one day people on the farm have speculated about herself and Cory. That isn't a good sign. She'll have to keep her distance from him a lot better when he returns. She just hopes he does.

Chapter Four
Cory

"Drop it, kid!" Dave barks at the young man pointing the gun at them and making demands.

"You drop it and hand over your vehicles and food," the idiot yells.

His voice quavers, though, so the effect isn't all he'd hoped it would be. Everyone else in their group has retreated to the inside of the RV.

"Kid, I've got a machine gun on the back of that deuce and a half and trained soldiers ready to put a thousand rounds of lead into that RV. I'm assuming that's your family, right?"

"Michael!" a woman from inside the RV yells as three of Dave's men come forward carrying fully automatic rifles.

"Shut up, Mom! Get back," the kid calls angrily.

"Look, kid," John starts, "I don't really like killin' kids. What are you, sixteen, seventeen?" The young man's mouth turns down into a frown. John's hit a nerve. "Just lower your weapon, so we can help you. We've got other things to do today and places to get, so drop the weapon and let us help your dad."

He looks quickly toward the man they'd originally approached and spoke to. The only thing he's holding is a wrench in his greasy hands and has an expression of terror on his face. He is obviously this boy's father. He nods to his son, and the kid lowers the gun. Then he places it on the pavement. Cory fast walks over and takes it.

"Good decision," Dave says. "Now what the fuck was that all about? Not too fuckin' neighborly if you ask me."

Cory has to suppress a grin. He's still too angry about the situation, so he bitch slaps the kid across the cheek, nearly knocking him down. "That's for tellin' your mom to shut up."

The boy says nothing but holds his stinging cheek and stares with shock and a lot of fear at Cory. He doesn't feel bad for doing it. The kid was being a dick to his own mother

"Show some fucking respect," Cory remarks and backs away toward the men again. The kid disappears into the RV. Cory hopes his mother also bitch slaps the little shit.

"Sorry," the father says and extends a hand to shake Dave's. "Our son's just jumpy. He's scared. We got robbed yesterday not far from here. They took just about everything but the gas. My son was just hoping to recoup some of our stolen goods. We thought you might be with the ones who robbed us. Sorry. My name's Thomas. You've met Michael."

Dave's men are already checking the RV for any other threats. They emerge from it a few moments later with two handguns and another shotgun before saying, "All clear."

Dave sends them to keep watch on the people and the road. Dave, John and Kelly make quick introductions with Thomas but refrain from anything further. Cory notices that Thomas also doesn't offer any more information about his group, nor does he ask the women to step out and say hello. He is cautious of them. It's smart.

"Were you with the group that was south of here, the ones who are dead on the highway?" John asks.

"Yes, sir," the man answers. "We were traveling east. I was gonna take our group to Nashville. Well, a little west of Nashville. A small town over there. Some people who were in our group went there to find their family members. They sent someone to tell us to all come down to their town since it was safe, basically abandoned. It seemed like a good idea. Louisville was getting more and more dangerous. Once we were attacked, most of us got split up… or killed."

Cory can attest to Louisville being dangerous. He found that out firsthand when he traveled north on his own.

"So why are you headed north if you were going south?" Dave asks.

"Figured it was too dangerous. Gonna just head back to Louisville. That's where we were before. We took a vote and decided to caravan south to this small town. It didn't work out."

Thomas hangs his head with defeat. Cory understands that this man must feel responsible for what happened. Maybe he was a leader within his group, someone people trusted to make good decisions, and now they are split up or dead.

John tells him, "Traveling the freeways and main roads usually isn't safe. What town?"

"Ashland City. It's small. You probably never heard of it."

"Oh, yes, we have," Kelly tells him. "It's more of a ghost town than anything else. That's where your friends went?"

"Yes, sir," he answers with a nod. "They said it's safe there."

"Yeah," John says. "It pretty much is safe. Not too many folks still around."

"What all did they take?" Kelly asks, interrupting further discussion of the small town they've all raided before. Cory has never seen anyone there. His friends must live somewhere on the outskirts.

"Not sure. I got my family and a few of the stragglers and took off on foot, headed for the woods. Some of the others did, too. They didn't chase us down. I don't think they saw us escape. I saw them raiding and taking everyone's food and water, gas. Didn't get the gas out of this clunker, though. They were beating up the men, shot anyone they saw running. We got lucky. We hid in the tree line until they were gone. Then I had to take my son down onto the road to look for survivors. As you know, there weren't any. It's bullshit. Those were our friends. I couldn't even bury them. Honestly, I didn't even feel like it was safe to stick around long enough to give them all a proper burial. With my son and I being the strongest ones in our

34

group, there's no way we could've buried so many people even if it was safe. Makes me sick. People like that don't deserve to live if you ask me. Why would they rob us like that? It's not like we have a lot. Mostly just food and supplies to get us to where we were going. We're traveling with women, children, and the elderly. Why rob us?"

John answers, "Because it was easy."

"Where were they from?" Kelly questions. "Did you get any impression of where they could've been from?"

Thomas shakes his head and sighs, "I don't know. I think they must not have been from far away because they also drove on motorcycles and four-wheelers. Some jumped out of a truck. When I saw your group comin', I figured you were them comin' back to finish us off. I was surprised they didn't take the RV. They ransacked it for what they could. Took most of our food and water."

"An RV is hard to maneuver easily in," John explains. "That's why they left it."

"You're damn lucky they didn't kill you," Kelly comments.

"Yes, I know. My family is all I have left. I have two daughters and my wife besides Michael. That's it. My little family."

"Who all is traveling with you?" Dave asks. "How many people are in there?"

"There's eleven of us," he answers honestly. "Six people other than my own family. Mostly older and a few young kids."

John nods. Cory is wondering if they are going to help these people or leave them to their own devices. He doubts they'll get far.

"So you think it's your radiator?" Dave asks and approaches their RV.

Yes, they will help them. It's the right thing to do, and Cory had a feeling Dave would do exactly as John and Kelly would. They work for a few hours on Thomas's RV to no avail. It's not the radiator. If Cory were to guess, he'd say it is the engine. It seems seized up. He has no doubt that the multiple bullet holes punctured into the side and front of the vehicle are causing a bit of the problem.

"Let's find them another vehicle," Kelly suggests when they meet up a few yards away from Thomas's group. "Then we'll syphon the gas out of the RV and get them moving again."

"Get them moving where?" John asks.

Cory is curious to see what plan they will devise with regards to these people. They seem pretty helpless.

"If we send them toward Ashland City or even one of our towns, they might not make it," Dave observes. "We could be sending them back into a fight with those assholes again. This time, I don't think they'll get so lucky."

"I agree," John says quietly.

Cory watches as Thomas's group discusses their own situation in a huddle near their vehicle. Some of the women have come out of the RV. He hadn't been lying. Mostly his group consists of older people, a few women and children. Cory has no doubt they'll all share the same fate as their friends down the road if they send them that way. He'd like nothing better than to turn around and track those bastards. It is unfortunate that they have liabilities traveling with them. He would like to suggest leaving Robert and his wife with this group while they backtrack and catch those thugs, but he knows his brother will never go for it.

Kelly interrupts his nefarious idea before he can verbalize it, "We should let them follow us to the base. They obviously aren't a threat. We let them come up to the base with us. It'll be safer than sending them on their way, no matter the direction. Geography ain't their problem, if you know what I mean. Then if they want to get to Ashland City, we'll have them follow us when we leave to head back home."

John nods, "At least we'll know they make it."

"So we're in the security providing business now?" Dave jokes as he lights a cigarette.

"Looks like it," Kelly says with a nod.

Cory adds, "I'll start scouting for a vehicle."

"Take Booker and Jameson with you," Dave orders.

Cory joins up with the other men from Dave's battalion, and they jog down the road looking for a suitable vehicle. They chat as they run, but Cory keeps to himself and concentrates on finding a vehicle. They separate when they come to a group of broken down cars. Some of them are wrecked, which isn't going to help their situation. There are eleven people, so they will need a full-sized van or more than one car.

Booker comes up with a mini-van, but after looking under the open hood, Cory realizes that the vehicle has been looted for parts. The battery is gone. Cory spots a bigger vehicle further down the road and jogs there with his search party comrades on his heels. It's an ambulance, older model but in fair shape. Nothing is absent when he checks under the closed hood.

"Oh, shit!" Booker says when he opens the back door.

Cory runs around to see what has upset him. There is a dead body strapped down onto a stretcher.

"Looks like he ain't makin' it to the nearest hospital," Jameson says.

"Nope," Cory agrees. "This is what you'd call a 9-1-1 fail case."

Booker looks like he'd prefer to puke. "Think we can get it running?"

"Sure," Cory says with optimism. "Still don't think they'll all fit in here. They had some boxes of shit with them in that RV, too."

"Yeah," Booker says. "Probably all they own now since they got robbed."

"I'll run back and tell the guys. See what they wanna' do," Jameson offers.

Cory gets to work while Booker keeps an eye out while his back is turned. He hotwires the ambulance and almost gets it to turn over. That's a good sign. The battery gives that tell-tale clicking sound. Once they charge it and fuel it, the ambulance just might run.

Within an hour they have it running and Thomas's group crowded into it. That was after Cory and Jameson took the body away into the woods, cleaned up the patient cabin a little, and let it air out. Leaving the back doors open helped immeasurably. They don't all fit, however, and some will need to pile into the back of Dave's deuce. It's their only choice. Robert has awakened and went into the woods to relieve himself. Cory also heard him vomiting again. That can't be a good thing. He plans on discussing it with John and Kelly later.

They take a break and feed the people in Thomas's group. Many of them looked weak. They had brought plenty and will not miss a few items from their stockpile if they share. There are children in the group. Not sharing is not an option. Cory is used to going without. There were days on the road when he was by himself when he had to ration his food items, especially when the weather was bad. He hopes when they make it to Fort Knox that they'll find food and accommodations there. If not, he and John will have to do some hunting to provide meat for the group. He knows that his family wants to get back to the farm as soon as possible. Cory does, as well. Leaving them behind had been hard.

Once they are on the road again, Cory drives this time while John rides in the back to catch some shut eye. Robert and his wife are doing the same. Out of habit, Kelly turns on the radio to static and immediately shuts it back off. Then he chuckles.

"That'd be nice, huh?" Cory asks his brother.

Kelly nods and says, "Yeah, no doubt."

"Think those people will be ok?"

"Yeah, as long as they don't piss off Dave or his men," Kelly jokes with a snigger.

Cory chuckles, too. "Those kids seemed scared shitless."

"They've been through a lot," Kelly reminds him. "Thomas said a few of them are now orphaned and in his care. Their folks probably got murdered yesterday. I'm surprised they're holding it together as well as they were."

"Yeah, that's bullshit."

"We were talking while you were dickin' around lookin' for that ambulance…"

"'Bout what? Your menses cycles?" Cory gives it right back.

"We might do a little recon on the way home," Kelly informs him as he scans the horizon and the surrounding forest out his window.

"Good," Cory says in agreement. "I was wanting to do the same thing. Those creeps are a little too close to home for my tastes."

"It's still pretty far from the farm if they're holed up anywhere around here," Kelly says with more confidence than Cory feels.

"Too close for my comfort," Cory says decidedly.

Kelly laughs softly at him, "Hell, Cor, the state of Kentucky's too close in your opinion. People are out there. Sure, not as many as there used to be, but there's still people living in this country. Most of 'em are good people."

"Not all of them are good," Cory adds with determination.

"No, not all," Kelly agrees with a sad sigh. "We called it in to Derek at the farm. Just in case. He said that two of Dave's men just got there."

"Hm," Cory says, not sure if he likes strangers, strange men to be more precise, snooping around on the farm when they aren't there to protect it.

"Hey, it's cool, bro."

"Yeah, so you say," Cory agrees through gritted teeth.

Kelly pats his shoulder, albeit a little roughly. "They're fine. Relax. You think this is the first time Derek's had to deal with shit without us? We weren't always deployed with him. He's smart. Got a lot more promotions than us. He knows how to run a secure base camp. Not his first time being in charge of subordinates. He's got this. Besides, the sniper's with him."

He knows Kelly means Simon. It does allay some of his stress knowing his best friend is on the farm. Even with an injured shoulder from that asshole stabbing him at Sam's house, he's still deadly with a rifle, boo-boo shoulder or no.

Cory looks at his brother and nods.

"And Paige and Doc," Kelly adds.

"What? She's in no shape to do anything if they're attacked," he reminds his brother of her state of being.

"I know that, but she's still capable of contributing if something happens. She can reload for Simon," Kelly offers in a chipper tone and a smile.

"Yeah, that's about all."

Kelly scratches at his right side. "Does it seem weird that every time I think of her getting shot it makes my side itch?"

"Like phantom pain or something?"

"Yeah, maybe. Makes me sick remembering that."

He'd like to confess everything to Kelly right now, let his brother know of his feelings for Paige, let him know that it makes him physically ill remembering her being shot, too. He refrains.

"Nah, sounds normal," Cory says instead.

Kelly shakes his dark head and adds, "Still can't believe she did that. She's one tough little cookie. She could've died."

He'd like to tell his brother to shut up. He doesn't like thinking about that day. It makes his palms sweat and his heart race.

"Yeah, no kidding," he remarks and wipes his hand on his pants leg, then the other. "She's tough 'cuz she was out there for a long time without anyone but her two friends. I don't think she even thought twice about jumping in front of a bullet for you."

"She's a really good person. She's strong but not as hard as she used to be. She's come a long way since she first got to the farm," Kelly tells him. "Oh, yeah. That's right, you weren't there."

"Nope," he says. "I was backpacking Europe. Seeing all the sites, meeting the locals, staying in hostels."

Kelly chuckles again. "Yeah, right. More like hostiles."

Cory smiles. "Exactly.

"But she's changed a lot. She trusts us more. She was very standoffish when she first came to the farm. Honestly, I think she just wanted Simon to leave with her and never look back. She wasn't wantin' to hang around. That's for sure."

"Nomad syndrome."

"Something like that, I suppose," Kelly says. "You're a lot alike in that way."

In the back, someone is snoring. It's probably Robert. Cory knows that John is likely just resting his eyes. He's not much of a sleeper on a good day.

Kelly just keeps talking about Paige, "She's a very loyal person, though. I like her a lot."

"You just like her because she took that bullet for ya'."

His brother laughs quietly. "Maybe. But she is a good woman. She'll make someone a good wife someday."

This upsets Cory, and he grips the wheel a little tighter, the leather making a squealing sound.

"She doesn't need to get in a hurry to get married," Cory remarks, trying hard to sound flippant, although he feels nothing of the like.

"I don't know. Her friend's gonna have a baby. Usually when women's friends and family members start having kids, then they want kids, too."

"I don't think she's like that. I asked her if she was gonna look for someone else in town since that dick Jason ditched on her, and she definitely didn't seem interested."

Kelly says, "Hm."

It irritates Cory further. He sure as hell doesn't want her finding someone else. He wants her for himself. However, he can't confess that to his brother. Their situation is complicated. The hurdle of Simon must be conquered first.

"Too bad Simon's your best friend," Kelly remarks. "She'd be a great wife for you."

"What?" Cory asks on a long exhale of surprise. Has his brother turned into a mind reader? Is Hannah rubbing off on him?

"Yeah, you and Paige. She's going to make someone a good wife someday. I mean, it's not like she's going to up and leave the farm. Not if Simon doesn't. I think they'll always be a package deal."

"Well, I sure as hell hope they don't leave. It's too damn dangerous out here for them to leave."

"No shit," Kelly says grimly. "Look at those folks on the road back there. I don't want them to leave, either."

"I only wish Sam hadn't left. That pisses me off."

"Yeah, you and John both. He's really pissed at Simon right now."

"Why's that?" Cory asks. He also speculates that she left because of his friend. As a person with their own relationship issues, Cory has no right to judge them.

"He's pretty sure she left because of Simon. I don't know why. I haven't had a chance to talk to Hannah about it. I'm sure she knows the whole situation."

Cory chuckles. "Yeah, no doubt. I kind of wondered about that, too. I know she wants to be with her uncle, but I was surprised she was willing to leave us for him. Seems odd. We were her family for the last four years."

"Yeah, and everyone's missing her. Kinda' depressing for the little kids. They all worshipped Sam."

"Doc's been upset over it, too."

"I've noticed. He's got his new grandkids to watch over now, though. That ought to keep him busy for a while, getting to know them."

"Another weird situation," Cory notes. It is very unusual that Robert McClane is so completely different than his father. Doc is loyal to a fault to his family. Robert only seems to have loyalty to himself and his cause. Cory can't imagine leaving his own kids behind on a farm that he hadn't visited in years, occupied mostly by strangers, and not being sure when he'd be able to send for them. He doesn't like to pass quick judgement on people, but Robert doesn't seem like he's even half the man that Herb is.

"His kids seem nice," Kelly comments.

"Yes, they do. G's a crack-up. Lucas is pretty serious, though."

"Agreed. He always has a serious expression on his face, as if the weight of the world is on his shoulders."

"Probably like Simon is about Paige."

"Yeah, he feels responsible for her, especially now that their parents just left them with us."

It reminds Cory that he and Kelly used to feel the same way about Em. He squelches those emotions to the pit of his gut and swallows hard. It is too difficult to think of his little sister. He prefers not to at all. Someday when the pain subsides just a tad bit, he'll allow himself to remember Em. Right now she is just a ghostly shadow constantly lingering along the perimeter of his subconscious. Kelly clears his voice quietly. Cory is left wondering if his brother has had the same thought about their little sister.

"They seem to be learning really well on the farm," Cory says, changing the subject as fast as he can.

"Yeah, Lucas is actually a pretty good shot. Derek took them out the other day to practice again. Gretchen's good, too. She just doesn't seem as interested."

"She can spin those six-shooters she likes carrying," Cory says with a smile. "Little shit thinks she's Clint Eastwood or something."

"Yeah, she might be deadlier than we thought," Kelly jokes. "I guess Huntley took them riding the other day. He says they are doing well with the horses."

"Good," Cory says. "The way it's going with fuel, we might be progressing in reverse on the fossil fuel front."

"Pioneers," Kelly acquiesces. "Who woulda' thought?"

"Who woulda'?" Cory agrees. "At least I got a motorcycle. We can get around on that. It takes less fuel. Even though little Doc already threatened me about it."

Kelly laughs a little louder this time. "Ha, I bet she did."

"I reminded her that we needed any form of transportation we could get."

"Uh-huh. And how'd that go?"

Cory looks at his brother. "Not well. I got a lecture."

"Sounds right. Just be careful on it."

"Yup."

Kelly resumes looking out his window for potential threats. "It isn't going to be good for going on runs. Can't hardly bring back supplies on a bike. But it could be good for emergencies and running to town or taking someone somewhere close."

"Yeah, that's what I was thinking, too. Plus, those four-wheelers are gonna come in handy."

"Those are great. Not so great in the winter, but they'll be helpful when the weather clears."

"Speaking of," Cory says as a light snowfall begins. They will never make Fort Knox today. The sun is already setting. They have spent all day helping Thomas's group and being delayed. "Are we gonna push through and try to get there tonight or stop somewhere?"

"Let me radio Dave," Kelly says.

They discuss the turn in the weather and decide to find a place to crash for the night. They aren't far from the Army base, but they don't particularly want to roll in there in the dark. They plan on doing a recon of the place first to ascertain its safety.

Dave leads the way, and they end up in Horse Cave, Kentucky, where they park their vehicles around back of a large hotel. Dave sends his men in to clear the building. Cory can tell it, as well as the entire town, is abandoned. They come out a few minutes later and declare it all-clear. They decide to stay on the second floor in a party room overlooking the parking lot where the vehicles are parked. He suspects this is where they would've held wedding receptions and the sort. There is a massive, stone fireplace at one end of the dance floor. Tables and chairs are set up as if the event coordinator had ordered them to be so for some big wedding that should've taken place. White dinnerware and linens cover the tables. Champagne glasses stand at each plate unfilled as if time has stood still in this place. It kind of gives him the creeps.

Two of Dave's men will remain on the ground floor to watch at the back door in case anyone decides to steal the vehicles. Cory helps Thomas's people get settled in. When they try to spread out down the hall into rooms, he limits them to the reception room only.

He and Kelly carry quite a few mattresses into the big room for them. It's easier to keep everyone safe if they aren't in individual rooms down the hall from them. Dave's men help gather supplies and mattresses while John and Dave hold a planning meeting at one of the nearby tables. At least these people will sleep in comfort for the night, even if the pillows, sheets and blankets are covered in dust.

"Huddle up for warmth," Cory tells one of the women. "Get as many of the kids into one bed as you can. It'll keep them warmer. It's the best we've got for the night, but it's better than the truck or out in the woods without a tent."

"Thank you so much, sir," she returns and smiles with appreciation.

He nods, tips a hat and leaves her with who he presumes is her daughter. He helps carry broken chairs and wood from outside to the stone fireplace where Booker already has a roaring fire going. This would've been a nice room full of ambiance with the fireplace lit for special occasions. Cory almost laughs. He wonders if Booker's specialty in the Army was pyrotechnics. Some of the little kids are standing in front of the blaze with their small hands turned up to absorb warmth. Others are sitting on the mattresses in dazes staring at the fire. He doesn't like their sunken, bloodshot eyes or the lack of life showing in them. He's sure these ones are orphans.

He and Booker, who he has come to like, take off for the kitchens. A hotel this size would've had a lot of food and supplies. They find the kitchen easily enough. It looks ransacked but not badly. Locating boxes of pre-packaged foods, he stuffs a discarded cardboard box full of items. Booker also discovers a pantry full of dried noodles, beans and rice. He knows as long as they haven't been tampered with by mice, then the dry goods are still viable. There is spaghetti sauce in bulk cans tucked away in plastic storage bins and cans of soda and juice. Some of it shows expired dates, but the canned goods should be all right.

It doesn't surprise Cory when Booker hands him a bottle of liquor and says, "This'll be great back at our clinic for treating wounds."

Cory just smiles and nods. That's the same thing he would've thought. The irony of the world is not lost on him. Young men their ages should look at a bottle of vodka and be thinking about making mixed drinks in red, plastic cups followed by doing something reckless and stupid. Instead, they both realize that their medical clinics need supplies like alcohol more than they need to get buzzed. Besides, it's also a pretty damn good anesthesia when there isn't anything else available.

They find so much that Cory has to fetch a rolling luggage cart to haul it. There is still a lot that they left. They'll likely come back in the morning for more.

Within an hour, some of the people in Thomas's group have huge pots of spaghetti made for them cooked over the fire. He notices that some of the children only eat a few bites. They are sitting on the floor in a tight circle, heads mostly hanging down. These aren't like the spoiled, pre-apocalypse kids who threw tantrums for not getting the latest Lego set or Barbie. These kids just lost their parents, security, and almost their lives. Their depression does not go unnoticed by the entire group. It infuriates him. He also observes the same, barely veiled anger on the faces of Dave's men. Children are innocent. They don't deserve this. He has an inkling they'd all like to join him for a late night rendezvous hunt. However, the local deer would be safe on this type of hunt. He and the others stand against the walls with their plates, eating quickly and glancing at one another with unconcealed loathing of the predators still lurking out there preying on the innocent.

He leaves to scout around in the kitchen again. This time he's looking for something different. He knows they used to hold weddings and other events in this hotel. Cory finds a two-pound bag of soft, sugar mints, the kind that would be bundled into small fabric sachets for guests, and takes them back to the kids. Maybe a little sugar will help. He's not sure, but he gives it to the woman who had thanked him. She smiles and nods. There is a quick spark of interest in her blue eyes as she looks up at Cory with more than just appreciation for the candy. He just nods curtly.

"I'm Rachel," she says with flirty eyelashes.

"Cory, ma'am," he returns cordially and leaves her.

She can disperse the candy as she sees fit to the children. She seems to be in charge of them. Perhaps no one else volunteered. It's going to be a big burden of responsibility taking care of so many youngsters. He's glad they found these people. Keeping them safe for a few more days, alive and thriving, seems like the right thing to do. Giving the orphans some candy may help the kids trust them just a little. It's the least he can do.

He volunteers for first watch with John and some of Dave's men while they hold a meeting and then bed down for the night. The hotel is dark and quiet and, if he's being completely honest, eerie. He and John walk a beat on the third floor just to double check that nobody is in the rooms who shouldn't be.

It seems like the perfect time to bring up Reagan's father and his state of health, "I think Robert was puking today when we stopped. I saw him doing it again when we found Thomas's group."

"Yeah, I thought I heard it, too," John says with a crease between his brows.

They are carrying oil lamps care of Dave's men. His group is very efficient and prepared for almost anything.

"What do you think it is? Think it's that smallpox shit again?" Cory asks with concern. He really doesn't think Robert should've been allowed onto the farm grounds. He is a liability. He is proving to be a pain in the ass, as well.

"Not sure. Hope not. Heck, we've got these people now plus Dave's men with us. If he's sick again or if it's flared up again, he could wipe us all out."

"Maybe we should talk to his wife," Cory suggests as they walk up a dark stairwell to the next floor.

John shakes his head and shrugs. "Doubt if it would do any good. If he doesn't want her to tell us something, she's not going to."

"Yeah, he's a control freak," Cory agrees as he glances out the window on the fourth floor. It overlooks the parking lot where their vehicles are stashed. He can just make out the faint red ember of a cigarette's tip glowing like a lighthouse's safety beacon in the night. He knows it is one of Dave's men. The area is secure. If it weren't, there would be holy terror being rained down on someone right now. Cory smoked a pipe with Doc a few years ago. He hadn't particularly cared for it. He'd smoked cigarettes a few times while on the road and a couple more with Kelly back at the farm, far from the bloodhound nose of Hannah, of course.

"That's an understatement for sure," John agrees. "I don't think his wife is allowed to think for herself. According to Reagan, he was like that with her mother, too. I believe he's like that with everyone."

"No joke. He was sending some pissy looks down the table when we first discussed this trip whenever you or Kel or Derek would disagree with him."

"I think he thought he was gonna blow in there and take control," John says with a shrug.

"Fat chance," Cory says.

"Right," John agrees. "Rank doesn't play anymore. I respect him as a military man, but not as a father or my leader. My general dismissed us. That's as much as I needed to hear. Robert isn't going to get this family into trouble. I won't let him."

"Is that why you wanted to come?"

"That's exactly why," John answers pointedly.

"How come she came with him, do ya' think?"

John shrugged again, "I don't know if I buy the story of her being good at public speaking or crowd control. I've personally only heard her say about two sentences since they arrived at the farm. I think he just likes her by his side."

"That had to be hard for her to leave her kids behind," Cory observes. Knowing what he does of Robert's three daughters, he can confidently surmise that they'd never do the same with their own kids.

"I get the impression it happens often," his friend notes. "I think that's why Lucas takes such full responsibility for G. I don't think it's the first time he's had to."

"Strange," Cory remarks.

John hits him with a knowing expression and nods. They don't discuss Robert any further. There is nothing to talk about. They are stuck in a shitty situation because of him, but Cory is glad that they could be of service to the stranded motorists. At least that's one positive thing that will come of this trip. He is very sure it will be the only outcome that is. A feeling of dread hits him when he finally lies down for the night and allows others to take his place on watch duty. In a secluded corner, he mostly tosses and turns on the dusty mattress beneath him. It isn't because the banquet hall is too warm or too crowded for his likes. It isn't because others are on watch duty because he trusts Dave's men, his brother and Dave. It is because he sees no good ending in their future now because Robert McClane is leading them into a situation that will eventually be a problem.

Chapter Five
Reagan

"John just called in," Derek says as he enters the kitchen the next morning. "They're back on the road."

"Do they still have those people with them?" Reagan asks, knowing about their situation on the road and the people they rescued.

"Yes, moving a little slower because of them, too," her brother-in-law answers as he kisses Sue's forehead.

Paige hobbles slowly into the kitchen with Huntley close on her heels. Derek pulls out a stool at the island for her to sit. She waves it away. Reagan notices that Huntley does not back away from her. He's getting so tall, nearly passing Paige in height already. She knows that Simon ordered him to stay close to Paige when he cannot be there for her. Reagan found it odd when she heard that Cory issued the same policy as her brother.

"I'd rather stand a little. Getting tired of sitting around," she tells them.

Her red hair is braided on either side of her face. This is a style that Huntley sometimes wears and always make his Native American features stand out even more. Sometimes he'll tie a bird feather in with a strip of leather. She knows he harbors a very small box of his mother's belongings somewhere in his room, but, as far as Reagan knows, nobody has ever asked about the contents of that box. It may also contain items that belonged to his twin brother, as well. It is simply too depressing to contemplate.

"I'm going out to milk," Derek says.

Huntley steps forwards, "Should I come out to help, sir?"

"Sure," Derek says and slaps Huntley on the shoulder. It makes a loud crack. None of the men in the family treat one another with anything that would be considered a gentle touch. "I think the women can babysit Paige for a while. We'll be back in for breakfast."

"Gee, thanks," Paige says flatly.

He laughs, kisses Sue again and leaves with Huntley, who glances at Paige. She waves him away with a chuckle.

"The guys are all right," Sue explains to Paige. "That's what Derek came in to tell us."

"Thank God," Paige says.

Grandpa comes into the kitchen next carrying a stack of patient files and a legal pad. "We should thank Him, indeed."

This earns a smile from Paige. "Amen to that."

"How's my favorite, red-haired, feisty shooting victim today?" he asks in a light tone.

"Fine," she replies. "Just a little sore."

Reagan is quick to say, "You overdid it yesterday. Not so much with the walking around, woman. Take it easy means just that. If you stumble and fall outside, you're really going to be sorry."

"Mm, smells good, Hannie," Paige comments, changing the topic.

Reagan would like to vomit from the smell of bacon grease but refrains out of decorum. Instead, she is relieved when her grandfather entreats her to speak in the music room. She gladly follows.

"Derek said that the men had a discussion last night about Robert's health," Grandpa says as he rubs his chin thoughtfully. He hasn't shaved in a week or so if Reagan were to guess. He often does this now, and she's not sure if it is because Grams is gone or if he forgets.

"What about his health?" she asks.

"It would seem that more than one of them witnessed Robert vomiting when he thought they wouldn't see."

"Does he have a fever?"

"Not sure. They said he slept most of the day and all night last night. John told Derek he saw him throwing up again this morning before they loaded up to leave the hotel where they were staying."

"Shit," she says without thinking. "This could be bad. I thought his flare-up was getting better."

"This is puzzling, indeed," Grandpa says. "I wish I would've gone with them now. If Robert is sick, he's going to need care."

"His wife will know how to treat him," she says.

Grandpa nods and says, "Yes, that might be true, but I don't know if they have any medicine with them. If he starts running fevers, he could contaminate everyone within that group, including the people they are helping, as well as Dave's men."

"Damn it," Reagan swears. This is typical Robert behavior; selfish, greedy, thinking only about his own needs. "They shouldn't have taken him up there."

"We'll keep in touch with the men. If Robert starts spiking fevers, I'm going to tell them to get out of there, leave him at the base and come back. I'll travel up there and take care of him."

"What?" Reagan screeches. "Bullshit you are!"

Grandpa places a hand on her shoulder and says, "It's the right thing to do, honey. He's my son. I'm not going to sit on my hands and watch him die. I would do the same for you or your sisters or anyone on this farm."

"No way," she argues stubbornly. "You aren't going."

"Let's just wait and see what happens," he tells her calmly.

Reagan feels anything but relaxed. Her heart has sped up with anxiety. Why did they ever agree to take him north?

Her grandfather continues, "He wasn't completely recovered when he left. It could just be fatigue. Let's keep in mind smallpox is very debilitating. People can be affected by it their whole lives.

Robert has taken very ill with this disease. I've never seen him like that."

"No kidding," she says with derision. She remembers her father as a big man, muscular, not an ounce of fat. Of course, he'd kept himself in impeccable shape. Anything less would've been imperfect, and he'd never stand for that.

"We'll wait and see what the men say when they call in later," he says. "I'm only discussing this with you because you're my partner. Right?"

He wraps an arm around her shoulders and squeezes. She looks up to find her grandfather smiling down at her. Reagan releases a hard exhale through her nose and smiles. Then she nods.

"I won't tell anyone else," she says, knowing that's what he wants.

"Good girl," he returns. "Now, what have those girls made for breakfast? It smells wonderful in this house."

Reagan groans.

"Not feeling well, honey?"

She groans again, this time more dramatically as Jacob and Mary bound into the room with their usual noise and energy.

"I'll make you some tea," he suggests.

"No!" Reagan says with a laugh. "I'll be fine. That stuff doesn't work all that great, and I'd rather we save it for other expecting mothers in town."

"Nothing much has ever been proven to help with morning sickness," he admits.

"It lasts morning, noon, and night," she reveals what he already knows. "Morning only sickness would be nice."

"Hormones," he says. "It'll eventually let up."

"I sure as hell hope so. This sucks. I have no life. The only time I feel good is when I'm asleep."

"I've had many patients who were like that," he confesses. "Perhaps if you felt well, you'd be doing things that you shouldn't."

"You mean like riding or running or having some semblance of my normal life before this thing invaded my body?"

"Exactly!" he says with too much chipper optimism for Reagan's taste. "You could've miscarried early on if you hadn't been so sick. This has forced you to slow down and rest."

"I feel like that's all I do," she says. "I know I studied pregnancy extensively, but until it happens to you, you just don't get it."

"No, I suppose I don't," he says with an empathetic chuckle.

"The fatigue is a pain in the ass. Did I tell you that I fell asleep the other day reviewing smallpox case studies? I literally fell asleep upstairs in my room at my desk. I woke up in a puddle of my own drool. Ridiculous!"

"That's not exactly exciting reading material," Sue says with satire as she passes them in the hall. "I'm going to the greenhouse in a minute if anyone wants to know where I went."

"It is interesting actually," Reagan argues. "It's very interesting! And nobody cares where you go!"

Sue just laughs at her as she heads downstairs to roust her kids. They are sleeping unusually late today.

Grandpa loops an arm through hers and pats her hand gently. She looks down at his long, gnarly, bent and crooked fingers and hands with the age spots and thin skin. She loves her grandfather's hands. They show that he lived a life, that he did things, important things with these hands. Reagan worries that her hands will not show the same signs of a long, productive life someday that his do.

"Sleep is good. It's normal at this phase of the trimester, especially with twins," he consoles.

"Not funny! Let's not jinx me even more. Besides, that was the first thing I made sure of. No twins! And I know about the fatigue. Of course, I know that. It just seems bizarre. It's like I have no control of my own damn body!"

"Not in the kitchen!" Hannah says as they approach the kitchen again. "Does anyone know where Simon is?"

"Out in the shed," Grandpa answers as he deposits her at the island with Paige, who has taken them up on their offer of a seat after all.

"Already?" Paige asks with a dubious expression.

"He's been working on the smallpox problem," Grandpa tells them. "I'll be back in a little while. You girls take it easy while I'm gone. Doctor's orders."

He's pointing at Paige and herself. Reagan just rolls her eyes at him. He laughs and leaves out the back door. She watches as he walks to the shed to join Simon. Grandpa just doesn't get around as fast as he used to. He worries Reagan.

Gretchen comes into the kitchen a moment later and plops down at the island with them. Her short black hair is sticking up on end. She doesn't look like she slept much. There are matching circles under each eye. Reagan has to admit, her new half-sister is very pretty, even if she doesn't wish to be and has the appearance of a post-apocalyptic goth kid tomboy. She looks like she belongs in a teen indie rock band of equally angry girls.

"Didn't sleep well, G?" Paige asks as she sips her tea that someone must've made for her.

Reagan hopes she isn't still in a lot of pain. Any damage to the liver is a slow and agonizingly painful recovery process. In Reagan's estimations, it is probably equivalent to pregnancy.

"Not really," she answers glumly. Then she looks around, "Did Lucas come down yet?"

"He's already outside doing chores," Hannah informs her.

Of course Hannie knows where everyone is. Reagan wouldn't know. She slept in. Again. The fact that Simon slipped past Hannah this morning undetected means he was up before dawn or just never went to bed in the first place.

"Worried about your parents?" Paige asks. "They'll be fine. Don't worry. They're in good hands."

"It's not that," G says on a yawn. "I just wish my mom woulda' stayed here. He doesn't need her. He just wants her with him."

"Well, maybe that's a good thing, though," Paige counters. "She takes really good care of your dad. It's probably smart that she went with him in case he gets sick again and needs her help."

55

G just snorts. "She's simply too submissive to say no when she needs to. Heck, everyone is when it comes to the general."

"Yes," Hannah agrees, surprising Reagan.

"And he didn't need my mother to go with him to take care of his health. If he has a problem at this new place, some of the doctors from our bunker were planning on escaping, too, and will be coming in this direction with the soldiers."

"Wait, what?" Reagan asks. "This is the first we've heard of this."

"It's not that big of a surprise, or it shouldn't be. My dad- our dad- has a lot of followers out there in the new capital. All kinds of people will probably show up. Who knows how long it will take them, though. It was hard getting out of there. I have no idea how long it will be before they are all able to get out of there. Once we left, I'm sure they amped up security."

"If people don't want to live there, why would the new President force them?" Hannah asks.

"More people, more laborers. He needs people to build the new country. He'll need scientists, farmers, doctors, engineers. More people, more control," Reagan answers.

Paige butts in to add, "I find the sheer number of people out there in this new Colorado staggering. I traveled the east coast with my friends trying to find our families. I don't think there were that many people left on the whole coast. It's crazy that so many people found their way out there."

"It's not like it happened in a week," G explains. "It took the last four years of this crap to gather people and reinforce our city. He would send caravans of soldiers and broadcasts on the radio to alert people to come there. It was a big effort."

"Did you like it there?" Paige inquires.

She frowns and sighs, "It was ok. I felt safe. I didn't feel safe like that when we lived up in Oregon."

This piques Reagan's interest, "Why not? You were living out in the middle of nowhere. It should've felt safe like here on the farm."

"No, not really," she says. "There were a lot of wild animals around. Sometimes people would pass through the woods, too."

Her eyes drop to the counter, and she stops talking.

"What would happen when they did?" Paige presses.

G shrugs and says, "Sometimes they'd just leave us alone. Sometimes they wouldn't even find our cabin."

"What if they did? What if they got too close?" Reagan asks.

"Dad or Luke would take care of it," she answers.

"How? Scare them off?" Reagan pushes. She knows almost nothing about her extended family and is curious to find out about their lives before they arrived on the farm.

She bites her lower lip before answering, "That was back before my dad got sick, so he and Luke would do patrols -kind of like you guys do here. I don't know if the general ever killed anyone, but I know Luke killed a few guys. He told me about it the same night he did it. I think he's killed others. We shared a bedroom there, too. Actually, we shared a bedroom at the bunker, too. He's really protective, and I don't really..."

She doesn't finish her sentence, so Reagan prods, "Don't what?"

"I don't really like being very far away from him. He's always been my big brother."

"You two seem really close," Paige comments. "I know the feeling. It was all I could think about, finding Simon again. It was the only thing that kept me going."

"I don't know what I'd do if I got separated from Luke. Probably die!" she says with teen angst.

"So," Reagan says, getting back around to her new brother's murdering of people, "he told you that he killed someone?"

She nods, sending her short hair across one eye, which she blows back with exasperation. "He said they were bad. He knew they were. He saw them in the distance out in the woods and stalked them to make sure they were gonna leave. Well, they didn't. He overheard them talking about robbing people. I think he shot them. Not totally sure. He didn't share the deets. He never told Mom, made me promise not to, either. He didn't want her to look at him like that, like a killer."

"I doubt if she would," Paige remarks.

"I don't know about that," Gretchen counters. "Our mom's really super religious. She was always lecturing our dad about going to church more when he was home. She was raised really strict. I don't know if she'd be able to handle it if she knew Luke killed people. She thought we should go back to the city, help people out, start a shelter or something." G groans with disapproval.

"It's self-defense now," Paige points out. "It's kind of a kill or be killed world. Nobody has a choice. That was taken away from all of us a long time ago. We've all had to do things that we'll struggle with for the rest of our lives. If we haven't, then we'd be dead, we wouldn't be here now. That's just the way it is."

"I know," G says and hangs her head. "I just don't think my mom could handle it."

"Women are a lot stronger and usually smarter than we give them credit for," Reagan says and swallows hard to keep from throwing up. Hannah's cooking may smell great to everyone else and usually her, too, but not in her current state of alien invasion via pregnancy.

"True," G says with a coy grin. "If we were in charge, there wouldn't be a worldwide apocalypse that ruined everyone's lives and killed millions."

"Perhaps," Hannah says with skepticism. "People are corruptible. Men or women."

"Yeah, just look at this new President," Paige reminds them. "I wish my dad was still alive. He might've been involved in this new government."

"What happened to him?" G asks.

"He was a senator and in London when the first bombs hit there," she explains. Reagan can tell it is painful for Paige to remember her father. She knows they were very close.

"That sucks," Gretchen says like a typical fifteen-year-old and twirls two, silver stack rings on her middle finger. "Sorry, Paige."

"It's ok," she answers. "I know he wouldn't have gone along with any form of this new government, which sounds a lot like socialism. My dad was a constitutional patriot to a fault. I don't think he would've like this new President guy."

Reagan asks, "Does the new President have a family, G?"

"He has a little boy, but that's all. His wife caught the flu and died two years ago. He took it really hard. His little boy is all he has for family. If he had any other relatives, then they must not have made it to the bunker. But I've never heard him say anything about them, either."

Reagan nods knowingly. This man has next to nothing to lose if all he has left is his young son. She couldn't say the same thing about herself. Her whole family is alive on this farm. Now she's bringing another being into this world, so she has even more to lose. This President is nothing like them. He has a much less complicated list of entanglements.

"He's an even bigger control freak than our dad," G comments.

Hannah says, "Robert is rather controlling. I hope he's changed, though."

"Don't get your hopes up," G says before Reagan can even get a word in. "Look, you seem nice," their half-sister says to Hannie, "but don't think he's changed. He's probably the same selfish, control-freak he always was when you were kids, too. He's always been like that with me and Luke. Mister Perfectionist. He was always riding our cases about something." She lowers octave and puffs up her chest, "'Your shirt's untucked, Lucas!' 'You were late for school again, young lady!' 'This stain on the carpet looks like it was from soda. Which one of you drank soda in here?'"

She groans loudly. Reagan laughs at her imitations. "Yep, sounds like Robert."

"People can change," Hannah argues in a gentle tone.

Gretchen snorts again. "Not the general."

Reagan is curious about her half-brother, with whom she's shared maybe one full sentence since they've been on the farm. "He's the same with Luke?"

"Yes, pretty much," she answers. "He'll give him a little more freedom, but that's not much. Luke will kill himself to please the general, too. He always pulled straight A's in school and college. Never broke curfew, was never late to school- unlike me- always did everything our dad wanted or was ordered to do. The general was really pissed that Luke wasn't going into the military like him."

"You don't think he would've?" Hannah asks. Reagan figures her sister is probably curious about Lucas, as well, and lets their new sister off for the swear.

"No, he was always interested in sciency-stuff. He wanted to cure cancer. He was fascinated with DNA and cells and research crap," she chuffs through her pert nose. "Good luck with that, right?"

"I don't know," Reagan says with a shrug. "We were making great strides with cancer research. The biggest problem was the government- namely the worthless FDA. But even with those idiots involved there were still improvements in treatment and cures. And he was on the right track. DNA and cell research was the key."

"Yeah, well, if the world hadn't gone to crap and my brother had been allowed to study what he wanted instead of having to put up false pretenses of wanting to be a lawyer to please our father, then maybe he would've cured cancer and I could've met my grandmother."

This hits Reagan right in her chest. It is agonizing to think of Grams. She swiftly looks at Hannah, concerned that bringing up their grandmother will hurt her even more. Her soft features have screwed up into a solid grimace of discomfort. She surprises Reagan by speaking to Gretchen about Grams. She doesn't talk about her much, none of them does. It is just too painful to do so. It still feels like a fresh wound, one that none of them wants to poke a hot branding iron into.

"She was… everything a grandmother ought to be, G," Hannie explains.

"Sam talks about her sometimes," Gretchen says. "She really liked her a lot. I wish I could've met her. Grandpa is really cool. I bet she was, too. She had to be, right? I mean, she was married to Grandpa."

"You would have loved her, too," Hannah expounds. "Everyone loved her. She had a lot of friends in town. Everyone looked up to her. She was kind and gentle. There wasn't a mean bone in her body…"

"Unless you said swear words in the house," Reagan says with a smile of fond memories. Her sister smiles, too.

"Oh, yes. She was a lady through and through," Hannah adds and searches, finds and squeezes Reagan's hand gently.

G says as she plucks a piece of bacon from a platter, "I saw a picture of her in the upstairs hallway. It looked like her and my grandfather were going to some sort of fancy dance or something. They were all dolled up. She was really beautiful."

Reagan says, "She was. Even in the end, she was beautiful and lovely and sweet. I know the picture you mean. Yeah, it was some sort of doctor's conference in Chicago. Grandpa was being recognized for his work."

"What kind of work?"

"Research, gynecology. It was when he lived in Boston a long time ago. I guess he was in a practice up there before he came back to Tennessee."

Hannah frowns and says, "I thought he was a family physician up there, too. Strange."

Reagan doesn't discuss it further. She knows what kind of a doctor he was in Boston. He discussed it with her once before she went off to college. Her sisters do not know of their grandfather's past. His heart had been broken when he'd told her. He didn't want anyone else in the family to know about his practice or the services that he and his partners provided to women in Boston.

Reagan covers for her blunder, "Well, he did gynecology and obstetrics work there, too. Just like he does with his practice in town now. He's just brilliant, I guess. One specialized field of medicine just wasn't enough for our grandfather."

Hannah smiles, which alleviates Reagan's concern about Hannah ever discovering their grandfather's dark past.

Gretchen says, "Luke must take after him then, 'cuz I sure didn't inherit any of his brains."

"You seem plenty smart enough to me, Miss Gretchen," Hannah corrects. "Reagan's smart, too. I'm quite sure you inherited a lot of their talents."

"What do you like doing, G?" Paige asks. "Well, what did you used to like doing?"

"I don't know. Nothing special," she answers.

It's difficult to remember that Gretchen would've only been about eleven or twelve when everything started. She never even had a chance to develop interests that would've carried into her adult life.

"What about now?" Paige redirects.

Reagan would like to point out her new sister's affinity for smoking cigarettes when she thinks no one is looking but refrains from doing so.

"I like reading books and writing," she answers shyly.

"Really?" Hannah perks up. "That's wonderful. What do you like to read?"

"Anything. History books, fiction, doesn't matter. I just like forgetting stuff for a while…"

She trails off, and the expression on her face makes Reagan feel sorry for her. She's just a kid. It pisses her off that so many kids are stuck in this mess. She can understand wanting to get lost in a novel about time travel or a history book on the American Revolution for a few days. Reality is sometimes unbearable now. Living in that bunker for so long would've been miserable, too, so she's glad they had books for the kids.

"And what do you enjoy writing about?" Hannah pries.

"I don't know. Just stuff."

"Like what?" Hannah asks again, not one to be put off. G would do well to learn this about Hannie.

"People that I've met and stuff. Things that we've been through. Travel and where we've been."

"So you're writing your own history?" Reagan acknowledges.

G shrugs and nods, "Yeah, I guess so."

Paige says, "Very cool."

"And a good idea," Hannah, ever the pragmatist, comments. "It's important to keep a written history of our life now. Grandpa does the same."

"He does?" G asks, her face lighting up with an expression somewhat akin to hope.

"Oh, yes," Hannah explains. "He says it's important to document everything. History has reset itself, and we must document as much as we can. It's a preservation of our new history, the one we're making."

"You're making breakfast," Reagan teases and gets a testy glare from her sister. She hastily adds, "Breakfast is important, too!"

"Heck, yeah, it is," Paige is quick to add.

She probably realizes it's better than going hungry. Reagan has always found her intelligent.

Gretchen says, "It's just hard to find paper and pens and writing supplies sometimes."

"Look no further," Reagan says, turning and pointing toward the basement door. "There's a ton of paper and writing utensils down there on shelves. It's one of the few stock-up things we have left. We don't use a lot of it. Grandpa is about the only one who does. Sam always used art paper, which is also hard to find, probably harder. But we still have boxes and boxes of notebooks and loose paper."

Gretchen asks with disbelief, "Really?"

"Help yourself," Hannah remarks with a grin.

"Thanks," Gretchen answers and dashes excitedly to the basement door.

Sue comes in the back door a moment later and lays a bunch of long carrots with their frothy stems on the butcher block side counter.

"Mm, smells good, Hannie," their sister says and presses a kiss to Hannah's fair cheek, causing her to flinch.

"You're freezing!" Hannah squeals with a laugh.

"It's a little chilly out," Sue returns and smiles as Hannah runs her hand over the carrots. Sue sets a basket of treasures from the greenhouse down next. Hannah is quick to touch them, as well. "Thought we'd make a root stew later today for dinner. How's that sound?"

"You plan the meals; I will make the meals," Hannah says with a nod.

"You always say that, but it takes both of us to do both things!" Sue complains half-heartedly.

"It sounds good, though," she admits with a lopsided little frown. "Makes us sound like we have a plan."

"You do have a plan," Paige says. "Feed everyone, so we don't starve. It's a pretty good one."

"I'm in agreement with that," Reagan adds.

Sue walks over and places her dirty, cold hands on either side of Reagan's face. She jumps and waves her sister away. "Damn, that's cold, Sue!"

Hannah is quick to say, "Hey, heathen!"

Sue smirks and skirts away from Reagan's swatting to wash her hands at the sink as the children bound into the room. The aromas of food have finally awakened them. Baby Daniel cries from the other room, and Paige readily volunteers to collect him for his morning meal. Everyone is concerned about the baby, but she and her grandfather are even more so. He is too small, not gaining enough, and they are nearly out of formula again. She hopes the men find some on their trip north and are able to return soon. She spoke with Derek and Simon last night about the possibility of a short run somewhere to scout for more until the men can return. None of them have any idea how long they'll be gone, and they have enough formula for another few days at best.

They all gather for breakfast, everyone but Simon who refuses to come inside. Reagan is starting to worry about him. She knows that John is more worried about Samantha, but there isn't anything they can do to convince her to come home. They'd tried to prevent her from leaving and had failed. The one person she'd needed to hear it from had refused to speak with her after she'd made the announcement to leave, and now John is barely speaking with Simon. She hopes her husband returns from their trip north in a better mood. Knowing he is traveling with her father does not improve the chances of it happening. If anything happens to John, she'll never forgive her father. She's never forgiven him for so many other things that it would feel normal. However, where the matter of her husband is concerned, Reagan has zero patience for anyone interfering with their lives. She wishes that she'd never permitted him to leave.

Chapter Six
Cory

Cory wakes just before dawn to a strange, warm feeling against his back. He rolls slowly to find a small girl tucked against him sucking her thumb and lightly snoring. Her cheek is covered with a smear of dirt, and her curly brown hair is tangled in a rat's nest. She is clutching at the hem of his jacket with her tiny fist. She must be a stealthy little bugger to have sneaked up against him sometime in the middle of the night. She can't be more than three or four years old. He wonders where her folks are and if they are with the group of people they rescued.

When he tries to rise, the little waif clings tighter. This is a conundrum.

"I see you have a friend," a woman's soft whisper elicits.

He twists his head to look above him. The woman with the flirty, blue eyes from last night- who he can't remember her name- is lying on a mattress that is right at the head of his. Cory distinctly remembers dragging his own twin mattress to this secluded spot in the banquet hall so he could be alone. He wonders if she did the same or followed his lead.

"Does she belong to you?" he whispers back.

"No, she's an orphan," the woman returns. Her blonde hair is smooth as if she just brushed it.

"From the other day? Her parents were…?" he leaves it at that since they both know the incident to which he is referring.

"No, no. She's with our group but didn't have parents in our group. As a matter of fact, we just found her last week. Some of the hunters in our group found her out in the woods all alone."

"Oh," Cory says softly, feeling terrible for the little girl.

"Her name's Tessa. At least that's what we think it is. She says her name, but she's hard to understand. She doesn't talk much. Actually, she hardly talks at all. The guys tried to find her family and walked for miles looking but nothing. Not a soul was in sight. She told us her family is gone. That's all she said. Just gone. I'm assuming they're dead."

Cory looks down at the sleeping angel and wonders how the hell she stayed alive out in the woods by herself and for God knows how long. It makes his stomach clench just thinking about it.

The woman reaches over and extends her hand, "Rachel. From last night. Remember?"

"Um, yeah."

Her smile is a bit too bright and hopeful for Cory, so he eases over the child and stands.

"Gotta make the hay," he tells Rachel and escapes.

Dave's scouts return after dawn to report movement at Fort Knox. He'd sent them ahead to check out the place. Robert hadn't been happy. He'd wanted to head straight in without the scouting party clearing the area first. He was overridden, and he hadn't taken it well. However, nobody wanted to walk into a trap, especially not when they had the extra responsibility of Thomas and his people with them. They reported that there were ordinary citizens, men, women and children among the soldiers. The soldiers were all armed. They were walking patrols and had guards posted near the entry gate, which wasn't much of a gate anymore according to his men.

A few of Dave's men stay behind with Thomas's group as the rest of them head to the base. Cory rides in the back of the deuce with his brother and John and the rest of the men as well as Robert's wife. When they roll up to the sentries at the wrecked gate, Robert and Dave exit the deuce and approach. Cory watches from the bed of the truck as the soldiers salute Robert. He has changed into a general's uniform and has somehow managed to get his act together this morning.

Cory leans over and asks his brother, "You weren't ever stationed here, were you, Kel?"

"Nah, not here," he says.

"Derek was for a short period," John tells him.

They are permitted entrance, which puts Cory on high alert as the truck trolls slowly onto the base. He has a feeling his brother and John are feeling the same level of nerves. He notices that his friend's hand tightens on the stock of his rifle.

The truck comes to a stop near a brick building, and it is clear to Cory that the Army base has been raided before and that nobody had chosen to live here before now. The scouts were right, though. There are people, including women and children, walking around, some doing chores, others working with the men. His group is instructed to follow a pick-up truck. They pass a school that has long since rung its final bell for the day. The front doors are barely hanging on by their hinges. They pass a smaller building, and Cory can just make out the word Patton before they go by it. They pull up to another red brick building and are waved into a spot. They park beside the other vehicle as a group of men come out of the building. Cory and the rest of Dave's team hop down and await orders.

"General!" a man with short cropped, pale blonde hair in his late forties says in greeting and holds out his hand to shake Robert's. "We were getting worried, sir."

"No need," he says, trying to allay their concerns. "Ran into a few delays, Parker."

"Well, we're glad you're here, sir," Parker returns.

"How long have you been here?"

"A little over two months, General," he explains. "Others are still coming. The first hundred of us got here a few months ago. More have come since."

Dave asks, "How are you feeding so many people."

They all look around at the many people moving about. Cory would like to know how they're doing it, too.

68

Parker says to Robert, "We can go over everything. I'm sure you all have a lot of questions. Let's get you inside, show you around. We've set up a headquarters here. Your men can come, too."

Parker smiles at them, but Cory would like to tell him that they are not Robert's men. They are simply the security detail that got him to the base. They don't work for him. It's something Robert would do well to learn also.

They are shown to a conference room where most of Dave's men stand against the wall. Cory follows suit. Robert introduces them, and introductions are made on Parker's side of the table, as well. Cory notices that a few of the men look at one another quickly when his brother and John are introduced to the group. He wonders if they know John and his brother.

"Tell me what I've missed," Robert orders as soon as everyone is seated or is standing where they wish to be.

Parker says, "It was rough getting outta there, sir. The sheer number of people I took with me made it more difficult, but we managed."

"How many people are on this base now?" Kelly asks.

"Over four hundred," Parker answers.

Dave repeats his question from outside, "And how are you maintaining this? Feeding and housing?"

"It hasn't been too hard yet," Parker says. "We've been hunting, fishing, brought produce with us."

"How'd you bring enough to feed hundreds of people?" Kelly asks.

Parker looks at Robert briefly before answering, "We have been taking from the storage facility in the bunker for some time. We had people working on the inside. Plus, we took seeds. Don't look at me like that," he says to them. "We helped harvest everything that was canned. We had farmers and workers out there who were on our side of the argument. We didn't steal. We didn't take more than we left."

"And don't you think that might piss off the new President when he sees that a lot of their supplies have been taken?" Dave asks, shifting in his seat.

"Like I said, we didn't wipe them out. There is plenty left for the people still there. We only took enough to hold us over until our first season of harvest comes in."

Robert breaks in to further explain, "In the new capital, we had certain emergency stores of food and supplies also in place in case we had a drought harvest."

"And we also brought dehydrated fruit for the children and the elderly," Parker explains. "We had many fruit trees in Colorado and berries that the workers in food prep took care of. They made fruit leathers and dehydrated packets of fruit like blueberries and apples. Again, we only took enough to hold us over, mostly hold over the children, till our spring starts here. We'd never leave people out there without enough to hold themselves over till the summer harvest. Sergeant Winters, we still have a lot of friends out there."

Dave nods, but Cory sees a certain amount of skepticism in his eyes.

"Food prep?" Kelly asks. "What's that supposed to mean?"

Robert says, "Oh, it's a wonderful and organized system, something I'd hoped to put into place in our own town."

"What kind of system?" Dave questions.

"Everyone has a job," Robert explains. "If you can farm, then you farm. If you can do canning, then you'll be in the food prep division. We have divisions and place people within them according to their skill sets. Doctors and nurses worked in the medical building."

"We've already established a medical clinic, sir," Parker tells them.

"Oh, good. That's great, Parker," Robert says.

"Yes, sir. We've already had an outbreak of the flu. We lost two people on the trip here," he informs them sadly.

"How exactly did you get here?" Dave asks next.

"Cars, vans, it was a caravan."

"How did you all sneak out at the same time?" Kelly asks.

Parker sighs and runs a hand through his pale hair, "We didn't all leave at the same time. Others will still come. A small group of twenty or so would sneak out and rendezvous. Then a few days later, twenty more. Eventually, we all met up on the road at the meeting point. It took some time, but we managed."

"And you think they're just going to let any others escape? Why all the escaping anyway? If people don't want to stay, then why is he not allowing them to leave?" Dave asks.

Robert says, "It's not that he has forbidden anyone from leaving. It's just been made very clear that it is frowned upon."

"There's a jail," Parker says. "A few years ago, a small group left, and a month later we found out they were in the prison a few miles away. When we questioned him, the President said it was because they needed to be reeducated. We knew then that we had a problem on our hands."

Cory isn't sure what the rest of them think of this information, but it pisses him off.

"You're tellin' me he took away free will?" Dave asks with unspoken anger.

"He didn't want people to leave. He said it was because they could tell others about the place and we would be overrun someday. He said he was protecting the interests of the citizens," Parker explains.

"Bullshit," one of Dave's men says. "Nobody could overrun a city that size."

"We started questioning his motives after that," Robert tells them.

"And soldiers?" Kelly inquires. "How many soldiers are here in this camp?"

"Nearly three hundred are trained soldiers," he says. "Some of the older teenagers are showing a willingness to learn, too. They want to be involved."

"Involved in what exactly?" Kelly quickly asks before Robert can say anything else.

Parker doesn't know what to say and defers to Robert, who also says nothing.

"How dangerous is this new President at the bunker?" Kelly redirects.

"Um," Parker mumbles. "Sir?"

He is looking at Robert to take the lead on this topic. For some reason, he seems to be the general's right-hand man, and yet he doesn't behave particularly forthcoming with information.

Robert says, "We have to be prepared for anything."

"Do you think the President will come all the way this far east to pursue a war with you?" Kelly asks. "It doesn't exactly make a lot of sense."

"There are a lot more people coming," Parker finally answers. "It's not just going to be the four hundred of us. Many more will come, and we'll be gathering people from local communities around here that are barely hanging on. He'll see it as a threat. I don't think he'll allow us to establish such a large city without seeing us as a potential threat."

"Did you learn that technique of harvesting more citizens while living out there under this new President?" Kelly asks.

"Yes, sir," one of the other men answers who is sitting next to Parker. "We got good at finding people. It's effective. We offer them a safe place. They provide the growing community with their skills or education. We've already established a school here, as well. A few of the teachers from the bunker came with us. We're using the elementary school here on base."

John shakes his head and says, "It can't be that safe if you're planning on waging war with this other army."

He hasn't spoken much, but neither had Cory expected him to. John is more of a listener, an observer.

"We aren't planning that," Robert says. "We just want to start over somewhere else. This is our group escaping his tyranny."

"But why build the army then?" Kelly asks.

Parker's eyes dart to Robert's before he says, "Preventative. And a military force should be the first step in building a new country."

"We have a country," Kelly reminds them. "Nobody needs to split it up or rewrite our Constitution. That's just bullshit."

"And you don't exactly have the numbers it would take to defeat an army of thousands," John comments.

"We know that," Parker says. "We're a long way from being ready. But we feel with the proper training and some time, we could be. We're glad that you all will be coming on board, too."

"What?" Kelly asks with surprise.

Robert is quick to say, "They aren't exactly on board with us yet. The situation at the farm was different than I'd anticipated."

He doesn't say anything further, which leaves Cory to speculate exactly what Robert thought he'd find at the farm. He wonders what his plans were for his family or the farm. Obviously, Robert hadn't known about all the extra people living there, but if it weren't for them, Herb and his family would've been killed years ago.

"So what are you planning?" Kelly asks pointedly and with unveiled irritation brewing in his deep voice.

"Fortification," Parker answers.

"Reinforcements," Robert adds.

"We'll keep you posted on what we need," Parker says.

Cory rolls his eyes.

"We won't be supplying your community with anyone or any supplies," Kelly says tightly.

"What?" Parker asks as if surprised by this. "I assumed you'd be working in a capacity of assistance since you came with the general."

"No," Kelly returns. There is a long silence.

"This situation could be a turning point in our country," Parker points out. "I don't understand how you can't be involved. You men have a military rank. You need to be involved. You are involved whether you want to be or not."

"You don't even have a plan on how to handle this man if he shows up," Dave remarks. There is slight disgust in his voice.

"We will soon," Robert says. "Now that I'm here…"

"Wait," one of the other soldiers lining the opposite wall says, interrupting Robert. "Sorry, sir. But, I for one would like to know what Sergeant Harrison has to say. No offense, but…"

"What?" John says with surprise.

"Well, sir, you're a Medal of Honor recipient. I remember you, sir, what you did," another man says. "We want to know how you'd handle this."

Cory had no idea John received such a prestigious medal.

"General McClane is the ranking officer here, men," Parker reprimands coolly. He is clearly disappointed in his soldiers for questioning them. "You'll take your orders from the general or myself."

"Seems to me I don't remember gettin' a paycheck for the last four fuckin' years, so I'd say we're all done takin' orders from just about anyone," Dave remarks with hostility. Parker backs down. "'Cept maybe from our wives."

There is laughter which helps calm the mood in the room. Cory doesn't laugh. He's not sure if he's going to like this Parker dude. He's more certain that he doesn't like Robert at all after this meeting.

"Yes, sir," one of them says to Parker. "We know that. We are aware who's in charge around here. But Harrison is ex-Delta and earned the Medal of Honor. We'd like to hear his side of this. He's had a lot of experience in the field dealing with shit. Seems like we ought to consider his opinion on the matter."

Parker and Robert both turn their attention to John and wait impatiently for him to speak.

"You have a problem," John says. "We pretty much strolled in here untouched, unvetted, and without any resistance. You're outnumbered, out machined if he has tanks or weaponry of that sort, and probably outmatched by the looks of the place."

"I have a lot of years under my belt leading men, John," Robert says as if offended.

"It's not that, sir," John returns. "You don't have soldiers anymore. You have some farmers. You have some doctors. Maybe a few construction workers. You don't have soldiers with the exception of the few in this room. I saw the soldiers you were referring to. Those aren't soldiers. Those are former civilians."

"That's insulting," Parker says. "The soldiers we have are trained. They have experience."

"Experience doing what? Training in Colorado at a bunker?" John asks rhetorically. "That's not on the ground, boots in the mud experience. Being outnumbered isn't your biggest problem. You are tactically short in live war experience. We just sent a scouting party in here a few hours ago to check the place out first. You didn't even know we were there."

Parker and his men seem startled by this.

"If he shows up with three thousand men, you'd better be ready to negotiate a verbal treaty because you sure as heck aren't going to defeat him militarily. I respect the opposition to tyranny. I don't respect the idea of splitting our great nation into two countries or changing our Constitution. That ought to be left alone. You'll never get any of our support on that one. And if you are going to wage war against someone who is supposed to be our President, well, then you'll have to do it without our support."

"Bullshit!" Parker says, spittle hitting the table in front of him. "You'll do as you're told. The general is in charge."

"He's not in charge of *us*," John says, leveling a glare at Parker that lets the other man know of his loss of patience. "Nobody's in charge of us anymore. Our general, General Gregory D. Loveland, released us from our service to the United States Army. I will not be pulled back in. Our group has small towns and families back home that we're all responsible for, and that's where we'll be heading tomorrow morning. We lived up to our promise to bring Robert here, and we did just that. I heard what you've had to say. It's all we promised to do. We never agreed to re-up and join the general in this fight."

"You'll be sorry you said that when your families and your little town are under the socialist thumb of the President," Parker says.

"How would that even happen?" Dave asks. "He's in another state. There are very limited communications. Zero long-range transportation options. How the hell's he gonna enslave all of us?"

"He'll eventually destroy the rest of the framework of our Constitution, and someday it will spread this far," Parker persists.

"His own citizens will only tolerate this for so long," John points out.

Kelly holds his hand up and says, "We're fifty years from even having power restored in this country. Have you seen the coastlines?"

It is clear that Parker has not. Some of the men standing behind him nod. By the looks on their faces, they've seen the devastation out there.

"The only way we'll rebuild this country is to band together, build cities, and grow our military again," Robert argues.

"Well, then we'll wish you luck with that, General," John says and stands. "But we're not going to be a part of it. We'll be back at the farm taking care of your family for you."

With that, they file out. Cory looks back and notices that Robert's face has flushed to a dark crimson. He does not believe it is from being overheated. He's downright pissed off.

Chapter Seven
Simon

It seems strange that Lucas is older than him. He is so completely opposite of Gretchen in every single way that it's also hard to remember that she's related to him. Simon does enjoy working with Luke, though. He's a no-nonsense kind of guy and totally devoted to his research. At first, he'd been worried that Lucas might be interested in Sam, but then he realized that Luke was just curious about everyone on the farm.

Unfortunately, neither of them are doing research on smallpox or cancer or influenza or anything remotely interesting. They are treating the cattle for ringworm. Derek had noticed the first outbreak last night and had discussed it at breakfast, which hadn't been smiled upon by the other diners at the table.

They are treating the smaller, easier to handle calves first and will move on to the full-sized cattle later. Dealing with an eight hundred pound beef steer is easier to do when they are trapped in the head gate apparatus. Derek will be herding them into the chute with Huntley's help while Doc, Luke and he treat them. For now, they are still taking care of the babies with G and Reagan's help.

"Hold him, G," Reagan says as she rubs the rag soaked in lavender oil and apple cider vinegar over the calf's thick, winter coat. The calf is wiggling and whining to be free. Simon isn't so sure Reagan should even be handling any of the livestock while she's pregnant. She could be bumped or hurt, and the baby could be put in danger. He knows telling her this would likely only irritate her and cause her to sneer at him meanly.

"I can't!" G cries out. "Hold still, you little shit!"

Simon has to hold back a chuckle. It's a good thing Hannah's in the house taking care of the children with Sue or else she'd be whacking G to the back of the head. He can't blame Gretchen, though. The cows are generally stupid animals of low intelligence which always seem to do the exact opposite thing that you want them to do. He figures what happens in the barn can stay a secret between the people working there. Animals can be very frustrating. So can humans, especially one very defiant and annoying person he knows so well.

"That's it, Miss Gretchen," Doc says, encouraging her. "You've got him now. That ninety-pound calf has nothing on you!"

She shoots Herb a glare for his teasing. Then she laughs and swears again. Justin and Arianna also wrestle the calves, helping greatly and making the process move more efficiently. Paige mixes the medicine. It is the only job they will allow her to do. She does it from a position outside of the pen on a hay bale so that she is out of danger. Cory's stupid dog is lying at her feet. For some reason, the mutt has taken to Simon's sister.

Reagan has both of the kids each sit on a calf once it is lying on its side while she inserts the long, plastic tube into the animal's mouth and down to the stomach. Doc pours a small amount of the homemade antibacterial, antibiotic solution down a funnel and the calf is dosed and then set free. The garlic and oregano oil mixed with a small amount of apple cider vinegar and salt should kill the invading ringworm. They'll need to be careful of it spreading to the other animals and also themselves. If they don't treat it, some of the smaller cattle could be killed by the outbreak.

The work is laborious and filthy, but by late afternoon, they have all of the livestock including the horses treated or pre-treated for ringworm. Doc has him and Derek stretch the long, ten-foot back rub into place between the two wide entry doors to the barn. Usually they'd pour homemade fly deterrent solution onto it, but

78

today Doc will pour the rest of their homemade ringworm solution onto the material and let it soak in. Every time one of the cows walks under it and rubs the worn, cotton material of the bolster, it will be dosing itself again with the solution.

They finish the day off with feeding the animals and tending to the sick or injured ones. Simon allows Paige to follow him around, but he slows his pace considerably since she is still recovering and has a long road ahead of her. Cory's dog is right on her heels the whole time.

The sun is already getting low, and another day is gone. He'll have to work in the shed this evening after everyone goes to bed. Derek, Justin and Huntley head to Derek's cabin in the woods for showers while the rest of the family clean up in the big house. He'd like to move back into his and Cory's cabin, but he isn't sure if Robert and his wife will be returning to it. He checked on it earlier in the morning during his patrol walk and had found it pretty bare. They must've taken most of what they owned and brought to the farm with them because it was cleaned out. Everything was wiped down, the beds made, and the bathroom polished. It was if they had never stayed there in the first place.

He waits on the second floor for Luke and G to get their showers first since Ari is using the bathroom in the basement. Paige is busy drawing in her bedroom, so he pops in to visit with her.

"Whatcha' working on?" he inquires over her shoulder.

Her hair is pulled up into a wet bun on the top of her head since she already caught a quick shower. She's wearing a black sweatshirt, which he's fairly sure belongs to Cory since it has the logo for a car manufacturer on the front. It makes him uneasy, even though he knows that his sister hadn't come to the farm with much. He'd like to suggest wearing one of the women's clothing selections available but holds his tongue. She probably doesn't even realize it belongs to Cory.

"I thought this would be neat to build someday in the vacant lot next to the library. You know since they're trying to hold classes for kids there. Well, they were before part of the library burned down."

"What is it?"

"A playground for the kids. They could go out during school breaks. Plus, when school isn't in session they could play and hang out here. It would give the kids in town somewhere to feel more normal."

"Keep in mind that some of these kids will never know what normal is or was for us. They will grow up thinking that holding class in an old library is the norm."

"True, but they still need somewhere that is just theirs, not something that belongs to the adults."

"It's a good idea," he praises.

"Really?" she asks, raising her eyes to meet his. "It's probably a waste of resources right now to use wood and salvaged things to build a playground for kids."

Simon shakes his head, "Nah, I don't think so. I actually think it's a very good idea to waste materials on it. Kids do need a place to feel like kids. There's nothing like this in the section of town we walled up. All they do is work like adults on chores and helping. It would be good for them to have a place to relax and just be kids. Now that the wall is getting closer to completion and the threat of the other town is gone, I don't see why they couldn't have somewhere to play outside this spring and summer. It'll be good for them."

"I just thought that the kids here on the farm have a playground and barns and everywhere and anywhere they want to go to play and feel safe, but the little ones in town don't have any of that. They are confined within the walls of the town and their homes, and nothing much is there for kids."

"I think if we gave these plans to the men in town, they'd think it's a good idea, too. Heck, they'd probably have this built by spring."

"That would be nice," she says with a smile.

"They talked about cutting out Jay's section of the town from the wall's city limits, but I don't know what's been decided."

"Yeah, with them gone, I don't see the point of having that be a part of the town. Nobody lives over there now, so why use the time and building materials to extend the wall?" Paige asks rhetorically.

"Exactly," Simon agrees with her. "Plus, if they don't extend the wall over there, then it doesn't have to be patrolled, either. That's more important."

He studies her sketch, noting that she has made a playground that resembles a small castle, complete with a drawbridge, a slide, and numerous climbing areas. They could use old tires to make swings, and there's always scrap wood laying around, especially from the wall build. She has even included a fireman's pole like all children enjoy going down. There are heavy gauge ropes hanging down from the one side so they could swing to and fro and climb up and down. It's a well-thought-out drawing. It's also odd since she doesn't have kids. She must be learning a lot about them living on this farm.

"See?" she says, pointing to a small section that has a roof and a floor. "This could be like a clubhouse where the kids could hang out up here and play games."

"Cool," he remarks. "We could use galvanized sheet metal to cover it. The material lasts longer and wouldn't warp if it gets wet like plywood. I think this could be really fun for the kids."

"They could even pitch in to help," Paige tells him. "We could search for some paint or stain, and they could seal it with a coat when it's done."

"Yeah, great idea."

Gretchen comes in a moment later, "Simon, you can have the shower now. We're both done."

"I'd better hit it while I can," he tells his sister.

"Yeah, hurry," she says. "Remember, some of Dave's men are stopping by for dinner and to help with night watch while the men are gone."

"Yeah, can't forget. I'll have to put on my Sunday best," he teases with sarcasm before leaving.

The hot shower feels great, leaving him with enough renewed energy to make it through the rest of his night. He balls his dirty clothing into a pile and leaves them in Paige's hamper. She has vacated her room, probably so that he'd have some privacy getting dressed. He pulls on clean khakis, a t-shirt and a blue flannel shirt. It wasn't too cold out earlier, but he knows the temperature will fall tonight when he's out on a patrol or working in the shed, and he'll need the layers under his coat to stay warm.

"Simon!" Sue calls from the first floor.

He grabs the hamper full of soiled clothing so that his sister won't have to make the trek down the steep stairway with it. She is still recovering and shouldn't even be lifting anything over a few pounds. He jogs down the stairs and is met by Doc and Derek. One of Dave's men, Gunny, is standing with them. Another one of Dave's men, someone of whom Simon cannot recall his name, is also with Doc and Derek. Sue is behind them holding baby Daniel. She seems concerned. Simon knows that Gunny, or Henry as is his real name, had looked with a certain amount of desire at Samantha once. He hates it that she's living over there on Henry's farm. It makes his stomach twist into knots at night when he can't sleep and lies awake tossing and turning over her abrupt departure.

"We've called Chet and Ryan Johnson over for a meeting," Doc explains.

"What's going on?" he asks. They were supposed to be having dinner and nothing else.

"We'll explain everything once the others arrive," Doc says.

Henry and the other man shake his hand. He nods but feels his apprehension level raising. Something is afoot if they want a meeting of this caliber. Fifteen minutes later, they are in the dining room with the doors closed off to the children's ears. Reagan and his sister are also present while Gretchen and Huntley keep an eye on the kids. Talia has come with her husband and has also brought along little Maddie. The sisters allow her to sit in on the meeting next to Paige while they watch Maddie for her. Everyone seems on edge.

Hannah and Sue are putting the finishing touch on their dinner in the kitchen. He can hear the pots and pans clanking. Usually, it is a comforting sound. Tonight, it does nothing to calm his nerves.

Doc announces, "We've called this meeting to discuss an incident on the highway near Dave's town."

"What happened?" Paige asks.

Lucas also seems nervous. He likely feels a great deal of responsibility for his little sister since their parents are gone.

Derek explains, "There was an attack. It was just like the one our group found on the road to Fort Knox yesterday."

Henry jumps in to say, "There were only four survivors out of their group twenty-six. They were hit hard, with brutal violence and a lot of force. They said they hid until the attackers left."

"How close was it to your town?" Chet asks.

Henry frowns and says, "Too close for comfort. Maybe ten miles from us."

His light brown eyes are concerned about his people on the farm. Simon can see it written there. Henry is slightly shorter than Simon but built like a bull. The t-shirt he wears under his jacket is stretched tightly across his chest and neck.

"How many people are living on your farm now, Gunny?" Derek asks. "I know you and Dave took in quite a few of those women from the camp."

Simon knows he means the sex camp but has refrained from referring to it as such. There just isn't a nice way of phrasing such an atrocity.

"We're up to forty-seven, but that doesn't count the people in our town. We have another few hundred living there," Henry explains with a deep frown. "Some of the women we all rescued from the camp had family members we allowed in to the town once we went out and found them. Others are living on my farm. Some of the other women have… well, some of our men are with them now."

Doc is quick to say, "Sounds like we need some wedding officiating over there."

"Yes, sir," Henry says sheepishly.

Doc is a stickler for propriety, and Henry must realize it. If Dave's men are sleeping with any of those women or have moved them into their barracks, then Doc is going to want them married and soon.

"We can deal with that soon enough, son," Doc reassures him with a wink.

Henry simply nods, probably not sure if his men would want him speaking for them. If their situation weren't so grave right now, it would be a funny moment.

"Yes, sir," Henry says quietly. "We are going on a scouting mission tomorrow to see if we can't locate these men who are attacking people on the freeway. They are getting too close to our towns."

"Wait, it was close to our town, too?" Paige asks with growing concern.

"And how close to our farms?" Chet asks.

"Yes, sir. Close to your town. Not too far from here, either, bout ten miles," the other man from Dave's camp says. "South of here near Lickton."

"That's two," Derek says with seething anger. "Two attacks in the last week."

"No, sir," Henry replies. "We got a radio call in just a few days ago saying that our friends up north of Millersville saw the same thing on the freeway. They heard from someone else about a similar attack about a half hour west of there. It seems," he says, opening and spreading out a map and pointing, "that they're hitting this area."

There is a red circle already drawn on the map. It makes Simon's stomach sink. To see it in plain writing, circled in red, is hard to process. There are small, red stars marking each of the hits. Gunny's circle encompasses their own small town and their neighbors and the McClane farm.

"Dave didn't mention the call you got from your neighbors," Derek remarks.

"We weren't sure it was gonna turn into anything," Henry answers. "We hear about situations like this all the time. Usually, they aren't connected. Sergeant Winters usually sends a group of us on an intel run to check out whatever issues our neighbors have."

"We do the same," Reagan tells him.

"Yes, ma'am," Henry returns. "It seems to be the only solution to keeping the…enemy at bay."

Sue comes in with a tray of sweet rolls and a teapot. She pours those who want it hot tea and passes the tray of sweets around. Simon is too consumed with the events of the moment to concern himself with food. He is literally sitting on the edge of his chair with anticipation. Many scenarios are playing through his thoughts, but none of them has a good outcome.

"Thank you, ma'am," Henry and his partner say with grateful nods and take huge bites of their sweet rolls. "Been a long time since I've had something this good. My mama used to make something like this for breakfast on Sundays before church. These are mighty tasty."

Sue smiles and says, "Don't have too many. You'll spoil your dinners. Chet, are you guys staying for dinner?"

"No thanks, Sue," he answers with a smile. "Bertie's got dinner waiting for us. Venison stew. Our favorite."

She smiles and leaves again.

"Like I was saying," Henry continues after taking a sip of his tea, "when we hear things like this, we always run out and check on it. Usually, they aren't related. Most groups we've had problems with aren't this coordinated."

"How well-coordinated are they?" Derek asks.

Henry frowns again before saying, "Very. We've got a pretty good guess of the size doing the raids. We think there may be as many as thirty people doing this, maybe more."

"Thirty?" Doc asks with unconcealed surprise.

Chet jumps in to ask, "How did you come to those numbers?"

"Well, the survivors of the groups are calling in the numbers at twenty or so. We figure it'd take at least another five to ten people keeping watch, hunting, running whatever camp they've got. We could be looking at fifteen. We could be looking at fifty. It's hard telling until we gather some intel on them. But the one thing we're pretty sure of is that we're dealing with more than a couple."

"It's gonna take a combined effort with your battalion to take out a group this size," Derek comments.

"Yes, sir," Henry says. "I'd agree with that assessment, Major Harrison."

Simon can see the soldier in Henry. When he'd first met him on the street in Nashville with John, Kelly and Cory, Simon hadn't seen this side of him. He'd acted casual, cool as if he hadn't a care in the world on top of that deuce while manning the fifty cal. He'd winked at Sam, which had pissed Simon off, but he hadn't looked like much of a fighter. Now a light has been flicked on behind Henry's brown eyes. There is something intense and dangerous in his visage. Simon sees the same thing in Derek, who is much older and more conservative about showing this side of himself. He has perfected the act of hiding this part of himself away, especially from his wife. Simon can see it anyway. He feels the same way right now. He'd like to hunt them down tonight and kill them all, even if he doesn't like killing people. They are a menace to their fledgling society and their newfound, short-lived peace. If these men are targeting people on the road, who usually don't have much to begin with in Simon's experience, then they need to be stopped. Robbing innocent people is unacceptable. Most people moving on foot have whatever they can carry on their backs or the meager amount of possessions they can stuff into small, compact vehicles. Perhaps they are like his sister, still traveling around the country finding lost loved ones or other survivors like themselves. It angers Simon that this group is picking them off like they have the right. The McClane family has never bothered with nomads moving from one area to another. They are never a threat. People are targeting them because they aren't a threat and because they can.

"We'll be scouting tomorrow," Henry repeats. "We'll try to gather some intel on them first before making a move. We'll wait for Sergeant Winters to return to issue the order if we find them. Or you, Major Harrison."

Even though he is the sole inheritor and rightful owner of his farm where Dave's men are camped, Henry obviously heeds to the military rank of Sergeant Winters. Dave is a good man in Simon's opinion, so everyone over there must trust him to make the right decisions for their group. Simon does not envy that amount of responsibility.

"No, I agree with you, Henry," Derek says. "And just call me Derek. No need for rank anymore. I'm not gonna order a strike until the guys come back."

"If we find them, I'll wait for you and Sergeant Winters to make the call then," Henry says.

"Good idea," Derek says, clasping his hands in front of him on the table. "Can you spare some men to help keep an eye on the farm tomorrow? Simon and I could help you on this intel run."

"I want to go, too," Chet says. "Wayne can watch the farm while I'm gone. Maybe a couple people from the Johnson's can come over to help him."

"I'd rather you and your brother stay local to keep an eye on our three farms, Chet," Derek says. "If they already hit within ten miles of here and we're all gone, we could have a problem."

"Right, you're right, Derek," Chet answers.

"I don't have a problem with you going, Derek," Henry says. "Yeah, that'd be great, sir. I can bring four or five men from our town over to help out."

"Are they trustworthy?" Reagan asks with apprehension.

"Oh, yes, ma'am," Henry says quickly. "You don't have to worry. I'd never send someone over here I didn't trust myself with any of our people."

"Cory's our best tracker, but he went up north with Dave," Derek explains, running a hand through his sandy brown hair which is slightly longer than his usual shortly clipped style. "But I figure we could help. We've gotta nip this in the bud before it ends up at our front door."

"Yes, sir," Henry says. "Agreed. We'll pick ya'll up tomorrow, say oh-five-hundred hours?"

"Sounds good," Derek says and stands.

Once their neighbors are gone, the discussion starts again.

"I can go, too," Reagan volunteers and is at once rejected by everyone in the room.

They have waited until dinner was served so that Sue and Hannah can be a part of the talks. Henry and his friend are eating like ravenous wolves. It leaves Simon to wonder if the meals are as well-prepared or even as plentiful at their farm. It leaves him feeling concerned once again about Sam's well-being.

Reagan says, "Wait a minute. It's not dangerous. It's just a run to gather information. I can help."

"I'd rather you were here in case something happened," Derek tells her. "What if something happened on the farm and you were gone? Your grandfather would be on his own if someone needed emergency medical care or if the farm was attacked. If the Reynolds or Johnson farms are also under attack at the same time, there could be a problem defending ours."

"True," she concedes, chewing her lower lip thoughtfully.

"Were any of the survivors needing medical care, Henry?" Doc asks, not surprising Simon that he would think of the victims first.

"No, sir," Henry answers between bites of roasted root vegetables. "They were mostly scraped up and banged up and just plain scared. They were pretty shaken up by the whole thing. Many of them lost family members and friends."

"What about the other survivors from any of the other attacks?" Reagan asks. "Were any of them needing medical attention?"

"Not sure, ma'am," Henry answers. "Our friends to the south have a medical facility of sorts. It's not as high-tech or as organized as you all's clinic, but I know they've got a doctor and a couple nurses or something. I think he might be a veterinarian or some such."

"Vets are good, too," Reagan assures them. "They had to study just as much as we did in school. You'd be surprised how many animals have similar organs, structure, and physiology as humans."

With that comment, she gazes off into the distance, likely thinking about the similarities. Simon notes the dark circles under her green eyes and worries anew over his friend. She probably isn't sleeping much since John is gone. She gets like this when he is away from the farm. Actually, she's usually even worse. She normally gets mean and nasty, but Doc's been keeping her especially busy lately. It's a smart move.

Sue asks, "So you don't think anyone needs help?"

"Anyone who was actually alive and injured was dealt with, but mostly I think the survivors were just shook up," Henry says.

"I can imagine," Doc replies. "How hard it must be to come upon bandits on the road while trying to move your family to a new location, likely leaving a bad situation for the promise of something better. This is a travesty, indeed, that has happened to these people."

"Yes, sir," Henry answers solemnly.

Derek says, "Don't worry, Herb. We'll handle this. These people and their terrorizing of innocents will end soon enough. We just need some time to plan it."

Doc nods, but Simon can tell that his mentor is profoundly disturbed over the situation.

"We can go over a radius to cover tomorrow," Henry suggests as he reaches for another slice of freshly baked bread.

"Have you heard from John or Kelly?" Sue inquires.

"Not yet," Doc answers. "The last we spoke was this morning."

"Everything's fine," Derek says, trying to dispel the need for worry. "If they were having problems, they would've called for help. No call means no bad news."

"Right," Hannah says with a soft sigh. There are tiny creases in her normally smooth forehead.

"Henry, how is Samantha doing over there on your farm?" Sue asks. Her eyes dart furtively to Simon's before looking away.

"Uh, she's doing just fine, ma'am. I'd say she's adjusting to our ways. We do things a little different in some ways and probably pretty much the same in others as you all do here. But, she's fitting right in, making friends. She's a real asset to our community, ma'am. Everyone really likes her."

"And her uncle?" Hannah asks next. "How is he doing?"

"Great, ma'am," Henry answers. "The two of them are workin' real hard on getting the clinic up and running. Guess she's gonna work with her uncle there, just like you all do with your clinic. Miss Patterson's been real helpful. Nice girl, she is."

Henry's friend nods in agreement with his assessment of Sam. Simon would like to punch them both in the throat but refrains. They are supposed to be allies. He excuses himself a moment later and takes his plate to the kitchen. He doesn't want to hear any more about Samantha or her fine and smooth transition to a perfect stranger's farm. It proves how independent she is of them. He hates this about her.

After dinner, they plan for the morning before going about their duties. Simon agrees to take first watch with Huntley as Henry and his friend are forced to leave for their own farm again. Simon can't say that he's sad to see them go. He'd rather work alone anyway, and he sure as hell doesn't want to hear stories about Sam from either of them. Three hours later, four men from Henry's farm show up to keep watch the rest of the night over the McClane farm. They seem harmless. They are highly trained, however, and it shows in their maneuvers and communications. It helps to alleviate some of his fears that the farm will be in danger while he and Derek are gone tomorrow with Henry looking for societal leeches. Simon and Derek crash for a few hours since they'll be back up and on the road bright and early with Henry. Simon tosses and turns. He tries reading a book about wound care, but the words blur and become one big, jumbled mess on the page. He turns his light back off and resumes the tossing and turning portion of his night. He stares at the ceiling

90

willing himself to sleep. It doesn't work. Nothing works. He is in total misery and knows the source. The swish of her dark ponytail, the fierce blue of her eyes, the soft curve of her waist, these are what keep him awake. He tries to tell himself that she's in a good place, that it's safer for her over there away from him, that she's better off. These lies are hard to swallow and cause stomach bile to rise in his throat.

When he finally exhausts himself, Simon falls asleep. Sam haunts him there, as well. He will never be rid of her, but at least in his dreams he can be with her in any fashion he desires. It is the one place where they can forget their pasts, move on, be together and find happiness at last. These are only fantasies. Reality is much crueler.

Chapter Eight
Cory

They are invited to dine with Robert, Parker and their men, but instead, they head back to collect the rest of their group from the hotel. They'll spend the night within the walls of Fort Knox, which seems to Cory to be a smart idea. Instead of eating dinner with Robert and his men, they cook and eat the food they brought with them for the trip. Then they are shown a sleeping barracks where they leave Thomas and his people from the road. Robert sends a man to collect them for another meeting. Cory catches his brother rolling his eyes to John.

They are escorted to a brick building where Robert will be housed. Cory walks beside his brother while Dave is in front of them with John as they are shown down a long hall to a small apartment. Cory's not sure if this space was actually an apartment before or if they've converted it to one for Robert since he is their leader. Robert's wife greets them and asks if they want something to drink, which they decline. They are shown into a room that looks like it will eventually be his office. Chairs have been brought in for the meeting, so they each gladly take one. There is still much to be discussed with Herb's son.

Robert comes in a few minutes later and says, "Sorry to keep you waiting. I was in a meeting with the security team."

"That's good," John remarks. "That's something important to get worked out. Security is the most important aspect to establish first."

He nods and says, "Yes, agreed. We have to keep up the security to protect the people here. The same as you've done on the farm and in your town."

Robert crosses the room to sit behind his desk. His color has returned, and he doesn't look as sick as he did earlier. His wife takes a seat in the corner.

"I'd like to ask some of you to stay on for a while," he starts with, which is a bad decision on his part in Cory's opinion.

"Not gonna happen," Kelly says with decided finality.

Dave also shakes his head and says, "No way. I'm heading back tomorrow morning first thing. I've got a compound to run and people to look after."

"What about you, John?" the general asks.

"With all due respect, Robert, it takes all of us to keep the farm safe," he answers.

"But you and your brother, Kelly and Cory, and Sergeant Winters and his men are the kind of soldiers I need here," Robert pleads. "I need men with experience in the field. I can't run an army without quality leadership. You've all got that. You've led men before. You've been in this type of situation before."

"And what about the farm, General?" Kelly asks.

"I can send men from here to look after the farm while you're here on the base," Robert suggests.

"That's not a good idea," Kelly argues.

Cory thinks it's an idiotic idea but doesn't give his opinion. He is content to sit back and watch this discussion play out, confident his brother and John will handle it.

Robert's next idea is even worse, "Then why don't you bring your family here? It would just be like living on a base as if you were stationed here."

"We're not stationed here," Kelly returns.

"The government stopped reassigning us to bases a little over three years ago," Dave reminds him.

"I realize that, but this is a matter of national security, the security of our country," Robert says.

"No, this is a matter of your own security from this dude you've got a beef with," Dave points out.

This pisses Robert off because he sends a contemptuous glare in Dave's direction. From what Cory can tell, Dave isn't fazed by it in the least.

"Bring your families here," Robert reiterates. "It's safe and will be even more so once you all are running the security and training the soldiers."

"You want me to bring my Hannah here? *Here?* To an Army base," Kelly asks in an incredulous voice.

"She'd be…"

"No way," Kelly says bluntly. "That's never happening. Are you serious? I don't even allow her to go to town when we go. She's never leaving the farm. Neither is our daughter. It's the safest place for them."

"I disagree," Robert argues. "I would never compromise Hannah's safety, or the baby's. This base will eventually be even safer than my family's farm."

Cory is pretty sure the general is bullshitting. Plus, he'd like to remind him that the farm isn't his at all. It will eventually be inherited by Kelly and Hannah, not Robert. It seems a touchy subject, so Cory doesn't point this out.

"No," Kelly says simply. Then he expands, which causes Robert more discomfort. "I make the decisions for Hannah now. She and Mary are my responsibility and mine alone. She's my wife."

"Ok, I understand. But you could come for a short time, and when you want to return, then you could. All of you could. And I'd really like to get Derek here. He'd be perfect. He has a lot of experience leading men."

"I doubt he'll share your enthusiasm," John says of his brother.

Dave says next, "This is just so that you can insulate yourself from this idiot out west if he comes here. He has the sheer numbers. We've already warned you."

"You misunderstand, Sergeant Winters," Roberts says in a very diplomatic and yet condescending tone. "We need strong leaders. As we rebuild the government, we'll need men like you."

"There's nothing to govern," Cory finally says. "I've been out there. Have you? It's caveman days again. There's no infrastructure, no electricity, nothing. What exactly are you wanting them to govern?"

Robert straightens his jacket sleeve and says, "There will be. I believe it will happen sooner rather than later. Out in Colorado where the bunker and new capital city are located, significant progress has been made."

"Through blatant acts of socialism," Kelly remarks. "From what you've explained, I don't want my kids being raised in that kind of country anyway, so why would we get involved?"

"Yes, but it wouldn't have to be like that here."

John shakes his head with doubt before saying, "Yes, it would. It already is. You've said it yourself. You have divisions set up here by that Parker guy. Farming division, security division, cooks. People aren't living free here. You've taken away personal property ownership and free will. This is a socialist setup."

"For a while, it will have to be this way," Robert says. "Once things are established, then people could own land and work jobs."

"For the greater good of the government," John says. "This is why you told us you fled the bunker."

"It was," Robert tells them. "Look, you don't understand. I want the country to be like it was before. It's just going to take a while to do that. I need leaders. We'll need to establish a government here. Eventually, we'll need law officers, as well."

"You need a small town, not an army base the size of Knox," Kelly tells him.

"I must confess, I'd hoped to establish a home base at the farm and turn Pleasant View into our military post."

"What changed your mind?" Cory asks, too curious not to. He had an inkling that Robert had plans for the farm and that was why he took it so hard that he wasn't ever going to own it.

"It's not out of the realm of possibility," Robert says. "I hadn't expected to find the town already established. However, my father doesn't want the base of command to be the farm."

"Ya' think?" John asks impatiently. "You aren't ever putting them in danger by bringing the enemy to the farm."

"I realize that now. I had no idea so many people were living there," Robert tells them. "Realistically, though, it could work. We have hundreds of acres. Our neighbors could be a part of it, too."

Cory can see the spark of a bad idea coming into his eyes. Running any type of military operation out of the farm is the worst idea possible. Bringing the fight to them is irrational. There are women and children living there. Of course, from the looks of the base, there is the same established military post here with women and children. Cory doesn't understand where they are supposed to go when the fighting starts. It makes him wonder if he even had a plan.

"Where would everyone go?" Cory asks what he's thinking. "You couldn't have the kids in the way if a fight hit the farm."

"The farm would only be a base of operation. The military would be stationed in town," Robert says.

"I think that's a dangerous idea, too," Kelly says. "There are a lot of women, kids and old people living there. What would we do with them?"

Not to mention that they could torture people in town to find Robert's whereabouts, which would be the McClane farm. Same outcome: the farm in jeopardy and the children in harm's way.

"Move them into the neighboring town, the one that Jay fellow was trying to establish," Robert suggests.

"We've been building the perimeter wall around our town to keep people safe, not around Jay's village," John says angrily. "We're hardly gonna throw them out, kick them to the curb so that your group of people here, your army, can just move in. That makes no sense. They have homes, gardens, families in that town. They aren't moving."

"Perhaps they could all accommodate the people here," Robert suggests. "There are plenty of empty homes in that town. I noticed that when I went to the clinic. If we did make the move there, you could all be involved more, lead the people that have come here."

Cory sits quietly as do the rest of them while they mull this over. Having a lot more people in their town could be a good and a bad thing.

"How long until you think the President is gonna come after you or send people?" Kelly asks, changing the direction of their discussion.

Robert's suggestion would very suddenly take their numbers into the thousands. They would need a full local government and law enforcement agency to keep the peace. Doc's plan of allowing the community to grow slowly seems more practical.

Robert regards his clasped hands on the desk as he pauses a long time before answering. "Maybe three months. Maybe less. Hopefully longer if winter sets in again."

"What are the chances he doesn't come?" John asks.

"Slim," he answers.

"Why would he risk men and resources to chase down people who don't want to be out there anymore?" Kelly asks.

"Because he needs the manpower we took with us. Some of his doctors and scientists are here, too. Some of his planners. It wasn't just all farmers and women and children who made the trek here to this base. He needs everyone who can make a difference in the new capital. Taking any of his important people with me when we left is like a slap in the face. Remember, I told you that I was one of the architects of the new capital's system. He knows I knew exactly who to persuade to leave. Some of the doctors were CDC scientists. Some of the planners were former governors and city councilmen of big cities. They know how to put a country back together."

"Nobody knows how to fix this," John argues.

"Not true," Robert says with confidence. "You'd be surprised if you saw the capital. They were making advances in vaccinations for the children, water purification for the city, planning buildings and roads. The only thing we hadn't figured out was electricity. That being said, they were very close to getting somewhere with the electricity, too."

"That's great, but the rest of the country is still in the stone ages," Kelly remarks. "But I believe that someday, it'll get better. It already is in Pleasant View, and they need us more than you do. Actually, it sounds like you need us a lot less than they do if you have so many people with skills here."

"More are coming, but they don't have military leadership value," Robert says.

"Value," Dave remarks quietly, noting the use of Robert's wording.

"Yes, Sergeant Winters," Robert says without missing a beat. "I know it sounds harsh, but this is how we have to see people. Everyone has a value. People living in the capital city had value, or they were let go. I wouldn't necessarily do such a thing, but we do want people living here who have something to bring to the table. Unfortunately, I don't have strong military leaders. Not like all of you."

Kelly chuffs, and Cory knows it is with contempt.

"Look, our scientists could be working with our doctors at the farm and in town. They could pool knowledge, work together. They could make so many advancements. I know Reagan would love to get her hands on their research."

"She's not coming here," John says emphatically. "She's pregnant, Robert."

"I know. I know," Robert says as if he finds his daughter's pregnancy an inconvenience. "But if we established Pleasant View as our capital city instead of here, then she'd be able to work with them. Obviously, the facilities here would offer more opportunity, but we could build them a research hospital there instead."

"Did you discuss this with Doc?" Kelly asks.

"Not fully, no," Robert answers.

"We'll think about it," Kelly says with finality. "But we're all still leaving in the morning. Are you coming with us?"

"No, I can't do that to these people."

"What about your kids?" Kelly demands.

Robert looks at his wife in the corner, who has said nothing during their entire conversation. She looks down at her hands.

"I'll have to ask that you all look after them until a decision is made here," Robert says. "I appreciate your help with the matter."

Cory has to hold back a rude chuckle. His children are not a 'matter.' But making Robert see his children for their actual worth as human beings is never going to happen. From what Cory understands on the topic, he also ditched the girls on Grams and Doc years ago and rarely visited. He's a bastard. Cory could never leave his kids behind, not even if the fate of the country were at stake. His children would be more important. Paige is also more important, and he has no intention of staying on the base, either. He is anxious to be home to check on her.

"I want you all to consider staying on or coming back," Robert says. Then, to Cory's shock, he adds, "I'd hate to pull rank on any of you."

Kelly laughs a great, obnoxious guffaw and rises from his seat. The rest of them follow suit. John does not share Kelly's defiant laughter. He is quiet, in a deadly mood. Cory has seen this many times in his friend.

They leave Robert and his mute wife and head for their bunks in one of the housing buildings. There are a few hundred people sleeping in the same room. He's used to a lot more seclusion and being on his own or out in the cabin with just Simon. The men discuss their conversation with Robert while making their way through the base. The vibe is angry and resentful. Dave the Mechanic, being Dave the Mechanic throws a lot of the f-word in for good measure on how he feels about the general. Cory feels the same about the man. He's an ass.

Cory finds a bunk under a window where he can look up at the night sky. His brother, John and Dave are close by. They are talking quietly. Cory just wants to rest up for the night. He knows they have plans on stopping at a few places on the way home to scout out formula for baby Daniel back at the farm. Plus, they need to deliver Thomas's group safely to Ashland City where they had intended on traveling.

He sleeps with his boots on and will be glad when they drive away from this place in the morning. Shortly after he lies down for the night, Tessa comes to his bed and climbs in. He rolls his eyes and tries to convince her to return to her own bunk. She's sucking her thumb and holding a threadbare stuffed bear.

"You can't sleep here, kid," he whispers so as not to awaken other sleeping people. "Where's your bed? I'll take you back."

She ignores him, stays silent and looks up at him with pleading brown eyes. He has to remind himself that this is how he ended up with Damn Dog.

"Come on, kid. You need to be with the other kids…or at least one of the women." Cory isn't even sure she understands him. There is a certain amount of vacancy in her eyes. He doesn't think she has a learning disability; it just seems to him that she has been traumatized and has become mute as a result of it. Whatever happened to this kid, she's messed up. Maybe he can see it in her because he recognizes it. Huntley was like this when his twin brother died from the pneumonic plague at the farm when they first arrived on it. Cory knows that he was the same way when he lost Em.

She grabs a fistful of his shirt and doesn't let go. Her little face has fear written all over it. Cory swallows hard.

"Hey, there you are," Rachel with the flirty, blue eyes says as she approaches his cot and squats beside them.

"Looks like I've got a buddy."

"Yeah, looks like it," she agrees with a nod.

Her blonde hair drapes in thick, cascading waves over one shoulder. She's very attractive in an obvious sort of way. She's just missing an earthiness about her that he has come to like in women. Or just one woman.

"Want to go back with the kids, Tessa?" she asks in a whisper.

This earns them a shake of her head. Her tangled, light brown curls bounce around. She burrows harder into Cory's side. He has no idea how to handle this. He wonders if she'll start screaming if he tries to dislodge her away. If he allows her to stay, will she pee the bed? Is she too old to do that? These are questions better given to Sue or Hannie.

His brother walks by Cory to go to his own cot. They must be done sorting out the conversation they had with Robert.

"Kinda' young for you, isn't she, bro?" Kelly teases. "Always the ladies' man."

"Ha-ha, funny," Cory remarks quietly. Most of the people in the room are dead asleep. "She's a clinger. I don't know what to do with her. She's been shadowing me all day. I can't seem to shake her."

Kelly chuckles and bunks down in front of Cory without another word or some helpful damn advice.

"Maybe you remind her of someone," Rachel suggests.

"Usually most kids run the other way when they see me coming," Cory tells her. "I guess she can stay."

"Ok," Rachel says and presses her hand gently to Tessa's head. "I'm just over there," she adds softly. "If you want to join me later after she falls asleep. I found a nice, dark corner."

"Oh, um…thanks, but I'm pretty beat," Cory tells her, knowing she is inviting him to her cot for sex and not a hand of gin.

"Maybe another time then," she says, leans in and presses a kiss to his closed mouth before he can do anything about it. Then she stands and leaves.

A moment passes and then another before the surprise wears off.

"Good night, ladies' man," Kelly remarks in the dark.

"Shut up," Cory scolds quietly to the sound of his brother's low, guttural laughter.

He doesn't know why this little girl wants to sleep beside him, but if it makes her feel safer for the night, then he's fine with it. Perhaps he does remind her of someone, her father, her brother, likely dead. Perhaps she feels like he'll protect her like her father would have if he were still around. And Cory will, too. He'll look after her for the night. He just has no idea what he's going to do with her in the morning.

Chapter Nine
Sam

She pulls on a pink hoodie and her black coat and heads out of the women's sleeping quarters. Carrying an oil lantern, Sam walks to her favorite spot in the long pole barn where she can watch the horses in the pasture. She perches on a bale of straw and sets her oil lamp down. The amber glow from the lamp is plenty enough for her to see by. The distant moo of one of the dairy cows sounds off through the shadowy, foggy valley.

She'd started a drawing the other day of a foal with her mother. It was the first time she'd picked up her sketch pad since leaving the farm.

It doesn't take long before a few of the horses realize she's in the vicinity and come over to the gate separating the barn from the pasture. It is still dark out, only four a.m., but she couldn't sleep anyway.

Sam works with charcoals on shading the neck of the mare and filling in the tiny, thin hairs of its mane. Their eyes are always a bigger challenge. A horse's eye is large and round and quite soft, gentle and expressive. It is sometimes difficult to convey the depth of their feeling in a sketch.

"Sam?" a voice says in the dark, startling her. "Sorry, ma'am. I didn't mean to frighten you."

"Hello, Henry," she returns to her host. "You didn't scare me. I was just concentrating on this a little too hard I think."

He steps closer and peers over her shoulder. "That's amazing. You have a real talent."

"Nah," she criticizes. "I just love animals, so it's not like work for me."

"Yes, ma'am," he returns. "I've noticed how great you are with the animals around here, especially the horses."

"Henry, I told you to just call me Sam."

"Sorry, habit," he explains for the twentieth time.

Sam notices that he's carrying a large backpack over one shoulder that looks very heavy and a thermos in his hand.

"Where are you off to?" she asks as she taps her pencil on the pad.

"The McClane farm, ma'am… I mean, Sam," he corrects.

Her heart skips a beat at the mention of the farm. She tries to play it cool but figures if he can read people at all, then he saw her flinch.

"Would you like to go with us? You could visit with your friends," he offers kindly.

Sam swallows hard and says, "Um, I'm not sure if that's a good idea."

"You'd be on your own for a while," he says.

"What do you mean?" Sam asks, wrinkling her brow with confusion.

"Derek and their sniper… can't remember his name…"

Sam scowls. Her voice suddenly feels tight as if she cannot inhale deeply enough to form words through her mouth. She whispers hoarsely, "Simon."

"Oh, yeah, Simon. They're goin' with us on a run," he tells her with a firm nod.

"But the others from the farm are gone up north. I know they took General McClane to Fort Knox. It's not a good idea for Derek and…anyone else to go with you while they're gone."

"I'm takin' men with me over there to keep an eye on the place while we're gone," he explains more thoroughly. "It'll be safe, as safe as here."

"Oh," she says softly. Her heart aches at the sound of her McClane family. She pines for their companionship, her sisters, her brothers, and when she allows herself, for him.

"You're welcome to ride along," he says. "We'll be gone for probably most of the day. You could visit with the ones who'll still be there."

She bites her lip with indecision.

"I have to get goin', though, ma'am," he says.

Sam hits him with a disapproving look.

"Habit," he says sheepishly.

"Ok, fine. I'll go, Henry. I think it'll be good to visit with them," she resigns herself. "Give me five minutes."

"I'll wait for you at the truck," he says with a smile.

Sam jogs to the bunkhouse and grabs her pack. If Simon had been staying behind on the farm, she definitely wouldn't have wanted to visit with them. Since he's going to be gone with Henry and Derek on this run, she'll gladly go and see her family. Her uncle and the few friends she's made while living on Henry's farm are no substitute for her McClane family, and Uncle Scott is always so busy working with the men to get a clinic up and running that she hardly sees him lately.

She climbs into the pick-up in the extended cab right next to Henry. She's glad he isn't driving but that one of his men is instead. It would make her nervous sitting in a truck full of strange men. At least she knows and trusts Henry. Some of the six men and also Annie are riding in the bed of the truck. She has met Annie and knows that she is one of Dave's trusted soldiers who helped during the sex camp raid. As far as the rest of them goes, it means that she does not trust them. She may never trust them.

Henry hands her a gray, wool blanket, a military issue blanket that is like the ones they use in her sleeping quarters. She doesn't question from where they've all come.

"Thanks," she says and wraps it around her legs. She'd been shivering, but only partly from the cold. Henry just nods. He is quiet and pensive and mostly staring at a map in his lap with a pen light.

He's studying it extensively. "What's going on? Why are you guys going on a run with the McClane men?"

He pauses, frowns and replies, "Nothing to worry about."

Now she is worried but figures she'll get the truth from the women on the farm when she gets there. Something is about to go down. She can tell by the body language of Henry and his men. She sees the red circle on the map and that it encompasses Henry's farm, Pleasant View, and the McClane farm. She wonders if this has anything to do with Jay's group that was forced out of Pleasant View. That was weeks ago, though. She can't imagine them coming back. She knows they went south because the men followed them for a long time to ensure it.

They arrive at the farm just a little after five a.m. and are greeted near the back porch by Grandpa and Derek.

"Sam!" Derek calls out and grasps her in a bear hug, lifting her off the ground. "Hey, kiddo!"

"Hi, Derek," she greets with a smile. There are tears pooling in her eyes, but she somehow manages to hold them back.

Doc is next, but his hug has less strength than Derek's. It is even more comforting and tender, though, and she lingers a long time within his embrace. A few tears trickle down her cold cheeks before she can stop them this time.

"So glad you could come for a visit, honey," he says and kisses the top of her head. "Go inside and warm up. The girls will be so excited to see you. Sue's in the kitchen feeding Daniel."

She nods, whisks away the tears that have fallen, and enters the kitchen. It feels just like she never left. The kitchen is warm and already smells good like rising bread and salted meats. Sue is just as shocked to see her and rushes over to greet Sam with a one-armed hug. Baby Daniel protests and cries out.

"He's getting big!" Sam notes with a smile. "So adorable."

"Wanna' hold him?" Sue asks, to which she nods vigorously.

She cradles him close and holds his bottle. He suckles hard at the nipple and makes the tiniest sounds imaginable. Some of the women on Henry's farm are pregnant, and she is anxious to be of help to them. She misses being around little kids and babies.

"He's not really growing as well as Grandpa and Reagan would like," Sue tells her as she takes a seat at the island. Sam sways back and forth in a comforting manner while Sue sits and sips at a hot beverage with steam coming out of the mug.

"He seems bigger to me," Sam says and presses her mouth to the baby's head. He smells so good and sweet and pure. Perfumeries should've learned how to bottle the scent of a baby. They could've made big bucks.

"We're almost out of formula," she tells her. "The guys are gonna try to find some today. Kelly and John and Cory are also going to scout for some on the way back."

"How'd it go up there with General McClane?"

"Not sure yet," Sue tells her. "I guess they're planning on coming home today sometime, so apparently not well enough that they want to stay any more days."

"What are..." she starts but is interrupted by Simon walking into the room.

"Sue, I left a .38 pistol in the music room under the seat cushion..." he says and stops dead in his tracks at the sight of Sam.

If he could be more surprised, he might just die on the spot from shock. His jaw temporarily hits the ground. Then, he sets his mouth in a tight line, immediately regaining his composure.

"What are you doing here?" he asks with a touch of rudeness in his tone.

Sue answers for her, "She came to visit with us while you men are out doing your thing today. Isn't it great?"

Simon shoots Sue a squinty-eyed glare. He even slightly wrinkles his nose. Then he adjusts his ball cap and raises his unshaven chin just a notch. He is back in complete, typical Simon control again.

"Hello, Simon," Sam greets coolly.

"Samantha," he returns through gritted teeth.

Sam can't decide if he looks more like he wants to murder her or lock her away chained in the basement so that she can never leave again. His expression is pained and tormented. Again with Simon, as it always is with Simon, she is left feeling confused and unable to gauge his feelings.

"Did you ride over here with Henry?" Sue asks.

Sam looks at her as if she is a simpleton for the question that is quite obvious and has already been covered. Sue already knows the answer to this. Sam hasn't a clue as to why Sue would ask that right now.

"Yes, of course," Sam answers, earning a coy smile from Sue.

"He's very kind to offer such a generous thing," Sue says.

Again with the rueful smile that is puzzling to Sam.

"Yes, he's been great, very kind and… accommodating," Sam answers her. "My uncle and I couldn't ask for a better host."

Simon growls. He growls deep in his throat and storms out the back door after grabbing his jacket from its hook.

Sue actually chortles.

"What's so funny? And what was that all about? You knew Henry drove me here. I didn't walk," Sam reminds her friend in jest.

"I know," her adopted sister says and smiles again before sipping her drink.

"I don't understand," Sam admits as she places Daniel's empty bottle in the sink to be washed. The little stinker is out like a light, likely dream-scheming to be up again in two hours. She rests him against her shoulder and pats his back trying to get him to burp.

"Oh, Sam," Sue starts, "there is so much you still need to learn about men."

"What do you mean? I don't know anything about men!" she says with a laugh.

"I don't think Simon liked you hitchin' a ride with Henry to get here," Sue admits with the smile again.

"Well, I couldn't hardly take a cab," Sam says and praises Daniel when he belches.

"No, of course, you couldn't," Sue agrees. "But I think Simon would've preferred it. I don't think he likes Henry too well."

"Why ever not?" she asks, appalled. "He's a good person. He's been so kind to my uncle and me and… well, gosh, so many people. He didn't need to take in so many people on his farm, but he did. I'll not have anyone besmirching him."

Sue grins and says, "Oh, no, he's a good man. I know that. I'm sure Simon realizes it, too. But that doesn't mean he has to like Henry."

"He'd better never talk badly about Henry to me. That's just ridiculous."

"Not if he's jealous of him," Sue finally tells her. "And he is jealous of Henry. He's not jealous of him as a person. He's red-in-the-face pissed that Henry has you on his farm and that you left this one. Simon has been a real bear lately."

"Well, it…he…I wanted to live on Henry's farm to be with my Uncle Scott."

"Uh-huh," Sue says with bold skepticism. "Sure ya' did, kiddo. But it might just work."

"What will work?"

"Leaving our farm to get Simon to come after you. It worked with John and Reagan. It's certainly taking Simon a lot longer to get it all figured out, but it might work."

Sam's cheeks burn with embarrassment. She doesn't want everyone on the farm to think of her and Simon like that. He wants nothing to do with her in that manner. It had been difficult to swallow, that pill of rejection, but she has been trying to make a new life for herself on Dave's compound.

"No, Sue, he won't," Sam says with resignation. "He's never going to feel that way about me, and I don't really want to hash it out with you. Simon and I are…just friends."

"That sure as heck didn't seem very friendly just now the way he stormed out of here," Sue remarks.

"No, but that's fine. He needs his space. So do I. That's part of the reason I left, but I also wanted to be with my uncle, too."

"I know," Sue admits. "But your uncle could've moved over here onto the farm or into town with you. There wasn't a good reason to uproot your life and move twenty miles away to a whole new town with strangers."

"I had to," Sam says and turns her back to Sue. Daniel has fallen asleep on her shoulder with his face pressed against her neck. She's pretty sure he's leaving a wet spot of baby drool there.

"I know, kiddo," Sue says. "Things will work out. They always do."

"Don't be so optimistic," Sam tells her as she watches the men and Annie board Henry's truck. "That's Hannie's job."

Sue chuckles, and Sam smiles.

"I'll put him down," she tells her. "Where do you want him?"

Sue rises from her seat and says, "Follow me. We've got him in with Hannah and Kelly, but when I feed him in the morning, I try to put him back down in Grandpa's room so Hannah can sleep."

"Sleep?" Sam whispers. "While Kelly's gone? Yeah, right."

Sue smiles over her shoulder at her as they go down the long hall to Grandpa's room.

"He's still getting up about every two to three hours," Sue tells her.

"That's fun," Sam remarks dryly.

"Arianna was like that for a few months," Sue tells her as Sam places him in the wooden cradle that Kelly built for Mary. It is intricately carved and even has a bear, trees and birds whittled into the headboard.

"Yikes."

"Then I called Grams, and she told me to put about a quarter teaspoon of baby rice cereal in her bottle," Sue says with a grin. "It worked. It was just the thing to hold her little tummy over for a few more hours."

"Bet you were glad for it, too," Sam says with a smile.

"Oh, yes," Sue replies. "Let's go make some hot milk. The kids like it in the winter with their breakfast."

"So do I," Sam agrees wholeheartedly.

110

When they return to the kitchen, the lights from the truck are gone, and the back porch light has been turned off. She notes that the door is locked. She can see one of Dave's men standing on the back porch in the pre-dawn dark and cold. Grandpa must be in his study because a soft glow extends out from underneath the door. It makes her smile softly.

They collect the glass container from the refrigerator containing a half gallon of fresh milk and pour the entire contents into a large saucepan and light the stove. Sue turns it down to low so that it doesn't scald.

"Tea?" Sue offers and lifts the kettle from the other burner.

"Sure," Sam accepts and takes the honey pot down from the cupboard in the pantry before joining Sue at the island.

Paige rushes into the room holding her side.

"Did they leave?"

"Yes, they just," Sue informs her.

"Damn him!" Paige swears in earnest.

Her hair is disheveled, and she is still wearing her pajamas, which are soft and worn out flannel pants with a long-sleeved tee, equally faded.

She continues in anger, "I told him not to leave without waking me."

"Sorry, Paige," Sue says with caring eyes. "I would've awakened you if I'd known. Men! They are so irritating. Can't live with them…"

"Can't reach things without them!" Sam finishes in jest.

"Well, not you. I can reach things just fine," Paige says and walks over to hug her. "Hey, Sam."

"How are you feeling?"

"Fine, wimpy, whiny, weak," she says with a frown. "Damn. Three w's. That can't be good."

"No, it surely can't," Sam agrees with a smile and kisses her friend on the cheek. "Enjoying the extra space in our bedroom?"

"What? No! I want you to come back. I'm laid up. I'm sickly and weak. I need my roomy back," Paige says and hugs her again.

Sam doesn't say anything this time. She misses her friend desperately but knows she can't return to the farm. She also doesn't want to hurt Paige's feelings by telling her that the reason she left the farm and abandoned her companionship was because of Paige's own brother. Paige is dealing with enough right now without getting involved in her and Simon's relationship, or lack thereof. Sam actually wanted Simon to get proactively involved in their relationship, but that hadn't turned out so well for her. She's quite confident that he is more than relieved to have her gone from the farm. Now he doesn't have to be bothered by her anymore and can pursue other interests or other women. Perhaps he has a certain affinity to someone in their town. She hadn't considered this possibility. If he has any sort of romantic pull toward someone else, then it would explain why he isn't attracted to her.

"How have you been adjusting over there?" Sue asks.

"Great," Sam lies. She hopes it comes off as truthful. She doesn't want them worrying about her. She does love being with her uncle and her new friends, but it can't fill the gap in her heart from the loss of her McClane family.

"Oh, good," Paige says after she has taken a seat. "Making friends?"

"Sure," Sam says and realizes that if she doesn't embellish on this a little, then they won't believe her. So she sticks to the truth. Mostly. "I sleep in a bunkhouse. There are a lot of other women in there with me. I've made friends with some of them. Everyone's been really nice."

"Well, kiddo," Sue says, "if you're happy, then we're happy."

She offers a grin that she hopes comes off as genuine. Never has she been so ashamed of herself for telling a lie. To offset her guilt, Sam reminds herself that it isn't a total mistruth. She does like a lot of the women in her new town. She also likes Henry and Dave and Dave's wife, who is really sweet if not a little rough around the edges. She doesn't put up with much, not even from Dave. But she's a devoted mother and wife and has helped Sam make the tough transition to their farm, although Sam has tried to conceal her loneliness and depression from them. Explaining the reasons behind it would be too painful to share.

"Right," Paige agrees. "We're happy for you, but you definitely have to come over for visits more often."

She slides her hand over to rest on Sam's on the island's marble countertop.

"And when you get better, you can come visit me, too," she returns with a smile.

"I'll have Simon bring me," Paige says with a nod.

Sam tries not to wince. Instead, she changes the subject and inquires after their reason for the run they've gone on. Once Sue has explained it, Sam feels her heart sink. So many people killed by this group of highwaymen. A new panic sets in, and this time it's not from visiting the farm and having to see Simon for the first time in nearly a month. Now she's worried about the men running into these killers on the road.

"They'll be fine," Paige says as Huntley walks into the room. "They're just checking it out, seeing what they can dig up on these people. They aren't going to engage in a battle with them, or at least that's what Simon told me."

"Ak'is," Huntley greets in his native tongue.

He likes to call Sam this or sometimes other Navaho words. He told her they all mean friend. He hugs her tightly, causing all the breath to leave her lungs. She has missed him dearly. They've been through so much together, all the way back to when they were forced into traveling with Huntley's father's group of bandits. He never speaks of his father. Actually, he never speaks of any of his family. Sam can only imagine the pain he must carry with him. Losing his twin brother must've been more devastating than anyone could possibly understand. Sam lost her family, too, but to lose a twin sibling, the other half of one's natural self would be like losing a limb. She understands the acuteness of his pain.

"Huntley, I can't breathe," she teases, to which he releases her with a sheepish smile.

"I am glad you are here," he says.

"Me, too," she returns and watches him pull on his green, rubber boots to go to the barn. "Want some help?"

"Sure," Huntley replies. "That'd be great. Then Sue or Reagan or one of the others doesn't have to come out and help with morning chores. Or Paige. She's not really in fighting shape just yet."

"Hey, I might be," Paige protests.

"Ha!" Sue exclaims on a laugh. "Don't get overly confident. You're still a mess."

"A hot mess, Paige," Huntley corrects with a wink.

"Well, at least I've got that," she returns with a weak chuckle.

They laugh together, which feels good to Sam. It feels like home. It'll be hard to leave today when Henry gets back. Maybe coming for a visit wasn't such a brilliant idea after all.

She works with Huntley, G and Lucas on morning chores, milking the two dairy cows, feeding the younger cows, tossing some alfalfa hay to the dairy goats, sprinkling grain to the chickens in the barnyard, and cleaning the horse stalls. It takes a few hours, but with the help of two of Dave's men, who volunteer, they get it all done. It's usually a faster process when all the men are home. Kelly and Cory usually take care of the dairy cows and the milking. John will feed and drop bales of hay from the loft. Simon tends to the goats and pigs, and Huntley does whatever else they need of him, including mucking stalls and cleaning up after the milkings. This morning proves what it would be like on the McClane farm and also on Henry's farm if they didn't have the men to make the jobs easier and faster. The last thing she does is collect eggs from the coop before joining Huntley on the trek to the house. He's carrying two buckets of milk. One of Dave's men who helped is bringing the smaller bucket of goat milk. Before she even gets to the back porch, she can smell the delicious aromas of a hearty breakfast awaiting them. Her stomach answers with a loud grumble. Sue calls out to make sure Dave's men join them. Sam knew they wouldn't allow the men who are helping them today go hungry.

The children are awake and greet her with squeals of delight and vigorous hugs and kisses. This makes her eyes tear up. She has missed these little hooligans.

Their breakfast consists of grits, fried potatoes, eggs, biscuits, peach preserves, sausage flavored with sage, apples and fennel seeds. They, together with their neighbors, make a variety of flavored sausages. Sam's favorite is Hungarian, which is heavily seasoned with garlic and paprika. It's not a great idea for date night, but, then again, her calendar has been empty in those slots for a long time. Dave's men are more than grateful and express their gratitude multiple times. The food at Henry's farm is plentiful but usually a lot plainer in taste. She would love to start an herb greenhouse over there to help with food seasoning.

After breakfast is finished, Huntley asks if she'd like to go for a ride with him and check the perimeter. There is no way she's passing up an opportunity to take out her favorite mount for a while. The crisp air nips at her nose and cheeks, but she doesn't care as they settle in and set the pace at a walk through the woods. Her gelding is tossing his head in defiance. Sam can tell that nobody is riding him with enough frequency. He's behaving feistily. It just makes her laugh at him, which earns another head toss coupled with a snort this time.

"Do you think you'll ever come back, Sam?" Huntley asks, startling her. "It's not the same here without you."

He rides bareback, almost always does. He told her once that his grandfather taught him this way when he was young but that he didn't remember much of it. He has rekindled his love of horses and riding since he came to live on the farm. Saddles just seem to get in his way. He is very skilled with the horses and has a natural fearlessness around them. He doesn't believe in riding one until it has become a friend first.

As he usually does, Huntley is carrying a pistol on his hip but also has his bow slung over his back. A quiver made from deer skin is perched there, too, along with six arrows. He and Grandpa like to craft their own arrowheads from flint and use real feathers for the quills. She knows that Grandpa wants to give Huntley a small bit of his Native American heritage. He teaches him little things like hunting for flints to make his arrowheads and the best feathers for the quills. She notices that he has his hair separated into two, thick braids on either side of his head today. Grandpa encourages him to embrace his Navaho birthright. He believes it is important for him to remember his family's customs and culture. He has given Huntley many books on his people. Sam believes Grandpa has borrowed them from the library or had the men pick up more when they've come across them over the years. Thus, today there are blue and red clay beads in his paint mare's mane which is also sporting three, tiny braids mixed in with the thick hair. He wears matching beads at the tips of his own braids. His permanently tanned skin is flawless and unmarked with high, hollowed-out cheekbones. The only thing that gives away his mixed race and his white birth mother are his light, hazel eyes, which are striking against his dark skin. There is a troubled past concealed behind the greenish tint of his beautiful eyes. Someday soon he'll be a handsome man. She loves sketching Huntley, but he rarely sits still long enough for her to do so. Sam is grateful to know and call him her friend.

"I don't think so, Hunt," she admits. "I think I need to stay over there. Moving back doesn't seem like a good idea."

"Damn Simon!" he swears angrily, startling his horse.

"Hey, don't curse," Sam scolds.

"He's an idiot, shadi," he says, referring to her as his sister as he so often does.

Sam loves it when he speaks in his native tongue. The Navaho have a lovely language with glottal stops and strangely placed consonants, and he's taught her a few words over the years. It was not an easy task learning them. No wonder the military used the Navaho to conceal and deliver secretive codes during World War II. Breaking off a syllable in the middle of a word is not something that one does when speaking normally.

"No, he's just not in love with me, shitsili," she says, returning the endearment for brother in his native language.

"He is a fool," Huntley says without missing a beat.

"We're all fools," she says teasingly but not without hiding her own sadness from him.

"I hate him that he's keeping you away from us," Huntley grumbles.

Sam reaches over and touches his arm affectionately. "You could always come over there with me if you want."

They ride in silence for a few minutes while he contemplates the offer. Huntley is like this. He takes a long time to make decisions. He never acts rashly.

"No, I can't do that, shadi," he says. "I'm needed here. If I left, then the younger kids would have more duties, chores. It would tip the balance. I have much to learn still from the men. I can't assume I would be able to gain that insight on Sergeant Winter's farm."

"Henry's farm technically. Dave just runs it all."

"Are they treating you well?"

Sam smiles at her little brother and says, "Of course. They're all really good people, Hunt. I don't mind it there so much."

"You're sad," he states simply, even though it cuts straight to her heart.

"I'll get over it. The wound is just still fresh," she confesses. There's no sense in trying to hide it from Huntley. Her little brother knows her too well. He'd know if she was lying. He also knows she left because of Simon. For a fourteen-year-old, he's insightful and wise. It probably comes from his people and also shadowing Grandpa for the past four years.

"Do they at least have horses to ride?" he asks, concerned for her well-being.

"Yes, they have horses," she says with a smile.

"That's good," he concedes.

"Wanna' race?" she taunts and bumps her horse into a trot.

Naturally, he puts his heels to the mare's sides, and within seconds they are racing across the top meadow and back into the woods again. When they return to the barn, Sam helps him wipe down the sweaty horses before turning them out. She has also been longing for the nostalgic smells and sounds of the McClane barns. She just hadn't known how much until she returned to it today.

Sam spends the rest of the afternoon playing with the kids in the back yard, in the barns and eventually in the music room. She even plays a song for them on Grandpa's violin since hers is over at Henry's farm. The instrument is out of tune and has mostly always been hanging on the wall of his office as decoration, but it works well enough. Being slightly out of key on some notes lends a sad tone to her song. It mirrors her feelings being back on the farm.

Chapter Ten
Simon

"Over here!" Henry's man calls out to the group from the ditch beside the road.

Everyone joins him there, including Derek and Simon. They have been searching for hours. Finally, they've found one of the scenes left behind by the highway attackers. There are dead people in the ditch. It's a ghastly sight, indeed. Simon holds down his bile and turns away to keep watch instead. Anything is better than staring into the sightless eyes of the children and women in a state of permanent repose, left for dead in a dirty, muddy ditch.

These people were innocent victims, not deserving of this sort of treatment. It makes him feel rageful. It also makes Simon wonder if he isn't a lot more like Cory than he tries to pretend he's not. There is a sudden need within him to tear off and track these bastards down, to exact revenge for the dead. Instead, he waits patiently for Derek to make the call.

The victims' vehicles are still parked in the middle of the road. Three of them have clean windshields. The other abandoned cars and trucks on the four-lane road are covered in years' worth of dust and dirt and now snow. Simon also assumes the three without snow on them belonged to those people because two of the mini-vans' doors are open and the dome lights are still on. This attack had to be within the last few days. The two vans and the car behind it, also with the doors open but without a dome light still working, have been raided. The gas caps are left in the open position. He knows they weren't pumping gas recently and just forgot to close the caps. The gas has been syphoned by those creeps. Personal items are strewn about on the cold, damp blacktop like the forgotten memories of their former owners. Even the battered and worn toys of the dead children lay discarded. These bandits likely don't have children in their group because toys, unless they are homemade like the ones given as gifts at the McClane farm and handcrafted from wood usually by Derek, Cory or Doc, are never left behind. Even the plastic, tattered Barbie doll staring lifelessly back at Simon has been left. A small, chipped and faded Matchbox car is peeking out from beneath the mini-van.

"They were ordered to stand down here in this ditch," Henry says behind him. "Execution style. I haven't heard of it going down like this anywhere else."

"Maybe they realized that they let some get away with the other attacks," Derek comments.

"Can't let that happen," Henry's man says.

Simon believes his name to be Bruce. He was the big soldier who watched so diligently over the young woman from the sex slave camp at their medical house in town after she'd been knocked unconscious. It was touch and go with her, and Doc wasn't sure if she'd ever awaken. Simon has heard through the grapevine that they are together as a couple now. He feels sorry for anyone who would even think about attacking her again, not with Bruce the bull as her protector.

"Right," Henry agrees. "They'd escape and tell someone like us what happened here."

"And they definitely don't want that shit to happen," Annie says.

Simon remembers her well from the night they raided the sex slave camp. She'd been partnered with Cory and had been injured. She obviously healed well and, in his opinion, very fast.

120

She adds, "We're about the worst case scenario that they haven't come up against yet."

"Never underestimate the enemy," Derek warns softly.

"True, but we have the firepower to take them out," Annie says. "We just need to find them first."

"Exactly," Henry says in agreement.

They load up again in Henry's truck and drive west, following tracks in the light dusting of snow. He sits in the back with Henry and Annie while Derek rides up front with Bruce and navigates. The trail eventually goes cold after a few miles where the blacktop has melted off the remaining snowfall.

"Keep going," Henry tells Bruce. "We'll see if we can't keep trackin' them."

"Watch out your windows for tire tracks in the mud alongside the road," Derek instructs. "They may have had to maneuver around a car or two left on the freeway."

"Right," Henry agrees.

Another hour creeps slowly by as they search in vain for the bandits. They pass exits on the freeway but don't see fresh tracks on or off the road. They pass through Coopertown and head towards Springfield, a city with a small town feel that is slightly bigger than Pleasant View and probably still more populated. However, they've been there before and haven't run into people. He hopes they don't tonight, either. Just because there isn't an established new community like their small town doesn't mean there aren't people living somewhere hidden in Springfield.

"There used to be a Walmart and some other stores like that down off the highway," Bruce informs them.

"Were you from Tennessee, Bruce?" Derek asks their driver.

"Me? No way. I'm from Minnesota," he answers proudly. "I met up with Dave after I got in touch with some of my family. I only had a sister, and her husband was a Marine, so I knew they'd be all right. We always had a plan for shit like this."

"Really?" Simon asks with surprise.

"Yeah, sure," he tells them. "She and I were to meet at our family's bugout location up in Kentucky. Our folks always raised us to be ready for something like this. Heck, I guess I never really thought it would happen, but it did. My family went together and bought eighty acres out in the boonies. We figured the weather in Kentucky woulda' been a little bit better for survival than those cold ass Minnesota winters. Plus, my mom was from Kentucky originally and enjoyed going back home for visits. My brother-in-law's family is full of operators. I knew they'd be all right."

"And are they?" Simon asks.

Bruce nods and says, "Oh, yeah. They're cool. I just didn't want to live there with them anymore. It was gettin' crowded if you know what I mean. My sister's got kids. Her in-laws are living there. His three siblings and their kids. Too many people for the two cabins we had built. Plus, when I got the call from Dave, I knew I had to go with him. My sister's still close, not too far at all. I can visit. Plus, I like knowing she's north and her group's covering the area up there and we're securing the area around here."

"Yeah, it's good to have allies," Derek says thoughtfully.

"Well, we *were* securing the area," he corrects. "Got some idiots to deal with first. It'll get sorted out again."

"Yeah, we got this," Annie says with confidence.

Simon looks at her and nods, although he doesn't share her self-assurance. He looks out his window again. Dave's truck is a lot nicer and newer than their truck on the farm. Or maybe the truck belongs to Henry. Simon isn't sure.

"Let's stop at some of the stores in this town," Derek orders as they pull off the exit toward a large shopping area. "We need baby formula and some other supplies."

"You got it," Henry replies.

"Having any luck with the CNG system for your vehicles, Derek?" Bruce asks as he swings the truck into a parking lot.

"Somewhat," Derek answers. "Cory just about has it tweaked. We had some issue with the fuel pump, but once we got that fixed, it seemed to work. Now we're having trouble with the

122

regulator. It's blowing into the intake. We'll get it worked out. We've just been busy as hell around there."

"Planting season's coming, too," Henry reminds them.

"Ready?" Bruce says as he cuts the engine.

Derek nods and opens his door. Simon follows suit with Annie on his heels.

"I'll be here with the truck," Bruce says. "Radio if you need help."

"Got it," Derek says. "Give us an hour or so. This is gonna be a tough find."

"I'm not going anywhere," Bruce says with a grin as he props his rifle on the seat beside him.

Bruce has backed the truck into a parking spot almost between two buildings, a Japanese hibachi restaurant and a video game store. Years ago, Simon would've wanted to hit that place. Now, he just wants to find formula for an orphaned newborn. He slings his rifle and draws his pistol instead. Simon consults his watch. It's nearly three o'clock in the afternoon already. They've spent all day on the road. He hopes they head for home soon. This is a long time to be away from the farm. At this rate, John and the rest of them will beat them home from the Army base.

He pairs up with Derek, and Annie takes off with Henry. They have promised to be on the lookout for baby formula, but they are likely also searching for anything that they can use over on their farm, too.

"It's a longshot, but let's hit that Walmart over there," Derek says and starts out at a brisk pace.

"Yes, sir," Simon agrees. "We don't have a lot of daylight left."

They enter through the front doors, stepping over the usual debris and broken glass. Most retail businesses resemble this store. It is nearly pitch dark once they get twenty feet from the front doors. Stores like this weren't going for feng shui with wide, panoramic windows. They didn't care about the pleasing aesthetic of their business, but rather the moving of goods in bulk quantities.

Overhead fluorescents were thought of as the most efficient and economical choice in lighting. He and Derek whip out their flashlights and shine them on the space ahead of them.

"I'll look for the formula. You check for anything else," Derek orders, to which Simon nods firmly.

They waste no time and begin searching. Derek heads to the baby department while Simon moves toward the pharmacy. The metal gate separating the half wall of the pharmacy counter from the rest of the store- also meant for closing up shop at the end of the day and keeping their drugs secure from theft- has been damaged beyond repair. He climbs over the counter, shoves at the bars and is admitted into the pharmacy without security hampering his cause. There isn't much left: a few inhalers, which he takes, some bandages, various bottles of meds that people must not have deemed worthy and a cash register laying on its side on the ground. It has been looted. This causes him to smirk. People were such fools at the beginning.

He remembers overhearing a lot of conversations among his father's friends and Senate colleagues about their stock portfolios. What a waste of time and effort that was! They would've been better off stocking up on rifles, canned goods, and socks. The most valuable commodity being socks, in Simon's opinion. They never seem to have enough pairs on the farm.

Once he has his booty stashed safely in his pack, Simon climbs back over the counter and begins searching the shelves in the area for powdered baby formula or anything else of use. He grabs a few pairs of reading glasses from the floor and stuffs them into his bag. Perhaps someone in town will have a use for them. Four bottles of aspirin and another of Vitamin E capsules are stuffed into the pack, too. Vitamin E oil is ideal for wound care. The rest of the vitamins and meds are gone. Most of the shelves are bare or contain items he knows they don't have a need for. He comes to the women's hygiene aisle and finds pregnancy tests, stuffs them in his pack. They will be able to use these at the clinic. There are a few bottles of mouthwash and four tubes of toothpaste on a shelf in the next aisle, also which get pocketed. Everything else is wiped out, picked clean.

A few aisles over, he finds a can of protein powder, but it's expired. Simon considers it and decides to take the container anyway. It is a slim possibility they could use it to feed baby Daniel. He's probably too young for his newly-formed digestive system to handle such a heavy dose of protein.

Next, he moves to the household items, hardware and automotive departments. He finds little but does take a few extension cords and two, jute ropes. There are many gallons of paint on the shelves. Apparently, remodeling wasn't on anyone's minds when the country fell. Those fixer-uppers were just going to have to wait. He grabs a gallon of deck stain and sealer. Then he pockets two cans of black spray paint. He thinks that maybe if the town does build the children a playground, they may be able to use this paint. They can always come back here for more or to a closer town for painting supplies. There's never a shortage of items like paint. This would get them started, though.

He doesn't even waste time on the gun department. He knows from experience that those were the first areas to get looted when it started. Instead, he heads to the bedding and bath department where he finds a few towels and washcloths, something they always need at the clinic. He works his way toward Derek's department and stops long enough to find a few t-shirts in the men's clothing area that are laying on the floor. He takes those, too. Then he grabs a ball cap for himself and one for Huntley. Several boxers are in the undergarment department, so he jams them into his backpack. Women's socks are next. There isn't much left, but he finds a few random pairs on the floor. Everyone's socks get patched and repaired often. Everything is recycled and handed down. He jogs to the craft department where he comes across needles and thread. He takes everything he can because he knows how much of these particular items Sue goes through.

"Hey," Derek says as he jogs up behind him. Simon heard him coming. "Doing some painting in the cabin?"

His friend is joking, causing Simon to smile. "Nah, Paige has an idea. Thought I'd grab this for her."

"Cool."

"Find any?"

"Nope," Derek says with a scowl. "But I did grab some baby clothes and rags. I found some bottles of this stuff, but I don't know what it's for."

He shows a bottle of it to Simon. The label reads "Pedialyte."

"Oh, I've heard Doc talk about this before," Simon tells him. "This is for baby dehydration, like if they contract Rotavirus or something extreme while they are still infants or toddlers, which can make them very ill. It can actually cause more diarrhea, so it can be dangerous if used too abruptly in treatment. It's like Gatorade."

"Whatever you say, man," Derek remarks with a chuckle and tosses it back down into his pack. "Let's split. We got enough from here. We need that formula."

"Yes, sir," Simon answers.

They radio Bruce to let them know they are returning to the truck. Simon dumps some of his heavier loot into a separate, cotton bag and leaves the items and especially the gallon of paint stain in the bed. Derek does the same with his finds. Bruce tells them that Henry and Annie are still gone. Simon takes a swig of water from his canteen and screws the cap back on. Derek lets Bruce know they are still looking for baby formula and that they'll be back soon.

Simon jogs beside Derek, relieved to have left the awkward paint can in the truck's bed when he spots a pharmacy a few blocks away.

"Hey, maybe they would've sold formula," Simon points.

"Let's hit it," Derek says with a nod and leads the way.

They approach the building the same way, from the front and head inside. The doors are surprisingly still intact. The windows are also undamaged. However, the building has been flooded either from faulty plumbing, vandals, or broken pipes from the winters. There is mold crawling up the wall where women's cosmetics are displayed. They scan the entire store and right away come to a clear conclusion.

126

Everything is infested with black mold. Nothing here will be salvageable, even if they did find the formula. It could still be contaminated, and they can't take that chance.

"You know the good thing about this pharmacy being here," Derek asks rhetorically. Then he raises his eyebrows and smiles. "There's always another one around the corner."

They leave out the back door, and true to his theory, another pharmacy is only a few blocks down the street. Derek uses their radio to inform the others of their new destination. Bruce tells them that they will head in their direction and pick them up since Henry and Annie have returned.

This time they must climb over a four-door sedan parked in its final resting place right through the front doors of the pharmacy. Glass is shattered everywhere and crackles loudly when they step on it. There is a dead man behind the wheel in a state of late decomposition. Simon averts his eyes and keeps going.

This pharmacy has been looted as every other one he's ever been in, but it isn't flooded. There is more to take here, and so he works on looking for items while Derek heads straight for the baby products aisle.

Simon finds a few bottles of vitamins, which they regularly hand out to pregnant women at the clinic. There is a bottle of iodine and two bottles of rubbing alcohol on a lower shelf way in the back. These will come in handy at the clinic. He helps himself to the pharmacy drugs behind the counter and actually locates a few bottles of prescription drugs they can also use at the clinic. There are many types of anti-depressants, which he knows Doc won't give to anyone. He was never a big believer in the modern psychiatric drugs. Not having the experience that Doc does, Simon deferred to his superior's better judgement on the subject. He only knows the names because he has studied the lists of prescription drugs and their uses so that he knows what to search for on a run and what to give a patient at the clinic in case he can't consult with Doc or Reagan. He does take a bottle of Metoprolol, which is used for heart conditions, a large container of high dosage Hydrocodone, which is a pain reliever, and two bottles of NSAID's, which are useful for thinning the blood and mild pain relief. Lastly, he finds a glass jar of Hydrochlorothiazide on the floor, which is a diuretic pill meant to help release excess water. It is especially good for heart patients who might be suffering from heart failure, or kidney failure patients, or patients ill with any type of edema.

Derek interrupts his search by saying behind him, "Found some, Simon."

He stands again and swings around. "Great!"

"It's expired," Derek admits. "We'll just have to test it."

"He needs it," Simon says with a sympathetic nod. "How much did you find?"

"Eight cans. There was a whole shelf of it," Derek tells him. "I don't think it'll last long, but it gives him more time to grow so we can put off trying the goat milk. Find anything?"

"Oh, yes," Simon answers as he tips his bag toward Derek. "These will all help a lot at the clinic."

"Good," Derek says. "Ready?"

"Sure," he answers.

"Let's get outta' here and head home. I'm getting hungry."

"Ditto," Simon replies with a grin.

They exit the store and walk down the middle of the deserted street in hopes of connecting with Henry and his team. The weather has soured on them and turned colder. The wind is whipping through the barren landscape of empty buildings, sidewalks and alleyways. Thick, wet snowflakes have begun to fall, limiting their ability to see very far down the road. It turns fast to blizzard-like conditions with near zero visibility. Luckily, it doesn't take long before they glimpse the approaching black truck, which sticks out like a sore thumb in the heavy, white snow.

"Can't wait to get in and crank the heat," Derek remarks.

"No doubt," Simon agrees and blinks hard a few times as snowflakes hit him in his right eye.

The truck is speeding toward them. They, too, must be anxious to get on the road for the farm. Henry still has to pick up his men from the McClane farm and drive home to their own. Being on the roads after dark isn't always a great idea, but Simon has a feeling that Henry's team will be just fine on that account, especially after they pick up their extra men. Beside him, Derek waves his right arm wide to alert them of their presence in the road since it is becoming difficult to see more than ten feet in front of their faces.

"They're in a hurry," Derek says with a chuckle as the vehicle approaches.

Only it doesn't slow down in the least but accelerates.

"Hey!" Simon yells too late.

Their friend's black truck is not their friend's at all but a black SUV that speeds past them. They are nearly too late to jump clear. Simon dives to his left and skids on the wet pavement, slamming his shoulder into a lamp post. Out of the corner of his eye, he sees that Derek is struck by the vehicle. It clips him good. Neither of them could've anticipated this. They'd foolishly assumed Henry was in the vehicle coming to fetch them.

Gunfire blasts through the open, back passenger window of the vehicle as it accelerates again. He steals a fleeting glance, sees Derek lying on his side not moving. Simon rolls to his stomach and raises his rifle to his shoulder. He takes slow aim. The shot will be difficult in this blinding snow, but he can make out the taillights.

"Shoot their tires!" Derek calls out weakly before moaning.

Simon breathes slowly. The vehicle is at least a hundred yards away now. He squeezes the trigger, allowing the shot to startle him. It connects. Gunfire bursts emit from both backseat windows toward them. Simon aims again. Screw the tires. He squeezes, absorbs the shot into his shoulder and watches through his scope as it pierces the back window to the hatch and hits with a thud into one of the shooters. He's struck someone. He feels no remorse for this. They ran his friend down in the road. Simon fires two more times, hitting their vehicle until it is gone, disappeared like a violent phantom and swallowed up by the blowing snow.

He jumps to his feet, slips and falls on the slippery ground and half crawls in a panic to Derek's side.

"Son of a bitch!" his friend curses. "My leg's broke, Professor."

"Let me have a look, Derek," he requests and begins feeling his friend's leg. It's fairly obvious. The lower half of his leg from the knee down is turned sideways.

"Help me get to cover in case they come back," Derek groans through gritted teeth.

"Right," Simon says with a mild hysteria brewing in his gut. Remembering his training is the only thing he can focus on right now. He drops his pack, removes Derek's, and gets into position behind his friend. Simon jams both hands under Derek's arms, hooking them under his armpits and drags him over the curb, causing him to cry out in pain. "Sorry."

"It's cool. Just get us outta here, Simon," Derek cries out.

Simon forgets being gentle and hefts Derek higher. He drags him into the closest building which is a former burger restaurant. Simon pulls him further until he has Derek resting against a wall behind a cluster of tables and chairs, some of which are knocked over. They will provide a little cover but not much. He props Derek's M4 right next to his friend and rushes back out to grab their packs.

"Good job, little brother," Derek says.

Simon can see blood trickling down Derek's forehead. He kneels beside him and drops his pack to the floor. Digging around, he finds his medic bag, which he always carries and pulls it free. Derek has a four-inch gash on his scalp. It needs stitches, but those will have to wait. He presses gauze to it and tapes it down as best as he can to prevent it from gushing down his face anymore. He knows how badly blood stings when it gets into the eyes.

"Stay here," Simon warns.

"Where else would I wanna' go?" Derek tries at teasing.

It mostly fails because Simon can see the pain on his friend's face. He must leave him for a moment to find something to splint that leg. Derek shouldn't be transported until he is stabilized. Simon can hear him trying to reach Henry's team on the radio. They must not be answering.

His heart stops because he hears the low murmur of a motor at a slow, trolling pace approaching the area.

"Derek!" he hisses and rushes back to his friend. "They're back."

"Stand down, Professor," Derek orders. "We can't engage. This could be their friends comin' back. We'll evade."

"Yes, sir," Simon replies and squats. He isn't happy about the order but knows that Derek has more experience than he does. He positions himself so that he is between Derek and the doors near the front of the restaurant. Those bastards are going to have to go through him to get to Derek.

The sound of the engine comes closer as Simon's heart pounds harder. He can just make out the headlights as the vehicle rests in place near the front of the building. Men shout to one another and then it moves on again.

He signals to Derek that he's going to check it out, to which his friend nods. Simon sneaks to the nearest window and watches as the vehicle turns around in another lot and then speeds past them as if its passengers have some urgent, new destination they must get to. He resists the urge to shoot at them again. Derek's right. They could have reinforcements nearby, perhaps fifty men. He rises to a stooped over, hunching walk and starts searching for the items he needs.

The dining chairs in the restaurant have metal legs, so Simon swiftly busts off two so that he can splint Derek's broken leg. He can hear Derek trying to reach Henry or Bruce again. Next Simon manages to bend the seat backward until it also breaks free. It has a slightly cushioned vinyl covering which he'll place under Derek's leg for more stability.

Simon rushes back to his friend and kneels beside him but not before he looks out the window to ascertain that their drive-by accosters have not returned yet again. Then he gets to work.

"They aren't answering," Derek says angrily.

Simon shakes his head as he pulls duct tape from Derek's bag, "Strange. They said they were on their way. Maybe they stopped for some more supplies."

"I wonder if they ran into those assholes," Derek remarks with concern.

"This isn't going to feel good, sir," Simon warns before lining up the splints. "I have to lift your leg to place the brace under it."

"Do what you gotta do, Simon," he says bravely and grits his teeth. "I'll watch our backs while you work."

"Yes, sir," he says nervously. He wishes that Reagan or Herb were here with them. They aren't, so he has to man up and help his friend.

"Try to hold still and bear with me," Simon issues with slightly more nerve.

"You got it," Derek says tightly.

Simon gently feels through Derek's pant leg and thermal long johns. He doesn't look at his patient's face. He knows not to do this. They are in pain, and dwelling on that fact and allowing their emotions to control him will not get this done any faster. He needs to move quickly to stabilize Derek to get him home to the farm.

Derek's leg is twisted to the side. Simon knows the break is bad. He places the broken metal chair legs on either side of his calf, and the seat back under it. Then he wraps it in his hoodie, which he removed. Duct tape will hold it all still enough until they can get him home. He'll have to sit on the back seat of the truck with his leg out straight while Simon rides in the bed, which is fine with him. Being cold for a few hours is better than Derek being exposed to the elements, and he certainly can't allow his patient to bend this leg in any way. This is not a simple broken nose that can be reset easily.

He is halfway through wrapping the leg in tape when a rustling outside the store alerts him. Simon instantly pulls his sidearm and faces the door, again putting himself between Derek and whatever might come through it. The sun has almost set. The store is nearly pitch dark. They are in a corner where they may not be seen. He is hoping that this spot was the right one to choose.

"Derek!" a man's voice cracks as he calls softly. "Simon! You guys in here?"

It is only Henry. Thank God their friends have found them.

"We're here!" Simon calls out loudly. "We're back here!"

He watches as Henry stumbles through the front door and falls flat on his face. Normally, they'd razz one another about tripping in such a way while on a mission, but something about the way that he rises slowly to his knees and falls again lets Simon know that this is not an ordinary trip from being awkward or clumsy. He rushes to their new ally.

"Hey, man," Simon says, squatting next to the bulky man. "You all right?"

Simon rolls him over and is astonished at the amount of blood on the dirty tile floor. Henry has been shot in the abdomen and is nearly unconscious.

"What happened? Where all are you hit?" Simon questions, leery of being in the open doorway lest they be seen.

"Gutshot," Henry reveals. "Had to run here to find you guys. Radio's gone."

"Where's the truck? Where is your team?"

"Gone. They're gone. Truck's gone."

"What do you mean? They were taken?"

"No, they're dead. Truck was taken. Me and Annie decided to hit another place since you guys weren't ready for us yet. Bruce waited in the truck. We heard someone shooting outside and ran out of the store. The truck was driving away in the other direction, and Bruce was on the ground. Then some other SUV sped past us shooting. She was dead in an instant. When I returned fire, they took off."

"We didn't even hear the shooting," Simon remarks.

Henry groans and then says, "You must've still been in a building."

Simon is reeling. He feels as if he has been punched in the stomach. Annie is dead. Bruce, their new friend and comrade, someone who seemed and looked invincible is also dead. He has no idea what to do. They are stranded away from home. And he is the only one capable of getting them out of this.

He does the same for Henry as he did for Derek. First, he drags the beefy man into the same corner for their safety. Then he gets to work treating his wound. He has lost a lot of blood, but the bullet has passed through. There are clear, clean entry and exit wounds. Simon first hits him with a tiny dose of lidocaine directly into the fatty tissue of the wound to handle the pain. It's the best he has with him. Simon hands the flashlight to Derek and has him hold it so that he can see what he's doing.

"We've gotta call in for help," Derek says on a moan. "We have to get out of here."

"My radio is gone," Henry rasps. "It was our link to my men."

"We'll call the farm," Simon tells them.

Derek says, "We're out of range, Simon. There's no way they'd get the call."

"We have to find a vehicle," Henry says and then coughs. He tries to hold his hand over his painful abdomen, but Simon shoves his hand out of the way. "Damn."

"Hold still. Don't worry about it, Henry," Simon tells him. "I'll take care of it."

His eyes meet Derek's just briefly before looking away. Simon can read the concern in Derek's gaze. There isn't anyone else to get them out of this situation. These men are going to have to rely on him. The family wouldn't even know where to find them right now. The radius on the map was at least a forty mile circle. They hadn't left exact directions with Doc as to their search parameters. They're on their own, and essentially Simon's on his own.

Simon presses gauze to Henry's exit wound and tapes it down tightly. Then he repeats the process to the entry wound. If he has to, he has enough supplies with him to close the wound with sutures, but for now, he just wants to stem the blood flow until he can get them the hell out of the area before those murderers come back.

"Stay here," Simon tells them both, although Henry seems to be losing consciousness. "I have to find us some wheels."

"Simon, take my rifle. Don't take your sniper rifle. You need something better for close contact."

"Yes, sir," he answers.

"Got your pistol?"

"Yes."

Derek grabs his arm before he stands. "Be careful out there, Simon. If this is the group from the freeway, then they're deadly. And they've got numbers. I don't know how they got one over on Bruce, so use extreme caution, brother. Don't engage. Just evade."

Simon nods once and stands. "Do you want something for the pain before I leave?"

"No, it'll make me muddle-headed. I need to stay frosty," Derek tells him. Simon just nods again.

He questions the silence outside and wonders if their attackers are waiting for them to exit the building. Simon listens near the front door where he can see without going outside. He double checks Derek's rifle, makes sure a round is in the chamber. He's locked and ready to roll. Seeing no lights approaching down the street, Simon steps outside. He has to secure a vehicle. The snow hasn't let up. They've had a mild winter so far, but apparently, this is going to be their token, late-in-the-season snow. He's glad he wore work boots as he steps into the slosh of the street. The sun has set. At least he is going to be covered by the camouflage of the night and the thickness of the snowfall.

Simon easily finds vehicles. None of them have fuel in the tanks. Only one even makes an attempt to crank over. He sprints to the next parking lot where abandoned cars and vans are parked haphazardly and not within the dedicated parking lines. Simon goes from vehicle to vehicle and doesn't find a single one that will run. He knows how to hotwire a car, learned this from the men on the farm, and is confident he can do it again, but finding one with gas and the ability to start is another thing.

"Damn it," he says to himself.

The only good thing he can say is that nobody is stalking him. He has been watching diligently for headlights or taillights and even flashlights. He left two, seriously injured comrades behind. He has to find something to transport them all home safely. They are counting on him, and he's never felt more pressure in his life. Except, of course, when he'd been responsible for Sam that night in her home when they'd been surrounded by those scumbags. At least Sam was able to keep mobile with him. Derek and Henry are both in a bad way.

He jogs back to check on them and to reassure Derek that he is still searching for a vehicle. Henry is out. This has Simon very concerned. There could be a million complicated scenarios if he has passed out from blood loss.

"I'm going out again," Simon tells Derek.

"Be careful," his friend says. "We're fine. Take your time. Nobody's gonna get in here." Derek pats Henry's M16 now on his own lap.

"Yes, sir," Simon says to his ranking officer.

As he is about to walk through the front door again, Derek calls out, "Simon! Check behind the buildings, too. There could be a car parked behind the buildings where employees would've parked."

"Got it," Simon calls back quietly. "I'll try to be fast."

He wastes no time doing what Derek has instructed. Unfortunately, the employee lots are also sparse, and none of the vehicles will start. Most of them have their gas caps open, so he knows they have been looted for fuel. His frustration grows as the wind picks up, making visibility in the snow more difficult. He has to get them out of here in case those men come back. As he crests the next hill, he spots an auto dealership. The location is far from Derek, but it may be their best chance of a running car. He sprints as speedily as he can, thinking only of getting them out of this town. It is the last thing he is even able to reflect on before slipping, sliding and falling and cracking his head against the concrete.

Chapter Eleven
Cory

They stop with Thomas's group south of Fort Knox and hit as many stores and buildings as they can to gather supplies. The town is desolate, as so many are today. It makes the salvaging of goods go rather fast. Within a few hours, they are back on the road. They stop again a little further south near Bowling Green, which is a much larger town. Cory has been through this city before. It's not abandoned. There are people living and surviving in the surrounding suburbs. They will need to be more cautious.

Dave orders two of his men to keep watch on Thomas's people since they don't have as much military experience. Dave and Kelly set security watching their vehicles and provide cover while Cory and John take off to find supplies. Thomas also takes his son to find their own group supplies.

The weather is starting to turn, a light snow falling and a crisp winding picking up. He'll be glad to return to the farm. He follows after John as they head into a shopping center. There are many different retail stores to choose from, but they'll stick together since the city is too large to vet for safety.

John hits a big box store first, but they don't find much. A few boxes of rice, a case of canned peaches, a bulk container of Band-Aids and three bottles of aspirin is their only loot. They leave immediately and head to a restaurant where they find some canned goods. Next, they hit a discount retail store that seems to have focused on household décor and clothing. Cory stuffs three sets of sheets into his bag and heads to the women's department. There, he finds two sweaters and a pair of khakis. He'd like to see Paige's legs in these. Actually, he'd like to see her legs in nothing at all. He grabs a few sweaters that don't appear to have been eaten by moths. Then he snags t-shirts and jeans next. He doesn't know the girls' sizes back at the farm, but they are all pretty slim, and these seem small.

There is a jewelry and accessories area next to the women's clothing. He snatches up a wool scarf, two pairs of sunglasses, and pair of black, leather gloves as he peruses. There is a pair of emerald-tinted earrings in the counter display. He reaches through the broken glass and puts them in his pocket. There are other necklaces and such there, too, so he takes them. The next aisle is women's face lotions and creams. He has no idea what they are used for, but he stuffs them in the bag. He knows she had chapped lips once. They sure felt soft when he'd kissed them, though. He wonders if she or the other women also have dry face skin, which is what he assumes this crap is for, so he'll pass the boxes out to them. Then he finds quite a few bottles of perfume around the other side of the counter. He remembers talking with Paige about her not feeling girly. He shoves all nine bottles into his bag. Scented lotions in fancy tubes and little glass pots are there, too. Women sure do get dry skin. Or maybe they just like smelling like flowers and bees and berries, which are all pictured on the silly labels. There is make-up, too. Cory takes all of it, which isn't much, and he knows almost nothing about any of it or what to do with it. He knows she wasn't a make-up wearer before, but if she is feeling dowdy, then surely his adopted sisters are, too. Hair ties and sparkly hair clip thingys go in the bag, too. Hand lotions, fancy bars of soaps, oils, and body washes are on the next shelf down. He swipes all of it into the bag. There are scented candles in the next aisle. These are actually practical, so he takes everything he can. Women's lingerie is next. There is quite a bit still hanging. Apparently, women weren't looking for sexy, slinky, silky slips and nighties when the country fell apart. Cory takes all that remains. He also snags the bras and panties. They always need these.

The men's department is next, so Cory does the same there, taking t-shirts, a light jacket, and three packages of boxer briefs. John returns with two children's coats and his own pack stuffed full of things. The kids are hard on their clothing.

"We aren't gonna find baby formula here," John tells him. "Let's roll."

"You got it," Cory answers and jogs with his friend.

"You found a lot," John remarks beside him, noting how full Cory's pack has become.

"Yeah, stuff for the girls," Cory answers evasively. He doesn't want to tell John it's because of Paige. It is best to let him think it is for all of the girls, which it really is.

"Cool," John replies with a nod.

They join back up with the group and place their loot into boxes they've brought.

"Any luck?" Dave asks, knowing full-well what they are searching for.

"Not yet," Cory answers.

"Ready to move to another area?" Kelly asks.

John shakes his head, "Nah, there're so many stores around here, we're bound to find some formula somewhere."

"And candy," Dave reminds him, to which John nods and chuckles.

"Ready?" Cory asks, getting another nod from John before they take off again.

They jog more quickly this time but head in the opposite direction. They find a grocery store, a big chain name, and get to work. The baby aisle is completely wiped out. They skip the rest of the search since the milk replacer is the most important part of their run. The next two stores also prove fruitless, other than finding miscellaneous supplies for the farm like canning lids, pectin, and two big cases of soda for the kids. John even finds a few bags of Starburst chewy candies, a family size bag of Twix in pale, Easter colored wrappers, a box of Junior Mints, Jolly Ranchers, and Laughy Taffy for his wife. Cory remembers back to when he first arrived on the farm. Reagan had given him and the other kids her stash of candy. She may be hard on the outside, but she is a caring and tender person. Most of the time.

"Shit," Cory swears with frustration. "We gotta find some damn formula."

"I know," John says with equal concern as they leave the store and walk down the sidewalk together.

John's radio scratches and Dave's voice comes over it telling them to return to home base. They pick up the pace and are back within a few minutes at the trucks.

"What's going on?" Cory asks as soon as they reach the others.

Thomas, his wife- who Cory can't remember her name- and their son- who Cory had slapped- are all standing with Dave and Kelly. Rachel and Cory's little shadow, Tessa stand nearby.

"Thomas has a proposal he'd like to offer us," Kelly starts.

"What is it?" John asks. "We're kinda' busy."

Thomas rings his hands in front of him and says, "I..we.. we found what you need, but we have a proposal to offer first."

"You found baby formula?" Cory asks.

"Yes, sir," his son answers. At least he's being more respectful.

"Where is it?" John asks directly and shifts his weight to his other leg. To Cory, he seems as if he is growing impatient. His friend probably wants to get back home to his wife to check on her. Cory can't imagine leaving a pregnant wife behind.

"We have it. Well, we found it," Thomas says. "But we'd like something from your group first."

"What do you want?" Cory demands with a degree of hostility. These people are in no place to make demands of them.

"We've discussed it, our situation. We don't think we want you to take us to Ashland City like we originally planned."

"Are you serious?" John asks.

"Yes, sir," Thomas says. "I know we asked if you'd stay with us to make sure we get there…"

"Yes, we would've anyway," John interrupts.

"But, our group realizes after…what happened," he says, his eyes darting to his wife, "that we aren't capable of surviving out here. We don't have the guns or the experience to deal with people like that."

"Where do you want us to take you?" Cory asks next.

"To your town?" Thomas answers.

Cory blows out a heavy breath of air. This might be a huge mistake. These people seem harmless, but they know basically nothing about them.

"We wouldn't be a problem. I promise you that. You've got my word on that," Thomas promises. "We could help. We have people with us that will help, who have something to offer."

"You're bribing us with the baby formula to let you stay in our town?" John asks angrily.

Thomas hangs his head. "No, John. No, we'll show you the formula. I'll take you to it. I just thought…it was stupid. I'm sorry. I shouldn't have tried that. You all have been good to us. We just don't know where to go."

"I thought you had friends in Ashland City or something," Cory says.

"Not really. The man who was with our group who knew them is dead. I don't know these people down there. He knew where their place was. I don't even know if I could find it. He was in charge of this move, not me. We were just going with him because he knew them. I guess they had a little farm outside of town. I have no idea how we were gonna make it work. There was only one house. We were talking about finding houses nearby that might be abandoned. It wasn't really much of a plan. Obviously! Look how it turned out."

"Yeah," Kelly says quietly.

"We're really desperate, John, Sergeant Winters, all of you," Thomas pleads. "I have no idea what we're going to do if we can't be accepted into your town. I don't feel comfortable going to our friend's relative's place without him. Somehow I feel like I still need to get word to them about what happened, too. They are probably worried since we were supposed to be there already. I'm responsible for these people now. We may have older people in the RV, but Rex is a former college professor, Tilly was a nurse when she was younger. They could teach people. It's what they were doing in our village. Rachel is really good with record-keeping. She kept track of our people and their families, made log books of our town members. That's important, ya' know?"

"I understand," Kelly remarks.

Cory sighs hard, feels a tug on his pant leg and looks down to find Tessa there. She's holding her arms up, so Cory indulges her. She immediately snuggles her face into his neck. Kelly shoots him a confused look. Cory just shrugs. He has no idea why this kid likes him. Most people are afraid of him, especially when his beard has grown out like it is now. Her tiny nose is cold against his neck. He unzips his coat and wraps her inside of it.

"I used to work construction, was a foreman with my own crew," Thomas expounds. "My wife ran her own restaurant. She really knows how to make food go a long way. She was in charge of that in our other village. We can help. We have value."

"Yes, so it would seem," John says.

"We'll give you the formula. We found it in a convenience mart gas station. We were looking for food for the kids in the truck. Found the formula in the back under a shelf. There's a lot there."

"Let us talk," Kelly tells him, to which Thomas and his family take the cue and walk away. "What do you guys think?"

"Not sure what to think," John says. "We don't know them."

"They hardly seem like a threat," Dave tells them. His opinion will hold a lot of weight in this decision. "They jumped in to help when we bunked at the hotel. I saw some of them working on the base helping out, too."

"That's true," Kelly says. "I saw it, too."

"They tried to withhold the formula for the baby in order to negotiate with us," John points out.

"They gave that up pretty fast, though," Kelly says. "I don't think he had the heart to follow through, and we knew it."

"What are you saying, Kel?" John asks. "Let 'em in?"

Kelly frowns, looks at his feet a moment before answering, "Yeah, John. I think they're probably all right. If we don't let them in, I don't think they'll get too far if you know what I mean."

"Yeah, I don't, either," Cory says, patting Tessa on the back. She's sucking her thumb.

"You think we should let them in, too?" John asks him directly.

Cory tips his head from side to side weighing out the decision in his mind before saying, "Yeah, I think so. Maybe they can help out in town. They don't seem all that bad. We may have gotten off to a rocky start, but I think that was bravado mixed with fear. I ran into a lot of those types out on the road."

"They did threaten us," Kelly remarks.

Dave jumps in to point out, "Yeah, but that was his dumbass kid, not Thomas. He seems like an ok guy. I don't think he's a threat. I'd feel comfortable letting him into our town if you guys don't want him."

"No, I think it's safe," Kelly says.

"You're the one who's gonna be making these decisions someday, so I'll go with whatever you want, Kel," John says. "I just wanna' get home. I'm good with whatever you decide."

"I want your opinion, though," Kelly tells his friend.

"I'd rather take the chance and let them into our town than send them on their way knowing their fates are probably gonna be predetermined by these highway jackholes."

"Agreed," Kelly says with a firm nod. "Cory?"

"Same," he tells his brother.

Thomas shows them the stash of baby formula he and his son found in the back of the convenience store. The storefront is wiped out. There are four boxes of it with eight cans in each box. There are also many other items they can take to the farm like lighters, matches, cigarettes, which will have to be hidden from Hannah, candy for the kids, motor oil, jumper cables, writing pens, a case of potato chips, three toothbrushes, dental floss, a case of window washer fluid, a box full of travel size Tylenol pill bottles, two boxes full of Tic Tacs, and a canister of propane on the outside of the building that is still full.

"The way this works," Cory explains to Rachel, who has tagged along, "is we take our loot back to our farm first. We take what we need. Then we transport the rest of the supplies we don't need to our town. The people within the town go on runs, too. The bounty is shared because the community is its own entity apart from us. The people in town who go on their own runs handle their loot the same way. Some is shared, some is kept."

"Seems fair," she says. "At least you guys try to share stuff with them."

"We also offer medical care twice a month at a clinic in town since we have doctors living on our farm," he says.

"Sounds cool," she remarks. "I'd like to see your farm sometime."

She is hinting at more than a visit to the farm; Cory isn't that naïve anymore that he doesn't recognize an invitation when he's issued one.

"Sorry, that's off limits," he tells her. "Nobody is allowed on the farm or to know the whereabouts of it. We offer services, but that's all. The town runs itself. If there are disputes, sometimes we're asked to step in and help. But we have it set up to run without us."

He can hear John warning Thomas and his group about stepping out of line in town and their recent problems. He also lets them know they will be banished if they don't follow the rules.

Rachel is still questioning him, "Is it safe, Cory?"

"Yeah, it's pretty safe. They've had problems on and off, but it's safe now. They have built a wall around it that's almost complete. In the spring, we'll be coming to town more often to help them get it finished."

"Oh, good!" she remarks and squeezes his forearm. "So I'll get to see you!"

With that, she walks away. Cory rolls his eyes.

"Ladies man all the way," Kelly says as he brushes past him, punching him in the shoulder as he goes.

"Whatever, man," Cory returns. He'd like to tell his brother why he is turning down the pretty blonde, but that is a secret best left unrevealed.

They pile into vehicles and move to another area of the city to salvage goods. An hour later, two more cans of baby formula and almost a full truck bed of other supplies in tow, they are back on the road for home. The sun has set and the weather turned nasty, so Cory is glad to be nearly home to the farm.

He has time to reflect on their trip as he rests in the back seat of the Hummer. It's nice not having Robert in the car with them. He has Tessa sleeping against his side, though. He has no idea how he's going to get rid of her once they get to Pleasant View. He also can't explain why she'd even want to be around him.

Robert had been downright livid this morning when they'd bade farewells to him and his men. He'd tried to argue his point again, but John had shut him down by pointing out that he had a pregnant wife to get home to. The fact that Reagan is Robert's daughter who is pregnant should've rammed the point home. Cory hadn't seen a shred of compassion on his face. He wonders just how much Robert cares for his children, or, if like Reagan says so often, he has single-mindedly pursued his own ambitions in life without a thought to his family. He has many times said that he's doing what he's doing for the betterment of them all. Cory questions the validity of this. He has not witnessed a lot of caring or loving, fatherly tendencies in Robert so far. He'd even thought for a minute that Robert might actually try to detain them. He'd reminded them again that he was their ranking general, to which Dave had snorted obnoxiously and loudly before climbing into the deuce and a half. Robert reconsidered his idea for pulling rank and detaining them, likely hoping for an alliance later on most likely. It would have instantly led to a war he didn't want. Plus, if he's going to start a war with the new President, he'll need more friends than enemies. In the end, his brother had shaken his hand, and they'd departed. Now

Cory is left to ponder whether or not this father of Reagan's will somehow eventually drag them into his civil war against the new government. Cory won't be leaving the farm. He won't be leaving Paige's side. The past few days was enough of that. He's ready to get home to check on her.

They drop Thomas's group in town, introduce them to the sheriff, and find an empty home with fireplaces for them to use. Their new neighbors immediately come out to introduce themselves and offer firewood. Thomas, although looking exhausted, volunteers to keep watch in a guard tower. He's promptly denied. The men in town now realize that people must be thoroughly vetted and trained for such a responsibility.

"Ok, kid," Cory addresses Tessa, who he is still carrying, "I gotta go. You stay with Rachel."

She shakes her head vigorously and clings on tightly. What the hell? This is like the Damn Dog situation. He didn't even feed this one.

"Yep, you gotta stay here," he says more firmly. "I'm going to my house now. You're gonna live here with Rachel and some of these other people. They'll take care of you."

"Come on, Tessa," Rachel says and pulls the child into her arms. She starts weeping silently. No sound comes out, but tears trickle down her soft cheeks.

Cory flinches. He doesn't like it when kids cry, so he rubs the top of her messy head of hair.

"Stop by and visit soon," Rachel says, leans in swiftly and kisses his cheek before turning around going into her new house.

John laughs at him when he gets back in the Hummer.

"Shut it," Cory orders and slams the door.

"Looks like you've got a ready-made family there, bud," John teases.

"Easy, John," Kelly warns with a laugh. "Don't scare him off. He'll leave for another year again."

"Not lookin' for a family," Cory says firmly. At least not with Rachel.

146

"What the hell is that smell?" Kelly asks.

"I don't know," John says. "I smell it, too."

"Yeah, me, too," Cory agrees.

Kelly swings around and looks at him. "It's comin' from back there."

"It is?"

"Yeah, bro. You been hittin' the cologne counter at the mall?" John teases.

"What?" Cory asks.

He remembers the loot in his sack.

"Damn!" Cory exclaims as he picks up his backpack and inspects it. The bottom is damp. He sniffs it and just about gags. One of the women's perfume bottles must have broken.

"Nice!" Kelly says with great exaggeration. "No wonder you're such a lady's man!"

"Lady's perfume, bro?" John inquires. "Couldn't have found something more…masculine?"

They both laugh loudly at Cory's dilemma. Cory has the stinky shit all over his skin now. He smells like a French whorehouse.

Dave follows them to the farm so that he can pick up his men, who should be there helping Derek and Simon keep watch over the family while they were gone. They park behind the old house and enter through the kitchen. Dave goes with them, but his men go off to join their friends loitering near the chicken coop. Cory can't wait to give the girly items to the women, especially one in particular.

He instantly knows something is wrong. The smell of food should be assaulting their senses but doesn't. Everyone is gathered in the kitchen. They all wear an expression of concern. Reagan is wringing her hands. Sue is running a hand through her rumpled hair. Paige is biting her thumbnail. And Sam is standing nearby holding baby Daniel with a forlorn look on her tiny face.

"Sam! What are you doing here, kiddo?" Cory says and goes to her, hugging her close.

"Hey, Cory," she returns without her usual enthusiasm.

He pulls back and frowns. "Everything ok?"

She shrugs. Her brilliant blue eyes are very troubled.

Kelly is the first to ask, "What's going on?"

"They aren't back," Reagan blurts and rushes to John, who hugs her close.

Paige is standing next to the island, gripping it so tightly that her knuckles are turning white.

"Who?" John asks.

Paige answers, "Derek and Simon. They went with Henry and some of his men to scout these creeps who are attacking people on the freeway."

"What? Why?" Kelly asks angrily.

Hannah explains, "They were just supposed to be checking things out, seeing if they could track them or discover their location."

"Gathering intel," Reagan says. "That's all they were supposed to do. They weren't going to do anything if they found them. They said they'd be back before dark. That was three hours ago!"

"It's ok. Don't worry," John says, kissing her forehead. "It doesn't mean anything's wrong. They could just be having car trouble or something."

His eyes dart to Cory's above his wife's head. There is concern in John's blue eyes.

"They felt it was safe to leave the farm since Dave sent extra help this way," Doc explains. "Henry came last night to tell us of another raid on the freeway. He said he was going out today to gather some intelligence on this group. Derek and Simon wanted to go with him to be of some help, so Henry brought Sam over to visit and some extra men to keep an eye on the farm."

Kelly adds, "Right, let's just get some info and figure out a plan."

Doc says, "Let's head to the dining room, everyone."

Kelly takes Huntley and Justin to the side and orders them to unload the loot from the back of the Hummer. Cory knows what is coming.

"I'll get my men. They might know where we should look for them if we have to," Dave says and leaves the kitchen.

Everyone takes a seat in the dining room. Paige sits right beside Cory and looks at him.

"Do you think he's ok, Cory?" she whispers with scared, wide gray eyes.

He reaches under the table and takes her frail hand in his. Cory doesn't answer her right away. He doesn't want to lie.

"I'll find him," he tells her. It feels better than a lie. Dead or alive, he will find Simon and the rest of them. It's the best he can offer. She does not pull back from his grasp, and her hand trembles in his.

Sam is sitting beside Paige and is very edgy and nervous. She keeps biting her lower lip and tapping her foot rapidly on the floor.

"When were they supposed to be back?" John asks as soon as the rest have found a seat. Dave is back, and some of his men are standing against the dining room wall.

"Yes, sir," one of them says. "Henry said they'd be back by sixteen hundred, seventeen at the latest. He didn't wanna' be out after dark."

That was over three hours ago, Cory realizes after he checks the wall clock.

"What vehicle did they take?" Kelly asks.

They all know that some of the McClane vehicles have been on the fritz.

"Henry's pick-up," the man tells them. "Annie and Bruce are with them."

"Was he having trouble with it?" Kelly presses.

"Not that I know of, sir," he says. "We just put a new alternator in it just last week."

Kelly just nods and asks Dave, "What color was it?"

"Black extended cab. Where were they going?" Dave asks his man.

"Wide perimeter, I think," he says. "He was heading north toward where that guy told us about the raid on the freeway."

"I'll get a map," Doc says and leaves the room.

He returns a moment later and spreads out their map of Nashville and the surrounding cities onto the table. Cory's heart rate begins to accelerate like it does right before a battle. Something in his gut tells him that this is no random breakdown of a vehicle. They're in trouble. His best friend needs him, but he will not convey his fear to Paige.

"North," John says, pointing to the map.

Dave's man points to the area where the suspected freeway raid took place.

"Yeah, it's about there," Dave confirms.

"They were going to check out the scene of the crime and see if they could track them down," his man says. "They had to have gone up into this area here."

He points to the same spot on the map as Dave.

Sue asks, "Why haven't they called in? I don't understand. If you guys are going to be late, you always call in."

"Maybe outta' range, Sue," John says.

Cory can see the dread building in John over his brother. His friend knows, just as Cory does, that something is wrong. They aren't just out of radio contact range. Soon, John's eyes will turn hard with determination and bloodlust.

"Should we give them more time to get back?" Doc asks. "Perhaps they are having car troubles or are simply having a problem because of the weather."

"I don't think it'll hurt to take a quick run north and just see if maybe they're having car problems somewhere along the road," Kelly says with a false smile and looks at Cory across the table. He can tell that his brother is playing it off as nothing to worry about, but Cory knows he is concerned.

"I'll take Cory," John volunteers.

"Sounds good," Kelly says.

Dave jumps in to help, "I'll go and take two of my men, too. The rest can stay here to help keep watch on your place while we're gone."

"Thanks, Dave," John says. "We appreciate that."

"Hey, man, my guys are out there, too," he says as he stands. "I gotta find 'em."

"We'll leave in ten," John says and exits the dining room with his wife, who is right on his heels.

"Can I go, too, John?" Sam asks and grabs his arm in the hallway.

"I don't think that's a good idea, kid," he tells her.

"But I could take Grandpa's medical bag in case someone needs care before we can get them back to the farm," she offers.

John looks at Doc and then his pregnant wife. Cory knows he's weighing this decision, and he knows John isn't going to want to take Doc or Reagan out there.

"I could go," Doc volunteers.

"No, sir," Kelly is quick to rebut. "We could need you here."

Doc steps forward and says, "Then I think it's a good decision for Samantha to go, John. She can help. She has a lot of medical training."

"See?" she says with a hopeful look on her sweet face.

John sighs hard and frowns harder before nodding reluctantly and saying, "Ok, kid, but grab a gun from the armory and warmer clothing."

"Yes, sir," she says and runs off.

"John, can I go, too?" Huntley asks, puffing up his chest just a bit.

"I'd love to take you, little brother, but Kelly needs help keeping the farm safe and secure while we're gone. I need you to do this for me, ok? Take care of the kids."

"Yes, sir," Huntley replies with a solid nod.

Cory leads Paige from the room and upstairs to the second-floor hallway where they can speak privately.

"Cory, I'm worried," she says, grabbing his hands. There are unshed tears in her light eyes. "Do you think something bad happened?"

"I'm not sure," he tells her. "Stay here and stay safe. Try not to worry. Let me handle this. It's what I do."

"They're so late. I just know something's happened. He's my brother. I know this isn't right. I can feel it."

"Don't think like that. Let's not jump to conclusions," he says and tries for a grin. He's sure it doesn't come off as genuine.

"I can't lose him, Cory," she says and chokes on a sob. "He's all I have left."

Cory pulls her gently into his arms and kisses the top of her head. He knows how she feels. He went through the worst case scenario situation when he lost Em.

"I'm not comin' back without him."

She nods against his chest.

"Be strong. Be there for Sue," he says. "Her husband's out there with your brother, remember?"

She nods again, this time with more force and leans away from him again. Cory presses a kiss to her forehead.

"I gotta go," he tells her and gets a nod, although she does not release his hand. "I gotta go, Red."

Cory kisses her mouth and pulls away. He goes slowly down the stairs with her until she is safely on the first floor again. Then, like John and Sam, he flies into action. He runs to his bedroom in the basement and pulls on thermal underwear and a warmer coat. Then he raids his drawers for warm, dry socks and a stocking cap. He may be tracking on foot for a while. The snow is piling up out there. There isn't going to be time to waste sitting in the car warming up when he's going to need to be on the ground. Next, he jogs back upstairs and out to the armory where he finds John and Kelly. They are both loading up heavily, although Kelly is loading ammo mags for Cory and not himself.

The family says their goodbyes before they pile into the Hummer again. Dave and his men have topped off the tank in the deuce, and they're ready to go, too. The last thing he sees out his side window is Paige standing on the back porch wrapped in a pale blue shawl with her arm around Sue's waist. He assigned Sue to her just to keep her mind from dwelling on her worst fears. He knows that sometimes taking care of someone else is a good distraction from one's own woes.

John and Dave are in the front seat navigating. Tracking at night is a lot more difficult than during the day. Cory has a lot of experience with it, though, from when he was on his own. Sam is sitting beside him in the back seat and is organizing Doc's medical bag. She has an AR-15 perched on the floor in front of her. She must've borrowed warmer clothing from the girls because Sam looks like she's wearing one of their barn coats with layers underneath.

"What do you think happened?" she asks him without looking directly at Cory.

"Not sure, kid," he admits.

"Trouble?"

He hesitates a moment before saying, "Maybe."

"Yeah," she agrees on a shakily exhaled breath. Then she adds what they are all thinking, "I figure the same."

They travel north for almost an hour when they come upon the carnage of the highway massacre that the men were supposed to be investigating. They aren't surprised by it. They've already witnessed another crime scene similar to this one. They continue north, but at each exit, Cory and Dave's men jump out and see if they can determine if their friends took the ramp. So far, they don't have shit, and every passing minute means his friend could be in danger. Cory climbs back into the Hummer with a heavy heart. He has to find Paige's brother, his best friend. He made a promise, and he's not about to let her down.

Chapter Twelve
Simon

He rolls to his side and notices blood on the snow. Then Simon touches his fingertips to the back of his head. When he brings them around to his face, there is blood on them that mimics the same that is dotting the snow. He winces as he touches the spot on his head again. He doesn't think he blacked out, but he sure rung his own bell hitting his head on the concrete curb. Shaking it off, he pushes himself to his feet. Nothing blurs, and he doesn't fall down again. It's time to move.

Simon runs as fast as he can to an Auto Zone store, thinking he might find a vehicle there. It doesn't take long to realize that there aren't any viable cars in the lot or behind the building. The store has been vandalized, and graffiti has been sprayed on the bricks. It has faded, and the message has become nearly unrecognizable. He tries the parking lot next to it that connects to a strip mall. None of the cars will start or even crank over once. Most of them have open gas caps, so he knows they won't have fuel, either. He sprints along the front of the buildings, staying close to them for protection, until he comes to a muffler shop a few blocks away, all the while feeling apprehensive about leaving Derek and Henry for so long. He leans his back against the cement block wall a moment to catch his breath and scan the perimeter before entering the building. His friend and new ally are all alone, and he's their lifeline to get them the hell out of this city. His frustration is growing in tandem with his apprehension.

He takes a few deep breaths and breaches the storefront. Broken glass crunches under his feet as the winds outside howl through the store and down a short aisle. This place would be great if he wanted to jack up his ride with an annoyingly loud muffler extension kit. Simon slips on something and almost goes down. At first, he thinks it is blood. Then he realizes that it is old, black oil spilled on the moldy linoleum floor. It is sticky on the bottoms of his lug sole boots. At the service counter, he sees sets of keys behind the front desk hanging on tiny hooks. Someone must've been selling candy bars for their kid's school charity because a nearly full box sits on the counter with a hand-written sign that reads, "$1.50". Simon empties the box into the cargo pockets of his pants. The sugar sustenance will be helpful for Henry and Derek since their food was in the truck that someone else now drives. Their night is long from over, and both are terribly injured.

Outside, an animal cries in the distance. He's pretty sure it's a screech owl. It reminds him of the Edgar Allan Poe poem, The Raven, where the man goes mad. Simon feels like he is going to go mad from his failure to find a vehicle to carry them to safety. The howling winds coupled with the shrieking owl feel ominous and foreboding. It also reminds him that Derek is lying helpless and could become the prey of a predator animal.

A door in the back leads to a garage where repairs would've been made to cars. Simon cautiously pushes it open, the hinges squealing in protest of not being used in years. A four-door, navy blue sedan sits in one repair bay while a mid-size SUV rests in the other. He hastily searches the garage and ascertains that he is alone. Then Simon opens the door to the sedan and reaches for the ignition. The keys are in it, but it won't turn over. He's getting nothing. He rushes to the SUV, a hunter green Jeep Grand Cherokee, and discovers that the keys aren't in it. He curses under his breath. Then he remembers the keys hanging behind the front counter, so he runs back inside to get them. He's not sure which ones might belong to the Jeep, so he takes both sets. He tries the first and they don't fit the ignition. Then he tries the other and breathes a sigh of relief when they do. He turns the key, but nothing happens at first. After a few cranks, the motor makes a rapid clicking sound. He knows that's the sound a battery makes when it needs to be charged.

Simon gets out again and starts looking around the garage for something to jump the car's battery. Being a muffler shop, there isn't anything like that here. He kicks the tire with frustration. Thoughts whirl through his brain at lightning speed. He wishes that John or Kelly was with him or even Cory. He's the motor head, the mechanic, Mr. Fix-it. Simon's the science nerd. He's fine with that label. He hadn't ever anticipated something like this happening where he'd be in charge of the survival of everyone on a mission. He has to think. His irritation level is at an all-time high. Then it hits him. The Auto Zone store still had a lot of things laying on the floor. Maybe he'll find jumper cables and a battery charger there. First, he looks in the trunk of the Jeep. There aren't any jumper cables in it. He checks the sedan, too, but doesn't find any.

Simon rushes through the stinging snow and travels back to the Auto Zone. He quickly finds the jumper cables but doesn't see anything he can use to jump it. There is a plug-in model, but that isn't going to work without electricity, which nobody has around here. At the farm, they have a product called a jump pack, but he doesn't see any of those. He needs to find a portable battery jumper. Then he needs to pray that it'll work. He rushes to the tall shelving units behind the check-out counters and starts rummaging. There are plenty of car parts and mechanic's supplies. If this were any other time, Simon would be stuffing his sack full of supplies and telling the lookout driver to bring the truck around. They could use so many of these supplies on the farm and on their neighbors' farms for future repairs.

He finds the battery aisle and is surprised that so many are still sitting on the shelves. Simon's not sure if he took a whole battery and changed it out if it would work or not. Finally, he locates the chargers, but most of them seem to be the kind that requires electricity. On the last rack, he spies portable battery chargers, or at least that's what the white label on the shelf says. He shines his

156

flashlight and mostly sees cobwebs and dust. A small box on the bottom shelf catches his attention. It's a portable battery charger, as small as most tablet computers. The box containing it is pink with white flowers on it. It looks like something a father would gift to his teenage daughter to teach her the responsibility of car ownership. Simon doesn't care. As long as it works, he's fine with flowers and pink.

He makes a fast dash back to the muffler shop and into the bay with the Jeep. Then he pops the hood and gets to work. The directions in the box say that the vehicle should immediately start on the first crank. He'll believe it when he sees it. The pink charger even has its own cables, so he drops the ones he found. He hooks the cable to the correct ports and turns the switch on the side of the charger to the 'ON' position. He almost passes out from shock when the little green indicator light glows. Simon wastes no time and gets in the driver's side. He tries the ignition again. It click-click-clicks in rapid succession but doesn't crank.

"Damn it!" he curses loudly and pounds his palms on the leather encased steering wheel. This has to work. He doesn't have any other plan. Running all the way back to the farm is out of the question. They must be twenty miles from home. Henry could bleed out. Derek could get gangrene. They could both be killed first by the jerks in the SUV or eaten by a bear or wolves or a cougar.

"Calm down," he reprimands himself more quietly this time. He has to go at this scientifically. He needs to use reason and logic. "Batteries take time to charge. Let's just give it a minute. Be patient, Simon."

This is exactly what Sam would tell him in a time like this. She was always a good partner when they were out on runs. He decides to give it exactly three minutes, even though he feels like minutes could be life or death in their situation. However, he has to try. Simon times it on his watch and tries the key again after three minutes. It turns over. The dashboard lights ignite with life. He feels like shouting to the heavens with joy.

He hops out of the Jeep, leaves it running, removes the charger and places it on the floor of the front seat in case he needs it again. Simon checks the gas gauge and sees that it only has less than a quarter tank. He's not sure if that will get them home or not. Still leaving the car running, which he knows will help charge the battery, Simon searches for a gas can. He finds one, but it's bone dry. He's going to need fuel. He finds a piece of hose on the ground, probably a car part that was removed and tossed into a debris pile. Inserting the hose into the gas tank of the sedan, he syphons the remaining gas out of the sedan and into the empty gas can. Then he fills the Jeep. After he gets back in, he sees that the gauge has gone up to nearly three-quarter's full. That's definitely enough to get them home.

Simon opens the garage bay's door and gets back into the Jeep. Overriding the headlights, he turns the switch to 'OFF.' There's no sense in drawing attention to himself. The brake lights are a bright enough beacon. He backs out carefully, runs over some debris in the parking lot that he hopes doesn't give him a flat tire and heads toward the restaurant. It feels good to be moving, mobile, in charge again. He skips the intersection since too many cars are blocking it anyway and drives up over the cement curb and down over the hill. He veers the Jeep away from a stone wall that ends in a drop-off and finds himself behind a superstore of some kind. Driving around the back of the building, he comes to another intersection and forgoes the laws of traffic. It feels like he is speeding, which he is for the tempestuous weather conditions he's driving in. But he is desperate to get back to Derek and has to drive around buildings and parking lots instead of just traversing right across them on foot. It takes him a moment, but he finds the switch for the wipers. They drag across the snowy windshield with a loud squeal. He turns them back off. Every little noise sounds deafening to his ears. He can't afford to be found out by anyone. He has to get the men to safety.

In the console cup holder is a full bottle of water. If this were another time, he'd be disgusted by taking a swig of some stranger's water bottle. However, this particular bottle has sat in this car for three and a half years. He's pretty sure the statute of germ limitations has been met. Plus, he's parched as if he's run through a desert for six hours straight. He wipes the rim after removing the lid, takes a drink and tries to forget that it once touched someone else's mouth. He'll save the rest for Derek.

At last, he pulls up beside the restaurant, hoping their new mode of transportation will be concealed well enough if those people return. He leaves it running. Simon has no idea if it will restart if he shuts it off. He can't take the risk that it won't. He's not Cory. He's not Dave the Mechanic or any kind of mechanic.

Simon calls out to Derek to let him know he is coming back in and wastes no time getting to them.

Derek is worse. He is sweating and very pale. "Any luck yet?"

"Yes, sir," he answers and kneels beside him. "I've got us a car."

"Good, let's get the hell outta' here before my wife comes out after me," he attempts at teasing.

Derek coughs three times. This frightens Simon that his friend has other internal injuries.

"Yes, sir," he says. "I must move you, Derek. I'm not going to lie. This is going to be painful."

"It's cool," he says stiffly.

"Let me give you some morphine. I have some from that hospital we raided," he tells Derek.

"No," he rejects and holds out a hand. "I'm gonna need to keep watch for you while you drive, Simon. I can't do that if I'm out of it. Henry's not gonna be much help."

Simon feels indecisive again. He presses his brows together and scowls. "Yes, sir," he finally agrees. "Ready?"

"As I'll ever be, Professor," Derek says bravely.

He swings his rifle to his back and lets it hang from its strap. Simon reaches under his friend's shoulders again and hooks his hands through Derek's armpits. Then he interlaces his fingers at Derek's chest and tries to block out his friend's cry of pain.

"Here we go," Simon tells him. Derek holds onto Simon's sniper rifle. "Drop it. I'll come back for it."

Derek does just that, obviously realizing that it is too long and cumbersome for him to hold onto while being dragged. Simon pulls as gently as he can. Every time Derek moans or groans, Simon feels the full extent of his own guilt and remorse. He knows down deep that none of this was his fault, and yet he can't help but feel tortured over Derek being this critically injured.

It takes him some time, but he manages to get Derek dragged all the way to the Jeep.

"Simon," he says through tightly gritted teeth. "Put me in the back, in the hatch. If I need to shoot, I can open the hatch and do it through the half-window."

"Yes, sir," Simon answers. He's in no position to argue.

He pushes the button on the tailgate, and it rises to its full height. Simon pulls Derek to the edge of the bumper. This is going to be the tricky part. He props Derek against the opening and climbs in. There is a backpack of the former owner's in the trunk. There are other miscellaneous items, but he just swipes them all to the side. Then he returns to Derek and tugs as hard as he can and manages to heft him up into the trunk space. Simon tugs him farther inside until he is resting against the back of the rear seats of the vehicle. It will provide him with some bit of comfort to make the ride home.

"Take these," Simon tells his friend, whose pallor is pale and sweaty. He hands him a chocolate bar and the bottle of water from the console. "Drink. Eat some sugar. It'll help until we reach home."

Derek is panting heavily and barely manages a nod. His friend is in great pain.

"I'll be back," Simon tells him, shuts the tailgate again so that the interior light goes off, and runs back inside for Henry.

First, he checks their new ally's pulse in his neck. It is weak, but it's there. Simon does the same with Henry. This time, the struggle to pull the other man is more difficult. He must weigh more than Derek, and both of them likely weigh more than him. Henry cries out in pain, waking about halfway to the Jeep.

"Sorry," Simon tells him in a rush. "You ok? I got us a vehicle. I'm getting us out of here."

160

"Help me up," Henry says, fully awake now. "Don't drag me anymore. Let me walk myself out."

Simon isn't sure how he's going to do it, but he does. He allows Henry to wrap an arm around his shoulders as Simon helps him stagger toward the Jeep. A moment later, he's out again, dead weight. Simon gives up and hefts the unconscious man over his shoulder and makes a mad dash before his own legs give out. He barely gets him into the back seat before he drops him. Simon tucks his feet inside and shuts the door. Then he runs back for his weapon and their packs. He opens Henry's door and props his lolling head with a backpack. Then he pulls a seatbelt down and clasps it in place over the man's hip. He certainly doesn't need any other injuries before they get home. Simon also takes a moment to inspect his wound. It is still bleeding, but the gauze is holding in place. He rips off a piece of duct tape and presses it down tightly against the wound to stave off further bleeding. He gently closes Henry's door and gets in behind the wheel.

"Ready, Derek?" Simon calls quietly as he puts the Jeep in drive.

"Let's roll, Professor," Derek says weakly.

"Drink your water while I drive," he orders and pulls away.

Simon drives around the city until he sees the rusted signs for the freeway. He was barely paying attention to their route, and now he has to navigate them back home. He tries the radio again. Nothing.

"We're still outta' range, Professor," Derek confirms. "You're gonna have to wait a while, get us closer to home for them to pick up a signal from us."

"Yes, sir," Simon says quietly. "Dang it."

"What is it?"

"Blocked road."

"Put it in 4x4 and go around. Keep it in 4x4 till we get home."

Simon locates the button to engage the four-wheel-drive unit and presses it. A moment later he can feel the car shift into gear.

"Hold on. This could get rough," he calls back to the only other conscious person in the car.

Simon veers around an overturned pick-up truck and a semi with a box trailer on its side. Dave has told them that his men always inspect semi-trailers for goods for their compound. This one will go unsearched tonight. He has other things on his mind. He must use the shoulder beside the right lane. The Jeep clings to the muddy bankside but doesn't slide despite the snow. After passing more vehicles left in the middle of the road, Simon slowly pulls back up onto it. He keeps to a snail's pace since he can barely see the road and definitely not the blacktop. It is hard to tell if he is even on it sometimes. A black void ahead causes him to stop altogether. He can't see the white of the snow on the road or any other broken down vehicles. Something is obstructing their passage down the road.

"What is it, Simon?" Derek asks from the hatch.

"Not sure," he says. "Stay here. I'll check it out."

"I'll cover you."

Simon exits the vehicle and approaches cautiously. He slips on the wet pavement but manages to stay on his feet. His pistol in hand, he walks towards the dark void in the road. He passes cars but after about twenty yards, there are no more vehicles and the road is empty of all but him. He's walking alone in the blinding darkness. He takes out his flashlight to better see where he is placing each footfall. As he approaches the dark area, Simon realizes it is a collapsed bridge, a huge void of blackness. He'd like to scream with frustration. He hadn't seen this when they'd taken the exit ramp before this one to get off the freeway. There is nothing there, no road, no way over the giant, gaping hole. Long pieces of steel rebar stick out of the concrete, wires hang down, light poles bent over and broken as if an earthquake has shaken the area. He will have to turn around.

"Damn," he curses in earnest this time. Then he turns and jogs back to the awaiting Jeep. "Bridge is out," he tells Derek after he's shut his door. "We'll have to find another way around."

"Yeah," Derek says with a lot of strain in his voice.

"How are you holding up?"

162

"I'll make it," he answers Simon.

He doesn't sound like he will. This sets him in a panic. Simon puts it in reverse and backs up until he can find a place to turn around in between cars. Then he steps on it. He has to get them home soon. The tires bite into the pavement and hold fast against Mother Nature's bounty polluting the scene with a winter wonderland theme. He must drive faster now. Neither of their wounds have been treated sufficiently.

Simon maneuvers back down the on-ramp and through the shopping plaza in the city. He speeds south until he comes to another road sign that has fallen over. Parking the Jeep again, he jumps out and runs over to the rusting sign. It is indicating a left-hand turn for the freeway going south again. This is what he needed. He manages to find the on-ramp and merges slowly around a garbage truck forever parked in the way. The freeway is just as congested and, since the last bridge was collapsed, he feels he must drive slowly in the dark or else be swallowed whole by the deep black void of another missing bridge.

They travel for about twenty minutes or so according to the clock on the dashboard with the incorrect time. Henry moans periodically in his sleep. Simon hopes this ride isn't jostling him too much. He is forced off the road two more times to pass wrecked pileups of vehicles. This is nothing new. They see this often on major roads and highways. People were in a panic to get places in the beginning. He finds himself wondering where they might have wanted to go in such a hurry. Static on their handheld radio draws his attention.

Derek says into it, "This is Big Bird here, go ahead."

They change their call signs often in case anyone ever brings in their signal with intentions of spying on them. The kids were the ones to suggest funny cartoon characters and the like. Mostly they agreed to it to appease the children. Changing their call signs was a wise move proposed by John. There's no sense in helping people who would mean them harm if they could find their location by listening in on their transmissions. There is enough of that out there without offering assistance, these people who would rob and steal and murder and run others over with a vehicle.

Nothing happens for a few minutes, so Derek repeats the transmission. Static comes over. Then nothing.

"Think it's them?" Simon asks. He hates the unconcealed hopefulness in his voice. It makes him feel weak.

"Not sure, Professor," Derek says. "Hey…I'm not…I'm not feelin' so hot, Simon."

"What's wrong?" Simon asks with heightening fear.

"Woozy. Not sure if I can stay awake. Here," he says reaching over the back of the seat. "Take the radio. If you get into trouble, yell. I'll wake up. I won't leave ya' hanging. I'm just nauseous and dizzy."

"Need me to stop?" Simon asks as he rests the radio on his lap. He's not letting it go for a second. It is their only lifeline to the farm.

"Hell, no!" Derek answers with more grit. "Just keep us moving southwest."

"Got it," Simon replies. "Did you hit your head? Maybe on that car or the pavement? I taped a cut closed on your scalp."

Simon knows the feeling well. He has a lump on his own skull from the same thing.

"No, don't think so. Maybe. It happened kinda' fast. Maybe something on the ground cut me when I fell. I've got a hard head. At least that's what the wife is always tellin' me."

Simon attempts a chuckle. It sounds nervous, so he stops doing it posthaste.

"Just rest," he tells him. "I've got this, Derek."

"I know, brother," Derek replies and falls silent.

Great. He wishes that his friend didn't have so much faith in him. He's not sure he has this at all. He feels like they just got their asses handed to them, and now he's running with his tail between his legs. He just wants to get away from that town and back closer to the farm, so he drives faster. He's very worried about Derek's leg. He's also concerned about Henry's bullet wound, but not as much. Derek is like a big brother to him. He doesn't want to let the family down.

Another half hour passes as he creeps along the freeway. Static comes again, and this time Simon answers it.

"Big Bird here, over," he says with urgency. "Come in, Cookie Monster."

Static. More crackling. And then: "Cookie Monster here, we gotcha' loud and clear, Professor."

Simon has to hold back tears. The breath he hadn't realized he'd been holding is expelled in a giant whoosh of relief.

"Doctor Death?"

"Yeah, it's me, buddy," John replies. "Car trouble?"

"No, sir. Worse. Derek's injured severely. Henry, too."

There is a long pause, and for a moment Simon is frightened he's lost them again.

"Position?" John asks.

"South of Springfield on forty-nine," Simon relays, hoping nobody else is listening in, especially not the jerks who attacked them tonight.

"Past Coopertown?"

"Not yet," Simon tells him. "I'm about two miles out from it."

"Stop there at the meeting place and wait for us. We're on the wrong road. Hold tight at that position and wait for us, Professor."

He breathes another sigh of relief. Derek has not stirred. He hadn't inquired after the radio call. Simon just hopes he's still alive back there.

Chapter Thirteen
Sam

Her palms are sweating in her gloves. This is bad, really bad. She nervously taps her right foot on the floor of the Hummer. Simon sounded scared and nervous. He's not like that. Even when they'd been attacked at her house a while back, he'd been relatively calm and in control like he always is, which is usually a sense of frustration for her.

They are moving fast, probably too fast for the weather conditions. Dave's men are leading in the big deuce. Whoever is driving must've been freaked out over the message they just relayed to Dave because his driver even plows into a small car in the road, taking out the corner of it so that he doesn't have to waste time going around it. She knows how close his men are and the tight camaraderie they all share. They are probably apprehensive about their friends. Sam is glad that Annie and Bruce are uninjured, though. At least there's that. She likes Annie a lot as a friend. She has also suspected that Annie is romantically interested in Cory because she asks about him often. Sam just smiles politely when she gets those sorts of inquiries.

They are on the wrong freeway. It's going to take some time getting caught up to Simon. She knows the meeting place is the mom-and-pop garage and repair shop in Coopertown. It's always been a safe place, unoccupied and desolate. Most of the town is also desolate, so it makes for a good place to meet anyway. It takes nearly a half hour to finally get to Coopertown. John flies past the deuce, probably thinking they don't know where they are going since Dave's group isn't aware of all of their meeting spots. He leads the way, barreling through the snow. He's a good driver. She's learned this about him when the weather is bad. John is careful and cautious and knows just how far he can push a vehicle. She's not so good at that.

They pull around back behind the shop. A dark colored Jeep is there with the fog lights on. Smoke comes from the tailpipe. It's running. This is not Henry's truck.

Cory raises his gun. Dave does the same. The driver's side door opens, and Simon emerges. Everyone lowers their weapons and exits their vehicles. John rushes to Simon first.

"What the heck happened?" he asks.

"We don't know. Not everything. Derek got hit by a big SUV. Henry's been shot…"

"Where's Annie and Bruce?" Sam asks.

Dave butts in, "Are they in the truck still out there somewhere?"

Simon's gaze falls to the ground, and he shakes his head. "I'm sorry. They're dead, sir. Henry told us they're dead. We were looting a town and split up, trying to find baby formula. I don't know what happened. It just all happened so fast."

John brushes past him to the Jeep and opens the back door to find Henry passed out on the seat. He peers over the back seat and rushes to the tailgate of the car.

"Derek!" he says when he has it open. "Hey, man. Wake up."

Sam and Cory are at his side in an instant as Dave's men attend to their fallen comrade in the back seat.

"We need to get to the farm as fast as possible," Simon tells them. "They need medical care I couldn't provide in the field."

"Right!" Dave yells, recovering quickly from the shock over his lost comrades. "Load up. Let's get them back to the McClane farm. Now!"

Everyone jumps into vehicles. John stays with his brother as does one of Dave's men. Dave climbs into the driver's side of the

Jeep so Simon can work on Henry in the back seat. Cory will drive the Hummer home. The deuce will lead their way, clear the path, and provide security to get them home faster.

"What the hell?" Cory says to her as soon as they are moving again.

Sam is sitting next to him in the front seat, "I don't know. It was confusing. I'm not sure I understand what happened."

"Yeah," Cory agrees and flips on the window wipers to clear away the accumulated snow.

"Oh, my gosh. I can't believe Annie is dead. He did say that, right?"

Cory blows out hard through his mouth and nods. "Yeah, he said that she and Bruce were both dead. That's messed up. They were good soldiers, really well-trained."

"This is bad, huh?" she asks rhetorically. Cory doesn't answer. "If they were caught by surprise or overtaken, then whoever did this is trained like you guys. What if they followed Simon? What if they find the farm or Henry's farm?"

"They won't, Sam," Cory says and reaches for her hand. "They won't. We're safe."

"Then how did it happen?"

"Maybe they let their guard down. Maybe those people run that area and are more familiar. It's hard telling until we get more of the story from Simon."

Sam hurries and sends up a prayer of gratitude that he wasn't harmed. She may be angry with him, may be for a long time to come, and doesn't want to live around him anymore, but that doesn't mean she wants him to be hurt.

Within a short time, that actually feels like hours, they are back at the farm. Someone must've called ahead because they are met at the shed by Reagan and Grandpa. Paige hugs Simon close, and he pats her back. The doctors are both in scrubs and are ready for whatever is going to greet them coming out of the vehicles. They begin calling out orders of where to put the men.

"Sam, prepare for surgery," Reagan commands Sam as she rushes around like a maniac. This is normal for her mentor, though. Sam just does as she's told.

She runs to the back of the shed where the sink is located and removes her coat and two layers, hanging them on hooks. She's down to her thin, thermal silk undershirt. Then she pulls her hair back with one of the rubber bands they keep on hand near the cabinets. She scrubs up at the sink with the familiar, strong and lemony-scented soap and tries not to let her imagination run wild with her. A moment later, Simon enters the space and mimics her procedures. He flings his coat to the ground, though, and doesn't even bother trying to hang it from an available hook. His hands are covered in blood, likely Henry's.

"You're assisting Doc. I'll help Reagan," he tells her.

Sam doesn't care who she is going to assist as long as she's helping someone.

There are two faucets that dump into the same utility sink, so Simon begins washing under the one beside her. Their shoulders bump every so often. She notices that his hands shake.

"Are you sure you can do this?" she asks.

"I'm fine," he says, but his voice sounds shaky.

"What happened?"

Simon shakes his head and looks at her. His eyes seem haunted. "Everything and anything that could go wrong did. Annie and Bruce were killed. Henry's gut shot. And Derek…." he lowers his voice to a whisper, "his leg's broke. I mean really broke. And I'm afraid he may have internal injuries, too. I don't know. He's in really bad shape."

"Oh my goodness," Sam frets and dries her hands. "Compound fracture?" she asks and prays his answer is to the negative.

"No, I don't think so, but his leg from the knee down is just dangling. I'm thinking spiral fracture? I don't know."

"Oh, no," she laments with true concern. She remembers her studies on broken bones and pictures in the textbooks that Reagan loaned her. Fractures of this type may need rods and screws and extensive surgery. She doesn't think they are capable of performing such procedures.

"I just…" he says and stops drying his hands.

Sam rests her hand on his forearm before saying, "It's not your fault. Let's just get out there and help."

He nods and looks at her, really looks at her. Simon is acting as if he is seeing her for the first time since she came to visit. He had barely been civil this morning.

Sam spins around and says, "Tie me."

He obliges and ties the strings of her gown behind her. Then she does the same for him.

"I'm glad you're here," he says.

"I'm glad I'm here to help with them, too," she answers and walks away. It is the truth. She wants to help. She loves Derek and has come to like and appreciate Henry. He gave her a home when she needed a new one without asking questions or passing judgment. Sam isn't about to read more into Simon's words than he likely means. Just because he's glad she's here doesn't mean he's in love with her. It is simply his way of saying that he appreciates the extra medical help. That's all. And she isn't going to confess her love to him again just because they are in the middle of a high anxiety medical crisis. He got that once. He threw it back in her face. She's not going to repeat that narrative. Not ever again. She's moved on from Simon.

Grandpa uses the small, portable x-ray machine and takes a picture of Derek's leg, causing the lights to dim. He has to wait to do it because Derek is in the middle of throwing up. John is right there beside his brother holding the bucket for him. Her father figure's face is as pained as his brother's. It hurts Sam to see John and Derek in so much emotional and physical agony. They have removed most of Derek's clothing, and he now sports a fashionable hospital gown.

Reagan is on the other side of the curtain with Simon working on Henry. He cries out from time to time. Sam can hear them talking about the injury.

"Hit him with more Lidocaine, Simon," she instructs, her raspy voice sure and confident.

"Yes, ma'am," he answers.

"Ketamine," she orders next.

Sam knows they are trying to get him numbed up and sedated. Performing surgery in the shed is nearly impossible, but they do the best they can with what they have to work with. If he has to be put all the way under, they can do that, too, but then they have to run an endotracheal tube and vent him. This complicates things so much more, and Grandpa would have to assist and run a spinal block for general anesthesia.

"Passed through," Simon informs her. "I found the exit wound."

"Good," Reagan says. "Clamp," she orders.

Dave the Mechanic must also be assisting because he answers, "Yes, ma'am."

Grandpa drills Derek with a hundred questions about his aches and pains, which he insists are only in his leg. However, Grandpa suspects he also has a concussion and needs a few stitches on his scalp.

"Why'd he vomit? Is it normal to throw up and stuff, Doc?" John asks with urgency.

"Yes, son. He's in a lot of pain. Also, I hazard a diagnosis of concussion, as well, which will also do that," Grandpa answers calmly before John walks away. He looks at the x-ray up against the bright light bulb hanging down in the corner. It's the best they could do. They haven't found an x-ray light box on a run yet, so the light bulb is the next best thing according to Grandpa.

"What do you think, Grandpa?" Sam asks at his side. He points to a particular spot on the x-ray.

"Can you name the bone, Samantha?"

"Yes, the tibia, sir."

"Good. See here, Miss Samantha, the blunt force of the vehicle must've hit him near the patella, the knee. Snapped the lower leg bone. He's lucky it didn't do more than this. I don't see shards or chips. That's about the only good thing I do see."

He starts mumbling medical jargon about distal, diaphyseal, spiral.

"Wow," Sam whispers as she inspects the picture. "That looks really dreadful."

Grandpa looks at her and then over at John across the room to ascertain that he isn't listening, "It is, Samantha. This is very bad. We're going to have to straighten his leg and cast it from the knee down, probably the thigh down."

"A cast?"

"Let's consult with Reagan," he says, leading her away. She is pretty sure he just wants out of John's hearing range.

Simon tells Grandpa the second he sees him, "I checked for pulses below the leg and got strong ones, sir."

"Good. PMS," Grandpa says with a nod.

Sam knows PMS stands for pulse, motor control, sensory feeling. It's basic first aid, and they were both taught these things by Reagan years ago. Sometimes she gets PMS, but that's something entirely different and usually multiplied by Simon.

"Yes, sir," Simon says. "He was giving me positive readings on all three counts."

"Yes," Grandpa says with a nod. "We're going to need to cast the leg from the thigh down."

"That bad?" Reagan asks.

He just nods, and she goes back to her sewing.

"Passed through?" Grandpa inquires, getting a nod from Reagan in return. "Good. That's good news."

"No organs were punctured that I could tell. He's lost a lot of blood, so we'll have to wait and see on that. Maybe do a count here pretty soon. I think this'll heal up nicely, though."

"Good again, Dr. McClane," Grandpa says while still looking at Derek's x-ray. Sam can tell he's weighing things in his mind. "Simon, why don't you finish here for Reagan? She's only closing. You can handle this."

"Yes, sir," Simon says quickly and trades places with her.

Grandpa takes Reagan toward the front of the shed, so Sam follows.

He shakes his head before saying, "Derek hasn't been as lucky tonight. He may not be able to walk again. It is a spiral fracture of the tibia with a possible comminuted fracture, as well. We're looking at six months minimum before we'll even know for sure if the casting and isolation will heal it well enough for him to walk again. I'm going to cast it, but the break is severe and in a critical place. He could be crippled from this."

"Shit," Reagan says with an exhausted sigh and removes her surgical cap and pulls her gloves off and folds them inside of each other to contain the contamination. "Can I look at the x-ray?"

He hands it to her after she has tossed her gloves into the trashcan. Reagan goes to the back where their x-ray lightbulb hangs and inspects the picture for herself. John keeps glancing at them with dread-filled, blue eyes. Sam feels bad for him. This may be a life-changing event for his brother. It reminds her how fragile life is. She's tired of thinking about how fragile life can be. They are reminded all too often.

John comes over to them and asks, "What's going on? How are you going to fix this?"

Doc lays a hand on John's shoulder and says, "This may not be fixable, son. We're going to set it as best as we can and cast it."

"Oh, good," John says with elation.

"No, John," Doc corrects and slowly shakes his head with the grave news he is about to deliver. "Derek may not heal completely or well from this or at all. He may be crippled. The bone is broken in a way that without surgery, it may not mend completely. I'm not an orthopedic surgeon. Even if I could perform the surgery, I would need rods and pins to stabilize the bones."

John doesn't say anything. He takes a deep breath and raises his chin. Then he swallows hard. "Let's not tell him."

"Whatever you wish. He's your brother," Doc says. "It's your call, son."

John shakes his head vigorously. "Don't tell him. If he heals completely by some miracle, then it'll be just that. If he doesn't, I'll deal with it when it happens. This is on me."

"I don't want you to get your hopes up, John," Reagan tells her husband and touches his arm. "If he can't walk again when this is over, I don't want you to be angry."

"He went through basic training, Ranger school, and special forces qualification. He's not going to take this lying down. If anyone can beat it, it's him. He'll walk again. I'll make sure of it. You guys put him back together and just don't tell him."

Grandpa's eyes narrow. Sam can tell that he doesn't agree with John's decision, but she also knows he won't go back on his word and tell Derek anyway.

"I'm not gonna lie," Grandpa says. "This is going to be painful. I'll knock him out with anesthesia first."

"Got it," John says.

"John," Grandpa says with gravity.

"Yes, sir?"

"We don't have the materials to make a cast," he admits with a fallen face. "I had a small box of casting materials at the clinic, but we used them last summer when that young boy broke his arm. We're out completely."

"Shit," Reagan says. "You're right."

"I'll take care of it, Herb," John says as Kelly comes into the back of the room, as well. "We'll go right now. You tell us what you need. We get it. That's how this works."

"Clarksville is going to be closest," he tells them. "There are a few small clinics and hospitals there. You'll find the materials I need either in the emergency room storage rooms or on a floor that specializes in orthopedic medicine."

"Right," Reagan says nervously, chewing her thumbnail. "Let me start a list." She grabs a notepad and pen. "It's not that difficult really. Plaster of Paris, bandaging, cotton. Damn. Grandpa, they also have the newer fiberglass materials."

"I don't want that. Get me the old-fashioned kind. The newer, high-tech materials won't mold tightly enough. We need this to be as perfect as we can get it."

"Agreed," she says thoughtfully as she scribbles rapidly. "And any type of morphine or pain killer you can find, too. This is going to be very painful, John. I don't want Derek to suffer. I'm not sure how much we have here for blocking pain. We took a lot of that to the clinic in case we have to deliver babies there soon."

"I will, babe," he says and takes the list.

"I'll go, too," Kelly offers.

John shakes his head, "No, stay. Stay in case it gets dangerous here. I don't know who did this, but they could be tracking us back to the farm as we speak with the amount of snow on the roads."

"True," Kelly agrees.

Dave has also joined their meeting and offers to stay on the farm to keep watch. His offer is met with appreciation.

"Unless you want me to tag along," he offers.

"No, man," Kelly says. "Stay here and help. We'll work and sleep in shifts. Unless you gotta get back to your farm."

"Nah, that baby's a well-oiled machine," he tries to jest. Sam can see that he is hiding his feelings behind humor. "Besides, I don't wanna' leave without Gunny."

Sam smiles. He is very loyal to Henry, but she doesn't know their history that well.

"I'll go!" Sam volunteers.

"Wait," Simon interrupts, to which Sam shoots him a deadly glare. He has no right to speak for her.

"I want to, John," she pleads.

"Fine, I'll take Cory and Sam," he says.

They return to Derek's side, and Grandpa tells him that he's going to set and cast the leg. He leaves out the part where he is unsure of whether Derek will be crippled.

"Hang on, brother," John says, leaning down and touching his brother's shoulder. "I'll be back. I've gotta get the supplies to make the cast."

175

Derek gives him a thumbs up. Sam guesses that it is all he can manage. Sue is at his side with tears on her cheeks. John touches the top of Sue's head, then kisses there.

"I'll hurry," he promises and turns to go. He steps toward Sam and says, "Find Cory and gear up."

Sam nods and sprints from the med shed. It doesn't take her long to find Cory. He is in the kitchen standing at the island wolfing down pork roast and mashed potatoes.

"We ready?" he asks Sam through a mouthful of food.

"John said to gear up. How'd you know?"

He smirks and winks at Paige, who is uncharacteristically waiting on him, handing him a glass of goat's milk across the counter. "I figured we were either going after whoever did this or something else."

"We need materials to make a cast for Derek's leg. Grandpa's sending us to Clarksville."

"Wait!" Paige cries out with alarm. "Again? You're leaving again? Tonight? So soon?"

"His cast can't wait," Sam explains, although Paige is not looking at her but at Cory. "A broken bone will begin to heal very quickly, so we can't wait. He's in incredible pain, too."

"I know. I know," Paige says sadly and looks at the countertop instead of them. "I'm just scared for you guys to leave again. Good grief. Especially after what happened tonight."

Sam rounds the island and wraps an arm around Paige's slim waist. "Don't worry, Paige. We're just going up the road to a hospital. No gunfights tonight."

"Well…" Cory interrupts on a tease and an ornery, lopsided grin as he pushes his half full plate away and stands. He is insinuating that perhaps they will go after those men, probably just to upset Paige. He gulps down the glass of milk without coming up for air.

"Cory!" Sam reprimands. "No, Paige. I promise. We aren't going after them. We're just getting supplies to make a cast for Derek's leg."

She can feel Paige nod against her own head.

"We're not going after them…*tonight*," he adds.

"Cory!" Paige complains this time. "You're incorrigible. Is my brother going, Sam?"

She shrugs and replies, "Not sure. Don't think so. We don't need him."

"Oh," Paige says quietly and seems forlorn.

"He looked tired," Sam corrects, not wanting to be abrupt with Paige because of her feelings toward Simon. "He should stay here and rest anyway. His nerves have got to be fried."

"Right, yeah, you're right. I'll get him to come in and rest and get something to eat. I don't know what they've had to eat today since they left this morning."

Cory says, "Probably not much since the truck was stolen."

"We'll make plates," Paige volunteers.

"That's a good idea," Hannah says as she enters the kitchen carrying baby Daniel.

"Make sure to get something for John," Cory says.

"Right," Paige agrees with a nod as she opens the refrigerator door and quickly makes a pork sandwich, wrapping it in paper. Then she places it and an apple in a sack.

"Oh, hey, Hannie," Cory says. "We found formula."

"I know," she returns with a wide smile of gratitude. "Huntley told me. He's in the music room going through the bags. I think the little kids found some candy. We'll have to check the formula, but hopefully, it's still good like the other cans."

"Yes, hopefully," Paige concurs.

"Do you wanna' grab some food, Sam?" Cory asks as he pulls on his warm winter coat.

"No, I'm good. I ate earlier," she tells him.

"Then let's roll, little sister," he says with a grin of mischief. He kisses Hannah on the cheek. "See you later, Hannie."

"Bye," she returns as she heads toward the kitchen sink near the big, wide window overlooking the back yard. "Be careful, Cory, and hurry back."

"Yes, ma'am. You got it."

Sam watches as Cory reaches for Paige's hand. She backs up just slightly and then looks furtively toward Sam. He pats his palm on the island's marble top instead.

"See ya', Red," he says lightly and nods.

She raises her eyebrows and nods. Together, they move to the back door. Paige rushes over and pinches his jacket sleeve with two fingers.

"Be careful," she murmurs with a soft voice filled with dread.

"We will," he promises. Before Cory can touch her, Paige backs away again.

"Bye, Sam," she says, hands her John's food, and hugs Sam.

"Look after everyone here while we're gone," Sam tells her and realizes instantly how stupid that sounds. She's still laid up and recovering from her own gunshot wound. "Well, just look after yourself. Leave the heavy lifting security stuff to Dave's guys and Kelly."

Paige salutes her and smiles. Sam follows Cory through the back door and out to the shed. Neither of them needs to restock on ammo. They did earlier this evening when they went looking for Simon and didn't use any of it. She hopes that trend continues as they hunt for medical supplies.

John meets them at the dark green Jeep that Simon brought home to the farm, and Sam passes him the sack of food, to which he nods with appreciation.

"This has enough gas, and Simon said it ran pretty well," John explains. "Let's take it."

"Fine with me," Cory says. "Want me to drive, old man?"

"Sure," John says agreeably as they all get in. "I'll eat my fuel and backseat drive."

Cory laughs. One of Dave's men gets in the back seat beside her. She hadn't known anyone else was coming. Sam met him once over on Henry's farm, but she can't recall his name. He's usually on night watch duty over there because she passes him occasionally when she's up and about and can't sleep.

"Extra help?" Cory inquires of John.

"Yeah, Zeke, this is Cory," John introduces, and the two bump fists. "You probably already know Sam."

"Yep, we've met," she says, hoping it isn't obvious she couldn't remember his name. He just nods and replies with "ma'am." She mostly trusts Dave's men. They have treated her with respect and have not attempted to bother her in any way with unwanted or unwarranted attentions. She appreciates that about them.

She stares out the window looking for potential threats along the dark tree line as Cory drives and John navigates. Sam's glad that neither of those responsibilities lay at her feet tonight. The roads are snow-covered, and she's not entirely sure how to find this hospital. They are also in a hurry, so Cory drives faster than she would have. Clarksville is nearby but usually takes quite a while to get to because of the need to be cautious and slow. However, within forty minutes they have made it to their destination. Cory pulls right up to the front entrance and puts it in park. He pockets the keys. It is quite clear upon first inspections that the building is empty. No light, either from candles or electricity, glows from within. There also aren't fresh tire tracks or footprints anywhere when they get out of the Jeep.

"Zeke, you wait here with the car?" John requests.

"Yes, sir," he replies. "Dave said to do whatever you asked. I'll wait with the Jeep."

Cory hands him the keys, which Zeke then places in the front pocket of his coat. Cory offers him a firm nod before they leave him to enter the hospital.

John pulls out his flashlight to guide them. They pass the front desk, but the receptionist isn't on duty. She also isn't maintaining hospital levels of cleanliness of her workspace. There is filthy debris and black muck coating the floor. Sam knows it is likely from a water line breaking above and raining down upon it. This usually causes mold, fungus, and eventually plant life to sprout right in the middle of a building. Most places look like they belong in a botanical garden now. This one appears to be no different.

John rushes over to inspect a tall, rectangular sign that contains a faded map of the hospital. He wipes away the dust with the sleeve of his coat.

"ER's around back," he announces and takes off.

Sam and Cory follow, and she takes special note of dark corners and hallways that open up into theirs. She can hear the swoosh of Cory's rifle as he also sweeps the area to keep them safe. John, in his attempt to hurry, trips over a discarded cord in the hallway.

"Dang it!" he swears.

"Careful," Sam whispers before they continue on. It takes them a few minutes of fast paced walking, but they eventually find the emergency room. They pass the triage desk that no longer offers a workplace for nurses and data entry clerks. The sliding glass doors to their right are permanently frozen in a half open position which has permitted the weather of every season to flow freely within. Tonight, there is a small mound of snow piling up just inside the doors. Near it, there is a corpse. Sam averts her eyes. She never likes seeing this.

Once they breach the permanently open doors to the actual medical treatment area, John suggests they split up to find what they need. He reminds them that they may have trouble getting into any stock rooms they find and to call him on the radio if they find what they need or if they require his help.

Sam walks beside Cory, careful not to step on the debris left behind on the floor. It is spooky, like walking through a haunted house attraction, the sort that used to pop up during the month of October every year. The out-of-business, metal fabrication factory suddenly became "The Haunted Factory of Terror." The elementary and middle schools that were closed down to consolidate into one mega-school building, thanks to taxpayers and school levies, were transformed for that one month of the year into "The Haunted Laboratory and School of Demons." Sam went to one of these once with her father and two of her friends. She'd been terrified and had never repeated that nonsense. Now she's living in an intensely more

180

terrifying reality. This hospital is dark and eerie, and she's pretty sure one of the corpses in the patient rooms is going to reanimate and chase her down with a chainsaw.

"There," Cory says as they come to the end of a dank hallway. A metal door to a room that says, "Hospital Staff Only" in black, bold letters is at the end of the hall.

Sam's fingers are cold beneath her wool gloves. "Maybe."

Cory tries the knob, but it's locked.

"I'll get it," Sam tells him, kneeling in front of Cory. "I've got my kit."

"I can just kick it," he offers.

"For some reason, I don't want to make a lot of noise here, if you know what I mean," Sam admits as she fiddles with the lock.

"Just spooked or something legit?"

"No, nothing real. Just creepy here."

"Got it," Cory says without judgement as he stands with his back to her keeping watch.

She feels the cylinder rotate forty-five degrees. "I'm in."

"Record time!" he praises. "I'm impressed."

Sam smiles at him and curtsies as she opens the door and enters the room. Cory is right on her heels as he shines the flashlight around to illuminate their path. It is clear that nobody has been in this room to raid it yet. Many supplies are stacked on shelves, but most of them are for cleaning or remaking beds. Linens are stacked on open, wire shelving units as well as blankets and hospital gowns.

"Shit," Cory swears.

Sam frowns, too, but adds, "Don't give up. This is just the first place. Let's keep looking."

They back out of the room, and Cory allows the door to close but makes sure it doesn't slam. Then he grins at Sam, who sticks her tongue out at him. He chuckles obnoxiously.

"Is everything ok with you and Paige?" she asks as they walk down another hall, an even darker, more shadowy one.

"Yeah, what do you mean?"

"Nothing. She just seemed upset that you were leaving. I was surprised is all."

"She's just been sensitive since the whole thing in town went down."

"Hm," Sam says but doubts his story.

"How do you like living with Dave's family?" he asks after they turn the corner and head in another direction.

"They're really nice," she answers honestly.

"Not as cool as me, though, right?"

Sam chuckles. "Of course not."

"Good, don't want you to be too happy over there," Cory remarks with humor in his voice. "Then you won't miss me."

"I miss you enough," Sam says. That's also the truth. Cory is like her big, annoying brother. She misses their camaraderie and mutual teasing of Simon. Her heart is broken that she had to leave her whole family behind, but she didn't have a choice. This broken heart will eventually heal. Living with Simon and being in love with him and not having that love returned was breaking her heart on a daily basis. That was never going to heal. Just being away from him has helped a lot. Spending time with her beloved uncle has helped even more. He doesn't push, but she suspects he knows she left the farm for a reason. She also suspects that he has some secrets of his own.

"Down here," he says, picking up the pace.

A door halfway down the long, dark hallway is standing ajar, even though it clearly states that it is not open to the public. Wires hang down from the broken ceiling tiles. She always ducks, even though there is no longer electricity feeding into them. Cory goes in first.

"Man, this place has been wiped out," he says. "Someone's already hit whatever was in here."

There are empty boxes strewn around the floor and equally bare shelving staring back at them. Static on their radio alerts them, and Cory answers John's call. He is approaching from the hall and does not want them to take a shot at him.

John enters the storage room. "Nothing? Me neither. I'd say the ER is a wash. Let's find the orthopedic floor."

They rush back to the map of the hospital and find the location of orthopedics, which also shares the floor with the same-day surgery unit. That could be a good source for items, too. Together, the three of them enter the emergency stairwell to get to the third floor. John leads and is hurrying more than normal. They usually approach places like this with more caution. Sam understands his sense of urgency. They continue on as a single team to the orthopedic wing of the hospital. There are suite numbers with doctors' names on the wall. John shakes his head with irritation and shoves through the swinging doors. There is a wide, circular reception area and a massive waiting room.

"I think Doc said they did surgery here, too," John says. "Why don't you two go and see if you can find some anesthesia or something. I don't know what. Sam, you're in charge of that."

"Got it," she says firmly.

John takes off at a jog, leaving them to find the same day operation unit. They leave the orthopedic wing and right away find the same day surgical suite located at the other end of the third floor. They enter into a long, open room with floor to ceiling windows and many comfortable chairs and tables provided for the patient's family members who were waiting for their loved ones being operated on. The double doors that lead to the surgery rooms do not open, however. There isn't even a lock on them to pick. Sam looks at Cory. He also seems dumbfounded. These doors would've whooshed open with the press of an electronic button at the receptionist's desk.

"Stand back," he says.

Sam steps a few paces back and watches as Cory kicks four times at the doors. They don't budge.

"I'll see if there's another way in," she offers and takes out her own flashlight.

Sam fast walks to the other end of the long waiting room and searches for another entrance door. There isn't one. She just finds more tables and chairs around the corner, so Sam rushes back to Cory.

"We need something to pry it open," he informs her. "Stay here. I'll go find something. I may have to go back downstairs if I don't find what I need. I'll be right back."

Sam would like to protest splitting up, but she doesn't say anything for fear of sounding like a wimp. They have already ascertained that they are alone in the hospital. It doesn't, however, mean that it is any less scary. She decides to raid the reception area for anything they can use. Slinging her pack onto the countertop, Sam digs in the drawers and finds pencils, pens and notepads. Someone always has a use for these, especially Grandpa and Reagan at the clinic. Of course, now that she is going to start a new clinic with her uncle, she may need to keep these supplies for them to use. There isn't much else to take, so she walks around the waiting area scouting for more items. She finds a drink station that would've been for the family members of patients. Opening the cupboard door below, she discovers coffee pods like her mother used to use in her Keurig. There must be sixty small containers of coffee, some flavored, some decaf and others just plain Columbian. There are packages of powdered creamer and sweeteners. She stuffs her bag full of them. Sam has plans for this find.

A noise at the other end of the room causes her to startle and jump. It's only Cory, so she exhales a heavy breath through her pursed lips. He acknowledges her with a lift of his chin and goes right to the double doors.

"John's found what he needs," he tells her when she approaches. "He's on his way over here. We have to hurry."

He has a piece of heavy duty steel and is jamming the pointy, jagged end into the narrow slot between the two doors. His tool looks like something he's broken off of a table or chair or shelving unit. She's not sure. But it does seem to be working because he has the door pried about six inches so far. Another few minutes and he has pushed hard enough to fit through.

"Let's go," he says. "We gotta hurry. They're waiting."

"I'm with you," Sam returns and follows him through the opening.

They try to move fast, but the layout is unfamiliar. The good thing is that the unit does not appear to have been raided before, probably because nobody couldn't get the door open. They weren't partnered with Cory, though. If someone says it can't be done, Cory will figure it out. He has a terrible stubborn streak.

"Split up," Cory orders. "Grab anything and everything."

Sam goes right while Cory stays straight. He disappears into a room as Sam finds another. It was definitely a surgical suite. The huge, round lights hang down from the ceilings on metal arms so that they can be moved into various positions. A bed in the middle of the room is where the patient would've lain. Sam hurries to a cart and grabs medical tools in packages, small vials, which she's pretty sure are anesthesia, and a box of rubber gloves. There are blue surgery towels on the second shelf down on the cart. She stuffs those in the pack, too. Then she sprints to the next room and repeats the same process. This time, she finds surgical masks, a bulk box full of hypodermics, and two bottles of heparin, which she knows reduces the risk of deep vein thrombosis during surgery. The last thing Derek needs is to grow a blood clot while he's laid up with a broken leg. Grandpa will know the correct dosage of heparin to administer. In another surgical suite, she finds a vial of propofol, and in another, a bottle of fentanyl, both used as an anesthetic.

"Sam, let's roll!" Cory calls to her when he sees her emerge into the hallway again. John is with him.

Sam jogs over and announces, "I found a lot!"

"Me, too," Cory says. "I have no idea what any of it's for, but I found a ton of shit."

They head out, jogging side by side with their packs slung and their rifles out front in the ready. Cory and John pull the double doors shut again so others cannot raid the surgery rooms. They'll soon be back for the rest.

"What about you, John?" she asks. "Get what you needed for Derek's cast?"

"With the weight of this pack, I think I got enough to make everyone on the farm a cast," he teases, although Sam knows how concerned he is about his brother.

They take the same route back to the Jeep where Zeke is still standing. Then it is home to the farm where Derek is waiting for them to save his damaged leg. The snow has stopped, and the clouds have disappeared again. The radiant silver glow of the half-moon illuminates their way. Sam just hopes Grandpa is wrong about John's brother sustaining a life-altering, crippling injury. She hopes that it is the first time in his professional career that he will be proven wrong.

Chapter Fourteen
Reagan

Setting her brother-in-law's leg was an excruciating process, terrible for her and Grandpa since he is not just a patient but a family member. At Grandpa and then John's insistence, Derek finally gave in and took the shot of pain blockers. Eventually, he was knocked out. Reagan isn't sure if it was from pure exhaustion and he just passed out or if the anesthesia knocked him out. She, for one, was thankful for the coffee that Sam found. Grandpa had been very appreciative. He's not a big fan of the herbal teas, either. And they didn't finish casting Derek's leg until nearly one in the morning. Her back is aching, her feet are sore, but her nausea has finally subsided. Unfortunately, Derek will feel a thousand times worse in the morning. They have left him in the shed with Simon, who'd insisted on sleeping on the cot in the back of the room so that he could check on Derek throughout the night. Henry is also out cold to the world, but his bullet wound will heal exponentially faster than Derek's leg. One of his men donated a bag's worth of blood. Sam volunteered to take the other cot to watch their patients, but Cory insisted he'd stay instead. Reagan hadn't missed the expression of disappointment that had flickered across Simon's face. Dave and his men are taking Cory and Simon's cabin in the woods since her father vacated it.

She climbs the back porch steps with Grandpa and goes straight to the mudroom to wash up. Hannah comes in a moment later.

"How'd it go?" her little sister asks.

"What are you still doing up?" Reagan asks in a reprimanding tone.

"I wasn't still up," she says. "I just got up to get Daniel's bottle ready and change his diaper."

"Oh, it went well," Reagan says. Then she amends it with, "It took a while, but we got it cast really well. I don't know. Maybe it went well. Hell, Hannie, who knows?"

"I heard," her sister admits.

"Does Sue know?" she asks, wanting to know if Sue understands that Derek may never be the same again.

Hannah nods. "Yes. Grandpa told her. Do you think he's right?"

Reagan pauses, considers lying and then immediately tosses that thought away because Hannah would be able to tell. "Yeah sis, I think he's right. Without doing multiple repair and reconstructive surgeries, this won't heal correctly. He needs rods and screws. We don't have that ability."

"Why not take him to that hospital they went to tonight to find the supplies to make his cast? Take him there tomorrow and do the surgeries he needs. Sounds like there were a lot of things still on that surgery floor Sam raided."

Hannah, ever the optimist. Reagan would like to shake her sister's shoulders to knock some reality into her thin frame but refrains. She, too, wishes that it were that simple, that they could perform some miracle operation. Things are never that simple anymore.

"Won't work, Hannah," she gently explains instead. "There isn't electricity. Even if we took the generator, we'd need a lot of tools, the right type of anesthesia, oxygen. Plus, neither of us are orthopedic surgeons."

"Hm, I don't know. You two seem to figure things out."

188

This time she chuckles. "Not this one. This would require an ortho with years of experience with trauma injury repairs. I was studying to become a general surgeon or a heart surgeon eventually. Grandpa's specialty was gynecology, obstetrics and then family medicine."

"Oh," Hannah says sadly, her sightless eyes dropping to the floor. "Then we need to pray for a miracle."

"Yeah, that'll do it," Reagan says and immediately feels bad for being sarcastic with Hannie. Her innocent sister doesn't deserve her cynicism.

"Prayer works, Reagan," Hannah corrects with irritation.

"Sorry, I know," she says and goes to her sister, hugging her close. "I know."

It will take a miracle, too. Reagan wasn't an ortho specialist, but she'd studied enough to know this type of injury is nearly insurmountable. Hannah pulls back and heads for the kitchen.

"Need help?" she asks.

"No, Reagan," her sister replies. "Go to bed. I've been asleep for a few hours. I'll be fine. I just need to feed him and get him back down."

"Did anyone have a chance to check that formula they found yet to make sure it's still safe?"

Hannah slides her hand along the counter until she reaches the dish strainer where the bottles have been turned upside down and left to dry after being washed.

"Yes, Kelly and Huntley checked it," Hannah answers. "They said all of the cans seemed fine as far as they could tell."

"Thank God," Reagan says.

"See? He always answers our prayers."

"Yeah," Reagan returns, although she doesn't necessarily agree.

"Now go to bed!" Hannah orders and even waves her hand through the air at her like Grams used to.

Reagan steps closer, kisses her sister's cheek, and heads upstairs to her third-floor bedroom. The room is dark and cool, perfect for sleep. But John is not yet in it, so the gray walls and hardwood flooring feel cold and dismal without him. He is like sunshine in a room as far as she's concerned. He has the ability to cause a room to glow, warming it with his brilliant smile and deep voice that is usually filled with humor.

She strips out of her clothing, thankful their son is in the basement sleeping with his cousins. She pulls on white, French terry shorts and a long-sleeve black tee that is threadbare and soft and silky, and crawls into bed. It doesn't take long before John joins her, snuggling against her back and warming her.

"Is he still doing ok?" she asks, knowing he was out in the shed with his brother.

"Sleeping."

"Good," Reagan says and arches her sore back trying to work out the kinks. John immediately begins kneading her back and shoulders. "Thanks. I'm glad he's still out. He needs to rest."

"Yeah," John says, his voice tight. "Simon said he'll run some pain medicine through his IV when he stirs."

"Yeah, we told him to hit him with some morphine in about six hours. He's going to need a pain management plan for the next few weeks. Grandpa and I are going to work on it in the morning."

Reagan isn't good with this sort of thing. She's great at sewing people back together, has had a lot of practice with just that during the last three and a half years. But feelings and emotions intimidate her. Telling people bad news is hard. There is a fine line between giving false hope and being truthful.

"He'll be all right, John," she says, trying to dispel her husband's fears.

He simply nods against the back of her head. Reagan rolls onto her back and hooks a leg over his hip.

"He's alive," she reminds him.

"Yeah, I just don't know if that's going to make him feel any better if he's crippled for life because of this," John says.

"Hannah's disabled," she tells him. "Doesn't slow her down. Derek's a tough man. He'll get through this, even if he ends up in a wheelchair."

"Do you think it'll be that bad?"

Reagan thinks about it for a moment before answering, "Honestly? I'm not sure, John. I hope not, but we can't do the surgery he needs. Hell, sometimes people in Derek's position and with his extent of injuries end up needing many surgeries, sometimes ten or twenty. This is just a bad break."

"Not funny," he says.

"What? Oh, sorry. I wasn't trying to be funny. But it's true. It was an accident…"

"No!" he interrupts with a fierce whisper. "It wasn't an accident at all. Someone did this to my brother on purpose. They're gonna pay for this."

And this is the last thing she wanted to hear from her husband. But this is also something she knew she would hear from John. He's going after whoever did this.

She tries to distract him, "How'd it go with my dad? You guys haven't even had a chance to tell us about it."

"We'll have a meeting about it tomorrow. Not much to say."

This is unusual for John. He's a sharer, mostly just with her, but he does like talking with her about everything. Sometimes they lie awake for hours just talking. Those are usually the nights when their son has weaseled his little butt into their bed. Neither of them ever minds, though. Jacob is a welcome distraction from the harshness of their reality. Cuddling with their son is something they both know will not last much longer. He's already trying to be one of the cool guys like Huntley, Justin, and the big men on the farm.

John slides his hand over her stomach, "How are you holding up? This was a long day for you. Too long."

"I'm better now that you're home," she admits the truth. She hates it when he leaves the farm, especially for something stupid like taking her worthless father somewhere far away. She thought they should've just given him a vehicle and a map and sent him on his way.

"Hey!" he says and jerks his hand away as if he's burned his palm.

"Oh, yeah," she says with a yawn. "That's been going on."

"He's kicking? That's the baby?" he asks.

"No, it's kicking. My baby alien is kicking," she says with irritation. Their baby started this a few days ago, or at least that's when she first noticed it. "It only does it at night. I haven't noticed it during the day."

"So cool," he says. "He's a little kicker, isn't he?"

Reagan can tell he's smiling. It makes her smile in return, even if she isn't very happy about this pregnancy. His joy seeps into her heart for their unborn child.

"Yeah, it's super cool. I finally don't feel like puking my brains out at the end of the day when I'm tired and want to crash, and that's when it starts kicking."

"Don't say 'it'."

"Ok, my alien invader."

He groans against her neck, then presses a kiss there. He smells good like always, making Reagan especially glad he's home. Maybe she'll actually sleep tonight.

"Our baby," he says and falls asleep with his hand on her stomach and his face buried in her neck.

He's exhausted. They haven't discussed her father or what happened with Simon and his group on their run that led to all of this. She got the basics from Simon but not the entire story. She'd like to know who they came up against that they were able to do this. Derek is very experienced. Dave the Mechanic is also experienced and so was his team. Simon is the most cautious person on the farm. It just doesn't make sense. Knowing that sleep is a long way off, Reagan slips out of John's arm, rises and pulls on her husband's discarded flannel shirt. It smells like him. She'd like it if it never got washed again. She goes down to the kitchen where she finds Sam and Paige sitting at the island.

192

"Can't sleep, either?" Paige asks.

"No," she answers. "Too keyed up."

"Want some warm milk?" Sam offers.

"Sure," she says and pulls out a chair for herself. "Grandpa go to bed finally?"

"Yeah," Paige answers. "He looked beat."

"But happy," Reagan tells her.

"Happy about what? This wasn't exactly a good day."

Reagan grins and points out, "Sam found him coffee. He said he thinks we should go back to that hospital to raid it more thoroughly soon. I think he just hopes we find more coffee."

Paige chuckles softly. Then she grimaces.

"Still tugging?" Reagan asks and gets a nod. "Just try to take it easy.

"Well, then don't make me laugh," Paige scolds playfully, holding her side.

"Cory and Simon still in the shed?"

Sam answers as she places a mug of steaming milk in front of Reagan, "Yes. I don't think we'll see either of them tonight."

"That's fine. Someone should keep an eye on the patients. It's a good job for those two knuckleheads."

Paige chuckles again and sends Reagan a warning look.

"Cory came in a short while ago to grab a thermos of hot tea and said that Henry woke up," Sam tells her.

"Oh, really? That soon, huh? That's a good sign."

"Yeah," Sam agrees. "He said that Simon gave Henry some more morphine that knocked him out. He's resting again."

"Good," Reagan concludes. "He is going to have to take it easy for a few weeks."

"All of this take it easy talk!" Paige complains. "It gets old fast."

"Yeah, I wouldn't know anything about that," Reagan says, reminding her of when she'd been laid up from her own brutal attack years ago. That had been a long and painful process. Some of the mental scars still linger.

"No kidding," Paige says with sympathy. "But we're talking about men here. They don't exactly do well with the laid up thing."

"No, and they get whiny a hell of a lot faster, too," Reagan complains half-heartedly.

"Aw," Sam complains. "That's not nice."

"They do!" Paige says. "My mom and I would get sick or a cold or something, and it was no big deal. We just went to the doctor or got over it with over the counter medicine. But, geesh, when Simon or my dad would get sick, you'd think the world was ending!"

"What's up with that?" Reagan asks rhetorically. "They conquer countries, run militaries, get broken and bruised in battle, but God forbid they get the sniffles. Grams used to complain about Grandpa the same way. She said he was worse because he was a doctor. And John's the same. Remember last spring when he caught a cold bug? I thought he was going to die. And then he gets stabbed, kills people, goes on raids, smashes his finger with a hammer and…nothing!"

"They are weird creatures, that's for sure," Paige agrees and takes a sip.

"Hey, be nice," Sam reprimands. "We're starting to sound like a bunch of angry feminists."

"I used to think I was a feminist," Paige admits.

Reagan nods and says, "I can see that about you. When you first came to the farm, I think you were still a feminist. I mean, you were self-sufficient and a survivor."

"Not really. I had a lot of help from my two friends and sometimes from the people we traveled with."

"I like having help from the men," Sam tells them as she stands on the other side of the island and sips her milk.

"When I first came here, I thought the men around here were sexist," Paige says.

"One of them still is, but he just does that to annoy us," Reagan remarks about Cory. They don't even ask. Everyone knows who she means. He's an annoying little shit sometimes.

"And you don't think they're sexist anymore?" Sam asks.

"No, I don't think so," Paige tells them with great consideration. "Well, of course, Cory's still a sexist caveman, but most of that is just for show like Reagan said. Or, at least, I hope it is. I think they just have a strong protection instinct over all of us women and the kids. They're just all manly kind of men. The way they act and the things they do would be considered archaic if the world was still the same, but it's not. They hold doors open. They carry heavy things. They also shoot people to keep us safe and do the really, really hard physical labor. They don't do it to lord it over on us. They do it so that we don't have to. It's kind of nice not being on super, high-strung alert all the time like when I was on the road. I mean, I still never sleep the whole night through. Obviously. Look at where we are right now. But I do sleep better."

"Yeah," Sam agrees. "Me, too. I remember when my mom and dad would argue, which wasn't often, and my mom would accuse my dad of taking her for granted. I think now that I'm an adult and have the ability to judge things differently that she was just using that as fuel in their arguments. My dad really loved my mom. I don't think he took her or us for granted at all. He was a really good husband."

Paige chimes in and says, "Couples throw insults at each other. It's what they do. They store up ammo and fire it off when they need to. I used to think adults just liked making their partners miserable. Like it was just what they did or something. I think my parents loved each other, but not like yours, Sam."

"What do you mean?" Reagan asks.

"I just think they were more like good friends," she confesses. "I know my dad loved my mom and vice versa, but they weren't really ever affectionate with each other. I don't think they were *in* love. Plus, they both had busy careers. They poured their affection onto us. I don't know. It's weird, I guess."

"Maybe sometimes people are just better friends than anything else," Reagan summarizes, feeling out of her league. Relationships are not her specialty. She only took the bare minimum of psych classes. If it weren't for John, she wouldn't be in a relationship. But from what she's learned from Robert, he seemed to think that his relationship with her mother was more like Paige's parents' marriage. Reagan never would've guessed that back then. She was focused on schooling, Hannah, and getting ready for college before her mother became ill. And she only ever saw one side of the story because he was never around. Her mother tried her best to hide her misery from her girls. Sue probably knows more about the subject than her. She adds, "I suppose everyone's different."

"I don't think the men here are chauvinistic, either," Sam says. "They just want to take care of all of us."

"Is it like that on Henry's farm, too?" Reagan asks, wishing Sam would just come home and even bring her uncle.

"Yes, pretty much," she tells them. "Big, muscle-bound Army dudes running around doing the heavy lifting. I think they may actually be worse than the guys here. Just the other day I had one insist on carrying an egg basket for me. An egg basket! Can you believe that? I think I'm a long way off from ever being allowed to go on a run with any of them."

"That's not the worst idea, Sam," Paige says with worry.

Sam argues, "But I like going on runs. I like contributing and being helpful. What am I gonna do? Be the town portrait sketcher?"

She groans and takes a drink of her milk. Reagan smiles at her headstrong, willful attitude. She is never going to age. She looks like a young teenager still but is angry about not being able to go on a dangerous mission where she'd be wielding a gun and in peril. Paige simply laughs. Reagan would, too, if she didn't think it would offend her little sister. However, the irony is not lost on Reagan that she looks like a little girl drinking her glass of milk while complaining about not being able to go on a dangerous mission.

"I guess that'll be up to Dave now," Reagan reminds her. "We're not exactly in charge of you anymore."

"I've asked, but he always comes up with a reason as to why they don't need me."

"Maybe your uncle told them he doesn't want you going," Paige suggests.

196

"Hm, I don't know. Maybe. But he's so busy, I hardly see my Uncle Scott."

"What's he doing?" Reagan asks, worried that Sam is all alone over there without friends and family. She and John have discussed the reason for Samantha's departure, and they both have concluded that it had something to do with Simon. Nobody has been able to pry any information out of him yet, though.

"Trying to get the clinic set up," she tells them. "It's a lot of work. They didn't have anything like that before, so it's basically being done from scratch."

"Are they building a whole new building?" Paige asks.

"No, it's the neighbor's old house," she explains. "They left when it first happened, so it's abandoned. A couple of Dave's men live there, so he said they could still keep their bedrooms on the top floor, but that they had to give up the first floor for a medical clinic."

"Wow, that's pretty charitable," Paige says.

Sam chuckles and says, "No, he's just the boss. What he says goes."

"Nobody argues?" Reagan asks.

"No," Sam explains. "He's a good leader. They know it. He has a group- Henry's a part of it- and they hold meetings like here. But Dave has the final say."

"So, the clinic will not be within the walls of Henry's farm? Will that be safe?" Paige asks.

"I think so. It's literally the next farm over. It wasn't a farm, not really. Just a few acres and a little white house. Uncle Scott's been treating patients there already, but they're trying to get patient beds and supplies and all that stuff for it. Plus, some of the rooms were open to the other rooms, so the guys installed some doors and partitions. They're supposed to be building walls next. I've been helping where I can by giving advice to make it more like Grandpa's clinic in town. That's about all they need me for. Dave's men go on runs to find medical supplies and meds, and I just hang out mostly on the farm or organize the stuff they bring back."

"Are you lonely over there, kiddo?" Reagan asks because she can't help herself.

"No, not really," Sam says and promptly looks down at her milk. "I've made some friends."

"That's good," Paige says and touches Sam's arm. "Still miss you, though. Maybe you could come over here and stay sometimes."

Sam looks up, smiles, looks at the back door with a forlorn expression and the smile fades as fast as it appeared. It confirms Reagan's suspicions.

"Sam, did you leave because of Simon?" Reagan asks bluntly because she is sick of not knowing. Sam has been gone for nearly a month, and everyone misses her desperately, especially the kids and Grandpa.

For a few moments, Sam just looks at the countertop without speaking. Paige regards Reagan over the rim of her mug. She, too, wants to know, Reagan can tell.

Finally, Sam says, "John didn't tell you?"

This stumps Reagan. "No, what do you mean?"

"I told him…" Sam starts but looks at Paige and stops.

Paige prods by saying, "Go ahead, Sam. You can say anything to us. I won't tell."

"I know," she says. "It's just that he's your brother."

"And he's inherited one of the numerous, unending supplies of dumb, man genes."

"Uh-oh, your feminist beast has reared its ugly head again," Reagan teases to which Paige chuckles.

"I'm cool with whatever you have to say," Paige tells Sam.

After a moment of uncertainty, Sam says, "I did leave because of Simon. But he wasn't the only reason, just the biggest."

"What happened?" Reagan inquires.

"Nothing," Sam reveals.

Paige looks at Reagan again before saying, "Something must've happened to make you so upset you'd leave the farm. Did you guys have a big fight or something?"

"No, *nothing* happened."

"Oh," Reagan says, understanding dawning. Sam doesn't want to tell them, but it is obvious that she left because of Simon. Reagan remembers walking in on them kissing in the back of their clinic in town. He'd commented so strangely to Reagan. She still doesn't understand what he meant. "I think I see what you mean."

"There was just too much sadness here," she confesses with unshed tears threatening to spill over. "I miss Grams and Em. I just wanted a fresh start. I've learned that time really does help to rid the heart of grief. Plus, I wanted to be with my uncle. I've missed him, too, and we were given a second chance."

None of this is believable to Reagan. She's not good with the feelings and emotions stuff, but she knows Sam is withholding the truth from them. Something happened with Simon, but Sam doesn't want to tell them. That's fine with Reagan. She won't push her because Reagan knows how hard relationships can be.

"Does he know how you feel?" Paige asks.

Reagan knows she means Simon, but neither of them wants to say the exact words.

Sam nods. This is the first truth to come out of this conversation.

"And he didn't return it?" Paige asks again.

Sam shakes her head this time.

"I don't get it," Paige says. "He seems like..."

Sam interrupts her with a forced smile, "I'm happy now. I am. I'm moving on, and that's a good thing. I trust Dave and his men, well, most of them. I don't know all of them yet. The women in the bunkhouse with me are really nice, too."

"What do you mean by bunkhouse?" Reagan asks out of curiosity.

"That's where I sleep. There are other women and some young girls in there. It's a big, long cement block building with cots and beds. It's...cozy."

"Do you have your own space, somewhere for your art?" Paige asks with concern.

"Um…sure," Sam says. "It's not like here. We don't have private bedrooms. A few people live in Henry's family home, but there isn't room for so many people to live in there. There's a bunkhouse for the men and another for the women. It works."

Reagan notices that she doesn't mention the fact that she does art in a particular place. She hasn't answered Paige's question.

"Plus, there are a lot of people outside of their farm living in the nearby town. I know Dave and Henry wouldn't allow people into the perimeter if they were dangerous. His men are always on high alert for nefarious behavior."

Reagan grins with melancholy. It sounds like she is trying to convince them that she has friends and everything is sunshine and roses.

"That's good," Paige says. "I'm glad you're safe. I've been really worried about you."

"Don't worry," Sam tells her. "I'm fine."

Paige doesn't say anything but regards her friend with the same sadness behind her smile that mimics Reagan's.

"What have I been missing around here?" she asks next.

Reagan shrugs and says, "Not much. My dad's gone, so that's good news."

Paige laughs, but Sam frowns and says, "Reagan! That's not nice."

"So what? He's not nice. I'm glad he's gone. I'm not going to miss him. You aren't going to see me crying a river over it. I'm even gladder that the men came back quickly. I didn't want them up there on that base with him. Robert can be very persuasive."

"I'm anxious to hear what happened," Paige says and pulls her blue shawl closer.

"Cold?" Reagan asks, getting a nod. "That's the blood loss. I told you it would take a long time to build your blood back up. It'll eventually work itself out, though. Just be patient."

"Patient. Sure," Paige says with a grin.

"G was talking to me earlier today," Reagan tells them. "She's pretty sure her mom's never coming back here. Her mom even told

200

her that when she gets settled in up there that they will send for her and Lucas."

"What'd she say to that?" Paige asks.

Reagan shrugs. "I think she wants her mom, but our mutual dad is another thing. I got the impression she doesn't want to leave the farm."

"Yikes," Paige remarks. "Sounds like that situation is going to get messy. I wouldn't want to be involved with those decisions."

"Me neither," Reagan agrees. "But I would definitely advise her to stay here rather than go with our dad anywhere. Plus, Grandpa will likely get involved. He had to for me and my sisters."

"Yeah, probably," Paige says with a nod.

"Those people they found on the road, the survivors, were brought to Pleasant View?" Sam asks.

"I guess so," Paige answers.

"They must be safe, or I don't think the guys would've brought them back. I wonder why they didn't want to stay on the Army base. Seems to me it would've been a better option if I were in their shoes."

"Maybe they met my dad," Reagan remarks sarcastically, earning two chuckles from the girls. "Hey, I'm going back up. Gotta hit the sack so I can be up bright and early so that this kid can make me nauseous all day again. We've got a schedule to maintain."

"Then you'd better stick to it," Paige says. "I'm heading up, too. I'm beat."

"You should've already been in bed resting," Reagan scolds. "And you, too, Miss Samantha."

Sam salutes and kisses her cheek. "Oh, I've missed my sisters."

Paige wedges in and hugs them, which they return in a tight, three-person embrace. Then they separate, and Reagan climbs the stairs to her husband, but not before she first stops to use the bathroom on the second floor. She can't imagine how women with twins do it. She slips into bed to find Jacob snuggled up against John's back. He must've had a bad dream and came upstairs while she was in the kitchen, the little sneak. Reagan is left cuddling her pillow. She's been too hot lately anyway. Pregnancy just sucks. She wouldn't recommend it to anyone. John is excited and wanting to talk about baby names all the time, and all she wants is for the baby to get out of her body and quit hindering her.

She hadn't wanted this. Between the two of them, John is the better parent to Jacob. Reagan is terrified that she won't want the baby even after it comes. She was never made for this. Her sisters were made for parenting. Not her. She was cut out to be a scientist, not someone's mommy. The idea of breastfeeding is horrific. Changing diapers on occasion for her sisters' kids is acceptable, but doing it all the time, all day and night is not. She has so many other things she needs to do. The constant neediness of her nephews and nieces with her sisters is just plain annoying. Jacob was never like that, and he spent a lot of time with John since she was always busy with the clinic or in the shed doing research. A baby that must be breastfed is another story altogether. It's overwhelming.

And none of this can even compare to her fears over the labor and delivery. What if she dies and John is left with the baby all by himself? They are having enough problems finding formula for baby Daniel. Another orphan on the farm would be an insurmountable burden. What if the baby dies? She's thought of that, too. John would be devastated. But Reagan's a realist. Her scientific mind cannot leave these thoughts alone. Either of them could die during this. Grandpa would never forgive himself. John would be ripped apart. It would be hard on the whole family. Plus, just giving birth is primitive and ridiculously difficult now. It scares the hell out of her.

She yawns and rolls toward John and Jacob, wrapping an arm around her son's tiny waist. Reagan falls asleep to the sporadic, yet strangely soothing thumping against her uterus.

Chapter Fifteen
Paige

The next morning comes hard, the blinding bright sunshine streaming through her windows unwelcome. She'd like to pull the blanket over her head and go back to sleep or draw the blue, toile draperies, but the family and chores and helping out are always waiting downstairs. Even though she is under many doctors' orders to take it easy and rest, she still tries to be of help, even if it's just holding baby Daniel while the other women prepare meals. It's not too tough of a job. He's adorable.

Paige rolls over slowly, surprised that it doesn't hurt her side. Usually, it does. That has to be a good sign. Sam is still dead asleep, angelic and innocent-looking as ever. She has both hands tucked under her cheek, which makes her look even more like a little girl. Her dark hair rests in soft, smooth waves around her shoulders.

Paige tiptoes to the closet, pulls out a change of clothing and slips out of the room as silently as possible. She wants Sam to sleep in as late as she wants. It doesn't sound- although Sam had tried to make it seem better than it was- like she is very happy over at Henry's. How could she be when her whole family is here on this farm? Paige wants her little friend back.

She dresses in the bathroom, uses the sink to splash cool water on her face, and looks in the mirror. Mistake. Her hair is a disheveled mess, so she rakes a brush through it. Not achieving the neat appearance she'd hoped for, Paige pulls the mess to one side and braids it, securing it with a rubber band she finds in a drawer. They are all meticulous about recycling rubber bands and removing them from their hair as carefully as possible so they don't break.

Paige walks gingerly downstairs to the familiar, comforting smells of a hearty breakfast being prepared. Apparently, she and Sam are the last ones to rise because the whole family in all its noisy glory is bustling around on the first floor.

"Hey, sleepyhead," Cory's deep voice comes from behind her, surprising her.

She spins to find him leaning against the doorframe of the mudroom. Cory indicates over his shoulder to get her to follow him. Paige looks around, sees that everyone is busy with their own agendas, and follows him.

She crosses the small mudroom and pulls down a gray sweater from the pile in the antique hutch because her long sleeve tee is not enough to keep her warm. When she turns around, Cory is right there.

"Where's Simon?" she whispers and peers anxiously over his shoulder.

"Still in the shed," he says and reaches for her hand.

Paige backs up and shakes her head in warning, earning a self-sure grin from him.

"What do you want?" she asks impatiently, keeping her voice low.

"There are so many ways I could answer that," he responds.

"Shh!" she whispers and holds her finger to her lips. "What do you want for real? I don't want Simon coming in here finding us. He's been acting really suspicious lately."

Cory frowns, looks off to the side, and then shrugs as if he doesn't care.

"I actually have a surprise for you."

This catches her attention, and Paige stops trying to see around his massive frame to the door's opening into the hall. Her eyes dart nervously, cautiously to his.

"Wait here," he demands and leaves.

Paige would like to tell him that he's not in a position to order her around. It's exhausting dealing with him.

He returns a moment later with a huge cardboard box that must be three feet wide by nearly four feet deep.

"What's in it?" she asks and steps closer. Knowing him, it could contain some sort of wild animal.

"Stuff I found on our run when I was looking for baby formula," he tells her.

Paige opens the flap to discover an entire box filled to the brim with women's goods from a drugstore or somewhere similar. There are perfume bottles, lotions, soaps, make-up and more.

"Now you can feel girly again," he tells her proudly.

"This…this is great," she says with unshed tears in her eyes. This was thoughtful and caring. She clears her voice and says, "I mean, it's great that you got this stuff for all of us girls."

"I got this stuff for one girl," he corrects. "But feel free to share."

Paige meets his eyes and offers a lopsided grin. "Thanks, Cory. This was really thoughtful."

"I took a lot of shit for it, too," he says.

She cocks her head to the side and asks, "What do you mean?"

"One of the perfumes broke in my pack, so I smelled like a woman all day."

She laughs at his distress, then holds her sore side. "This is still awesome. Everyone's going to be thrilled with this."

"You can pay me back later," he remarks with a wicked grin and steps closer.

"Hey!" Simon blurts as he enters the room behind Cory. His blue eyes dart to Cory and narrow. "Breakfast is ready. What's going on? What are you two doing?"

Her brother's questions are full of unhidden accusation.

"Cory brought all of these really nice things back from the city for us girls," Paige is quick to say. "Wasn't that thoughtful?"

Simon steps closer and peers into the open box. Then he looks at Cory and then her. He nods with leery hesitation, slowly and full of apprehension.

"You never bothered with stuff like this before," he says pointedly.

Cory shrugs nonchalantly, hefts the box and squeezes past her brother. "Never thought to. Your sister's the one who pointed it out that the girls needed this kind of crap."

Simon looks at her, and Paige nods.

"Oh! Well, then good. But from now on, just ask me to get you the things you need," Simon remarks and stomps away.

Her brother is in a terribly sour mood today for some reason, and she's pretty sure it has to do with the sleeping angel in her room upstairs.

"He's in his customary bear-with-a-sore-ass mode again," Cory also notices as he sets the box in the music room near the window.

"Yeah, probably because Sam is here I would guess."

Cory looks in the direction that Simon just went and glares.

"Hey, ignore him," Paige says, touching his thick, bare bicep.

"I also got a bunch of bras and undies and some clothes you guys can go through. I'm not sure where Huntley put that bag."

"That's really sweet, Cory," she tells him and watches his eyes drop to the ground with embarrassment. "You might not be a total Neanderthal after all."

"Nah, don't believe it. I still am," he remarks with ornery humor and a wicked glint in his eye. "Want me to prove it?"

"No," Paige says firmly and steps back. "I'm just anxious to hear about the trip with Robert."

"I'm going out to chop wood after breakfast if you wanna' go. I'll tell you all about it."

"Oh, all right. I thought they were having a meeting about it, though."

"Probably," he says. "If you wanna' sit in here and listen in on it, that's fine. I'm just not into hearing it explained twenty times.

206

I'm feeling cooped up. And we're getting low on our stack of wood out at the cabin, so I figured I'd get outta' here for a while."

This invitation is highly appealing. Getting a seat for the meeting is going to be tough since everyone is curious to know about their trip. Paige nods.

"Yes, I'll go with you to the shed," she says. "I need some fresh air. It sucks sitting around so much."

"You got it," he agrees and touches the tip of her nose.

Cory leads her from the room with a hand at her elbow as if she is fragile enough to fall and shatter into a million pieces. It makes her wonder if he'd actually been waiting for her to come downstairs. Just this past week she'd finally told all of the men in the house that she didn't need to be carried down the stairs anymore. She goes slowly and makes sure to use the handrail. They'd all backed off. All but one.

Everyone is scattered around the house for breakfast. She doesn't even sit in the dining room but in the music room with the little kids because there are too many people eating at the same time. Dave and one of his men join the family in the dining room. She doesn't mind, though. The kids are more entertaining. Their conversations are usually nonsensical, but Paige likes to think it's because they are still innocent enough of this cruel world that they are afforded the luxury to be whimsical because of the safety on the farm. She often wishes she was still the same way. Listening to their chatter, the making of big plans for the day, and funny stories are better than missions and runs and ammo and defense strategies. Simon joins her on the sofa as they balance their plates on their laps. Cory is stuck in the dining room where she can just make out the conversation, which is clearly about their trip. Soon, the kids begin to disperse, ever the most lightning fast consumers of food.

"What happened last night, Simon?" she inquires after his ordeal on their scouting run.

"I don't know."

"What do you mean? You were there."

He sighs and pauses in the middle of eating, "I mean I don't know. Derek and I were picking up supplies. Bruce was waiting with the truck. He called in to say they were heading our way. Henry and Annie decided to hit one more store since we weren't ready yet. The next thing I know, we were walking down the street to meet them, and a black SUV swerves at Derek and hit him on purpose. We thought it was the truck, Bruce coming to pick us up. It wasn't."

"Wow, that's terrible," she says with a frown.

"I dragged Derek into a building and started medical care. Henry shows up a few minutes later and tells us that the others were shot and killed and that he was the only survivor. We didn't even hear the shots."

"The storm?"

"Yes, it must've been. They weren't that far away."

"Maybe they had suppressors on their weapons," Paige contemplates.

Simon nods, "I hadn't thought of that. It would make sense, though."

"Why didn't you call the farm?"

"We were too far out of range," he explains. "I had to treat Henry and Derek both. Then I had to find us a vehicle to get home."

"That's amazing," she says with awe.

"No, it's terrible," he admonishes. "It wasn't amazing at all. It took me forever to find a vehicle, or I could've gotten us home sooner."

"But you did, Simon," she praises. "They were so lucky you were with them. I wouldn't have known enough to treat those kinds of wounds. Plus, how the heck did you find that Jeep?"

"In a muffler shop's garage bay. They must've been getting work done on it when the crap fell apart, and they just never went back for it."

"Thank God."

"Yes, true. I shot one of the men in the back seat. They were shooting at us, so I shot him. I tried to disable their car, but I missed.

It was hard to see. Once I took out the guy in the back seat, they stopped shooting at us."

"I'm sure. They were probably more concerned at that point with getting away from you," she says and takes his hand. "I was freaking out when you were late. A million things were going through my mind, and none of them were good. I knew something was wrong. Derek's never irresponsible like that, neither are you. You're both the most responsible ones on the farm. I just wanted to come and find you."

"No," he says and rests a hand over hers. "No, you did the right thing by staying here. Don't ever try to come and find me. I'll always find you."

"But I was so scared," she confesses, tears pooling in her eyes. She was terrified out of her mind last night, so sick to her stomach that her wounded side ached terribly. Reagan had threatened to sedate her if she didn't calm down.

"You found me once," he says lightly and wraps an arm around her shoulders. "That's enough. It's my job to make it home to you from now on."

Paige offers a grim smile. "Just don't leave anymore. At least not for a while, 'kay?"

He offers a dismal grimace but doesn't answer, which means he isn't going along with her request. This bothers Paige.

They eat in silence for a while before Paige asks, "How are the patients?"

"Henry's doing a lot better. Doc says he'd like for him to stay a few days to a week so that he can heal and we can watch for signs of infection or internal bleeding. I don't know if he will. He seems like a pretty stubborn person."

Her brother's expression has turned angry, and he wears a sneer on his face while speaking of Henry.

"Don't you like him?"

"What? No, he's fine."

Simon seems like he is muttering an untruth to her, but she doesn't press him on the issue.

"Derek?" she asks.

Simon's gaze falls to his plate, but he doesn't say anything. Paige nods. She understands what he isn't telling her. This is a horrible event that has befallen the family. Derek is the oldest of the men on the farm other than Herb. He is calm and wise, the leader of the soldiers. In so many ways everyone looks up to him, looks to him for sage advice.

"Is Sue with him?"

"Yeah, and Doc."

"This isn't your fault, Simon," she says, knowing her brother will blame himself for this tragedy. "Not only is it not your fault, it could've been a lot worse if someone else had been with him. Not everyone, myself included, would've known enough to treat either of their wounds. They were lucky."

Sam walks into the room a second later. She is dressed for the day and fresh and pretty in a pale yellow turtleneck sweater and black riding pants.

"Good morning," she says brightly with a wide smile lighting her doll-like face.

"Um…" Simon stutters as he rises. "I'm gonna head back out to the shed. Doc needs me."

He leaves without another word.

"Hey, Sam," Paige says, covering for her brother's social gaffe. He is a bear. "Sleep well?"

"Great," she responds, trying hard not to let her smile falter or her mood darken because of Simon's behavior. "Better than I have in a while. I forgot how quiet it is here."

"Is it noisy over there?"

"Sometimes. I share a room with a lot of people, so there's always one snorer," she jokes, making Paige chuckle. "Dave's men move around a lot at night, too. They do a lot of night patrols, so that wakes me sometimes when I hear them outside or see their lanterns."

"My room's still got an empty bed," Paige hints again.

"Thanks," Sam says. "I'm going out to the horse barn."

"'Kay, maybe I'll see you out there."

Paige takes her plate and cup to the kitchen where the kids are already working on clearing counters and washing the dishes.

"You ready?" Cory asks, coming up behind her and startling her with his deep voice again.

"I'm going to make you wear a bell," she says with annoyance.

"I'll get your coat."

She follows him to the mudroom where Paige has to remind him that she doesn't need help.

"I'm getting better you know," she complains.

Cory ignores her and says as he helps her into her jacket, "I told the girls about the box of crap I brought. I think they were just as excited as you."

"See? I told you it's a girl thing."

"I stand corrected," he says and pulls a black stocking cap from the pocket of his hoodie. Then black leather gloves and a gray scarf with purple plaid come out next. They still have their tags on. "I got these for you. I know you get cold."

She bites her lower lip. This is too much. He is going beyond just gathering items for all of them. He had purposely set these aside for her because he knows that her blood loss causes her to get unnaturally cold. Paige swallows hard and looks at his outstretched hands with the overly thoughtful gifts in them.

"Th…thanks."

"No problem, Red," he says, hands her the gloves, and walks to the sink where he cuts tags from the wool scarf with a pair of utility scissors. He hands her the scarf and hat.

"Ready," she says.

"Not yet," Cory returns and steps close again. He reaches into his pocket again and pulls out a pair of gold-framed aviator style sunglasses and puts them on her. "Now you're ready to go. Don't want you to go snow blind."

He smiles broadly, his charm and natural charisma catching Paige off guard.

"Total Hollywood hottie now," he remarks as they head out the door of the mudroom onto the side porch.

Paige snorts and says, "Yeah, right."

"Yeah, you are right," he says, piquing her interest. "They had nothin' on you."

"Shush," she scolds and lightly backhands his arm. He's only wearing a hoodie even though it is winter. The sun is out, but the temperature isn't very high. The snow from last night still coats the earth in a cold, white blanket that catches the sunlight and would cause her to flinch at the brightness. The sunglasses really do help.

"It was one thing to be nice and get us lots of girly items, but don't get all flattering and laying it on thick. I said I was thankful. I'm no more a glamour girl than you are a civilized gentleman."

"Civilized? Where the hell's the fun in that?"

"Cory!" she says with a laugh.

He chuckles. Paige follows him toward the equipment shed near the cow barn where they store wood for splitting. The wheelbarrow is usually already there, as well as a small wagon that they use for toting bigger loads with the tractor.

Cory extends his forearm and says, "Hold onto me when we go down this hill. I don't want you to slip."

"I've got it. I've got it," she complains.

"Don't get all cocky and confident on me," he teases like she had. "I said I was thankful you lived and took a bullet for my brother, but let's not tear anything open."

She smirks and takes his offered arm. It feels better having a firm hold on Cory's arm when she does slip as she gets closer to the bottom. He is right there to help her, though. She doesn't go down but does feel her unused, weak muscles strain. Cory gives up and sweeps her into his arms.

"Hey!" she reprimands. "Don't! Cory, someone could see."

"So?" he asks. "We've been carrying your bony butt around this farm for the last six weeks. It's not like this would draw anyone's attention."

"Maybe my brother's."

She doesn't want to inhale so deeply of his scent but does. He has his own smell, and it instantly stirs her senses. His beard is full and thick. She's noticed that Kelly, Derek and John all have more than a few weeks' worth of stubble. They are like hibernating bears around here in the winter. Simon is the only one who religiously shaves every morning. It wouldn't be like Simon to allow himself to look unkempt. He was always like that, even when he was a little kid.

Cory says, "Everything draws Simon's speculation. He's just a hovering male lion where you're concerned. He didn't like any of the dudes in town looking at you, either. Or when you had that boyfriend for a while there."

"He was hardly my boyfriend." Paige holds on around his neck as he cradles her under her legs and around her back. It feels natural being in Cory's arms like this. She has to push down other thoughts of even more intimate embraces with him as they sneak uninvited into her mind.

"Which was a good thing for him 'cuz I woulda' had to kill him eventually."

"Nice," she remarks glibly.

"Truth," Cory returns with a raise of his eyebrows.

"That's going a bit far, don't you think?"

He hits her with a wide, white smile, "No. I'm uncivilized, remember? I knew what I knew, and I knew I wanted you for myself."

Paige scoffs, "Ha! Hardly! You couldn't stand me."

"That changed pretty quickly. I didn't like your sassy attitude, but that doesn't mean I didn't still want you. I just wanted you with some tape on your sass mouth."

"Hm," she says, looking away on a pout. It's better than staring into the sultry, hooded eyes he's giving her. Cory is nothing if not direct and painfully blunt. "You don't have to carry me. I'm getting a lot better. I even went up the stairs yesterday without losing my breath. Herb said he'll test my blood at the end of this week. He thinks I'm doing great with this injury healing so fast."

"Fast? It's been a long time."

"Not really. They said it would be months before I felt better. I'm ahead of the curve."

His eyes meet hers with serious intent, "Don't ever scare me like that again."

When they reach the small wood shed a moment later, he places her gently on her feet again.

"I mean it, Red," he says, taking her face between his palms. "Don't scare me like that again. I can't take another one of those. I might croak."

She grins and stares at his chest. Cory tips her chin back with his index finger.

"Don't make me keep you under house arrest for the rest of our lives."

The way he says 'our' bothers Paige and she pulls away. "Hey, you aren't in control of me. We aren't together like that. You don't have the right to tell me what to do."

"If you'd just quit being so damn stubborn, this wouldn't be an issue."

"And if you don't stop talking like that, Simon's gonna figure this out."

"There isn't a whole lot to figure out lately," he bellyaches and places his hand on his hip.

"And there isn't going to be. Not ever again," she says, wagging her finger in front of him.

Cory laughs. "We'll see."

She stares daggers into his back as he leads her to the edge of a low-to-the-ground, utility trailer with rusty, metal sides that were once coated with black paint. First, he dusts off the wooden floorboards with his gloves before offering her a seat. Then he builds a small campfire near her on the ground just outside of the shed.

"Don't want you to freeze," he says as he gets it ignited within a few minutes.

Paige knows they never do this. They simply come out and chop firewood, split logs, and haul them to the house and med shed. They don't bother building fires or worrying about their comfort while doing their chores. This is for her. Again, with his thoughtfulness. He's making it very difficult to go back to disliking him before they had sex…a few times.

"Thanks," she tells him quietly as he remains squatted beside the fire. He blows on it to keep it from extinguishing. Cory glances over at her, and Paige feels a tug in her stomach. This time it's not from her injured liver. Sometimes, when he's not irritating her or vexing her to the point of wanting to punch him, Cory takes her breath away with just a single look. Just like he's doing now. His gaze is friendly and open, not the guarded, hard demeanor he usually puts off because of his haunting past. He walks around most days with a wall of stone that he keeps up to protect himself. He may try to hide his softer, inner emotions, but she's seen them. Today, his smile is infectious and kind. Paige returns his grin with one of her own.

"Wanna' go to the cabin?" he asks and winks.

Paige groans. And there it is. The irksome part of Cory that drives her nuts.

"No!" she spouts with anger. "Stop it."

"Shrew," he teases and stands.

"I'm only here to pick your brain," she informs him with superiority. Then she adds, "And watch you work."

"Lazy shrew," he further jokes and shoots her a lopsided grin that makes him look more like a little boy than a trained, hardened killer.

He starts working by splitting some of the larger logs down the middle with a tool Simon showed her once and called the 'monster maul.' She'd tried to use it to show her brother and Derek, who'd been with them at the time, how helpful she could be, but Paige could barely lift it. Her brother had promptly taken it away from her and lectured her about how she was going to whack her shin and break a leg or cut off her toes with it. Later, after she was done being outraged by his lack of patience and slight show of chauvinism, she'd secretly been glad that she didn't have to help split the wood. Doc says it is singlehandedly the number one reason the men on the farm are built like former NFL linebackers. She did help her brother stack the wood and load it into the bucket of the tractor, which Derek showed her how to operate. Stacking wood was also hard work. That day last summer when she'd first come to the farm still feels fresh in her mind. So many other days do, too, and Paige wonders if it is because she is making good memories since she came to the farm or if it is simply because she feels safe for the time being.

It doesn't take long before Cory becomes too hot and removes his hoodie, leaving him in a cream-colored thermal undershirt. He even pushes the sleeves up to his elbows, and Paige can see a sheen of sweat on his forearms.

"I wish I would've thought to bring you a jar of water," she remarks as she rubs her hands together. Cory may be hot, but the sun has not yet been permitted entrance into the shed. It doesn't usually touch this part of the farm until later in the day. The fire he built her is helping a lot, though.

"I'm fine," he remarks. "Why? Are you thirsty? I can run back and get you something."

She smiles and says, "No, I'm literally just sitting here. You're doing all the work."

"Nothing new there," he remarks.

She picks up a pebble and throws it at him. He just laughs at her.

Most of the time, everyone working outside carries a glass mason jar with a lid for water transportation. There aren't any imported, fancy water bottle companies delivering to the wholesale club anymore. Nobody's offered an Evian for their farm toils. For some reason, Paige thinks the spring water on the farm served in a glass canning jar tastes better anyway. Sometimes Sue will bring it to them while they are working. She'll flavor the water with mint leaves and frozen pieces of fruit. Paige can't wait for the weather to break for good and the berries in the woods to grow again.

"Gotta stay in shape somehow," he tells her and winks before going back to his work.

"You're hardly in danger of getting fat," she reminds him, watching the muscles of his back and shoulders flex as he swings the maul over his head with enough brute velocity to bust through a log that must be two feet wide.

"You won't want me anymore if I turn into a lazy sloth with a beer gut."

Paige grits her teeth. "I don't want you now."

Cory, being obnoxious as usual, throws his head back and barks loud laughter into the quiet, morning air. "Yeah, right!"

She just growls and decides on a new topic, "So how did it go with Robert?"

He turns to her and says wryly, "He's a real dick if you ask me. And smooth change of subject there, Red."

She chooses to ignore his jab. Why is he the only person who is so openly rude and who must challenge her at every turn? Damn, irritating man. Instead of arguing, she asks, "What happened? You guys ran into people on the road who were attacked? I'm fuzzy on the whole story."

Cory takes a break and sits next to her on the trailer, explaining his trip in full. He's patient when she asks a lot of questions. She can't help it. She is curious about Reagan's father. Cory seems more concerned about his motives. He tells her about Reagan's father and his plans and about the people they brought back to town who were, indeed, assaulted on the freeway.

"I think he wants to force us into this war he's about to start with the new President, whoever that idiot is," he tells her.

"You know who he is. He used to be the vice," Paige corrects.

"Red, I was into muscle cars and cheerleaders back then. I don't even barely remember the actual President let alone the moron that's now calling himself the President."

Paige finds herself digging her nails into her palms. For some reason, it bothers her to think about Cory chasing after pretty girls with short-skirted uniforms and bouncy ponytails.

"Right?" he asks and looks at her. Paige is caught off guard because she'd zoned out on their conversation. She blinks hard.

"You were a senator's kid. You were probably more knowledgeable about politics."

"I guess so," she answers and looks at her shoelaces instead of at his face and his knowing, brown eyes. "I don't really understand what they're fighting over. Seems stupid and worthless. Why can't they just part ways and agree to disagree?"

He chuckles. "Men don't usually do that."

"Exactly. And it's dumb. They're going to cause a lot of people to be killed because of their power struggle over a broken country."

"A lot of people from the bunker have already shown up at Fort Knox to be with Robert," Cory tells her. "He must have a pretty powerful message to get people to leave safety, security, and food to start over again fifteen hundred miles east."

"Reagan warned us that he's like that. Maybe those people just don't want to live like they were out there. From what I understand, it seems harsh. They kick you out if you aren't useful to them anymore. Who gets to decide something like that?"

"Greater good. Socialism. People are dumb, Red," he remarks.

"Yeah, but how long is it going to be before we're dragged into this thing?"

He doesn't answer, but instead, stands and goes back to his wood pile.

"What the heck?" Simon shouts angrily and comes into the shed a second later.

"Hey," Paige says softly, knowing she needs to walk on eggshells with her brother right now. She tries to keep it casual, "What's going on, bro'?"

"Why are you out here? I came into the house to check on you and found out you went out here with *him*."

"Cory's telling me about their trip. I wanted to know."

He storms toward her and says, "Then you can ask John." Simon pulls her gently and slowly to her feet. "Let's go."

"She was hanging out with me, Professor," Cory says, and Paige would like to punch him. He's not helping.

"No kidding. And I've warned you. This thing...whatever this is...it's not happening," Simon warns with a fierceness in his tone.

Cory just chuckles and holds up his hands in supplication. Then he asks, "Want me to carry her back?"

He's really not helping, and Paige would like to tell him that. Simon levels him with a deadly glare and leads her away. He fumes all the way to the house.

"Simon, calm down."

"I don't like the way he's been looking at you. Stay away from Cory."

"He's just thankful I took a bullet for his brother."

"You don't know him like I do," he says superiorly.

This piques her interest. "What don't I know?"

"He's a man whore. He sleeps around. He never wants a woman for anything but that. And I have news for him, he's not doing that with you."

His words hurt because she already knew these things about Cory and slept with him anyway.

"So? I'm not interested in him. And let me tell you, he's not interested in me like that, either."

These lies sting her tongue as if a scorpion has just pierced her there.

He chuffs through his nose with obvious disbelief. She finds his behavior rude, so Paige hits him with a low blow. "How's Samantha?"

Simon stops dead in his tracks. Then he simply continues on their march toward the house without answering.

"What? I didn't hear you," Paige taunts.

"Stop. That's not even subtle. Don't behave immaturely."

"So? You want to ride my ass about something you think is going on between Cory and me, but I can't even say Sam's name around you without you being rude or freaking out?"

"I'm not being rude, and I am certainly not freaking out," he replies in his usual, stoic manner.

That part is true. Her brother is not the kind of person to freak out. It's one of his more annoying qualities. Even when they were kids and would get into squabbles, he always acted more like professional, Supreme Court Justice handing down a decision than a kid. It used to piss her off that she couldn't get a rise out of him.

"Then why won't you talk about her with me?"

"Because she left. There's nothing to talk about."

"Lie."

Simon hits her with a hard stare. "Who's being rude now?"

They both turn to look as Sam laughs gaily in the horse corral about fifty yards away. She is with G and her brother, showing them some riding tips. Her cheeks are wind kissed and pink. She looks like she belongs in a professional editorial spread in a magazine for horse lovers; the beautiful girl and her meticulously groomed mount.

"I think Sam is in love with you and…"

"Why would you say that? Don't be ridiculous. She's too young to be in love with anyone."

"Not true. And if you don't pull your head out of your ass, you're going to lose a really good girl to someone else because Sam is sweet and caring and loving and kind."

"Of course she is. I never said she wasn't."

"So? Then why don't you love her back?"

Simon slows his fast pace, and Paige watches as his expression turns from angry to pained. He doesn't always hide everything from her as well as he'd like.

"We've been through too much together. You wouldn't understand."

This has her puzzled. "I don't get it."

"Exactly."

"Explain," she demands. When he doesn't answer, she follows up with, "Now."

220

He shoots her a look of impatience. "The things that Sam and I have been through has ruined any chance of us ever having a relationship like that."

"I don't understand. That makes no sense. Usually, when people go through a lot together, it bonds them to one another even stronger."

"Not this time. Not in this scenario. You aren't reading a romance novel. This is real life. You don't understand. Besides, I don't even look at her in that way."

"Lie number two."

"Stop being rude."

"Stop lying," she orders. This is just like when they were young teenagers living at home. Typically, her mother would have to split them up eventually. Also usually because Simon would irritate the hell out of her with his stoicism, and she'd lose her shit. If she weren't so angry, she'd laugh at their situation now.

"I'm not. She's like a sister to me."

He tilts his chin up just a notch. Paige isn't allowing him to get away with this. "Get real."

He looks over at her and frowns hard.

"I've seen the way you look at her. You don't look at me like that."

"Stop."

"Tell me and I will."

She knows this is painful. She can tell he doesn't want to reveal something to her. He's her brother. There isn't much he can hide, or at least not hide it forever.

"She deserves to be happy and find someone who will make her that way."

This is a surprising statement. Simon always seems like he doesn't want her to be with anyone.

"And you don't think you could make her happy, Simon?" she asks as they approach the back porch.

"Look," he says, his tone turning angry, his eyes flashing with ferocity, "I failed her on every possible level. I didn't protect her when I should have. How the hell am I ever supposed to be with her after that?"

He spins in an angry flash and leaves her. Simon never swears. She knows she might have pushed him too far. However, his statement leaves her pondering her brother and Sam even harder. Perhaps, she will find out more about their problems before Sam leaves the farm again. Maybe she could help them. Paige wants to help. She wants her brother and her friend to be happy together if that's what is best. She just doesn't know if he'll let her in enough to be of assistance in this situation. He is blocking her out of his life entirely. Unlike Cory's stone wall, Simon's is reinforced with impenetrable steel, as well.

Chapter Sixteen
Simon

Three days after his confrontation with Paige in the barnyard, Sam and Henry are ready to return to his farm. She stayed on to visit with the family, but Dave and the rest of his men left that same day. Simon feels terrible for snapping at his sister the way he had, but he hasn't had the opportunity to discuss it with her. Truth be told, he's also worried if he brings it up she'll want to talk about Sam again.

"Simon, give me a hand?" John calls for him near the back of the pick-up truck.

He rushes over to help his friend lift a heavy barrel of oats into the bed. John and Kelly are going to Dave's camp to trade with them and return Sam and Henry, who is anxious to be back on his own farm. Simon knows the feeling. Any time away from the McClane farm puts him in an irritable mood. The bed of the truck is full, items also having been contributed by their neighbors. They will share in the spoils of the trade with Dave's compound with the Johnson and Reynolds families. They do this often with their friends. If there is anything left, they take it to town to be donated.

"We need to get on the road," John tells him as he slams the tailgate into place.

"Yeah, you guys should get going," Simon agrees and nods.

"You're going with us," John says.

"Kelly's going," he reminds him. "I don't want to crowd the truck. Paige and Cory said they were going, too. She wants to see what it's like where Sam stays, and Cory wants to help."

"Kelly's staying," John tells him. "He's not feelin' so hot, so I told him to kick it here and help Luke and Huntley and Doc keep an eye on the place. With Derek down, the place needs to be watched with extra sets of eyes."

"Then I should probably stay," Simon argues. He doesn't want to tell John that he has no desire to take Sam back to Henry's farm. It burns in his gullet like a red hot flame just the idea of her going back over there. He's also had the last few days to watch her dote on Henry and wait on him hand and foot in the shed while he mended. Simon tried to avoid being in there when she was, but it didn't always work out. There were shifts that needed to be covered, and it's his job along with Reagan and Doc to take care of their patients.

"No, not happening. I need a sniper. Whoever is attacking people on the road in this area could hit us while we're moving back and forth between the two farms."

He has a point, but it irritates Simon just the same. "Yes, sir."

John slaps his shoulder roughly and says, "Great!"

Most of the family gathers as they usually do on the back porch to say farewell. The snow has melted, and the weather has warmed considerably, reminding him once again of the intemperate patterns in the weather here in comparison to Arizona. There was usually just one pattern out there: hot.

Simon hurries to the porch where he makes sure Paige gets down without slipping, even though she sends him a testy look. He releases her and takes a backpack from Hannah instead.

"Food for the trip back tonight," she says with a smile.

Simon hugs her close and says, "Thanks, Hannah."

"Stay safe out there, Simon," she instructs and pats his back.

"Yes, ma'am."

He takes his sniper rifle from Kelly's outstretched hand with a nod.

"Plink anything that doesn't look right, Professor," Kelly orders firmly.

"Yes, sir."

This is their first trip they'll make on compressed natural gas, the system they have been working on for months. Derek and Cory made two, short trips to town yesterday on it, and the system worked fine. John and Derek talked earlier today and decided it was time to fire it up and try for a real trip. Simon hopes it goes well. He also hopes Derek's healing process goes well. So far, it doesn't seem to be, or at least it doesn't seem to be a painless one. He is in total agony and most of the time won't take any pain medicine for it. Doc calls him stubborn. Derek says he's only refusing it because someday one of his little kids might need it more than he does. For now, he and Sue and their three children are living in the big house. They have taken Doc's bedroom suite since Derek is being pushed around in a wheelchair and needs to stay on the first floor. Their kids are in the basement with Huntley and are thrilled about it. His sister tells Derek often how it gets better. He was shot years ago in the beginning and barely made it home to the farm, but this is worse. Paige knows the slow trail to healing that the human body can meander along until it is fully recovered. His kids have been splendid at keeping him company, even if playing cards and watching them act out plays and puppet shows might not have been his idea of entertainment. Derek never complains. He seems very determined to beat this.

Since the house is too crowded, and nobody knows if or when Robert and his wife might return, Cory and he have moved back out into their cabin. It feels right. It's cozy and private. Plus, as an added bonus, Simon hadn't been forced to hang around the house and be near Sam while she stayed with the family. His sister had wanted to move with them, but he'd denied her. Simon still can't shake the suspicion that Cory is attracted to his sister. For the last three days, he and Cory have been like they used to be, just the two of them, living in their cabin, pals. He hopes it stays that way.

"Are you sure you want to go?" he asks Paige at the truck.

She rolls her eyes and says, "Simon, how many times are you going to ask me that? Yes. I want to go. I want to see where Sam is staying and what it's like over there. You may not care about her anymore, but I still do."

Simon flinches. Then he swallows the words he'd like to say. He does care about Sam. Too much. That's the problem. Instead, he opens her door and helps his frail sister up into the back seat. He worries that the ride will jostle her around too much, but both doctors assured him that she'd be fine.

As he is about to step in beside her, Cory says, "Hey, man, you gotta ride up front. We don't have room for your rifle back here, bro'. Henry's still gotta get in, too."

Simon scowls. This. This is the reason he suspects his friend all the time. "Fine, then Paige can ride over here by the window and you over there by the other window and Henry in the middle."

"Simon," his sister chastises, "be nice. Henry should have this side. I'll sit in the middle. Look, I fit the smaller, middle seat better. Good grief. It's no less safe."

Safety wasn't the concern. He narrows his eyes at Cory, gets a chuckle from his friend, and rounds the truck. John helps Henry into the truck last. He is still walking in a slightly bent over position since his stitches and abdomen are healing and probably painful. Simon opens the passenger door and gets brushed past by Sam.

"Excuse me," she says without any real feeling.

Great. Now he has to sit with her beside him. This is going to be a long day.

They wait while John finalizes plans with Kelly. Then he spends a long time hugging and kissing his wife.

"Hey!" Cory leans over and yells out the open front door of the truck, "Little Doc, isn't that how you got that way in the first place? Hurry it up, Doctor Death! We're burnin' daylight."

Reagan flips him off behind John's back where nobody else can see, especially Herb. Simon sees it. So does Cory because he just laughs raucously.

"Cory!" Sam scolds with a laugh then a groan.

"Neanderthal," Paige comments, making Simon smile. Cory may be interested in his sister, but she certainly doesn't return the sentiment.

"Nag," he returns.

It doesn't sound like he is as serious as Paige. Simon turns in his seat to send his friend a warning glare. When he turns back, Sam is looking up at him. Her shoulder is nearly touching his, her brilliant blue eyes regarding him with a look of puzzlement. The ache of her absence hits him like a punch to the chest. He has missed her terribly. She was always his friend first before all else. Simon spins the rest of the way and looks out the window. John finally joins them and, to his relief, they're on their way.

"Stay alert," John warns as they get out onto the open road.

"Yes, sir," he and Cory reply in unison.

For such a simple run, they wouldn't normally take three of the best shooters off of the farm. However, there are highwaymen out there killing people. The farm is safer than they are on the road. Condo Paul and K-Dog came over to speak with them yesterday about these highway attacks. They'd heard of another one south of Nashville. Simon wishes he could send out a warning to people not to travel right now until this passes. Unfortunately, there is no way to warn people. Doc had even expressed concern about his son up at Fort Knox, but Kelly had wisely assuaged his doubts by reminding him how well-fortified they were with arms and solid buildings. Even though it is only about a thirty to forty minute drive to Dave's camp, Simon knows that travel always takes longer because of the roads. He just hopes they don't encounter more than abandoned vehicles. Occasionally, John stops so that he and Cory can push them out of the way.

"Doc said he was talking to Dave about their clinic that Sam's uncle is getting started," John says, drawing Simon's attention.

He peers right back out his window again, though. It is morning still and easy to see with the sun high in the cloudless, late winter sky. Spring is around the corner. It's certainly in the air. He was even awakened this morning by the busy chatter of birds outside the cabin.

"Oh, yeah?" Cory asks from the back seat.

"He said that maybe you should stay over there for a few weeks and help them get it established," John tells them.

"Me?" Cory asks. "What the hell would I know about that?"

"No, not you, ya' idiot. Paige is right. You are a Neanderthal. I mean Simon."

This causes him to whip his head to meet John's gaze.

"What?"

"They need to know how to set it up, how to configure the supplies and stuff and get it up and running."

"Sam's uncle was a doctor. Don't you think he knows a little more than me about that kind of thing?"

"No," Sam tells him and adds haughtily, "my uncle was a doctor at a hospital, a staff doctor. He didn't have a practice outside of the hospital. He worked for the hospital and kept an office there in the pediatric wing."

"But he still knows what he needs to run a small, general medicine practice," Simon argues.

"Whatever you say," she returns impolitely. "You know it all."

John says, "They need to know how we run our days at the clinic and how many supplies it would take to get through a normal clinic day. That kind of thing. Plus, they need to know what other building materials to pick up and what medical equipment they might need and where to find it."

"Well," Paige adds from the back seat, "if anyone's gonna know that, it's you and Sam. Certainly not the rest of us."

"Right, if they need to know where to keep the smelling salts if someone passes out from the sight of blood, they'll ask Paige," Cory teases and then grunts. Simon assumes his sister has elbowed him. It doesn't work because he adds, "Or how to get out of working."

228

This time she just groans. Simon grins. If Cory irritates her, she won't be interested in him ever.

"It's not that hard," Simon tells John. "I'm sure they'll figure it out."

"If they were going to figure it out, the conversation wouldn't have come up," Sam corrects him rudely. "It doesn't matter. We don't need you. We'll be just fine without your help."

"I don't know," John says, lingering on a topic Simon would much rather move on from. "If nothing else, I think you might see if you can offer some advice before we leave today."

"Yes, sir," he says with humility. He doesn't want to argue with John. Technically, he's his commanding officer, so if he wants Simon to stay over there for a few weeks to help them, then that's what he should do. He'd just rather do anything else. Cleaning the toilets in the big house- even in the kids' bathroom- would be preferable.

They make it safely to Henry's farm without incident on the roads and are permitted entrance at the gate. Dave greets them with a smile as they get out of the truck.

"'Bout time you got your lazy ass home," he razzes Henry.

"I see you didn't burn the place to the ground while I was gone," Henry returns.

"We had a few close calls," Dave says, causing Henry to laugh.

Other men come to see Henry, as well. He is apparently a very well-liked person. Simon would like him better if he didn't think Henry was attracted romantically to Sam. He has been forced the last few days to endure Sam in the med shed tending to Henry. It had been painful to watch her light laughter at Henry's supposedly funny quips. Many times, he'd had to leave the shed for fear of losing his temper or his lunch. He wants her to be happy, just not with Henry.

"Let's hurry up," Simon says to Cory, who is standing at the tailgate of the truck.

"Well, that's a neighborly attitude to have," Cory remarks. "We're supposed to stay for a while, check out their place a little more, and I guess they're having a memorial service for Annie and Bruce. Dave sent some of his men to get their bodies."

Cory says his last sentence in a hushed tone so the others don't overhear him.

"Oh, I hadn't heard," Simon tells him.

"That's not a surprise," Cory says.

Simon's eyes narrow. "What's that supposed to mean?"

"Since she came for a visit and ended up staying on for a few days, you've been incognito, bro'. I think I've seen you about ten minutes out of every day."

"I've been busy," Simon says, a partial truth.

"Uh-huh."

"Whatever," Simon says with impatience. "Do I bust your balls every time you disappear?"

"Yeah, pretty much," Cory answers.

Simon finds his friend irritating sometimes. "I just want to get back to the farm. We're supposed to run a clinic day tomorrow. I have a lot to do tonight."

"Sure. Whatever you say, Professor. But we won't be leaving till the big man says we are."

He knows Cory means John. However, he'd like to jump in the truck and take off for home. Being here is torturous. It doesn't matter that their farm is like a military compound and as safe from an attack as the Alcatraz Prison.

They join Dave to walk to one of the camp's storage barns, and Simon is relieved to see across the drive as Henry is helped into his house by his friends. Henry's home is similar to Doc's but is smaller and less grand. It is the kind of home that one would see on a typical dairy farm- white, two-story, well-maintained but nothing architecturally inspiring or ostentatious. Their money as farmers probably always went into their outbuildings, fencing, and livestock. Henry seems like a pretty unassuming person, and so Simon figures his parents were, as well. It doesn't make him like Henry any better, though. He is also relieved to see Sam follow along with John to the storage barn and not Henry to his private residence.

The barn Dave is leading them to is a one-story structure with a low pitch roof and a concrete floor. When he slides open the wide door, Simon is surprised by what he sees.

"Whoa," John remarks. "Been busy, Mechanic?"

"Yeah, was worried about those fuckin' apocalypse rumors we been hearin' about," Dave jokes, causing them all to laugh.

There are rows and rows of supplies either on pallets or in tubs, crates, and boxes. The storage barn is neat, organized, and has aisles to walk down. They follow Dave into the building. Some aisles are taller than Simon.

"You brought stuff to trade, and we've got stuff I know you'll want," Dave says casually. "Look around. We've got everything labeled as best as we can. Call it out if you think it'll be useful, and we'll work a deal. We've got another building behind this one that's also full."

"Damn, dude," Cory remarks. "Now I know why most of the places we hit are usually empty."

Dave laughs. "Been storin' up our nuts for the winter."

John chuckles and bumps his friend's fist. With typical, military hand signals, John indicates they should split up, and Simon heads to the far right while Cory goes the other way. His sister follows after Cory and John, which pisses him off, and also leaves him with Sam. As they stroll down the first aisle, one with boxes stacked nearly to the ceiling, Simon uses his flashlight to better see.

"There's so much," he says to her but mostly himself.

At first, she doesn't say anything but then, "Yep. They go on runs almost every day. He has enough men here to do that."

"Yes, I suppose that would make a difference."

"Medical supplies are at the end of this row. I'm sure there are some things there that you can use at the clinic."

Her voice is almost monotone. She has lost the lightness with which she usually speaks, and it bothers Simon.

"Won't you need them at the new clinic?"

She shakes her head, "No, we've got more than we need. The stuff we don't have is equipment like exam room beds."

"Ok, thanks," he replies.

She slips past him and leads Simon to the storage shelves against the back and side walls filled with tubs of supplies marked, 'medical.'

"Here," she says and indicates with her hand. When he hesitates, Sam pulls down a box without his help and opens it, setting the lid beside it on the floor. "See? There's a ton of this stuff."

"Wonderful," Simon praises and squats.

There are tourniquets, bandaging, syringes and more. He has no idea what he should suggest trading. They can always use supplies like this, but he wishes that Reagan or Doc would've come instead of him because the decision seems too monumental to make. He digs and sorts through items but comes up short of everything except indecision.

Sam leaves a second later, and Simon finds himself watching her walking away. Her black hair swishes and vibrantly stands out against her bright pink jacket. He tries not to stare at her derriere. He tries really hard.

Simon places a few items on the floor beside him. And replaces the box to the shelf to take down another. He removes the lid and finds medicines in pill bottles, and liquids in tiny, amber glass bottles that would be pulled through a syringe to administer. He wonders how many more boxes they have like this.

A cardboard box hits the ground beside him, startling Simon out of his ponderings.

"Use this," Sam orders. "Dave said to fill it with whatever you want. That'll be the medical portion of the trade."

"Really? He's sure?"

She sighs as if annoyed by him and looks out the small window near her. Then she hits him with those blue eyes and says, "I'm assuming he's serious since he said it."

Simon nods and says, "Thanks."

She doesn't leave as he'd expected she would but kneels beside him and picks bottles out one at a time. Simon doesn't move at first. He's frozen in place staring at her. It's been so long since he's

232

seen her, so many weeks. Seeing her again is like a breath of fresh Sam air. Upon further close inspection, she seems a little paler than normal, and there are dark smudges under her sapphire eyes as if she isn't sleeping much.

"Are you helping?" she asks impatiently.

"Oh, yes. Yes, sorry."

She just shakes her head as if he is irritating her. Simon isn't used to this sort of treatment from Sam. He doesn't know what to do about it.

"Do you like it here?" he asks with great hesitation.

"Here's a bottle of aspirin," she says, ignoring his question and handing him the small, plastic bottle.

"Thank you," he says, taking it and trying not to let his fingers brush hers as he does so. Another moment goes by before he repeats his question. "So do you?"

She sighs again. "Sure."

He finds himself unable to look away from her. The soft curve of her cheek, the brilliant blue of her eyes, the high, pointy arch of her dark brows. They draw him in as if under a spell. And he dares not look at her soft, full mouth too long. His treasonous mind revisits that night at her parents' home all too often, most of the time when he's on watch duty at night and the farm is quiet and still. He prefers to keep busy. Work has been the only thing keeping him sane. So many times he's wanted to commandeer a vehicle on the farm to come and rescue her. But it doesn't seem like she needs to be rescued from anything. She seems just fine, and Dave's compound is more than safe. She's safe. She actually seems as if she's adjusting, too. Simon wonders if she thinks of that night or if she's moved on completely. Part of him wants her to remember. Part of him wants her to long for him. These are the selfish parts of his mind outside his moral compass. The rational, sensible side of him wants her to move on and be happy.

"Antihistamine," she says, handing him a package of over-the-counter pills.

Simon mutters another comment of appreciation.

"This is going to take forever if you don't help, and I know you want to get home to the farm as soon as possible," she points out, looking directly at him with sad eyes before looking down into the box again.

"Yes, I'm helping. Sorry," he says and starts digging. "How do you know I'm anxious to get back?"

"Because I heard you telling Cory. I'm not deaf, Simon."

"Right, sorry," he apologizes, although he doesn't really know why or what for. "I just have a lot of work waiting for me back home."

She shakes her head, snickers, and snorts through her nose. "Oh, ok. Is that what it is?"

Simon doesn't answer because he's too busy watching her hair fall artfully over her left shoulder near him. He gets hit with a wave of her scent. Sam always smells good.

She looks at him again, this time with less melancholy but angrier eyes, "What?"

"Huh? Oh, nothing."

"Antibiotic cream," she says, jamming a tube toward him, which he takes with a nod. "And here's a bottle of lidocaine. We always went through a lot of this with injuries."

"Thanks," he repeats, sounding idiotic to his own ears. "How's the clinic coming?"

"Fine. We are fine," she answers with staccato precision.

"That's good," he answers. What he really wants to say is: "Come home to the farm. Now. Today. Come back where you belong." But he doesn't. Simon can't allow himself to do so. This is why he's avoided her the last week. He can't be near her without wanting her, and that frightens him. It was his idea to move back into the cabin with Cory. He didn't trust himself in the big house when she was only upstairs. His longing sometimes disgusts him so much that he gets nauseous from it.

"I'm glad it's working out for you here, Sam," he says, trying in earnest to mean it.

She hits him with such a fierce glare that he's surprised it doesn't knock him over backward from the tempestuous force of it.

"Sam!" someone calls from the other end of the barn.

Her face instantly transforms into a huge smile. "Uncle Scott!"

She stands and greets him with a hug.

"Hey, munchkin," he says, obviously using his own nickname for her. "I heard you guys were back. I also heard about Derek and Henry. That's terrible."

"Yes, but they'll both be all right. They're alive, right?" she says.

Her uncle nods with solemnity. He seems like a man who has seen his fair share of tragedy.

"Everything else go all right?" he asks.

"Yeah, it was good. I got to see my friends again for a few extra days," she tells him.

"I know. That's good. You miss them a lot," he says, revealing a lot more than she had. "Hi...Simon, isn't it?"

"Yes, sir," Simon returns cordially and shakes his hand.

"Right, Simon," Scott says with a smile. He turns back to Sam and asks, "Your best friend, right?"

"Uh...just a friend, Uncle Scott," she corrects. Her uncle nods with confusion but doesn't comment.

"Need help?" he offers.

"We're packing supplies in this box because Dave's making a trade with Grandpa's group."

"Oh, great!" he exclaims. "That's super. What can I do?"

"I've got this under control. I'm not sure if John wants to see the medical supplies in the other building, though. You could show him those."

"All right," he says. "I'll see you at dinner, munchkin."

She smiles and nods at her uncle before he leaves. Then she returns to helping Simon rummage for medicine. They return the box to the shelf and slide a lower one out and onto the floor.

"It's good you're with your uncle," he says, trying to convince himself aloud.

"He said he'd move into town," she confesses. "When Grandpa wanted us to stay or move into Pleasant View."

"What happened? Did he change his mind?"

She shakes her head and looks directly at him, "No, I did. I wanted as far from the farm as I could get, Simon."

This strikes to his core. He didn't think he could feel any guiltier about Sam than he already did.

"You didn't have to go this far. The family misses you. Everyone misses you and talks about you all the time."

They are interrupted by a young woman who rounds the corner and squeals. "Sam!"

"Hey, Courtney," she says and hugs the girl.

"Man, I missed you. It sure got boring around here without you," Courtney says and notices Simon for the first time. "Hi, I'm Courtney."

"Simon, ma'am," he replies and shakes her hand.

She looks at Sam and says playfully, "Geesh, girl, you didn't tell me how cute all the boys on the McClane farm were. You were holding out on me."

The young woman with the dark blonde, straight hair and expressive, brown eyes smiles at him kindly. Simon attempts to return it, fails, and pushes his glasses higher on his nose.

"Courtney's my age," Sam tells him. "You two should hang out sometime. You'd make a great couple!"

There is a falseness in her expression that Simon recognizes. He knows that Courtney doesn't yet know Sam well enough to see it because she laughs gaily and slaps Sam's arm lightly.

"Subtle, Sam!" she jokes. "Gosh!"

"Well," Sam says, looking only at Simon with something akin to cunning in her eyes, "Simon's single, too. You guys would hit it off. I know you both so well."

"Look out, Simon," Courtney teases. "She's going to have us married by sundown!"

He smirks and stares hard at Samantha. She's doing this to irritate him, and he had underestimated her ability to be ruthless. She's trying to hurt him. It's not working. She's merely pissing him off. A healthy dose of her own medicine might give her something to think about.

"Yeah, sure. My schedule's open," he says, not dropping his gaze from Sam's. "First, I'll have to go on a quick run to find a tux."

Courtney just laughs with good humor because she doesn't realize there is an underlying tension between himself and Sam.

"Oh, yes," Courtney says, "Don't want to look too shabby."

"And you'll want a ring, at least four carats," Simon adds, making Courtney laugh again.

"Maybe five," Courtney joins their play.

Then Simon looks at Courtney and sees that she is starting to realize this isn't just teasing. Sam isn't joining them. He feels bad for using Courtney to get at Sam. Then he feels bad about trying to make Sam irritated, too.

"Or we could just pack this medical box," he says, trying to lighten the mood again.

"Hm, gosh, I'd love to stay and help, but I'm on chore duty," Courtney jokes. "I just wanted to come by and see my girl."

"I'll catch up in a little bit, Court," Sam says with a grin and hugs her friend before Courtney leaves.

"She seems nice," Simon says with caution and gets hit with an intense glare from her, blue fire lit behind her eyes.

"Too nice for you."

He flinches. "Probably."

Simon squats and pushes the box back into its low slot on the shelving.

"Maybe you can text her your number," she suggests.

"Left my cell in Arizona," he says, attempting another joke. Sam doesn't bite. When he stands again and turns to face her, she is still glaring. Simon sets his mouth into a tight line of uncomfortable silence. This is not how they used to be; silent, angry, arguing. She used to be the one person he always felt he could talk with so easily.

She starts tapping her toe. Her left eyebrow rises. She's angry.

"I was just teasing, you know," he reminds her. "I'm not interested in your friend, Samantha."

"Someone in town then?"

He shakes his head, "No. Well, maybe Mrs. Browning."

She's the librarian. She has a late fee card almost filled with Simon's dirty laundry list of tardy returns. She's also in her sixties.

The right side of Sam's mouth twitches.

"What about you? Fending off the guys around here with a stick?"

She snorts. "Hardly."

Simon knows this isn't true. She's lovely and tender and desirable. He is certain many of the men in this camp are attracted to Sam.

"Sure," he says with sarcasm.

She juts out her chin and says with defiance, "So? What's it matter? It's none of your business who I'm sleeping with."

"What? What did you just say? You're talking about sleeping with people? *Sleeping* with, as in having sex?"

Simon hopes she is just saying this to vex him. If not, he's going to drag her back to the farm even if he has to tie her to the hood of the truck to do so.

"I'm an adult. I don't need, nor do I ask for your permission, Simon Murphy, to date or sleep with other men. You don't own me."

"That's not even funny," he reprimands. "I'm just making sure you're safe here and being taken care of, and you're being childish."

"No, I'm being independent."

Simon is losing his patience.

"I'm still alive, aren't I?"

"Don't be nonsensical. There's more to it than that, Sam, and we both know it."

She shakes her head and says, "No, not really, not anymore. I'm alive and well and fine. You don't get to ask me about my love life. It's not any of your concern. You rejected me. You didn't want me, so you have no rights over me. You don't need to know anything about me at all other than what I wish to tell you."

He grinds his teeth together to stop himself from doing something irreparable. His sister walks around the end of the aisle and finds them in the middle of their argument.

"Everything ok, guys?" Paige asks.

"You shouldn't be walking so much, Paige," he says angrily. "Why don't you find somewhere to sit for a while?"

"Yes, I'll show you where I sleep, Paige," Sam immediately volunteers and takes his sister's arm, leading her slowly away. She sends one last nasty scowl over her shoulder at Simon before they disappear.

Simon wonders if Sam offered to do this just to be able to use the word 'sleep' once more to get at him. She's never been such a vindictive person before. He can't believe she'd be that way now. She really needs to return to the farm. This place and all the freedom it's affording her is a bad influence.

An hour later, they've made their trade with Dave, and John shakes his friend's hand on it to make it legal. They were able to make a fair exchange of materials and goods for both sides.

They attend the memorial service, given by their camp's pastor, for Annie and Bruce, who is leaving behind the young woman from the slave camp with whom he'd had such a deep connection. She cries uncontrollably and must be consoled by her friends. Courtney cries, as well, but Simon notices that Sam does not. She is standing stoically with her arm around her new friend's shoulders. This is unlike Sam. She is usually so tender-hearted and fragile. Simon wonders if this is because of her move or her new friends or if she didn't know Annie or Bruce well. It's strange. He feels bad about their deaths and not just because he was there with them. He knew them as well as Sam had. She would've known them even more than him because they used to live here on the same farm. It leaves Simon speculating about her hardness.

Dave then shows them the camp's medical clinic, which is not actually on the grounds of Henry's farm but nearby. They are making good progress on the house, but Simon finds it concerning that it is not as secure as the camp where armed guards patrol twenty-four-seven. He hopes Dave has a plan for security once it opens.

When they are ready to depart, Dave, his wife, Sam's uncle and Sam come to send them off.

"Call if you have trouble," Dave is telling John near the driver's door of their truck.

"It's lookin' great," Cory is saying to her uncle about the clinic.

"I'm going to miss you, little sister," Paige says as she embraces Sam close. "You need to come and visit sooner. Or maybe I can come here."

Sam doesn't answer Simon's sister. She only nods and backs away again. Then she hugs Cory.

"Take care of yourself, kiddo," Cory tells her. He pats her back and kisses the top her head with affection.

"You, too, Cory," Sam returns. "Take care of Paige for me."

This bothers Simon. It's his job to look after his sister, not Cory's. He lets this one slide, though, since they are making their farewells and everyone seems emotional.

John joins them and hugs Sam next. "Be careful, kiddo. Stay out of trouble and listen to Dave."

John's tone is fatherly and filled with love and deep inflection. Cory and Paige climb into the truck and wave to Dave. John finally pulls back and clears his throat.

"Ready?" he asks Simon.

"Yes, sir," Simon answers as John goes around him to the truck. He is left standing with Sam alone as John leaves to join Dave near the door again. Cory and Paige are talking through her open door to Dave's wife, who is really sweet. She told them a funny story about accidentally shooting Dave in the foot with a crossbow a few years ago. She had them all rolling with laughter. Simon could tell how much they love each other by the way Dave and his wife had laughed, teased, and then smiled into each other's eyes as many other memories swept over them.

"Stay safe, Sam," Simon tells her as her uncle walks away. He steps closer, anticipating a hug.

"See ya'," she says in an almost flippant, nonchalant manner and sprints toward Henry's house, going straight in through the side door without knocking.

Simon is left standing there feeling and looking like a complete idiot. He gets in the truck, slamming the door too loudly and doesn't care. She hadn't offered him a hug or a handshake or anything. Her manner was dismissive and rude. He would like to march up to Henry's house, pull her to the side and shake some sense into her. This new defiance is unbearable and bratty in his opinion. She is behaving worse than Arianna.

And why is she going into Henry's house when her bunk is in another building?

"She's going to check his bandages," Paige answers the question he thought he'd only said in his head.

He doesn't reply to his sister but stews silently and stares out his window. They pull away from Henry's farm, and Simon contemplates making John turn around to go back and force Sam to return to the farm. He reminds himself this is for her own good. This is what he'd wanted, sort of. He has to stop himself many times from yanking the door handle and jumping out to go back on foot.

Chapter Seventeen
Paige

The family is in full-blown work mode for the planting season, and the weather has finally leveled out to a seasonal, warm temperature. Six weeks have gone by since she last saw Sam when they took her home. The doctors, Sam's uncle included, have held joint medical clinic days in Pleasant View exactly twelve times, and Sam was present for exactly zero of those times. Paige suspects she will never see her little friend again, and she surmises that it is because of her brother, which somehow makes it sting just a tad more. Her loyalty to them both is being torn asunder. Simon's her brother, but Sam is her friend, a really good friend. She wants them both to be happy, and Paige knows this isn't accomplishing that at all if it's what Simon had in mind. He is miserable and grumpy. Actually, grumpy would be an improvement. He is no longer the bear but has become something else altogether, and Paige wonders if he isn't turning somewhat jaded and resentful from Sam's departure. Neither have ever admitted to being an item, but everyone, including Paige, deduced that on their own. They were always so close, so intimate. Sam used to hang on his every word. Simon sure seemed infatuated with her, as well. Now they are not speaking, visiting, or even being civil when they do see each other, which as far as Paige knows, was six weeks ago. She's not sure time will heal this wound in Simon. Perhaps Samantha is healing from their fracture slightly better, but

Paige hasn't spoken to her for so long she wouldn't even know. It breaks her heart to see her brother like this.

"Coming through. Watch your toes," Derek alerts her as he rolls his wheelchair down the long hallway from Herb's office to the kitchen.

"Sorry, Derek!" she exclaims and scoots back against the wall. She'd been on her way up to her room to grab a jacket to go for a walk. The sun will set in just a few short hours, and she wanted some fresh air. A few days ago she'd actually started jogging again. Doc had proclaimed her well enough to do it if she felt up to the task but had warned her to stop if she felt internal tugging or pulling. She hasn't felt that in weeks. It is a relief to be getting back to normal. Lucas was kind enough to go with her since he was free for an hour while the men worked the top fields. Without Derek's help on the tractors and plows, the workload is heavier on the rest of them. He has been complaining about it often. "Need help?"

"No, ma'am," he says as he wheels around the corner.

He is still in his cast and also in an extraordinary amount of pain every day. Normally he doesn't accept any of the pain medicine the doctors offer. The first few weeks had been the worst. He was in complete and total agony and hadn't taken well to being mostly bed-ridden. Being pushed around in a wheelchair also hadn't sat well with him. At least now he can wheel himself around without aid, which is better since he is as stubborn and bull-headed as his brother. John is resolute in his opinion that his brother will one day walk again and heal completely. Simon told her that the doctors do not believe this to be true. Derek needed and still does need extensive surgeries that they just can't perform. She doesn't think Derek is aware of this.

"I'll help you, Dad," Justin says and rushes to his father to push the wheelchair.

"Thanks, big man," Derek says to his son.

It's just sad to watch Justin push his dad away. It breaks her heart. Derek was so strong and sturdy, just like the other men. Paige prays that he'll heal completely.

"Heading somewhere?" Reagan asks when she runs into her on the second floor.

"Out for a walk," Paige tells her. "Wanna' come?"

"Hell no," Reagan returns. "I'm beat."

Paige just shakes her head and smiles, "And no wonder. You worked all day today at the clinic and all day yesterday in the shed."

"Yes, I'm aware," she says, pulls the towel down from her hair, and tosses the damp article into a hamper in the hall. Jacob runs out of the bathroom and down the stairs in a blur of motion. He's always in high gear. "Gee, wonder why I'm tired?"

"Need help?"

"Nah, John's on his way in," she tells her. "Cory is finishing up in the barn for him."

Paige tries not to let his name cause the emotion in her that it does. She simply nods and presses her lips tightly together to keep from expressing it.

"What are you working on in the shed?" Paige asks.

"Looking at slides under the microscope," she answers. "And studying premie care."

"Are you worried about your baby?"

"Me? No," she answers, although Paige doesn't believe her. "We have a lot of pregnant patients in both towns, and Sam's uncle can't be everywhere at once."

"Babies are a lot of responsibility for you guys," she remarks, referring to the doctors.

"Yeah, like I need to be reminded of that. Need to use the shower?" Reagan asks.

"No, I took one this morning so I wouldn't be in the way of everyone tonight. Let John get his. I'm not exactly getting dirty like everyone else."

"Not yet," Reagan comments. "You will be soon enough. You're doing great, getting stronger."

"Yeah, Doc checked my blood the other day and said I'm up to a twelve- whatever that means."

244

"That means good stuff," Reagan jokes. "That's all you need to know. I heard you went running the other day."

"I don't know if I'd call jogging for twenty minutes running, but it felt great to do it anyway."

"I'm jealous. I'll just be happy to stop puking long enough to start running again."

Paige offers a sympathetic look and says, "Are you going to run during your pregnancy?"

She rolls her green eyes and blows a loose curl out of her face before saying, "No, probably not. I can't imagine John going for that. I'd have to stop every ten feet to barf."

"Maybe there's a reason you're so sick. Maybe you would've miscarried if you'd been too active like riding and running."

"I still could," she says. "But I doubt it. I'm far enough along now that I should be out of danger."

Reagan places her hand over the small bump that is finally showing. She is so petite and thin that it really sticks out. And it's utterly adorable. Hannah teases her relentlessly.

Paige reaches out and lays a hand on her rounded tummy. "Is he kicking a lot?"

"Mostly just at night. I'm sure it's kicking during the day, too, but I just don't notice. That's normal."

"You'd know," she remarks with humor since Reagan is a super genius doctor. "Are you getting nervous?"

"Nervous? No," Reagan says, leaving Paige to estimate again that she is fibbing. "Getting fat? Yes."

"Oh, please!" Paige chastises. "You're still as tiny as ever."

"If my ass gets any bigger, I'll be wearing sweatpants for life."

Paige laughs heartily at Reagan, although her friend is still just as poker-faced as ever. "Hey, don't judge. I've been living in sweatpants for months."

It wasn't much of a choice. Anything snug against her waist or sutures was too painful to bear. Plus, they hadn't wanted her to damage the stitches or put too much pressure on her stomach. First, it had been hospital gowns. Then she graduated to her own nightgowns, paired with a robe when they brought her down to the first floor to be around the family. Now she wears sweats or loose fitting yoga pants. She feels like a bum and is hoping to upgrade to a pair of jeans soon.

"At least you have an excuse. I'm just turning into a fat cow."

"Shut up," Paige teases on a laugh. "You aren't turning into any such thing. And you have an excuse, too. You should be eating badly and consuming weird things and getting fat. You've got the rest of your life to lose it."

"John found candy last week at a gas station," Reagan relates. "Even Skittles this time. I gave most of the stuff from the run to Fort Knox to the kids."

"I know," she says. "That was a good find. You even shared some with me. Also rare." Reagan chuckles.

"I'm beat," Reagan admits and turns to go. "Hitting the sack so I can pass out for about twelve hours, which is what the alien seems to like."

"Nothing wrong with that," Paige informs her.

Reagan just snorts and sends a wave behind her head to Paige.

"G'night," Paige calls and turns to go to her own room.

Hopefully, the evening doesn't get too chilly since she's only wearing a tank top and stretchy exercise leggings for pants. She didn't think she was ever going to be able to give up her thermal underclothes. The chills have gotten better as her blood has built back up. She glances in the mirror before heading out. Her hair is down, which will help if it gets windy. They've had some strong winds lately whipping through the valley. She pulls on a hoodie, as well. There is a logo for a trucking company, Tennessee Steel Haulers, embroidered on the back with a picture of a semi. Cory found this for her a few weeks ago on a run to Clarksville. He'd given her an entire tub full of clothing items he'd taken from different stores. The men have also been bringing boxes jammed full of books for the town library to restock the shelves from the fire. They are also trying to build the basement reserves of stock-up items back up since so much of it has been depleted. Sam told her that when she first came to live on the farm, the basement had been full, stocked floor to ceiling with shelving units of items. Their reserves have been nearly depleted, but thanks to the men, most of the shelves are filling up again. Gretchen had been thankful for the jeans Cory found for her. John brought back a bag full of shoes, too. She and the other women have been living large with the other finds, which included perfumes and lotions, that Cory brought back this winter from the Marshall's discount store. It's just nice feeling girly again, even if it won't last forever. She and Gretchen even painted each other's nails the other night, and Paige actually talked her into a dark navy blue instead of the black she usually wears. Most of G's clothing is still grunge-style, rock concert tees, black jeans, baggy flannel shirts, which definitely don't belong to her because they are too big. Sometimes she even wears black eyeliner. She always has the same, tiny diamond studs and small, silver hoops in the three earring holes in each ear. Her fingers are usually covered in multiple silver rings, and she insists on keeping her hair in a short, pixie cut. She's a very pretty girl but definitely works hard to hide it.

They'd also painted Hannah's nails a pale rose color, and they looked great. Hannah's hands get drier than hers, so Paige donated all of the tubes of hand lotion to her and Sue. She'd been more than appreciative. Cory had also taken Simon and, for the first time, Huntley with him on a short run to Clarksville where Huntley had found a new crossbow. Doc had been concerned about the dangers of the high-power bow, but John and Kelly convinced him that they'd help Huntley learn how to use it. She's pretty sure Huntley was just glad that he finally got to go on a run with the men. He was ecstatic about it. For some reason, he prefers to deer hunt with a bow instead of a gun, but he has never owned a mechanical bow. He usually just uses an ordinary, wood bow with long arrows and a single string. Paige likes the deer jerky they process as a result of the hunt but doesn't really want to be involved in the killing of the deer to get it. She's had to kill enough animals for survival. She hopes it never comes to that again.

As much as she is grateful for the new items, Paige would rather the men didn't go out. Not now. Maybe not ever again. She knows they are secretly hunting for those men that ran over Derek. They tell the family it's only for supplies, but she sees the extra guns and ammo they take. The weather has been so good, they've even gone a few times on the new four-wheelers they took from those jerks last year whose leader was named Mike, the same bastard who'd shot her and had been shot and killed in return by her brother. It's not worth it to risk their lives exacting revenge for Derek, too. One of these times, she fears they will not get so lucky. They are also looking for the highwaymen, another reason she wishes they'd just stay on the farm.

After applying some cherry-flavored lip balm to protect against chapping, Paige goes back downstairs to the mudroom and pulls on her gym shoes, the same ones Cory took her to get at that store in Nashville. The house is quiet. This is the time of night when it gets this way. Parents are trying to get their kids prepped for bed. Sometimes Hannah and Sue will be in the kitchen doing work to prepare for the morning meal. Tonight they are not present. The kitchen is uncharacteristically empty. The children have cleaned it spic and span, though, after a big meal of pork and sauerkraut. It had hit like a brick coupled with mashed potatoes. All that shredding of cabbage she'd helped with last fall for canning was so worth it.

She sneaks quietly out the side door so as not to disturb if any of the kids are already asleep. The evening air is warm and soothing. In the rose garden, she can tell where Sue has been spreading compost all winter on her grandmother's flower beds. She knows how important it is to the girls to keep their grandmother's beds going. Reagan told her the first summer after her Grams had passed, they couldn't bear to enter her rose garden. The story had made Paige feel sad and miss her own mother desperately. Every day that passes makes the pain a little more bearable, though, and Paige likes to think her mom is somewhere peaceful and beautiful.

248

She decides to walk the perimeter of the horse pasture. She does like watching them and looking at them, just not riding them. Not fifty yards into her stroll, Cory's dog trails after her.

"What are you doing out here, Shadow?" she asks it and bends to pet the beast. "The kids sure did name you correctly."

Shadow is content to let Paige rub behind her ears and even returns the favor by pressing up against her black pants, leaving hair all over them.

"Of course," she says wryly.

Opening the gate to the pasture, she waits for his dog to follow her through and then closes it, making sure it hooks tightly. She doesn't want to get blamed if the horses go gallivanting across the countryside. By the time she makes it to the end of the pasture, Paige is slightly breathless. She stops and leans against the fence as the sun starts dipping low behind the tall pines on the horizon. She's so thankful the weather is once again warm. Shadow growls low in her throat right before rustling in the woods reaches Paige's ears. Her gun is on her hip, and she places her hand on the butt of it.

"Lost?" Cory calls out as he comes down a steep hill on the back of his horse and into the clearing. He manages to open the gate to the pasture and shut it again without dismounting.

"No," she replies and approaches carefully. She does not like his stallion. The animal is majestic and stunning, but he is definitely not trustworthy.

"Kind of far from the house, don't ya' think?" he asks rhetorically as he swings down and walks closer.

"No, just going for a walk," Paige explains. "It was too nice out tonight to sit inside and read again. Besides, I'm done with the books Simon brought from the library last week."

"You should've waited for me," he says in a slightly reprimanding tone. "I would've taken you."

"I have your giant wolf to keep an eye on me."

"She's not a wolf. Well, maybe. I don't think she has any wolf blood in her. She's just a big boned girl," he says with a grin. Then he winks and adds, "Don't tell her, though. Don't want her getting a complex."

Shadow leans against Cory's leg with her torso, begging for a petting, which he obliges. She is definitely his dog. She loves the kids and the rest of the family and has become protective of the farm and its people, but she's Cory's dog. Paige could tell it was hard on him when she was made to sleep in the barn since being in the big house was not a popular idea with the moms who clean it. Now that he and Simon are back in their cabin, Shadow is back to sleeping next to Cory on the floor out there, or at least that's what he told her the other day.

Watching him behave so affectionately with his dog tugs at her heartstrings. How can he be so caring and gentle with animals and family and then kill people brutally the next day on a run? It doesn't even bother him. He offers the muzzle of his horse's nose a rub, too.

"What's wrong, huh? You wanna' go free, stud?" he asks the horse, which actually responds with a low, rumbling nicker through its nose and prances in place. He pulls off the saddle and bridle, releases the brute, and the horse is free to gallop and play. The first thing it does is roll in a dry patch of dirt. Cory says without any real anger or judgement, "Idiot."

"Takes after his owner," Paige badgers. He just chuckles and picks up the horse tack.

"Yeah, we're both studs."

"That's a long way to carry all that. Want me to get something?" she offers.

"Sure," he says. "Grab his bridle."

"Gee, that's really tough," she mocks, picking up the lightest item that basically weighs nothing. Luckily, there aren't globs of foamy horse spit hanging off of the bit. She detests that when it happens. It's so gross. Sam laughed at her once for saying so. She hopes her friend has horses to ride over at Dave's.

"That's enough for you," he informs her and lugs the saddle, pad, and blanket over one arm. Paige knows how heavy those are and has no clue how he can carry it all like that. Her arm would be falling off before they ever made it to the barn.

"I'm stronger than you think," she announces. It's sort of true. Not lately, not since she got herself shot.

"You're getting stronger. That's true. But you just need to worry about getting better and leave the heavy lifting to me for a while. You do the heavy thinking. I'll do the heavy lifting."

"How is that a change from any other time?"

Cory says, "In a few months, I'll let you carry my saddle for me."

He is joking, of course, and she knows it. He'd never let her transport a saddle that heavy so far. His chivalrous and, usually chauvinistic, side would rear up first.

"Deal," she agrees with good humor. A few minutes later, she asks, "Can we rest a minute?"

He shoots her a speculative look and asks, "You ok, Red?"

"Just a little winded. Nothing new!" she complains as Cory leads her to a stump under a tree.

"Sit," he orders more firmly.

He drops the saddle, standing it on end on the horn. It lands with a big thud. Then he drops himself to one knee beside her. Without preamble, Cory takes her hand in his and presses two fingers to the pulse point on her wrist. When it first happened, just walking from room to room in the house would cause her heart rate to skyrocket. Doc and Reagan used to check her like this rather frequently. Apparently, Cory must've asked them about it and learned how to, as well.

"You don't need to do that," she says. "I'm fine."

"Shh," he demands impatiently.

Paige waits while he uses his watch to time her heart rate. She tries not to groan with irritation. After a few minutes, he releases her hand.

"See? I'm fine. I just still get a little winded sometimes."

He doesn't rise but remains kneeling beside Paige on one knee. He rests his elbow there and stares hard at her as if contemplating whether or not she is telling the truth. She stares back and offers a slightly less patient look.

"Stop. Everyone is so ridiculous about it. I'm fine. Don't be overprotective. Don't hover."

He snorts and smirks. "Sure. That's gonna happen."

Cory recently sheared off his beard and sideburns, and actually let Sue cut his hair. It's still longer than most of the other men's in the family with the exception of Huntley. He usually wears it pulled back in a very short ponytail. Today it is free and wavy and thick.

He rambles on, lecturing her, "It's my job. You took a bullet for my brother. I owe you for life, woman."

"No, no way," she says, holding up a hand to stop him. "Not for life. You've repaid me many times. You got me clothes, took care of me carrying me up and down the stairs all the time. I think we're even."

"Not even close," he says, hanging his head slightly to pick at sticks and pebbles near her foot.

For some reason, Paige feels she must offer him exoneration for the invisible guilt tether he insists on tying between them. She places her hand on the top of his head, leaving it there. After a moment, Cory's head rises, and he looks at her with intensity. She gives him a crooked grin that probably displays more melancholy than joy. Cory slides his hand onto her knee.

"You've lost weight," he remarks with a hard frown.

"I'm gaining it back," Paige informs him. "You won't be able to call me Beanpole for long."

He just shakes his head, but she doesn't know if he is disagreeing with her or if he is thinking about something else. When his brown eyes meet hers, she confirms the first theory

"I'll be fine," she insists, trying to instill some sort of peace within him. He carries too much remorse about so many things. She doesn't want to be one of those. Paige allows her hand to slide down to cup his shaven cheek. He reaches up to cover her hand with his own.

"You're so fragile," he remarks as if he is stating a fact.

"No, I'm not," she argues softly, shaking her head and offering a smile. "Don't be silly. I got shot. I lived for three years on the road. I fell through a floor. I've killed people to survive. I hardly think that counts as fragile, Cory."

He grins with rebellious intent. He's back. She lets her hand drop back down. She doesn't like Cory being glum and serious. She's used to him being a smartass and cocky and confident and irritating. Serious Cory is too intense for Paige. It makes her think of him differently.

"The people you claim to have killed probably fell and had an accidental weapon discharge and shot themselves," he says with a flash behind his eyes.

She scowls meanly at him and narrows her eyes. "Shut it. They were legit stateside kills, as the guys call it."

"Probably fell down a flight of stairs and broke their own necks."

She huffs and gets miffed. "Hey! That's bull. I did it myself."

"Got run over by a herd of buffalo or something," he harasses.

She chuckles, although she wants to thump him over the head with something. He is so damn aggravating.

"No, I did it!"

"Pack of wild ducks attacked probably. More likely."

"Shush!"

He lets his serious demeanor slip just slightly and grins. Then he adds, "Accidental electrocution."

"Cory!" she threatens but loses her momentum and laughs. She slaps his shoulder lightly.

"Old age," he teases, trying to maintain his straight-faced composure.

"Stop it!" she warns with a full-blown giggle.

"Butter knife in a toaster."

"You!" Now she is giggling uncontrollably.

"Hang-gliding accidents."

She wraps her hands around his throat and mock chokes him. Paige laughs, and he finally cracks a grin. Then he grabs her face between his large hands and pulls her mouth to his before she can protest. Within seconds, her resolve is gone. It's just the two of them again, just like it was in Nashville and again in town at the clinic that night. She thinks about those nights so often they are like reels of a movie picture playing out in her mind. It usually hits when she's alone in her bedroom by herself.

Cory's hands leave her face and slide down around behind her, pulling her gently forward. She is precariously perched on the edge of the log but knows he won't drop her. He'd held her suspended four floors above her certain fate of death. His palms flatten on her hips, fingers digging in. Then they move under her bottom and pull her up against him tightly as he deepens their kiss. Paige buries her fingers in his thick hair and pulls him closer, as well.

Cory groans into her mouth, breaking her trance-like state. She jerks back with a gasp.

"Cory!" she whispers raggedly and presses against his chest.

He doesn't reply but leans his forehead against hers while they catch their breath.

"I've missed you, Red," he admits as his hands travel up her back and hold her close.

"We can't," she says on an unstable exhale. She doesn't remove her fingers from his broad chest. She can't seem to stop them from stroking lightly through his thin, long sleeve tee. She also isn't going to say that she's missed this, too. Some secrets should never be uncovered.

"Too late," he teases and tangles his hands in her hair. Then Cory presses her head to his chest, inhaling deeply. "You smell good."

"You brought me perfume, remember?" she reminds him with a smile.

"No, not perfume. This is just you."

She tries not to let this affect her feelings toward Cory. He shouldn't say things like this anyway. They can never have a real

254

relationship, and Paige doesn't want one. So she doesn't tell him that she likes the way he smells right now, too. Cory always smells the same; like horse sweat, leather, his own sweat, and something slightly like pine needles. It is nearly intoxicating.

"Someone's going to see," she reminds him and bites the inside of her cheek to stop herself from saying something more like 'let's go over there farther into the woods where no one can see us making out like sneaky teenagers.' Instead, her responsible, mature, annoying adult side says, "We should go. It's getting dark."

He doesn't move for a moment but pulls her closer. Finally, he leans back, presses a kiss to her forehead and then her mouth. This time it is merely a brief pressing of his lips to hers as if he is saying goodbye. She finds herself wanting it to be longer. It leaves her disappointed when he stands and offers a hand. She takes it and follows on shaky legs.

"Feel ready to keep going?" he asks as if nothing has happened.

She is incapable of speech, so Paige nods instead. They don't talk about their inappropriate kiss or the fact that it shouldn't have occurred in the first place because even though they were out behind barns in the back of the horse pasture, someone could've seen. It was irresponsible. Shadow follows them to the barn where they store the tack in the room it belongs. It is nearly dark in the barns, the sun almost gone completely. A full moon has already started its monthly rise over the treetops. It makes it easier to see on the farm at night, which is nice when they need to move around on patrols.

As she walks down the aisle, a horse nickers and neighs to them in greeting. Cory picks up her hand and attempts to hold it.

"Cory, don't," she scolds. "Simon could catch us."

"Maybe we should just tell him," he suggests as if he is serious.

"Never happening," she informs Cory and dislodges her hand from his, although his had felt warm and comforting. The air is cooling down slightly and causing her to feel chilly again.

"He's bound to find out eventually," Cory says as if that makes sense.

She stops dead in her tracks and looks up at him. He simply cocks his head to the side with a grin.

"Not funny."

"You going back to the house now?" he asks and shuts the barn door, leaving it cracked open about ten inches.

"Yes," she replies. "Are you on first watch?"

"You know it," he says with a smile. "I'll be bored out here all by my lonesome. Wanna' keep me company?"

That sounds tempting and…interesting. It stirs her blood just imagining.

"No," she reluctantly answers. "I'm going to bed."

"That's sounding better and better," he says.

She glares at him, trying to keep her composure.

"It'll give me something to think about while I'm roaming around out here."

"No, don't. Think about something else," she says. She went with them two weeks ago to town for a clinic day and tried to be helpful. During her lunch break, she walked to the library to return some books before she got recorded for late fees. She'd taken a shortcut through a yard near an alley that backed up to a brick building. Behind the building, she'd seen Cory speaking with a woman, one she knows came with Thomas's group who were high-jacked on the freeway. They are staying in a home near there. Paige has no right to feel jealousy of Cory talking with some woman, but she had. She was a pretty blonde wearing a blue-jean skirt and a short, cropped top that fit snugly. Her name was Rachel. Paige had subtly asked around about her. She has never formally met her other than in passing or at meetings. However, Cory did introduce her to a little girl named Tessa, who seems to hold Cory in very high regard. She'd clung to his pant leg when they had to leave that day. Apparently, women young, old, and everything in between find him irresistible. She is beginning to understand why.

256

"Don't have anything else on my Neanderthal brain," he says with a grin, showing his dimples. She forgot he had those since they've been concealed all winter by a thick beard. "Correction. I don't have a lot on my brain other than tracking and killing the asshole who ran over Derek."

"I wish you guys wouldn't go out looking for them. You're literally just asking for trouble."

"Correction again," he says, waving his finger around. "They were asking for trouble, and they're gonna get some, too."

She grimaces and stops walking. "Cory, just let it go. Don't keep looking. I just have a bad feeling about those men. I can't explain it. You know the night the guys didn't come home and I told you I knew something was wrong with Simon?" she asks and gets a nod. "This is the same. I've got a bad feeling about this. What if I'm right? Is it worth it to lose some of our family by seeking out this danger?"

"Yes," he says firmly, a coldness entering his eyes. She's seen this before. "This has to be settled. You can't just let people get away with something like this. They have to be dealt with, Paige. Don't worry about it. We'll handle it. I'm tracking them. They can't hide from me forever."

"That's what I'm afraid of," she says, biting her lower lip.

Cory shakes his head confidently and says, "No, they've got a reckoning coming. They aren't getting away with this. There's a toll they have to pay. Someone's getting their ticket punched for this."

"What if they punch yours?" she asks with fear.

He laughs obnoxiously. "You've been with us on a run. This is different. We're not looking for baby formula. We're looking for vengeance. They don't stand a chance."

"What if the highwaymen are the same ones who ran over Derek?"

"Could be. Who knows?" he says as if he doesn't care. "Thomas said they didn't have a black SUV, but those morons could've robbed someone for it after attacking his group."

"But they seem...experienced. What if you guys have finally met your match this time? Don't you think that's bound to happen?"

He regards her as if he finds her humorous. It infuriates Paige.

"Don't be so self-assured, Cory Alexander," she reprimands and waves her finger near his chin. "There's always someone stronger or faster or smarter. And these men could have more experience, too."

He grabs her finger, presses a kiss to the tip before she can pull away.

"Maybe we'll turn you loose on them. You're quite the lethal killer... according to you."

"You're not funny!" she says, her temper and voice raising.

"What's not funny?" Simon asks as he approaches, startling Paige.

"What? Oh, that." She points at Cory and says, "Cory. He's not funny," she explains and takes a furtive step back from him so that it doesn't seem to her brother that they were walking too closely together.

"I could've told you that," Simon remarks with dry humor.

"I don't like you guys looking for Derek's accoster. I want you to stop."

Simon looks at her the same way Cory had just a moment ago only his is also laced with irritation. "Get real, sis. You really think John's gonna let this one pass? He's hell bent on finding them. He'll never rest until he gets justice for what they did to his brother."

She swallows hard and looks at her feet for a moment. "What if they get the take on you guys? Have you thought of that?"

"You can cash in the life insurance and retire to Maui," Cory jokes.

Paige raises her eyebrow and points to Cory, showing her brother what an ass he is being. Cory just laughs at her. Simon rolls his eyes.

"Whatever, Paige," Simon says. "We're not gonna stop looking for them. As long as we've got fuel- and we've got plenty now that the CNG is working more efficiently- we're looking for them. We owe John and Derek that much. Besides, those people could find the farm or attack the town and hurt more innocent people. The people in town aren't ready for an attack of that caliber yet. They're getting there, but they aren't there yet. We can't let that happen. We have to protect the farm and our people."

"And we like killing assholes," Cory adds. "There's that, too."

"I agree with you, Paige," Simon tells her, looking at Cory next. "He's not funny. Now, I'm going out to the cabin to get some sleep before my shift starts at four. Are you going in for the night?"

"Probably," she answers. Earlier she spent an hour in the armory room in the back of the shed working on shotgun shell reloads. It's literally the least she can do.

"No. Not probably. You are. Go to bed so I don't have to worry about you," Simon directs.

"I'm starting to think I should be calling you both Neanderthal," she tells her bossy brother.

"As long as you go inside and go to bed, you can call me whatever you want," Simon remarks without humor.

She groans aloud and rolls her eyes at Simon. "I am going in, but not because you said I have to."

"Get some rest, brother," Cory tells Simon. "I'll hold down the fort."

Simon bumps his fist against Cory's before leaving.

"You're a bad influence on my brother," she notes with an arched eyebrow and pursed lips.

"What?" he asks as if his feelings are stung just slightly by this. "Maybe he's a bad influence on me."

"That's believable," she remarks with sarcasm.

"Probably not, huh?" he asks, his dark eyes penetrating. "Want me to tuck you in?"

"No!" she cries, caught off guard by his question.

"Too bad," he says and grins crookedly.

Paige can't help the smile she returns. His mischievous humor is too much to resist sometimes.

"Yeah, maybe," Paige blurts before she can stop herself. Her cheeks burn with embarrassment.

"Maybe, huh?" he asks and steps closer.

"No, I didn't mean to say that," she corrects. "Um...g'night."

She fast walks the rest of the way to the side of the house and lets herself into the mudroom where she removes her shoes and stashes them under the table where most of the other shoes are kept. Then she grabs a glass of water from the kitchen and takes it upstairs with her to her room. She slips into a knee length nightgown of pale lavender and slides under the covers, letting the warmth comfort her. She tries not to think of their kiss in the field. She also tries hard not to think about the fact that she'd said 'maybe' to his invitation. Damn her stupid mouth. They can't be together. Not now. Not in the future. Not ever. She's not going to go through the pain of losing someone she loves again. Keeping Cory at arm's length is the best plan, and she's been doing really well with that until today. Her brother will never allow it anyway, and it would be a betrayal of him to pursue such a relationship with his best friend.

Within minutes, Paige is fast asleep, her long walk having done the trick to exhaust her. Unfortunately, her mind occupies itself with dreams of Cory kissing her again.

Chapter Eighteen
Cory

"All set?" he hears John say in the hall near Doc's old bedroom. Derek's low murmur comes next followed by Sue's. "Have Sue come and get me if you need help. I'll be up till four when Kelly comes on."

John leaves the hallway and heads into the kitchen where Cory is packing himself food.

"Ready?" his friend asks.

"Yep, just a minute," Cory returns as he folds the sack's top to prevent the items from spilling out.

"I was just talking to Derek and Kelly before they went to bed," John says.

"About their nighttime beauty regimens?"

John grins, "Sure."

"'Bout what?" Cory asks more seriously his time.

"Going on another run," his friend relays.

"Where to this time?" Cory asks. He doesn't particularly care where they end up as long as they are hunting those jerkoffs who ran over Derek. He likes Derek as much as his own brother. They pal around a lot in the equipment shed working on vehicles and tractors. Cory's learned a lot from him over the years about motors and mechanicals.

"We're thinking Nashville," John tells him.

"Seems like as good a guess as any. K-Dog and Paul said they heard from people moving through last week that another attack was spotted over that way. Seems we ought to take a pass at it. Can't hurt."

"They probably know to move around and not hit the same areas twice in a row," John ponders. "They have experience. That's for sure."

"Not more than us," Cory reminds him.

"Perhaps," John says quietly.

"We'll find them, John," Cory promises.

John's blue gaze meets his, "Oh, I know we will. I won't rest until they pay for this."

"How's he doing?" Cory asks.

His friend hangs his head and says, "Not great. I think he's getting depressed. Doc says we won't know how he's going to recover until the cast comes off."

"How much longer will that be?"

"Not sure. Few weeks maybe."

"That's good," Cory remarks as he grabs a jacket from the hook near the door. "That thing has to be getting old."

John chuckles and replies, "Oh, yeah. He's complaining about it day and night."

"Poor dude."

John laughs harder and says, "You mean, poor Sue."

"No doubt," Cory says and picks up his rifle resting against the door jamb. "Ready?"

"Always," John says with steadfast sureness.

They both head out the back door, leaving all other doors to the house locked. Then they split up after bumping fists.

Walking the nightly beat on the farm has transformed them all into nocturnal predators and creatures of habit. John is patrolling on the high ground up above the house toward the road. He likes to perch up there with a night-vision scope on his rifle to surveille the farm. Cory checks the barns and behind them about a hundred yards into the woods. With the moon full like it is tonight, he doesn't even need his night-vision gear to see his way. Damn Dog is right on his six, sniffing the ground and padding along.

"Come on, girl," he calls to her as he walks up a short hill behind the barns. She follows obediently.

Cory slings his rifle against his back and climbs a maple tree, going about halfway up. He can see everything from this position, and he often does this to get a broad, panoramic view. Having missed dinner earlier, he pulls a brown paper bag out of the pack on his back. Damn Dog sits patiently at the base of the tree waiting for him to come back down. He adjusts his weight on the thick branch and jams his foot against the trunk of the tree to hold himself still while he eats. He'd grabbed an apple pie pocket and a sandwich he'd made from leftover baked chicken. Piled with some lettuce from the greenhouse and herbed goat cheese and he's in heaven. He washes it all down with a canteen of cold water. He makes sure to save some of the sandwich for his dog and tosses it down to her. She is waiting for it, knowing her snack was coming.

"You're still a begging thief," he says to her, causing the big mutt to whine at him.

Cory is set to climb back down and move toward the pig and goat barn when he catches light in the horse barn. Then it flicks off again. A moment later, he can see someone using a low beam flashlight around the back of the horse barn. One of the horses offers a light whinny. Cory raises his rifle and looks through the scope. Before he can see the flashlight bearer, the person disappears around the corner of the cattle barn. He climbs down and jogs to the barn, earning a rustling of cattle hooves in the cement feed lot. As he rounds the corner, a feminine squeal of surprise erupts from the person he runs into.

"What the hell are you doing out here so late?" he asks Paige, who is completely startled by him. His shift is over in a few hours, the time being nearly two a.m.

She has a dark wool blanket wrapped around her shoulders. It looks like an old Army blanket that Doc had bought in surplus over the years and had stored in the basement. They are warm and

263

efficient, and the family takes them often when they go on runs in the cold season to stay warm in the truck. She flicks off the small flashlight and continues to stare at him with big, wide eyes.

"Everything all right, Red?" he probes.

"Um…yeah…yes. Everything's fine," she says.

"Why are you walking around out here?" he asks with concern.

"I was looking for you," she confesses and pulls her blanket tighter. "I woke up and couldn't go back to sleep. I've been waiting for you to get done with your shift."

"What's wrong?" Cory asks, his concern growing.

"Nothing's wrong," she says and looks at her feet.

"Then what is it? Why do you need me?"

She chuckles softly. "I wish I knew the answer to that."

"What…?" he tries to ask her another question, but Paige hurls herself at him.

She presses her mouth against his and sinks her fingers into his hair. Cory is at first stunned but recovers a moment later and returns her kiss. Strange questions and thoughts sail through his mind. Did she have a nightmare? Was she afraid of something and had turned to him for comfort? Is she sleepwalking? None of these things make sense, and he's not about to visit them again since she is pressing her chest against him. Cory pulls her up tightly against his frame and holds her there.

Finally, they separate and Cory is left with more questions than answers.

"Can we go somewhere?" she inquires.

At first, he has no idea what she means. She presses a palm against his chest, searching under his jacket to make a connection with his bare skin. Then it dawns on him that she means somewhere more private.

"Not the cabin," she says. "Simon's still out there."

"John's out here with me on the north hill," he tells her. "He'll see lights in the barn."

"We don't need lights," she says and takes his hand, leading him back into the woods.

Once they are near the area that Cory just ate his dinner in a tree, Paige places her blanket on the ground and stands before him.

"Wait," Cory says. "I don't know if this is a good idea. John could come looking for me or your brother."

She steps closer and presses her mouth again his again, this time with more urgency. Her hands slide up his chest to his shoulders and push his jacket down until it falls to his wrists. Cory leans his rifle against the tree. His jacket hits the ground, and so does hers.

"Wait," he repeats but forgets what he was thinking. He knows this isn't smart. He knows they could be caught. Unfortunately, he can't seem to make his brain form complete thoughts. All he can think about is her small waist in his hands and the way her loose hair is brushing against them, tickling the backs of his knuckles.

"I want you," she whispers huskily against his neck before kissing him there.

That seems to make the most sense, definitely more than any of his stupid questions and hesitations. He sweeps her into his arms and holds her close. Cory drops to his knees with Paige and gently lays her on the blanket. Nothing else seems to matter. She wants him. He always wants her. There's never a time he doesn't. He doesn't want to scare her off, so he keeps his plans for their future together concealed for the time being. But he wants this with Paige every day forever, not just one night here or there when the mood strikes her.

She yanks at his shirt until he pulls it off and balls it up to place it under her head. Cory leans over her, crouches and pulls her sweater up, exposing her stomach. He kisses there, traces her surgical scar with his fingers, then kisses again.

"This might not be a good idea," he says softly. "I don't want to hurt you."

"You won't," she insists, tugging him down on top of her more tightly.

Cory isn't as sure, so he is careful with her, tender and precise in the way he touches her. Paige isn't quite so gentle. She claws at him with a passion that has not been spent in months.

She has lost some weight, which makes it even easier to move her around where he needs her, even though she was never heavy before. His hand skims down over the soft curve of her hip to feel the bones jutting out just slightly. She'll gain some back, he has no doubt, but Paige isn't ever going to be the kind of woman who gains a lot of weight. She is slight and tall, made of fine curves and gentle angles. And she fits so perfectly in his hands. And in his life.

"God, I missed you," he says before kissing her deeply and thoroughly.

He removes her clothing but leaves her sweater on so that she doesn't get cold. He does slide his hand under it to cup her breast, though. He's not going to deprive himself of her if she's actually willing. This total and complete surrender doesn't happen often.

"I missed this, too," she says against his ear.

It bothers Cory that she doesn't say that she's missed him. He wonders briefly before squashing those thoughts if she is just using him for sex and has no real interest in him at all. It's not like she has a lot of other prospects, being stuck on the farm most of the time. He saw her turn quite a few heads over at Dave's camp, so he's glad she didn't move over there like Sam. She belongs wherever he is and not far out of reach. She cries out against his mouth as he slides his hand down between her legs to cup her through her thin pants. He hopes she isn't cold. She feels warm to the touch. She feels fantastic under his hands. She moans when he slips his hand into the waistband of her pants and pushes downward through her fortress of unnecessary clothing articles. Then he forgets all burdensome thoughts and is completely consumed by a fire as red as her hair until they are, a short time later, lying spent and exhausted in each other's arms under a full moon.

Neither of them speaks for a while, and they just stare up at the stars. It feels so right having her lying in the crook of his shoulder and sprawled on his chest. This is where she should always fall asleep. However, Cory knows they can't fall asleep.

"You with me, Red?" he asks and receives a soft groan in response. Cory chuckles and kisses the top of her head before allowing his fingers to drag through her long locks. "We need to get you back."

"Why? I just want to sleep here," she says with a drowsy, scratchy voice.

"That would be fine with me, but I don't think you're ready to tell everyone about us yet."

He feels her stiffen in his arms. Then she sits up and pulls on her jacket. Cory follows and tugs on his shirt and coat, having already dressed from the waist down the second they were done. He hadn't wanted them to be caught unaware by anyone nefarious who could've sneaked onto the farm and into their woods. No sense in being caught with their pants down literally. He jumps to his feet and tugs her gently by the hand.

Cory pulls her up against him and knows instantly that she is doubting her decision to be with him. She isn't so compliant and soft in his arms now.

"Are you ok? I didn't hurt you, did I?" he asks, praying her answer is to the negative.

"No, I'm fine. Just tired. I need to get to bed," she says and pulls free.

She isn't making eye contact. Ten minutes ago, she'd been digging her nails into his back and saying his name as she begged him for more. This may have been a mistake. He should've insisted on some sort of a commitment from her that she can't just sleep with him without offering more. He wants more.

"Let me walk you back to the house," he offers and takes her arm.

"I can manage," she says, rejecting him.

This doesn't sit well with Cory. He knows this routine; he's performed it with other women with whom he hadn't wanted a relationship. Maybe karma is about to kick him in the teeth where

Paige is concerned. Of course, he doesn't believe in superstition. He's a man of action and planning, not whimsical silliness and fantasy.

"I don't want you to trip and fall and get hurt," he says. "I insist, ma'am."

He tries to keep it light since he is getting a very strong impression from Paige that she just wants to keep their relationship to the occasional casual sex encounter. Not telling the family about them is the same as lying. It doesn't sit well with him, especially because of Simon. He takes her arm and leads her from the woods.

When they get to the other end of the horse barn facing the house, she pulls free.

"I've got it from here," Paige says, still not looking directly at him. She takes the blanket from him, leans up and presses a kiss to his cheek no more passionate than the kind Ari would offer.

Cory holds his rifle behind his back with his hand to secure it from falling forward. Then he snatches her around the waist with his other arm and pulls her up against his chest. He captures her mouth in a searing kiss that leaves her breathless and panting when it's over. No more being taciturn and reserved. Her color is high once again, and she regards him with doe-like gray eyes. Cory grins lopsidedly.

"Cory! Careful," she warns and slips from his grasp. "Jesus, someone's going to see."

"We're the only ones up. Sleep well," he says as she turns to go. "Think about me."

She waves her hand behind her dismissively and trots to the back porch in a rush to be away from him. Cory chuckles and leans against the barn. It's a good thing a band of heathens hadn't come to the farm to kill everyone while he was in the woods with Paige making love because he probably wouldn't have stopped. She has a very distracting effect on him, and there doesn't seem to be a damn thing he can do about it.

He pulls a cigarette out of the cargo pocket of his pants and lights up. Damn Dog returns and sits by his side quietly. Then she lies down there and looks up at him with big brown eyes. He can no more understand what she wants than Paige.

"You women are a pain in the ass," he tells his dog. The kids still call her Shadow, but she'll always be Damn Dog to him. Cory squats and scratches behind her ears the way she enjoys.

He takes a drag on his cigarette and can still smell Paige on his skin. He just wants to climb the back porch stairs, enter the house, go upstairs to the second floor, and crawl into bed with her. Paige's scent is heady and sweet like fruit mixed with lavender. He's not so foolish as to think this is coming from the perfume he found for her. This is just her own personal scent, and he'd like nothing better than to bury his nose in her neck and hair and crash out for about ten hours. That isn't about to happen any sooner than the ten hours of straight sleep. They've been going on nothing lately. Planting season, Derek being down, hunting for jerkoffs, and running the clinic days in town are taking their toll on all of them.

Damn Dog's head raises instantly and then lowers again more slowly.

"Hey," John says as he approaches from his south. "Trying to burn down the barn?"

Cory chuckles and John follows suit.

"Want one?" Cory offers a cigarette.

John chuckles quietly. "Are you kidding? The boss's sense of smell is off the charts right now. She can barely stand the smell of just me lately."

"Well, I can't say as I blame her on that one," Cory harasses.

"True," John agrees good-naturedly. "Thanks but no thanks. She'd kick my butt. Then lecture me on the dangers. Not worth it."

"Heading in for the night?" he asks his friend.

John nods and replies, "Yeah, I saw the kitchen light come on. Kelly's on his way out."

"After he raids the fridge."

"You know that's right," John agrees, and Cory laughs.

They stand there another moment before John states without preamble, "Simon's your best friend, Cory."

It takes him a moment to catch on to what John is saying. Then he swallows hard and stamps out his cigarette.

"I know," he says quietly, his voice full of guilty treason.

"Do you love her?" his friend asks.

Cory takes a moment but finally nods and replies, "Yes."

"Be careful there," John says and walks away without another word.

Cory sits on an overturned bucket while Damn Dog remains in her position at his feet. He's not sure if John saw him kissing her in this very spot or if John has just put two and two together on his own. John is perceptive when it comes to situations like this, a lot more perceptive than his brainy wife. He also knows John would never tell anyone. It doesn't make Cory feel any better about it. This isn't going to work forever. Secrecy and lies always turn sour in the end. He doesn't want it to come to that. They will eventually have to confront this head on and deal with their feelings for each other. Cory has been so busy and preoccupied with other things lately that he hasn't had the time to speak with Paige privately or very often. Actually, he'd mistakenly thought that she was avoiding him lately, but maybe he was just being paranoid. Winning her over is proving a difficult task, especially when her brother is constantly making sure they don't spend time alone together. Simon is his biggest obstacle. He's also, like John pointed out, his best friend, and Cory doesn't want to hurt him. Simon doesn't deserve that.

The kitchen light turns back off a moment later, and Kelly joins him at the barn, relieving John for the night.

"Sleepin' on the job?" his brother razzes.

"I learned from the best," Cory gives it right back.

Kelly reaches down and pets his dog. She's in love with his brother and immediately rolls to her back to earn a petting on her stomach. Kelly just chuckles.

"Anything exciting happen tonight?" Kelly asks.

Cory almost chokes. "Nope. Nothing."

"Good. We've had enough drama the last six months to last years. It'd be nice if assholes just kept to themselves for about the next decade."

"No shit," Cory remarks. "Not likely to happen."

"No, probably not," Kelly agrees and stands again.

Simon joins them a moment later and seems winded.

"Sorry I'm late," he says hastily and adjusts his baseball cap. Then he bends and ties the laces on his gym shoes.

"Lazy bastard," Kelly teases with wry humor.

"Sorry, Cor," Simon apologizes.

This makes Cory feel like an even bigger piece of cow turd. He just had sex with Simon's sister in secret, in the woods like an animal, no less, and his friend is apologizing for being exactly two minutes late for his shift.

"No prob, man," Cory says, guilt washing over him.

"Should I take the perimeter by the road?" Simon asks Kelly.

Kelly points at him and nods. "You got it. I'll handle the barns and the woods."

Simon jogs away, and Cory feels bad for being relieved because he doesn't want to face his friend anymore tonight. The shame is staggering.

"Luke said he wants to start on night watch with us," Kelly tells him, breaking his train of thought.

"Sure. We've been working with him for months. I mean, he's a general's son. I'd say he can handle some night watch duties."

"He's a hell of a good shot," Kelly says.

"So is G," Cory adds with appreciation.

Kelly smiles and says, "Hell, that little shit only has to give someone one of those nasty looks like she gives when someone brings up Robert. They'll run scared shitless."

Cory laughs and nods. "Yeah, I don't think she likes her dad too well."

"Does anyone?"

"True enough," Cory says. "I heard you talking with Doc yesterday about making another trip up there soon. Why do you want to?"

"I don't. Herb does. He intends to meet with the doctors there and discuss doctor shit or whatever. He also wants to make sure shit's getting done right and that nobody's being mistreated."

"Why would he think people would be? They left the bunker, too. They came to Knox of their own accord."

Kelly shrugs. "Probably knows his son all too well."

"I didn't get the impression that he was going to start treating people badly, though. He needs them. Can't start a new country without people in it."

"I could. Sometimes I'd like to turn the farm into an island and lock out the rest of the world," Kelly admits with a frown.

"Yeah, lot of assholes out there," Cory says, getting a nod from his brother. Kelly has so much responsibility on his shoulders now with Hannah and Mary and the eventual running of the farm. Cory's not sure he could handle that much pressure. "Mary's going to need to find a husband someday, though."

"What the hell? Are you trying to give me a damn ulcer?"

Cory laughs at his brother's distress.

"She's adorable already. Just wait till the dudes come knocking for her when she's of age."

"I'll punch you in the throat right now," Kelly warns with a lopsided grin.

"All right, all right," Cory lets up with a smile of his own.

"We need to find these highwaymen assholes," Kelly reminds him.

"We will," Cory promises.

"We aren't going down like a bunch of punks," his brother rants angrily. "That's bullshit. They wounded one of ours and killed two of Dave's. Speaking of, he called over. We're going to Nashville. It's confirmed."

"Are you going this time?"

"Not sure," Kelly answers. "With Derek down, I'd like to. Hannah gets upset, but we need to find these idiots and kill them."

When the women and kids aren't around, they can be themselves and not talk in code about subjects like killing people that would upset them. Some of the women like Reagan don't get upset.

"John and I can go without you," he says.

Kelly nods. "Yeah, we'll see. Dave said he'd send men over. K-Dog and Paul also said they'd come over for a few days. Dave wants to find them just as bad. He had a soft spot for Annie. Bullshit she got killed. Guess she really looked up to Dave like a big brother, and now she's gone. Dave's got skin in this game, too."

"Whatever you decide, man. You wanna' hang back here, that's cool. Either way, same result."

He bumps his fist to his brother's.

"Go get some sleep," Kelly orders. "We've got a busy week ahead of us."

"Nothin' new there," Cory says and turns toward the big house with his dog in tow.

"Goin' the wrong way, bro'. You moved to the cabin, remember?" Kelly reminds him.

"All that pot I smoked in college," Cory jokes and waves to his brother, leaving him at the barn. Cory never went to college. He wasn't a book nerd college type like Paige or her brother. The only subject he liked was history, and usually, he ended up getting his own books from the library to read more detailed accounts of what was skimmed over in school.

He doesn't want to tell his brother the reason he was heading to the house instead of their cabin. Cory was walking toward the big house out of instinct to be near her. Their secret is becoming more difficult to keep with each passing day. He'd like to shout it from the highest hilltop on the farm and be done with it. He doesn't want to hurt his friend, though, or any other family members by their deception and secrecy and their clandestine meetings. Mostly, he's afraid he'll lose her if he pushes too hard, and that would be an indomitable mistake. She's been through so much that Cory doesn't want to be just one more disappointment for Paige. Her friend was killed, both parents, she constantly worries about Simon. He wants to be something good in her life, and until she can see that he is, he'll have to be patient. He can never lose her. He almost did once, and it nearly wrecked his world. There's no way he can let that happen now. He has to win her. She has to see him for what he really is and not what she's heard about him or fabricated on her own. He's going to have to do something drastic with her and soon before he ends up without her *and* his best friend.

Chapter Nineteen
Simon

Another week goes by, and they still have no more leads than they did before regarding the whereabouts of the highwaymen or the others who ran over Derek. John's frustration has been off the charts. He wants to go on runs every single day, but they are in the middle of the planting season, clinic days have to be upheld for the people of their town, and the farm still needs to be run efficiently. They are all feeling overwhelmed by the lack of clues that will lead to removing those people from the earth. Simon doesn't enjoy killing people, has trouble sleeping at night because of the men he has killed, and would rather never have to do it again, but his logical side knows that they must take these men's lives. If they do not, those men could make their way to the farm and their town eventually. For all they know, the highwaymen may already know about their town and are lying in wait for the right time to strike. They have no idea how many are with the highwaymen group, either, so it makes them even more dangerous. They could have an entire battalion. They could have enough men to overrun the family. John often warns them not to be too confident. He has also ordered a refresher course on evasive maneuvers, tactical training, and shooting, which has been perfect for G and Lucas and even Huntley, too. Luke is now taking a few night shifts each week to help out. He seems like a pretty cool guy, even though he is quiet and mostly just hangs around with his little sister. Simon understands why John feels the extra training is necessary. Their adversary is unknown to them. Dave's men have also been hunting down their enemy. They lost two of their own because of the people who ran over Derek. They report in nearly every day on what areas they have covered and where they have searched. Just yesterday, they found an SUV, black with a dent on the front, left quarter panel that could have been from hitting Derek. It was located about ten miles from where the attack happened. Simon's not sure if it's the same one, but Henry had gone with Dave to check it out and had confirmed that he believed it to be the same vehicle. They found a lot of blood in the back seat, which is where the man was that Simon shot. Now they know that finding the black SUV is a dead-end, if it is, indeed, the same one that hit Derek. There were no people near it as it had been abandoned alongside the road empty of gas. There weren't fresh tracks anywhere near it to pick up their trail and hunt them down. Dave's men had run a five click perimeter checking for signs of them. Simon guesses that whoever left the SUV had a vehicle traveling with him that they were able to transfer into. It could very well be Henry's stolen truck that aided them in their escape again.

They have wrestled with the idea that the highwaymen are gone, moved on from the area since it has been weeks since they've heard of an attack. However, without the modern communication conveniences like telephones, they have no way of knowing for sure if they have moved on or if they have simply widened their hunting parameters, and the family and their contacts within the different communities just haven't heard of any more encounters. And Derek's attack could've been by people moving through that city never to return again. The black SUV was found ten miles south, so it is a possibility that they just kept on going. They haven't found any proof that the highwaymen's attacks are connected with Derek's or the deaths of Dave's people, Bruce and Annie. Henry's pick-up truck that they stole, however, has yet to be recovered, which leads them to believe that those same people still have it. There are just so many unanswered questions with both sets of criminals out there.

276

Today is a typical clinic day in town. They are setting up and getting ready for patients. Even Reagan felt well enough to work, although he and Doc had assured her that they didn't need her. There are many pregnant patients coming in today for their monthly "tummy checks" as Doc calls them. Herb and Reagan keep a close eye on all of their pregnant cases because they know just how dangerous pregnancy and birth can be now. Simon does, too. Obstetrics is not something he would've wanted to go into if he'd ever become a doctor. He was meant more for microscope work than patient interaction and certainly not baby delivery. Losing their patient, Mia, had been hard to deal with. Their defeat as doctors had been tremendous. Now they are raising her orphaned son. He knows Reagan and Doc carry a lot of guilt because of her. They don't speak of it, certainly not Doc, but Simon knows it lurks in the shadows of their doctor consciences. Even Doc has doubled down on his obstetrics studies and how they can better handle emergency births when they arise. The three have them have been formulating a plan so that they can perform emergency C-sections.

John, Cory and Paige also tagged along to offer help. His sister is getting stronger every day and wants to make up for lost time by helping as much as possible, although nobody expects her to. Cory is with them to offer extra security, and also to sit in on a meeting with Thomas's group to re-question them about their freeway attack. There has to be something they've missed.

"Good, Dave's here," John says and exits the clinic.

It is still early in the morning, the clinic not yet open for business, and they are unloading supplies from the truck into the storage room. When they go on runs looking for those men who hurt Derek, they are also picking up a lot of supplies. They are returning to Clarksville in a few days to finish raiding that hospital where they found the materials for Derek's cast. They have gone there twice since.

"I didn't know Dave was coming," Simon casually remarks to Reagan, who is helping him stock shelves.

"Yeah, he's bringing all the pregnant women from their town," she explains and hands him another small box. "We're doing a combined women's clinic day today. Sam's uncle doesn't have a lot of experience in obstetrics or gynecology, so he's coming to learn. It'll be good for you, too. I have no idea what sorts of medical situations these women may have with their pregnancies. Gestational diabetes, hypertension, placenta previa. Who knows what the hell we're about to see? Guess we'll find out."

"Oh, good," he says, hoping to gain experience. "How many are there?"

"Not sure," Reagan says. "I think at least a dozen. They're not all from Henry's farm. I mean, what the hell? They aren't rabbits. Most of them are from their nearby town and some of the neighboring farms."

Simon smiles at her crassness. "Hendersonville?"

"Yeah, or what's left of it. They have a small community there that they try to help when they can. Everyone knows about her uncle, so people have been coming to them for medical care. I guess Sam's uncle is comfortable with treating kids since that was his specialty, but he doesn't know shit about pregnant women."

"He could study you," Simon offers with a grin.

"No, thanks," she comes back with immediately. "I'm taking care of my own pregnancy. Nobody's going there, if you know what I mean."

"Well, eventually…"

She hits him with a malevolent glare and wags her finger, "Not even then, mister. It'll be Grandpa and me. That's it. I don't want a bunch of nursemaids and family members in there. It's bad enough it's even happening at all. Gimme a break."

Simon chuckles. He has no doubt that Reagan will be in total and complete control of this birth. She's like that with everything. And he's relieved, if he's being honest. He hadn't really wanted to be in the delivery room with her. That just seems a little awkward. Besides, with Reagan, someone could catch a foot to the face when the pain starts.

Sam!" Reagan exclaims with a warm smile. When she smiles, Simon can understand why John wanted her so much. She's so pretty and young looking. It just doesn't happen often.

He swings around to find Samantha behind him carrying a wooden crate full of supplies. He hadn't known she was going to be present, or he would've stayed home on the farm. She hasn't come around the family for almost two months, even though this isn't their first joint venture in a shared clinic day with Dave's group.

"I'm so glad you came!" Reagan says and shoves a box into his hands so that she can hug her young muse. She pulls back just a second later. Contact still isn't easy for Reagan. "We've got a lot to do today. It's good that you're here. Say hello, Simon."

Reagan's dictate surprises him, and without hesitation, Simon obeys her, "Hello, Samantha."

She does not offer him a kind greeting in return but shrugs and says to Reagan, "I heard Uncle Scott was coming and bringing the pregnant women. That's the only reason I came. I knew you guys would be super busy."

Reagan's face falls just slightly, but she recovers and says, "Great. That's great that you're offering to help us. You'll be in high demand today. We're mostly just doing tummy checks on late termers, and cervix checks on the early ones. Then there's blood pressure monitoring, that sort of thing. We don't have any charts on your uncle's patients. Do you know if he does?"

Sam shakes her head, "No, I don't think so. We haven't got that far yet. We're still working on setting up the clinic over there. It's a lot of work, and it's not going so well."

"Yeah, that's tough. It's hard to get the supplies we need now. Not like we can just flip through a catalog and order a portable INR testing machine from the supply company. Everything has to be found now. But it will be good when you guys do get set up," Reagan agrees. "Why don't you get ready to start some charts, and I'll have one of Dave's men or your uncle help me finish here. Simon, go with her and help. That's a lot of writing for just one person."

He hesitates for a mere second, gets the look of wrath from Reagan, and nods, "Yes, ma'am."

Simon pulls down a stack of clipboards and follows Sam from the storeroom. Going down the hall, he passes Doc, who must also stop to hug and greet Sam. Everyone is grateful for her help and overwhelmingly happy that she's here with them. Simon wishes that he could share that sentiment. It is so much easier to tolerate, his loss of her, when he doesn't have to see her.

"We'll just want to get their names and as much medical history…" he starts and is interrupted.

"I don't need your help," she blurts. "I've been working here as long as you."

"Right, sorry," he apologizes uncomfortably. "It's good that you're here to help, though. It'll make this go a lot smoother. Heck, they always complain that I don't write as neatly as you."

"Look, I'm not here for any other reason other than to help the family and my uncle and these women."

"I didn't say…"

"Don't think I came here to see you."

This hits hard. He doesn't want her to be so hateful with him, but then again, what did he expect from her? Smiles and sunshine and an offer to draw a lovely sketch for him? He rejected her. Simon knows this. It doesn't soften the blow anymore knowing he did it because it was the right thing to do. He can see the pain in her blue eyes when she looks at him. He knows he caused this. It makes him sick to think of her like this, but Simon also realizes he can't go back on his word. He can never have Sam. His own guilt would eat him alive first.

"No, I wouldn't," he admits. "Sorry. I just wanted to say that I was glad you came. I…I'm glad you're here."

She snorts and walks ahead of him. Simon catches up as they collect a stack of blank sheets of paper at the front desk.

"You're only glad I'm here so that you don't have to write out all these charts."

"No, that's not what I meant. That's not true. I do have to admit, though, it does help. At least nobody will be forced to decipher my chicken scratches," he says, trying his hand at teasing. Sam whips her head to the side to send him a nasty look. Teasing isn't going to work. That's not really him anyway. He's not Cory or John, who are both funny and charming. He's a nerd with no female experience whatsoever, and it shows in a cringe-worthy way when he tries to be cool.

"Your writing is fine," she says.

He tries at just being kind instead of funny. He doesn't like the tension between them. "I'm no artist. I don't have the dexterity to be so neat and elegant."

"Look," she says, turning to look up at him. "Let's just try to avoid each other today, 'kay? I have no desire to be near you, and I'm sure you feel the same. So, let's not try to pretend otherwise."

"That's not true," he says with a frown of growing concern. He certainly doesn't feel that way about Sam. As a matter of fact, he's been miserable without her company. She was his friend. She just unfortunately also happened to be a friend he couldn't stop lusting after like some sort of pervert.

"Whatever you say, Simon," she tells him. "You could've fooled me."

"You're the one who left," he says, stepping to the side to block her from exiting the receptionist's desk area.

"And you're the one that forced me to," she snaps and slides past him.

The feel of her brushing against the front of him has a staggering impact on his senses, and he is left standing there feeling like a fool. He recovers and grabs a pen.

They go outside, finding many women sitting on the street curb, the front porch to the practice, and in any available chairs talking with one another and waiting to get into the clinic. Simon and Sam split up and start making notes on single sheets of paper that will be transferred into a file for each woman. He collects as much of their medical history as he can and moves on to the next. It doesn't take long before the doctors are seeing patients. He joins in with Reagan since Doc is working with Sam's uncle, showing him the ropes, so to speak. It takes them three hours, but they manage to get the pregnant women through the clinic. There were a few that had minor complications like high blood pressure and one with a heart arrhythmia that will be monitored by the docs. Reagan notated the one with the heart condition that she treated and handed the chart over to Scott since it was a woman from their town. Simon learned a lot from his mentor. She is thorough and professional and even seemed to have a calming effect on her patients today. Many asked after her own growing bump, but Reagan had simply ignored them and redirected her own questions back at them. She seemed reluctant to acknowledge her own pregnancy. Simon's not sure, but Reagan doesn't act like she is too happy about her pregnant state. He doesn't understand why that would be, though. She and John are obviously in love, and they are both great parents to their orphaned son, Jacob. Most of the time, Reagan puzzles him. Most of the time, most women do. Sometimes his own sister does.

Their day is long from over, though, because they must still see their regular patients from town who need care and require their help. Sam and her uncle stay on to be of assistance. Doc has ordered Simon to shadow her uncle, who is going to see the children that come into the practice since pediatrics was his area of study. Simon makes notes like he usually does in a leather-bound journal. He always reviews them later on the same day and throughout the week to supplement his regular medical studies. Reagan teases him that he just started his residency a few years sooner than most medical school grads. Doc is convinced that Simon's hands-on work at the clinic is better than anything else anyway. He still has many more courses to go before he'll ever be a doctor, but Simon likes the work and is grateful for the opportunities he's had since he came to the farm. He enjoys helping people, especially the ones who aren't shooting at them, and the clinic affords him the chance to do good works. If he hadn't ever landed on the McClane farm, Simon really doesn't know what he would be doing out there. It has given him a sense of direction and a purposeful education in his life. He knows that Sam once felt the same and wonders if she still does.

Sam brings a small boy who lives in town into the exam room. He is clearly frightened, but her uncle is great with the younger patients. He was definitely cut out to be a pediatrician.

"Suture removal," Scott says. "Would you like to do it or assist, Simon?"

"Oh, um, whatever you'd like, Doctor," he says before setting the boy's chart on the counter.

"Have you done the procedure before?"

Simon nods, "Yes, sir."

"Then you can remove, and I'll just observe," Scott offers, to which Simon nods.

The child is rather hysterical, but with Sam's guidance and the fact that children love her, Simon is able to remove the little boy's stitches without him screaming bloody murder. This is definitely not his first time performing this procedure. He's done it countless times since so many people in town and on their own farm have been injured, shot, stabbed and wounded over the last four years. His own shoulder stab wound has finally healed completely. He's grateful that he had such excellent doctors take care of the wound. Who knows what would've happened if he hadn't had their skillset available? He could be living with ruined tendons and incorrectly healed muscles and ligaments.

Within minutes, the kid is running back to his big sister, who is his legal guardian. There are many of these orphan type situations in their town, likely in every town.

"Good job," Scott says. "I think that was our last patient."

"I'll clean up," Sam volunteers.

Simon jumps in to say, "I'll help."

"I don't need help," Sam blurts.

"Oh, don't be silly, munchkin," Scott corrects her and rubs the top of Sam's head. "Take the help. I'll go and start the other room we used and see where the other doctors are in finishing up for the day."

He leaves a moment later with a stack of patient folders and closes the door behind him.

She glowers at Simon, turns her back to him and begins sanitizing the room.

"Does…does your uncle know about us?" he asks hesitantly.

She snorts through her pert nose and offers a shrill laugh. "Yeah, I love going around advertising to people that I got jilted. That's always a great conversation starter."

Her words cut him like a knife. "You weren't jilted."

She scoffs loudly.

"Everybody has secrets they don't wish to share," Sam informs him.

Simon scowls with uncertainty. What does she mean by this?

"You weren't jilted, Sam. I just wanted you to be happy," he tries to explain. He'll never be able to make her or anyone else understand, not fully.

"Oh! Well, you did a great job," she remarks snidely.

"I never could've made you happy," he admits with defeat. Why did her uncle leave them alone? Simon wishes that he would've volunteered faster to go and clean the other exam room before her uncle did so.

"Guess we'll never know," she mutters angrily and swipes a wet rag across the countertop.

"Look, I've been thinking…" he starts but is interrupted.

"I doubt that."

Simon gnashes his teeth together to keep himself from saying anything untoward, "As I was saying, I've been thinking about this situation a lot. I feel bad that you left the farm. You're clearly not happy over there at Dave's camp."

"I'm perfectly happy, thank you very much," she responds in a haughty tone.

"I think we both know that's not true, Sam."

She levels him with a look filled with annoyance and something else, perhaps hatred. He doesn't blame her since he's been hating himself a lot lately, too.

284

He continues on as if she isn't staring him down like she wishes she had the ability to turn him to dust with those flashing blue eyes, "I could move into town. I'll take Paige and live in town here. It would be closer to the clinic to cover medical emergencies. You could move out to the farm with your uncle. I'm sure Cory would give you two the cabin, and Cory could move into the house again."

"How convenient," she says with a bad attitude.

Simon pauses, goes to say something and stops. Is she being sarcastic? He's not always sure. Women are a puzzle most of the time for him, so it figures that Sam should certainly not break that mold. She has always been a big mystery, especially when she is behaving like this. He has been considering a move, though. Moving his sister into town would also keep her away from Cory, although Paige seems to be steering clear of his friend lately. He's actually been quite content with that situation for a change.

"Are you...are you angry? Did you not like that suggestion?" he asks, treading lightly.

"You are the world's biggest hypocrite, Simon Murphy."

Simon's brow pinches with confusion, and he shakes his head. "I don't understand. I'm offering you an alternative."

"No, you've obviously heard that I've been spending time with Henry and that I like him. That's the reason for the offer. You can't stand it that you can't control me anymore. Too bad! I've also been spending time with other men on Henry's farm, too. Are you going to ban me from speaking with all men or just the ones you're jealous of?"

Simon is stuck on pause, temporarily in information overload. She's spending time with men? In what manner? Does she mean that they are lovers, friends, acquaintances, pals, good buddies? He hopes for the latter.

"What the heck's going on with you and Henry?" he demands, feeling his heart rate accelerate and his temper beginning to rise.

Sam actually looks surprised. She stares at her feet. "Oh. I thought you heard something."

"Like what?" Simon asks, his control slipping just slightly.

"Nothing," she evades and turns her back to him again. She begins stuffing items into their storage crate as quickly as possible.

"What's going on between you and Henry?" he repeats, his fingers curling into a fist.

Sam goes to the door carrying the crate and attempts to open it. Simon is right there and slams it shut before it separates more than a few inches from the jamb. He keeps his hand flat on the door, blocking it from being opened again.

"I don't owe you an explanation," she mumbles, her eyes darting to his. This time there is less anger and more uneasiness in her expression.

He boldly laughs as if he finds her humorous. "Right. Sure you don't. I want to know what's going on over there. Isn't your uncle keeping an eye on you at all? I'm going to need to speak with him."

"Excuse me?" she demands. "You aren't speaking with him about me, Mr. High and Mighty. Or anyone else! It's none of your business. You have got to be kidding me. This is outrageous."

"It is my business. It's the whole family's business. You are our business, Miss Samantha."

"You gave up the right to know anything at all about me when you rejected me, Simon. So back off!" she says, her voice rising in pitch.

"We're friends, and I care…"

"Oh, no we're not. Friends don't hurt one another, not on purpose. No way. We aren't friends. Not anymore."

This stings. Actually, it cuts deep if he's being honest. He's always considered her a very good friend, sometimes even more than Cory. Being around Sam was always different than hanging out with Cory. She's more tender and sweet. He shares things with her that he doesn't with his male friends on the farm, or at least he used to. She always gave him good advice. He misses her kind and delicate demeanor, her intellect. She was always so amiable and gentle. Perhaps not today, though, or right in this moment.

286

Simon swallows hard and says, "I still consider you my friend. I wish you wouldn't say that."

Sam looks at the crate in her arms. When she raises her eyes to meet his, there are unshed tears in them. It breaks Simon's heart to see her so tormented and to know that he is the one causing it when all he wants to do is make her happy.

She shakes her head and says, "It doesn't matter, Simon. You and I are through. I don't want you in my life in that way, not anymore. You can't be a part of my decisions. You can't give me advice and pretend like we're friends anymore. It doesn't work like that."

"That's ridiculous. If you continue on with whatever is going on between yourself and Henry, I'll be forced to intervene."

"Ha! You will not do any such thing."

Her sad eyes are replaced with the fiercely angry ones again.

He narrows his own eyes at Sam, hoping to intimidate her. Then he warns, "Don't force me to."

"And what are you going to do? Shoot him? Snipe him from afar?"

He hadn't thought of that, but it might be a viable option if this Henry jerk keeps snooping around after Sam. Simon knew he didn't like that guy. He should've let him bleed out. He is an untrustworthy snake.

She is still rambling, but he really doesn't want to hear what she's saying, "Henry is a nice, kind man. He gave me a place to live without question when I had nowhere else to go. He took in my uncle. He took me in…"

"Gee, I wonder why he performed such a noble deed?" he asks with spite and jams a hand onto his hip to keep from shaking some sense into her.

"Because he is nice. Nice, Simon. Unlike you!" she spouts off in his face, standing on her tiptoes, her sleek ponytail bobbing around behind her.

"Hey," he warns and points at her. "Don't push me."

"You are unbelievable, Simon. You don't speak for me. You don't say who I can be interested in. You don't own me."

"Now you're 'interested' in him?" he asks, using air quotes. Sam just laughs maniacally. There is a light trace of seething rage in her mocking tone, too.

"See? You don't get it. You don't have a right to know."

He tries to speak but is cut off again.

"And someday, when I choose to marry someone, you'll have no say in that, either. My uncle will. And he's not going to take advice from you because your opinion on the matter will not make a damn bit of difference."

"Don't be crude," he reprimands for the swearing. He never should've let her leave the farm. That was idiotic. She's using foul language, dating men- or whatever's going on over there. Now she's talking about marriage, too? Simon feels sick. He also feels angry and helpless and on the border between violence and hatred, but not toward Samantha. He wishes Hannah was here; she'd know how to handle Sam and talk her off this ledge of stupidity and insanity.

"Don't tell me what to do," she comes right back. "I'm going to continue to hang around Henry and whomever I please, and there's not a *damn* thing you can do about it."

"Now you're just being immature and defiant like a spoiled brat that needs to be spanked," Simon warns with fury.

"So? Henry doesn't seem to mind."

Sam grabs his hand and yanks it away from the door. Then she flees the room in a huff of righteous temper. Simon slaps his open palm as hard as he can against the wall, causing it to rattle. The sound reverberates loudly in the quiet calmness of their clinic. People are probably wondering about the source of such a noise, but he doesn't care. His hand stings, but it is not enough to cool his ire. He wants to hurt something, or someone, namely Henry or any other man over there making a play for her. He knows nothing about any of them. They could be just as bad as his aunt's group with whom he and Sam had been traveling. That situation had turned out so badly that many times he wasn't sure if he and Sam and Huntley and his

288

twin brother were going to make it out alive. Their dark past, so full of bad memories and painful ghosts, is the sole reason he cannot allow himself to even consider being with Samantha. But that doesn't mean he wants to see her abused again by someone. He just wants to keep her safe. His own impotence in this situation is frustrating. He cannot vet these men who will vie for her hand. It disgusts him.

Is she serious about Henry or any of the other men on that farm? Is she really considering marriage? She's only been gone about three months. Surely she has not found someone that soon. He wants her to be happy, but Henry is not the man for her. Maybe he and Cory should swing by over there on a run or a scouting mission in the next few days. It couldn't hurt.

They join John and Cory outside of the clinic once everything has been cleaned and sanitized and packed into the back of their truck and Dave's. Doc stays behind to finish some paperwork he wants to get done, but the rest go as a group to the city building where the town sheriff and his deputies work. Thomas and a few of the people from his band of attack survivors are waiting there for them, so John suggests since the weather is good that they sit outside. They gather around the picnic tables that have been pushed together. These, along with the new jungle gym being built by the teenagers in town for the little kids, are new additions to what they are going to name a park. It isn't much yet, but it's a good start. The wall surrounding their town should be completed by the end of summer, and this will give the people living within its walls a place to spend time, a safe place to gather, and most importantly an area where the young children can play outdoors and still feel protected.

Simon and Cory stand back while John, Dave and Thomas sit at the picnic tables with his group and review the maps John brought from home. John is bloodthirsty. So is Kelly and Dave. There is a barely leashed feral look about all of them lately that only seems to be building in intensity. Cory always has this look, so it is difficult to tell whether he is even more bothered by the attack on Derek or if he is just getting antsy for his next kill. Simon notices that Sam stands on the opposite side of the picnic table from them with her uncle. He has to force himself not to gawk at her like a moron.

Tessa, from Thomas's group, approaches Cory and raises her stubby arms to Cory until he picks her up. Then she actually grins and clings on like a baby monkey. Her guardian, Rachel, also approaches and insinuates herself between Simon and Cory.

"Excuse me, ma'am," Simon apologizes and steps to his left closer to Paige. His sister looks miffed. He shrugs and goes back to paying attention to the meeting.

John says, "So this is the area here where we found you guys." Thomas nods. "And which direction were they going when they left?"

Thomas points on the map. "East. They left us and went east."

"How many were there?" Dave asks.

"I sure wish I knew for sure, Sergeant Winters," Thomas answers. "It all happened so fast. I wish I had more. It was such a blur. Maybe seven or eight men?"

Thomas's son jumps in to say, "No way, Dad. It was way more, Sergeant Winters. It was more like fifteen or so."

"Is that a more accurate number?" John asks.

Thomas shrugs then nods. "Maybe. Like I said, it was so confusing and fast. We didn't have a lot of time to think and get a good look around. My first thought was to get my family to safety."

John nods. "I understand. What kinds of weapons did they have?"

"I told you. Handguns and long guns."

"Can you be more specific?" Dave asks.

Rachel steps forward and says, "Shotguns. I saw two of them had shotguns. I know what those are because my dad used to have one for hunting."

"Good," John praises.

They've spoken with these people before, but it's always worth it to try again. Maybe someone might remember some small detail or another that they didn't before.

290

"And their vehicles? What were they driving?" Dave asks. "Do any of you remember seeing a black SUV, like a Suburban or a Tahoe, something like that?"

They shake their heads.

Thomas's son says, "One group jumped out of a pick-up truck. Three or four of them were on motorcycles, even though it was snowy."

"Do you remember the color of the truck?" John presses.

"Dark blue maybe?" his son explains. "The others came in a car. Four or five of them jumped out of that. A dark gray color."

Rachel adds, "And don't forget the white van."

"What white van?" Cory asks her.

"It came after the others. I saw it. They parked farther down the road, but I saw it."

"I didn't see that," his son says.

"This is the first we're hearing about a white van," John says. "How many people got out of it? Women and men or just men?"

She shakes her head before replying, "No, not women. I don't remember seeing any women get out of any of the vehicles. Just all men. I think maybe four or five got out of the van."

John looks to Thomas, his son, and another man they've brought with them, an older man with white hair and eyeglasses.

"I don't remember the van," Thomas says. "But that doesn't mean Rachel didn't see it. It might have been there when I was trying to get people into the woods to safety."

Dave says, "Yeah, probably."

"What all did they take other than food and gas?" Cory asks.

"Um... I don't know what you mean, Cory," Thomas says.

"Did they take other supplies, car parts, anything that would strike you as odd?"

"Yes!" Rachel says, turning to Cory. "They did pop the hood on one of our vehicles. I think they took a hose or something."

"Interesting," he replies.

Rachel smiles up into Cory's face with open admiration. Simon crosses his arms and rolls his eyes with annoyance. Good grief. Everywhere they go, it's the same. His friend just ignores Rachel and bobs Tessa on his hip. Simon's not sure what the connection is between him and the little girl, but she is like this every time they come to town. So is Rachel.

"Ropes, a few boxes of medical supplies we were taking with us, and bungee cords," Thomas says. "They took things like that."

Simon nods knowingly. Those are the types of items they scout when sent on runs, too. Only the McClane clan actually loots abandoned buildings and empty hospitals, not from other, innocent and, usually in most of the cases they've come across, helpless people.

"And you say they didn't rape any of your women?" Dave asks bluntly.

"No, sir," Thomas answers. "None of ours. Of course, many of our women were older or young children. Rachel was probably one of the few they would have...taken advantage of, and she got out with us."

Simon isn't surprised because they've spoken to other people who were also ambushed by the highwaymen and so has Dave's group, and only one of them have reported rapes. So far, the rape scene they encountered is the second one they know of so far. They rob, then they murder. They take what they need, then they get rid of what they don't. It makes him so angry that people like this have to exist on the same planet.

John adds with confusion, "But we all saw the one woman who was clearly raped along the roadside on our way to Fort Knox. She was with your group."

"You did?" Thomas asks, knowing it was his group they saw scattered on the freeway on the road to the Army base.

John nods solemnly.

"I saw her when we went back after they left," Rachel says. "She was in the ditch with the others. I covered her with a sheet. It must've blown off."

"Who?" Thomas asks.

"We'll talk later," Rachel answers him.

292

"That's the only case we've heard of so far of rape, though," John says. "There's a possibility it's happening and, like your group, Thomas, the survivors are too busy fleeing to see it."

"True, but for the most part, they don't seem interested in the women," Dave remarks, to which John agrees.

"Maybe they have their own," John says. "If they have wives or girlfriends, then they might be leaving their women and families behind while they plunder."

"Maybe they're battin' for the other side," Dave remarks without humor.

"A gay mafia of professional thieves and hitmen?" John asks with humor.

"Right, doubtful," Dave says.

"They would've taken Thomas's son," Simon remarks.

"Yeah, true," John agrees.

"Or they don't have women and are operating alone," Cory suggests. "Or they take most of the women they can find with them and have them holed up somewhere that they can't get free. Maybe the woman we saw who was raped put up too much of a fight and they killed her. Perhaps that doesn't happen with most of them. Maybe they just go along with them to stay alive."

"I don't know," John says, his tone suggesting that he's not sure of Cory's theory. "They'll still want women, either by force or by submission."

Simon has to agree with him, but he hopes these men aren't going around the countryside raping women. Just because they haven't heard of it happening more than the two times, doesn't mean it hasn't. Perhaps they were worried about being gone from their base camp for too long, or maybe the others in their group don't agree with it.

"What were they wearing?" John asks.

"Wearing?" Thomas repeats as if he doesn't understand.

"Were their clothes clean, dirty, military issue?" John pushes.

His son says, "No, not military. No camo. Nothing official-looking."

Rachel adds, "But they seemed clean, most of them."

This will let them know if these people have a source of running water and soap and could have a compound nearby from which they are running this operation.

"Were they lean and wiry, hungry-looking?" Dave asks.

"No, not at all," Rachel answers.

Dave asks, "Did you get the impression that they were vagabonds, homeless types or did they say things like, 'we need to get back to base.' Sometimes the things that people say to one another can give us a clue as to their whereabouts."

Thomas shakes his head. He seems to Simon as if he has been deeply traumatized by what happened to them. He doesn't remember much or is blocking it from his memory as a defense mechanism.

"They were mostly just shouting at everyone, terrorizing them," Rachel puts in.

"Do you think they were ex-military like us?" John asks.

Simon knows they are all secretly hoping this isn't true. Nobody wants to think of once honorable men turning so evil, especially not America's men in uniform.

"I don't think so," Rachel says.

Thomas's son butts in to say, "I'm not so sure about that. I think they could've been. They seemed like you guys."

"How?" John presses anxiously.

He pauses a moment before answering, "They just…I don't know, they seemed really well organized and like…they knew hand signals to use and stuff like that."

"And radios. I saw two of them talking into radio thingys," Rachel offers.

"What about their weapons?" Dave repeats their earlier line of questioning. "Did they look like any of ours? Like they woulda' kept them when the country went to shit and took their military weapons with them?"

"Hm, no," his son says. "I don't think they had weapons like yours."

294

John asks, "But they acted like us? They used military language?"

"No, not words or anything. Not that I heard. Just the hand signals I've seen you guys doing."

John looks up at Cory who is standing near him. Then Dave nods to John and stands.

"Well," Dave states, "thanks for talkin' with us again. We just wanna' catch these rats."

"We want the same, Sergeant Winters," Thomas says and shakes Dave's hand. "We've all been praying you find them and handle it. Everyone's counting on it."

Simon walks away with his sister to discuss the meeting while others break into small groups, as well. Cory is stuck with Tessa on his hip and Rachel in his ear.

"What are you guys going to do about this?" his sister asks.

Sam joins them, standing next to Paige. She isn't glaring at him for the time being, so for this small miracle, Simon is thankful.

"They have to be stopped," Simon explains for the hundredth time to his worrisome sister. "They're killing people and taking from them. This can't go on."

"Maybe they'll move on from the area," Paige says with hope. "Maybe they came from somewhere else and hit this area and will move on to another place for a while again."

"And we're supposed to rest on our laurels while they flee?" Simon asks, his anger getting the best of him. "That would be knowingly allowing them to attack more innocent people."

"What if you don't find them?" Sam asks him.

He shakes his head and says, "I think we will."

"What if you can't best them?" Paige says hurriedly before he can continue.

Cory comments as he approaches from behind, "Not best them? Have a little faith, Red."

"*I* have faith in you, Cory," Rachel puts in, earning a sneer from Sam. Simon is surprised by her dirty look. Sam is usually kind to everyone.

"Faith isn't going to get it this time," Paige argues, glaring at him and Cory. "You could both be killed."

"Which is why we're training again," Cory says, sending a pointed expression at Paige. She doesn't wither from it, though. She never backs down from Cory.

"I can tell," Rachel says, taking the opportunity to squeeze Cory's bicep. He just belly laughs.

Simon watches as his sister and Sam send the other young woman dirty looks. He has no idea why they don't like Rachel. She seems nice enough to him.

"Fine!" Paige says in a miff. "Next time you guys go, so do I. I've been trained, so I'm tagging along."

"Me, too!" Sam puts in before anyone can even answer Paige.

Cory laughs, this time with more bellicose guffaws. Tiny Tessa just grins and presses her hand against Cory's cheek. His sister's face is almost humorous; she is so mad Cory is laughing at her.

"You two aren't going with us," Cory bats down.

"You don't get to make that decision," Paige says, walking away toward John. They all follow. He is rolling up his maps and tucking them safely away into his pack. "John, I want to go with you guys on the next scouting mission to find these highwaymen. Sam does, too."

"Uh…" he stammers, obviously picking up on the tension within their group.

"No, way," Cory rebuts again.

"I say no, as well," Simon interjects. "They shouldn't go. It's too dangerous."

"Everything is dangerous, Simon," Sam reminds him, as if he needed her to. He shoots her an aggravated look only to have her raise her stubborn chin into the air.

"Maybe not both couples at the same time," John says casually.

Simon wishes that he wouldn't have phrased it that way. None of them is a couple.

296

"Cory," John says, "you and Paige work well together. You can go with me tomorrow. Simon and Sam, you'll go after them. Sam will be with Dave's men until we meet up like we have been, and then she'll pair with you."

"I'd rather pair with Simon," Paige suggests before he even can. At least his sister sees the reasoning in this.

John slings his pack over his shoulder and pauses a moment before answering, "No, you and Cory work well as a team. Sam and Simon are used to being teamed up. She's an excellent spotter. You don't have the experience with that yet."

Sam opens her mouth to argue but is shut down by John.

"My order stands. Take it or leave it," he says and walks away.

Reagan, who has been sitting quietly at the picnic table rises and says, "Hey, you may not like each other, but at least you get to go. You could be me stuck on the farm, knocked up, and bored."

John leans down and kisses her forehead. "I'll keep you entertained, babe."

Then he kisses her mouth. He doesn't break their kiss but deepens it, slipping an arm around her back and pulling her to him, or at least as close as he can get her since her belly is in the way.

"Gross," Cory says good-naturedly. "We're outta' here."

They turn to go with John's laughter at their backs.

"Geeze," Rachel says as they walk away, leaving John and Reagan behind. "I guess I need to make a trip out to your farm. Sounds pretty romantic out there."

"Nobody is allowed on the farm," Paige informs her with a snobbish air of superiority. It makes Simon wonder at his sister's rudeness.

"Your last name isn't McClane," Rachel points out. "You're still living there."

"That was a different circumstance," Cory states emphatically to put out the fire. "She's right, though. Nobody is allowed to come there, even for a visit. Sorry."

"Then you just have to come to town to see me more often," Rachel hints, not subtly.

Cory places Tessa to her feet and hugs her one last time. "See ya' in a few days, kiddo."

She nods silently and takes Rachel's hand. Then, in a move nobody expects, not even Cory, Rachel leans up and swiftly places a kiss to Cory's mouth. He looks stunned. Simon is, too. Cory doesn't try to prolong the kiss or embrace her as John had with Reagan. He leans back just slightly until Rachel lowers down and backs away. Cory isn't one for public displays of affection, even with his long list of other lovers. This woman is bold, even for Cory's tastes. Simon is also surprised that his friend's eyes immediately dart to Paige. There is a nervous awkwardness in Cory's faces that Simon's never seen before, and he doesn't like it. Simon looks at his sister and sees a boiling fuse about to go off beneath her thinly veiled surface of emotions. Instead of saying something, she spins on the ball of her foot and heads toward the clinic in a pace that Simon can't keep up with.

He continues to walk along with Sam with no small amount of discomfort.

"What the heck?" Sam complains to him.

Simon isn't about to remind her how much she hates him.

"I know," he agrees. "That was…odd."

"Are they…?" Sam asks. "Are they seeing each other?"

He vigorously shakes his head. "No, not that I'm aware of."

"As if you'd be aware anyways, Simon," she jeers.

He doesn't care if she wants to make fun of him. As long as she's still talking to him at all is the only thing that matters to Simon.

"True," he concedes. "Hey, before you leave, I have something for you. I was going to give it to Dave to take back to you, but since you're here…"

This stops Sam in her tracks. Simon could kick himself. He always says the wrong thing, the idiotic thing. He never gets anything right, especially with Sam.

"I don't want anything from you."

"No, no, it's not like that," he says and jogs ahead the last few yards to the truck. He pulls out the box and takes it back to Sam, who is already walking away toward Dave's SUV. "Sam, wait. Hey, wait a minute."

He steps in front of her so that she has to stop or run him down. Her expression is dark and stormy again. He's hoping his gift will bring a smile to her soft face.

"Look," he says. "I found this stuff in a store south of Nashville last week."

"I said I don't want anything from you."

Simon considers the ramifications of telling lies. He knows the Bible speaks against it pretty firmly, but surely there are still gray areas that weren't covered. After all, it's a big subject to cover. Lying to someone you care about to make them happy again should be under the tagline: 'slipups and when they're ok with the man upstairs.' The lie he told her when he said he didn't care for her in the same way that she cares for him was the biggest lie he's ever told. Not caring for Sam would kill him. Letting her go was the hardest thing he's ever done, but it was the selfless, right thing to do.

"Oh, it's not all just from me," he fabricates. Of course, it is all from him. "Cory found some of this. I only found a few small things. It's actually mostly all from Cory and John." Also untrue. The lie got a little bigger than it was supposed to. Perhaps God did know what he was crafting in those verses that covered this subject.

"Oh," she says with caution and peeks into the cardboard box.

It is full of art supplies, 'girly' items as Cory now calls them, and a few articles of clothing, including a pink t-shirt, a pale yellow hoodie, and new riding breeches that he'd found at a tack and horse supply store just outside of Nashville. They are the size she took before she left the farm, but now she seems smaller as if she's lost weight since leaving. These pants may be a little big on her. Good. He doesn't think she should strut around in front of strange men in super-tight riding pants anyway.

She says with a sad sigh and then the tiniest of grins, "Wow, this is a lot. Thank you. Tell Cory I said thanks, too."

"You're welcome," he says, glad to see her mood lift just slightly. "You're very welcome."

"Ready, munchkin?" her uncle says as he approaches them.

"Yes, I'm ready," she answers her uncle.

He extends a hand and shakes Simon's. "Thanks for the help today, Simon."

"Yes, sir," he returns with a nod. "You're welcome."

Dave is right behind him with his men. Their pregnant town residents are already loaded into a few different vehicles and trucks, and look ready to be home where they can put their swollen ankles up for the night.

"Be careful," Simon says to her as John and Reagan approach, this time with Doc. They speak with her uncle a few feet away.

"The most dangerous thing I've done in a long time is come here today, Simon," Sam says to him, still looking down at the box of goods and not at him.

"Why? What happened?" he demands, his fear for her safety escalating. Had they run into trouble on the road and not mentioned it?

"Not all dangers are physical ones, Simon," she answers and wipes at her left cheek.

"What do you mean?" he asks stupidly.

She hits him with a look as if he is a complete idiot and turns around to leave. Sam hands the box into the backseat with her uncle and climbs in beside him. She immediately rolls up her window, and Simon believes it is because she doesn't want to see him. He also thinks perhaps she was wiping away a tear. It rips open the healing wounds inside his heart once more.

Chapter Twenty
Paige

Their trip to look for the highwaymen and the men who ran over Derek is postponed for nearly a week due to the planting season, which angered John. The beginning of summer is a busy time on the farm, she's learning. The garden has to be put in, the fields need to be planted with crops for the livestock, and everything must be fertilized again. Paige has been helping Sue in the greenhouse, reloading ammo, working with the younger kids on school lessons with Hannah, and designing an architectural drawing for their neighbors, the Johnson's. They want to add a dairy goat barn. They have recently traded with the McClane family for a few nannies and their kids for two hogs. They need an efficient design that will make the milkings go smoothly and an area where they can graze outdoors. She is glad to help them and is supposed to travel over there in a few days. Evie Johnson came yesterday morning to invite her to brunch and to go over the drawings. Paige is less enthusiastic about the brunch with Cory's ex-girlfriend, who seems to want to be her best friend.

Today, she, Cory, Kelly and John are heading to an area between the city of Clarksville and Fort Campbell, Kentucky. They are hoping to find those men, but Paige secretly hopes they don't run into them on the road like their other victims.

Dave and quite a few of his men are supposed to be meeting them, but he isn't bringing Sam. She is busy helping her uncle, and

John had said that she would work with Simon, who must stay behind to guard the farm with Luke, Doc, and Huntley. Chet is helping them, too, since Kelly is going on this trip. Plus Chet wanted to work with Simon on the bee hives. They have combined all three farms' hives into one area near the back of their joined properties. Paige is afraid of the bees, but she sure likes their honey. One of the things they traded with Dave was a dozen jars of honey, which he does not have in production over on Henry's farm. Their whole community had been thrilled with the sweet nectar. Sam said their food is mostly bland, so she will be coming for a visit soon to gather herbal starter plants. All of the meals that Sue and Hannah provide on the farm are tasty and plentiful. Paige isn't sure how they manage to make things more flavorful and even better than she'd ever had before the fall of their country, but they do. Chicken with rosemary, potatoes baked au gratin style with parsley and garlic, stews and soups flavored with sage and bay leaves, beef roasted all night and morning over the campfire spit in the backyard and coated with a rub of garlic, salt, and homemade vinegar- these are some of her favorite meals. So long veganism.

She hugs her brother goodbye, acknowledging the fact that he is angry with her for going at all.

"This is ludicrous," he whispers into her ear.

"Simon, I'll be fine. We need to build up our supplies. Daniel could use more formula again. I want to go. I'm well again. I want to help and contribute."

"You aren't well enough yet."

She chuckles and pulls back, "According to you, I'll never be well enough to go on a run, but I am. I'm strong again."

"You still get winded."

She shrugs. "I'll be fine. I want to go."

Cory walks up to them, and Simon turns on him so hard that Paige is afraid he's going to do something violent against his friend.

"Hey, man, don't blame me. I didn't want her to go, either," Cory explains and shakes his head as he places an ammo can in the bed of the truck.

Paige snorts, "I didn't ask your permission."

"If you had, you'd be keeping your bony butt on the farm," he complains, joining Simon's argument against her.

"Too bad," she retorts. "I'm going. If you don't like it, I'll pair up with John instead of you."

"Not happening," he says. "Kelly's with us today. You've worked with me before. It's how we do it. You'll stay with me."

Everyone turns to look as the family comes onto the back porch. John is right by his brother's side before following his wife to the yard near the corner of the house. Derek's cast came off, but he can't walk yet. He mostly hobbles around on crutches or a walker they found for him. He's also still needing the support of the wheelchair sometimes. To Paige, he seems depressed. He stopped shaving, and he mostly stares off into the distance. He and his family have not moved into their cabin again. It is simply too far for him to walk, and John doesn't really want them so far out there anyway. He argues that it's easier to help Derek out until he gets better if they stay in the big house. Paige has noticed that when John uses phrases like "until he gets better" that Doc and Reagan usually look down or away. He refuses to believe that Derek won't be whole again, but Paige suspects that Derek is starting to understand it.

Reagan is arguing with John about going on this trip. They are planning on being gone overnight, and she is not happy about it. Most of the time she's not too thrilled when he leaves the farm, but an overnight stay just seems to make it even harder. Paige knows the feeling all too well. She hates it when Simon does the same.

After ten minutes of final planning, safety instructions given to those left behind on the farm, and saying farewell, they finally get on the road. Paige shares the back seat of the truck with Cory while John rides shotgun and Kelly drives. The morning chill has not lifted yet from the air, so she keeps her black hoodie on over her black Jimmy Hendrix tank top, which she's pretty sure is a man's since the arm holes hang low. She coupled it with a navy blue cami underneath. She's also wearing the slim khaki cargo pants Cory recently picked up for her. They don't reach all the way to her ankles, but she doesn't care since she's used to it. On her feet are the sturdy hiking boots he also helped her get. Most of her clothing, even the clothes back on the farm are care of Cory finding them on runs. She doesn't want to read more into it than him gathering items for the family, and she just happens to be one of the family now. Paige has, unfortunately, noticed that most of the things he finds are usually given directly to her.

"Dave and his men are taking the eastern part of the city, and we'll work the west. I'm dropping you in the heart of the city, Cor," Kelly tells them. "You and Paige will rendezvous at seventeen hundred hours with us at the hotel. Do not attempt to travel up route 41 without us. We'll approach the base together after dark."

"Yes, sir," Cory says.

"Don't leave the four-wheeler exposed or you might be looking for a Schwinn," John teases.

Cory laughs and replies, "Yes, sir."

"Evade if necessary," John says with more serious intent. "Recon and call it in. Don't engage if you can avoid it. We don't know who we're up against yet. If you run into them, you could get yourself into trouble. Paige's with you. Keep that in mind."

"Yes, sir," Cory says with a nod and looks at her and winks.

They've brought two of their four-wheelers, the ones they confiscated from Mike's group of bandits. They are hauling them behind the truck on a small trailer. It will make traveling around the city scouting for items and the bad people a lot faster.

John and Kelly go back to discussing the summer crop season while Paige looks out the window at the wild landscape that has become America. Everything looks so different than it had four years ago. Most paved roads have grass growing right down the middle of them. Once perfectly-tended pastures are overgrown and wild, filled with weeds and pricker bushes that snag on clothing when walking through them. Homes have become victim to the ever-encroaching flora around them, their exterior walls covered with vines, their porches invaded by weeds that have pushed up through the cracks between the floorboards. She remembers staying in a house like that once with Gavin and Talia. Likely due to a windy thunderstorm, a tree had fallen on the stately old home, piercing through the roof and one window on the first floor. Its branches had continued to grow new leaves. The small, twig-like ones that hadn't fared so well in the crash they'd used to start a fire in the wood-burning stove in the living room. She always wondered what happened to the inhabitants of such homes. Many times after her friends had fallen asleep, Paige would wander around looking at photographs hanging on walls in beautiful frames or decorating the mantles or coffee stands of its former owners.

"Right, Red?" Cory asks, startling her out of her reverie. He gives her a questioning look when she turns to look at him.

"What?" she asks with confusion.

He doesn't repeat the question, whatever it was he wanted to know, but stares hard at her.

"You all right?"

Paige nods in answer.

"Nervous?" he asks quietly, even though Kelly and John are in the front seat in a deep discussion about some battle they were in once.

She tries to play it cool, but it probably doesn't work. "No, not nervous."

"You'll be fine," he says and takes her hand stealthily on the seat between them. "Just don't step on any rugs."

She grins and nods, slipping her hand out from under his. Then she stares out the window again. Paige had wanted to go on another run when she was better because she doesn't want to turn soft living on the farm with the creature comforts it provides. After their last trip out, she'd promised herself she was done going. She knew she couldn't do that, though. She started this thing as a survivor and plans to end her life the same way, whether that day is today or forty years from now. Sitting around doing farm chores and helping out with the kids isn't keeping her skills honed. This is the only way to do that. She'd just been hoping to go with her brother, not Cory. She's been playing the avoidance game with him since their last encounter in the woods, even though she'd like to sneak away every night with him. That's a foolish proposition with only unhappy endings, and she knows it. This isn't a romantic comedy where the girl gets the guy, and everything works out perfectly.

They stop twice on the road to push cars out of the way that have been left, wrecked, or abandoned. Paige waits in the truck with Kelly who keeps it running. It takes them a long time, but they finally make it to Clarksville where Dave and three of his men meet them on the designated side street behind the donut shop. Kelly pulls over in an alley where they unload the four-wheeler for Cory. Paige grabs her rifle and pack and meets them near the trailer. Kelly uncharacteristically gives Cory a hug. The men never do this. It's usually harassing and insulting one another, not hugs and kind words. His demeanor makes her even more nervous.

"Seventeen hundred hours," John repeats and bumps his fist against Cory's.

"Got it," he replies.

John tips his ball cap to Paige, and the men leave. This is when her nerves kick into high gear.

"Ready?" he asks.

"Yep," she says, trying to be nonchalant.

Cory steps closer and says softly, "Hey, I'm not going to let anything happen to you."

She nods and looks up at him, biting her lower lip. He takes her rifle, checks the mag, smacks it back into place and loads one into the chamber.

"You're the most important thing in my life, Red," he confesses quietly and hands it back.

His words take her breath away. Paige shakes her head with a frown to discourage him from talking like this.

"Yes, you are," he argues.

"Kelly and Hannah and your niece are," she reminds him.

Cory just shakes his head and looks her in the eye. Paige would like to run off, catch up to the truck again and ask if she can change partners for the day.

306

"I'll protect you," he says, turning to straddle the ATV.

Paige swallows hard and follows him. She wraps her hands around his waist, and they're off.

They hit a bakery first since it doesn't seem looted. Cory parks the ATV around back near the service entrance, and they enter unhindered through an unlocked door.

"Over here," he calls quietly and leads her to a shelving unit.

There are bags of flour, but they've clearly been rummaged by rodents. A jar of chocolate chips is on the top shelf.

"Yum," he remarks and raises his eyebrows at her.

"Gross, they might be spoiled by now."

Cory chuckles, unscrews the lid, and pulls out a handful. "Look good to me. Besides, they probably have enough preservatives in them that they'll be good until the next apocalypse."

She smiles at this and takes a few that he offers. The sweetness and taste of chocolate is almost too much for her senses. It's been a long time since she's had chocolate. Sometimes they'll find candy bars, but they usually give them to the little kids in the family. It was comical the first time Reagan's son Jacob tried a chocolate bar, Hershey's with almonds. His cute face lit up with delight. Paige knows the feeling. This is so much better than the vegan chocolate bars she used to buy at the health food store near her campus.

"We'll get Hannah and Sue on some cookies when we get back," he remarks with a childlike grin. "I think I read once that chocolate is an aphrodisiac."

Paige chuckles. "I thought you were into reading military history?"

"You'd be surprised how much sex is in those books."

She shoots him a stunned expression.

"Guess people gotta procreate even in war time," he adds.

"Wouldn't have been very many people on the earth if they hadn't. I guess it makes sense."

He laughs before stuffing the chocolate chip container into his pack. Paige finds a smaller container of white chocolate chips, and they take those, as well. She has no idea what the shelf life of items like this might be, but it's worth the risk. Vanilla, coconut and peppermint extracts also get pocketed. The bottles are large, bulk sizes and will likely last for years.

They leave the bakery and take the ATV to another section of town since, other than the bakery, the buildings in that area were well-looted or burned to the ground. Cory parks them near a group of chain restaurants and shopping centers with grocery stores. They usually don't find much in grocery stores. Most of what hasn't been looted has been destroyed by the gases given off by the spoiled produce, the bugs that infested, or the rodents who invaded. She's never been to this city before, so Cory will make the decisions on where to hunt. All she knows is that they are heading north. They leave the ATV behind a dumpster and take the keys.

They quickly discover that the grocery stores, as they expected, are completely cleaned out. The restaurants prove the same other than some dishes and supplies that they don't need and leave behind. They hit up a bookstore, making Paige wish she could go to the coffee bar and order something cold and icy. Instead, they take a satchel full of non-fiction books for their librarian. Paige also grabs two romance novels on paperback, since she knows how much Mrs. Browning likes them, although she won't admit to it. Paige has seen her covertly reading them behind the librarian's desk, which she still mans every day like it's just business as usual.

"Check these out," Cory says, coming up behind her in an aisle of young adult fiction and setting his stack on the floor. She picks out a novel she thinks G will like and stuffs it in her pack.

"What'd you find?"

He shows her two small electronic gadgets and the coordinating charger packs.

"What would we use those for? They're for reading books on them, aren't they?"

"Yeah, but they play music, too," he says. "You can also play games that are pre-loaded. Think the kids would like them? They won't draw a lot of power to charge. We only have the one iPod back at the house. The kids might like having music players."

"You mean other than the piano in the music room?" she asks with a smile.

"Yeah," he says and chuckles. "It's not quite as portable."

"They might like them," she remarks as he packs them into his bag.

"Found a book on historical architecture of the south," he says before squatting and handing it to her. Paige kneels beside him. "Thought you might like this."

He says this all the time when he brings loads back to the farm from a run. He never brings her nothing at all. There is always something, even something small that he finds just for her.

"Cory, you have to stop this," she says, holding the book and looking directly at him.

"Stop what?"

His brown eyes are soft and gentle despite the fact that they are on a mission. She knows firsthand how instantly they can become intense and calculating.

"Bringing me stuff all the time. Finding things for me. It's too much. We aren't... we aren't..."

"Aren't what?"

"We had fun a few times, but that's all it can ever be," Paige says, hating how flippant she sounds. Her mother would not approve of this behavior. She was not one of those modern moms who were cool with doing whatever you wanted as long as it didn't hurt anyone. She was more like Herb McClane, and Paige knows he would definitely not approve of her and Cory's trysts. She never even told her mom about her boyfriend in Georgia until she caught him in bed with her friend.

Cory laughs softly and chucks her under the chin. "Okay, Red. Whatever you say."

This pisses her off. "I mean it!"

Paige stands and stuffs the book into her pack telling herself that she'll donate it to the library, but knowing full well that she'll thoroughly peruse it first.

"Did I tell you how sexy you look today?" he says on a low murmur that nearly causes her knees to buckle.

As she is about to retort a reprimand, the sound of an engine outside of the store permeates their conversation. Cory grabs her hand and leads her to the front of the building, all thoughts of teasing and arguing and their stolen loot forgotten.

They crouch behind a twelve-foot long, wooden magazine rack, and Cory risks a peek. Paige silently crawls to the other end to catch a glimpse. Then she hears a car door slam shut. She can see the vehicle, a blue sedan across the street in another shopping plaza. Four men get out and stretch as if they've been in the car for a long road trip, except that she knows that nobody does the family road trip to sightsee anymore. Three of them have rifles.

"Psst," Cory whispers to her.

Paige crawls back just in time for him to haul her to her feet and sprint to the back of the bookstore. Her heart hammers in her chest as they exit the building and mount the ATV again. It puzzles her because Cory is not the type to flee. However, his brother and John ordered that they do so.

As he starts the engine, she prays those men don't hear it. She wraps her arms around Cory, and he drives them away from the spot where the men were loitering. He goes about two blocks east and parks behind a tall building.

"Leave your bag," he orders, and she places it on the ground beside the ATV.

Without preamble, Cory jumps off and sprints into the building with Paige on his heels.

"Where are we going?" she asks, trying hard not to notice a corpse lying in the revolving door that they must step over.

"High ground," he explains and whips open the door to the stairwell. "I wanna' see what those dudes were up to. I need to see from up high."

She tries to keep up, forcing Cory to slow his pace, which he does without her asking first. They arrive on the fifth floor where Cory listens first, then opens the door and enters the hallway. This building is long ago abandoned. She can tell by the amount of dust, dirt and mold on the floors and walls. They go up one more flight to the roof and cross the space swiftly to take up a position behind an industrial heating and cooling unit so that he can spy down over part of the city. Paige rests back against the metal box to catch her breath. Cory is already looking through his binoculars.

When she can, she asks, "See them?"

"Not yet," he answers.

"Think that's the highwaymen?"

He doesn't answer, which leaves her to think he either doesn't believe it to be them or that he doesn't have enough information yet to hypothesize about them. Either way, she is content to rest a minute. They stay there for a long time, nearly a half hour as Cory scans the area.

"What are they doing?"

"Looting, same as us," he answers.

"Is it them?" she asks again.

"Not sure," he finally says. "Looks like they're moving on."

"Really?"

"Yeah, they're heading this way."

"Oh, no," Paige frets.

He just continues to look through the binoculars as he calmly says, "Don't worry. They can't see us up here."

She can hear the approach of their engine, which isn't very quiet or practical for being stealthy. Their muffler sounds like it needs to be replaced. She holds her breath until it passes. The rattling sound doesn't stop but keeps going until it fades into the distance.

"They're gone," he tells her and continues to spy. "I'm calling it in."

He does and gets a response from his brother, who tells them that they'll be on the lookout for it but that they haven't run into anyone all day on their side of town.

"Ready?"

She nods and stands again. "Guess I'm done working on my tan."

"Better not get too tan. Your brother's freckles stand out more when he gets tan in the summer. So do yours, I've noticed."

"Oh, the joys of being a redhead," she says as they go back inside and down the first flight of stairs.

"I like your red hair just fine," he confesses and even reaches out to stroke it before she can back away. Then he opens the door to the stairwell for her.

"I thought you might prefer blondes lately," she says, instantly wishing she could kick herself if it wouldn't be so obvious.

"Blondes?" he asks casually. "Nah, boring. I like red. Probably always will. You've ruined me forever with that fiery color."

"Bah," she scoffs.

"What blonde?" he asks as he does a fast search of the rooms on the fifth floor.

It was a former office building, so they likely won't find much that they can use.

"Nothing, forget it," she says, trying to drop the subject.

"No, who? Who's the blonde I've supposedly got the hots for, Red?"

"Rachel? In town? She's always hanging on you," she says, regretting her inability to stop herself first. Unfortunately, Paige is curious if he returns the woman's affections.

"Ha! No kidding," he admits and heads to the exit door again. "Not my type."

"Blonde, cute, hanging on your every word?"

She follows him down the stairwell to the first floor again where he picks up her fallen bag and hands it to her.

"No, I like women who just want to use me for sex and then ignore me for weeks on end."

He is staring pointedly at her, which makes Paige blush hard. What he's saying is true, and they both know it.

"That's not true," she attempts to fabricate anyway.

He chuckles and nods.

"We're not in a relationship," she informs him and slings her bag. "You should date Rachel if you want. And I'll date other people, too. We aren't exclusive. You shouldn't look at us like that. Just keep it casual, ya' know?"

When he doesn't answer, Paige looks up to find him glaring at her angrily.

Cory asks, "Do I look like the kind of man who likes to share?"

She swallows hard and shakes her head.

"You can't stop me from seeing other people." Her voice cracks. She doesn't even believe this. There is no way he's ever going to allow her to see other men.

He smirks arrogantly, the only way he knows, and says, "Try me. I don't think you'll like the consequences."

"Look, Cory, we aren't an exclusive thing. We aren't together, not like that. I can date anyone I want. You really can't stop me."

"I don't have to," he says with a sly smile as he adjusts his rifle strap over the front of his chest.

"What's that supposed to mean?"

His grin turns crooked and self-sure. Then he folds his arms across his chest.

"I'll just tell your brother."

Paige is infuriated. "That's not even funny. Don't be an asshole. You better not push me, either. I'll...I'll start seeing someone in town."

She doesn't really even know anyone in town other than the librarian.

"Do you know all the different ways I've been taught and learned on my own how to kill someone?" he asks and swings a leg over on the ATV.

"That's morbid. Don't be like that."

"Test me on the seeing other people thing, and I'll show your new boyfriend some of my finely tuned skills."

Before she can retort her outrage, he starts the four-wheeler so that she can't answer with a response. Then they are moving again. He is making her so mad. His behavior is controlling and chauvinistic. Of course, this shouldn't surprise her since she's come to know him so well.

They stop again at two different convenience marts and find a few items in the back that they can take home to the farm like lighters and flashlights. An auto store is next where he takes many items foreign to Paige. They take two bolts of fabric from a craft and sewing store after the car store looting. Cory bundles the fabric into a square in the bottom of his pack. Paige takes the scissors, boxes of needles and thread and places them in hers. Then they hit a children's superstore and search for formula. There is some sort of pre-mixed stuff in jars, but it is expired and looks it. Paige takes a minute to grab six complete outfits for Daniel. He'll look so cute in them. Cory snags a few toys for the smaller kids.

"What is this crap?" Cory asks, picking up a package.

They are walking down one of the baby gadget aisles near the back stockroom. It is nearly dark and very spooky in this particular area far from the front windows. Cory already ran ahead to scout the stockroom to make sure nobody was squatting there. The ATV is parked one building over between two dumpsters in an alley meant for shipping and receiving.

She smiles. "I have no idea. You aren't looking at the right person to answer that question."

"Maybe I am," he says and cocks his right eyebrow. "You'll have kids someday, probably mine, all boys, of course."

Paige snorts. "I don't think so. I'm never having kids."

"Why do you say that?"

She picks up a package of plastic nipples and stuffs them into his pack, which he obliges by turning his back to her.

"Because it doesn't make sense to. There's no point in bringing more kids into this wretched world so that they have the same miserable existences as we do."

"I don't consider our existences miserable."

He places a pack of disposable wipes in his pack. They often use these when they are on a mission and don't have access to running water.

314

"Mine *was* for three years while I lived on the road. I don't ever want that for anyone else, especially not my own kids."

"It wouldn't be like that. Our kids would be safe on the farm."

"There isn't going to be an 'our kids' situation, Cory. And you don't know that they'd be safe on the farm. Maybe the farm won't always be there. Maybe someone will eventually overtake us, burn it to the ground or something. Then what? Would you want your kids to have to live on the road like I did? Nothing is for certain."

Cory grasps her upper arm lightly to halt her. "Hey, it'll always be there as long as we're always there. None of us will ever let anyone take the farm."

She knows he means the soldiers in the family, but there are things that happen in an instant that can change everything. She knows this firsthand. Some strange disease could wipe out over half of them in a matter of weeks. Even the toughest of them could be killed by illness or even accidental injury.

Paige shakes her head and says, "You can't know that. Nobody can predict the future. If they could, none of this would've happened in the first place."

He reaches out and cups her cheek in his warm palm, and Paige tries not to lose herself in its comforting strength.

"I'm thankful for some of it, though," he says softly. "If it didn't happen, I'd have never met you."

She tilts her head to the side and frowns. "Cory, that's ridiculous. Look at all the people we've lost. Your parents, my parents, your sister."

Her last word stings him. She can see it in the way he flinches with an almost imperceptible twitch.

"Sorry," she apologizes immediately and touches his forearm. She feels genuinely bad about it, too. He never speaks of his little sister, only that one time in the cabin when they were alone, and he'd only said the briefest of sentences about her. "I didn't mean to bring her up. I just don't think anything's worth losing all of our family members over."

He nods and says, "I wish they were still with us, too. But I promise you that you won't lose anyone else or the farm. Not while I'm still alive."

She turns away and resumes their walk toward the back of the store. There is a puddle of water at the end of the aisle that she sidesteps. When she looks up, she can see a small hole in the roof where light is filtering through. Paige doesn't want to tell him that he may not always be alive, either. She's watched so many people she cares about die. Life no longer has an expectancy rate with tables and charts and theories about what can improve one's timetable like not smoking or lowering one's cholesterol.

"And my sons will be big and strong like me, too. They'll take care of their mother and the farm."

"Oh, brother!" She just groans with annoyance. "Don't be your usual irritating self, caveman."

"Fine, I'll be my usual charming self and seduce you instead."

"Like that could happen," she informs him as if he doesn't have a chance. She snorts for good measure.

"Wanna' bet?" he asks and stops walking.

Everything in Paige screams at her not to taunt him. "Sure, I'll take that bet. You don't intimidate me."

Then she wonders how many times in a single day that a person should contemplate kicking herself in the shin. She tries to act casual and picks up another package. It looks like something for pumping milk. She turns to look at Cory, thinking perhaps he wandered off since he is being quiet. He is standing there leaning against a shelf. He isn't looking at the items they should be trying to find but at her. His gaze is methodical and slow as he peruses her from head to toe making Paige feel highly scrutinized.

"Stop it," she orders as a blush spreads on her cheeks. He is purposely embarrassing her with his examining stare as if she is wearing no clothing at all.

His lopsided grin is followed immediately by him walking forward. Paige backs up, bumps the shelf behind her and squeaks out a protest as Cory takes her face between his hands and pulls her up against him, his mouth capturing hers. Within moments he has her breathless and panting, clawing and tugging at him as he explores her mouth at his leisure.

He pulls back but lowers his face to her neck.

"You shouldn't have done that," she scolds without much real weight.

"You shouldn't have asked for it," he says, forcing the blame on her. His fingers are tracing her forearm and then against her side, causing a tremor to pass through her.

Not one to accept defeat, Paige comes back with, "You shouldn't act like a Neanderthal all the time."

Without warning her, Cory takes her gun and pack.

"Hey," she exclaims. "What the…? I can carry those myself."

Her words are cut off as he ducks and flips her over his shoulder next.

"What are you doing?" she hisses, trying not to make too much noise.

"If you're going to call me a caveman all the time, I figure I should start acting like one."

He carries her to the stockroom and sets her to her feet. Then Cory pulls a shelving unit in front of the solitary swinging door. For added safety, he reaches up and sets the lock into the door frame to prevent it from being opened from the other side.

"What are we doing back here?"

"Shh," he says impatiently, holding his finger to his lips.

This makes her frown. Is he shushing her?

Cory stalks toward her, takes her hand, and leads her farther into the dark room. She trips over debris, but he yanks her back up.

"Where are we going?" she asks again.

He comes to a stop near a side wall and reaches up onto a shelf where he pulls down a small, twin size children's mattress. Then he sets his gun on the floor, propping it against the shelving unit.

"What are you doing? Are you crazy?"

"Caveman," he replies simply and unfastens his belt.

"Wait, are you thinking... Do you think we're just going to do that here? Have you lost your mind?"

He grins and tugs her close.

"Cavemen don't need candles and romance and ambiance," he explains while kissing her neck.

"This is nuts, Cory," she states. "You need to stop."

Her words sound weak and very flexible to her ears. She doesn't sound at all convincing, and they both know it.

"You need to stop," he argues. "Stop denying me. Your caveman wants you, woman."

He emits a guttural grunt to be sarcastic. She chuckles against his mouth as he kisses her deeply.

"This is so stupid," she declares when he pulls back, his fingers working the button of her pants.

"Most of my best plans usually are," he admits with a boyish grin and kisses her neck.

A moment later, they are on the mattress and Cory is kissing her stomach. He doesn't remove her shirt or his own. Neither does he remove and discard either of their pants. But he does take one leg out of hers and his own so that they can dress in the blink of an eye if they need to. Normally when he makes love to her, it is slow and methodical, unhurried. Today he is speeding through the process, but his hands are igniting her baser emotions, making her ready for him. She has wanted him so badly lately, wanted to sneak out to him when he's on watch duty at night or when he's working in the equipment shed by himself in the evening when everyone is busy doing their own leisure time activities, or when he's in the top field using the tractor to plow up the earth for corn. There has been opportunity, but Paige always denies herself. She doesn't want a full-blown relationship with him, not the kind he seems to want, at least.

Static on his radio interrupts what has so much promise, and Cory instantly grabs it from the floor where he'd placed it.

"Catfish to Marlin, we've got you," Cory says to his brother.

"Problem here," Kelly says. "Meet at grid cords…"

There is a long pause before Kelly comes back on. She has already pulled her pants back up and her shirt down. Cory sets the radio down to do the same.

"Magic Mason," his brother says.

She looks at Cory and frowns.

"Got it. Be there in five."

"What the heck's that mean?" she asks.

"Country club," he answers.

"It's called that?"

He grabs his rifle and leads her out the back door to their ATV.

"No, Mason was that pro golfer kid, remember?" he asks.

"Oh, yeah, Michael Mason. Wasn't he like sixteen or something? Some kind of prodigy golf whiz?"

"I guess. It's what we call any country club. His nickname was Magic Mason. We use that for code."

"Smart," she remarks as she climbs on behind him.

"It's like we've done this before," he quips and turns to wink at her. "We'll pick up where we left off back there tonight, Red."

"I don't think that's a good idea."

"It's another one of my brilliant bad ideas," he says and starts the engine before she can rebut.

Chapter Twenty-one
Sam

She's been cooped up for over a week helping her uncle at what will be the new practice at the neighbor's former home. The work is mostly tedious, and she has been cleaning and sanitizing the small patient rooms that the military men have constructed for them. The drywall dust had been the worst part. Dave's wife came by frequently to help with bedding and towels that will be a permanent part of the clinic. The house doesn't have electricity or solar panels, so they will need to use the small generator that Henry is donating to them for power until the solar panels can be constructed. They have natural gas on Henry's farm, but it isn't plentiful and often fails. Their primary source of heat is wood-burning stoves and fireplaces. The home they are using for the new practice doesn't have a wood-burning stove or a gas well. Dave's men brought over a small, antique cast-iron stove out of their plethora of looted items in the storage barns and have been working on getting it installed. They likely won't need it until fall, but there is some amount of conversion that will have to take place for the chimney and proper venting of the wood-burner. They may need to heat buckets of water for instrument sterilization, and the wood-burning stove will be the only way to do that for a while. At least it will be warm when they need to work there in the winter. The few men who stayed there from Dave's group only lived in it during the summer months, but her uncle is considering keeping his permanent residence in the top of the house.

If he does, Sam will probably follow him. It's only next door to Henry's farm, so they will be safe from harm. Plus, Dave said if they move there, he'll also post one or two of his men at the location on a permanent basis to keep them from being robbed or hurt by would-be marauders. It isn't going to be nearly the setup that Grandpa's practice is in Pleasant View, but they are going to provide people with much-needed care as best they can. Many of the citizens in Hendersonville have not had medical care since the country fell. Nearly two hundred civilians are still trying to make a go of it. They also have a registered nurse and a former dentist who will be helping them.

She is glad to be leaving Henry's farm today, though, because Dave's wife and a few other women are smoking fish outside, which doesn't exactly smell so great in Sam's opinion. She's not a big fan of seafood, never was, and they seem to eat it about once per week on Henry's farm. Some of the people on the farm go to the local ponds and lakes to catch fish, even in the winter, and others already knew how to cure it. Every once in a while on the McClane farm they'd have fish for dinner, but it was always freshly caught out of Grandpa's lake, and it had a good flavor, cooked to just the right tenderness, and seasoned nicely. The canned or smoked fish on Henry's farm doesn't compare to the careful and thoughtful ministrations of Hannah and Sue's culinary skills in the kitchen. Before the smoking began after breakfast, very early this morning, it had smelled wonderful because one of the men has fashioned a metal cooking oven, which is really just a square metal box, on top of the wood-burning stove in their bunkhouse where she sleeps with the other women, and one of the older women had risen early and baked fresh bread in it for their breakfast. The whole bunk was filled with the comforting aromas of rising yeast and warm dough. They had freshly churned butter to spread on it, along with their scrambled eggs and skillet-fried potatoes. Soon the plan is to add an actual working kitchen in their bunkhouse so that they can be more self-sufficient and make their own meals instead joining the massive effort it takes to ensure everyone on the farm is fed at the same time.

Another idea they are working on is adding more showers that will run hot water from a solar panel on the roof of the bunkhouse. The water is not always particularly hot in their two current shower stalls since it runs off of the natural gas that is unreliable.

It is midday and Sam is traveling with Henry and three of his men to the McClane farm. They are going to offer added protection and supply the farm with security while Sam collects herb starts from the garden, the woods around the farm, and the greenhouse. She's relieved because Simon won't be there. Sue had sent a letter back to Henry's farm the other day after clinic day in town since Sam hadn't attended it again. The letter stated that she could come to the farm and she'd help her collect herb starts for Henry's farm. Sue had also included in the letter that Simon and Cory wouldn't be there because they were planning a run for supplies. Sam isn't stupid. She'd picked up on the subtle, or not so subtle, hint in the letter. The coast was going to be clear for Sam to come over for a visit without the burden of Simon being present.

"Have everything you need, Sam?" Henry asks, standing at her open door. They are taking a mini-van since Henry's truck was stolen and Dave has the other truck. There are other vehicles on the farm, but not many that will transport a lot of people at the same time.

"Yes, Henry," she answers with a smile. "Thanks."

"We'll be there overnight," he reminds her.

"I've got my bag," she says, patting the backpack on the floor between her feet. She can't wait to get to the farm. She misses her sisters, especially Paige and is looking forward to staying up all night talking.

"Good," he says. "Let me know if you need to stop."

"I'll be fine. Thanks," Sam returns and presses the button for the sliding door to close. One of his friends will drive them since Henry is still healing from being shot. He props his rifle between his feet on the floor in front of him and keeps one hand on the forearm.

"Feeling ok?" she asks as they drive away from the farm.

"Yes, ma'am. Thanks to you, I'll be just fine," he answers and winks.

"Thanks to the doctors, not me," she corrects.

"You nursed me back from the brink," he teases her.

"Just doing my job," she tells him.

His friend in the front passenger seat plugs his music player into the outlet, and country music sweeps through the vehicle. Henry just smiles at her since conversation is more difficult with the radio going. He has kind eyes, troubled, but kind, nonetheless. He is always well-mannered and patient, even with the other people on his farm. Henry is gentle and sweet, but Sam is not interested in him romantically. She does spend time with him since his friend is the man that her friend, Courtney, has fancied herself in love with. Sam would like to warn her new friend about the dangers of falling love, but she doesn't want to spread her cynicism to others. Sam knows that true love does exist. She's seen it in some of the couples on the McClane farm and again on Henry's. There is an older couple, survivors of a home invasion at the beginning, and Dave and his wife, who clearly love each other. She's not giving up on the idea of love itself. She has just given up on finding that in Simon. She's not always very good at reading people, but Henry has let his interest be known by going out his way and doing little things for her.

"Be on alert," Henry warns his men, getting responses to the affirmative.

Two of them are sitting behind her and Henry in the trunk. They've removed the third row of seating and have also taken out the rear window. The other man is pointing his rifle through the open hole, guarding the rear against being attacked. The man driving is older, a retired commercial airline pilot who was also an Air Force pilot in his youth. He lives in Hendersonville, not on Henry's farm, but they are still friends and were before the fall of the country. He comes to visit often. He is a friendly, trustworthy man and a widower, who is also raising his three grandchildren. They are parentless since he lost his daughter and her husband, as well. Jerome is a good man, and Sam likes and trusts him.

The trip to the farm is one filled with nerves for her since she knows they are still on the lookout for the highwaymen. She also knows from Sue's letter that the men are gone on a run for supplies, but Sam is smart enough to know that a supply run is not the only mission they are on. She keeps her hand on the pistol on her hip. Even with her anxiety for their safety, they make it to the farm unscathed. Henry calls the farm on their radio and makes a connection with Derek.

The farm comes into view as they crest the top of the short hill on the oil well access road behind the Reynolds farm. Sam tries not to become emotional at the mere sight of her beloved home. Jerome parks them near the horse barn. She's glad she wore her riding boots because she'd like to grab Huntley later and go for a nice long ride.

She walks to the house with the men and notices that Derek is still on crutches. Sam prays that Grandpa is wrong and that he'll walk unassisted someday. He hugs her close.

"Hey, kiddo," he says.

Derek's embrace feels like a mug of hot chocolate, warm and comforting and familiar.

"Hi, Derek," she returns.

"The girls are inside," he offers. "I've got some things I need to go over with Gunny and the others."

She knows it has to do with the highwaymen but doesn't press for more information. Sam pulls off her riding boots and leaves them on the porch as Henry helps Derek down the stairs. Then they go to the picnic table. Derek sits slowly, plopping down the last twelve inches without the ability to stop himself from doing so. Then he grimaces. She knows he is in pain, although he wouldn't want anyone to know. She can see it in his face even if the men near him cannot. He pulls papers from his back pocket, including a map. Sam goes inside, leaving them to their meeting. It's not like she's going to add anything to the planning and scheming to catch those men.

"Miss Samantha," Grandpa greets from the island where he is adding cream to a ceramic mug. It is probably the coffee she found him in that hospital.

"Hi, Grandpa," she says and hugs him around his slim waist.

"How's my favorite nurse?"

She chuckles. "Fine, just fine."

"You need to eat more, sweetheart," he reprimands. "You're withering away to a little stick."

Sam smiles. "Hardly."

"Maybe you need to stay a few days," he suggests without subtlety. "Hannie will fatten you up lickety split."

"I am. I'm staying tonight. Then I need to get back to help my uncle. We're getting closer to opening the clinic."

"Great, honey."

They chat for a few more minutes until he excuses himself and joins the men outside.

"Hey, Sam!" Hannah calls from the music room. "You get in here right now."

Sam strides to the other room and hugs Hannie close. They embrace for a long time until Daniel squawks from the cradle near the window.

"Oh, I'll fetch him, Hannie," she volunteers and picks up the baby. "He's getting big!"

"Yes, finally. Growing like a little weed," Hannah says.

She walks to Sam, seeks and finds her, resting her hand on Sam's arm. She pushes a fair wisp of hair from her face, her long, loose braid unusually unkempt for Hannah. They sit and talk for a while, sometimes as the kids run in and out of the room. Sam just laughs and hugs them, too.

"Where's Sue?" she asks.

"In the greenhouse," Hannah answers.

"So the men are on a run?"

Hannah's head hangs, and she nods. "Yes, I'm afraid so. Kelly went, too. I'm not happy about it. They're even staying overnight. That makes me even more nervous."

325

"I know, but they'll be ok, Hannie," Sam says and touches her hand on the sofa between them. "John, Cory and Simon will keep him safe."

"I'm not sure how Simon will help. Simon's here," Hannah says, her head raising. "John, Cory and Paige went with Kelly."

Sam's heart sinks while Hannah babbles on about who went and what they are trying to accomplish. "Wait, Sue sent a letter to the compound yesterday saying to come for a visit. She said that…he'd be with them on a run."

"Oh, she must've got confused, Sam," Hannah says, although it doesn't seem convincing. "Simon stayed behind to keep watch on the farm. If he'd left too, then there wouldn't have been enough people to protect it."

This makes sense. Sam isn't sure why she hadn't figured that out on her own. They never send that many of the fighters on a run and leave the farm unprotected.

"Right," she says and stands to place Daniel down in the cradle again. He has fallen asleep, his tiny eyelids fluttering every once in a while.

She feels angry with Sue for meddling, which she's sure is what's happening here. Sam wants to leave, go back to Henry's compound, get away from the farm as soon as possible, not have to see him at all.

"And Paige? You said she went with them?" Sam inquires, hoping she can avoid him by hanging out with his sister.

"Sorry, Sam," Hannah explains, "she's with them. I sure wish she wouldn't have gone, too, but she did."

Sam nods. "She'll be fine. Cory and the guys will watch out for her. John did say that we could both take a turn and go with them."

Hannah frowns before saying, "Sue's in the greenhouse. I know she wanted to get some herbs picked out for you to take back to Henry's farm. I'm glad you're going to add a greenhouse."

"Yes, it'll make an excellent addition to his farm. The food is a lot blander over there. Plus the medicinal herbs will be great at the new practice."

"How's that coming along?"

"Really well. Slow, but Dave's men are doing a good job."

Hannah nods and finds Sam's hand again, patting it. "Wonderful, Sam. I'm glad you're making progress and that you will be heading up the greenhouse project."

"Oh, no, not me. Dave's wife and one of the women the men rescued from that camp are in charge of it. I'm just taking them the starters."

"You should help, too. You know a lot about the herbs from Simon. It's good to stay busy."

"Yeah," Sam agrees with a gloomy nod. She knows this all too well from the months she's been gone from the farm.

"Why don't you go out and fetch Sue for me?" she suggests. "If you can work without her for a while, I could use help with dinner. Just send her in."

"Oh, sure. You don't want me to help instead?"

"No, she's making her famous chicken parmesan, and I'm not great with Italian dishes. I need her help."

Sam laughs and nods vigorously. "I love Sue's pasta dishes."

She hugs Hannah, grabs a messenger bag from the hall hook to gather herbs, and leaves the house, Arianna on her heels.

"Are you moving back, Sam?" Ari asks and takes her hand while they walk.

Sam swings her little friend's hand and replies gently, "I don't think so, Ari. That's not a good idea right now. My uncle needs my help."

"I miss you, though," Arianna says as Huntley approaches.

Sam can't believe how tall he's becoming, and handsome. His hair is down and flowing today and seems as if it has grown another inch since she last saw him.

"I'm going to collect some herbs if you wanna' tag along," she offers them both.

"I can't," Huntley says as he hugs her. "I'll catch up to you later, and we'll go for a ride. I've gotta help Lucas right now. He's cleaning out the loafing shed."

"Want help?"

"Nah," Huntley is quick to reply. "It's bad enough that we gotta shovel cow poop. You don't need to get involved in that, too."

"Not like I've never done it."

He laughs and jogs away. Ari follows closely after him. She'll likely try to entice him with a game of tag or hide-and-seek when he's finished cleaning out the barn. Sam wonders if Lucas will be dragged into their play. With Ari in charge? Likely.

Sam goes to the greenhouse and enters, finding Sue covered in dirt up to her elbows. She greets her with a big smile.

"Sam!" she squeals with delight. "I'm so glad you came."

"Thanks for sending the letter," she says, although she'd like to be mad at her for concealing parts of the truth.

"Sorry, Paige isn't here. The guys changed their minds at the last minute and let her go instead of Simon," she explains, which makes Sam feel a lot better.

"Oh," Sam says. "Doesn't matter. I'm glad for the visit."

"See you've got your bag," Sue says, indicating the messenger bag. "Going picking?"

"Yep," Sam answers cheerily.

"Got a gun?"

"Yep," Sam says and pats her hip. "See you in a little bit. Oh, and Hannie said she needs your help in the kitchen."

"I've got a nice selection set aside for you," Sue tells her, pointing with her small spade to the corner where a collection of plants rest in a tray.

"Awesome," Sam remarks blandly. She just wants to get to the woods before she has to see him.

"I'm so glad you're here, Samantha," Sue says, kisses her cheek and leaves.

Sam fast walks past the barns and into the woods, enjoying the warmth of the afternoon. There is a low cloud cover rolling in from the west which promises rain. Sam squats near the base of an oak tree and digs up wild chickweed. She knows there is a hill behind the cattle barn where mint grows and another near Grams's rose garden. Later she'll dig up a start for that, as well. Mint is particularly useful for stomach ailments. For now, these herbs will work for grinding and using medicinally at the new practice. Grandpa is also sending back with them antibacterial creams, salves, and two gallons of antibiotic tincture. Sam moves farther along the forest's edge selecting and storing plants in her pack.

"What the hell are you doing out here?" Simon barks loudly as he approaches, startling her and causing Sam to fall backward onto her bottom.

Before she can stand on her own, Simon is towering over her. Then he grasps her upper arm and pulls her to her feet.

"Gathering herbs if you don't mind!"

"In fact, I do mind. This isn't safe," Simon states angrily, his blue eyes fierce and strangely irrational.

"Henry and three of his friends are on guard, so it is perfectly safe," she informs him.

"I already saw your boyfriend and his three goons," he says with uncharacteristic tactlessness for Simon. "They're going over their intel on the highwaymen with Derek."

Ignoring his insinuation about herself and Henry, Sam changes the subject and asks, "What have you guys found out? Anything new or helpful?"

He pauses, scowls and says, "No, nothing new. Don't change the subject, Samantha. This isn't..."

"I know, I know. Gimme' a break, Simon," she orders and turns her back to him to choose more herbs.

"I wouldn't even have known you were out here if it weren't for Sue telling me about your visit just now," he informs her.

"So? I'm safe and sound. I don't need you to be my babysitter. I've got my pistol, and I'm not going far from the farm."

"Why are you being so needlessly bullheaded? All you had to do is ask, and I would've brought you out here."

Simon steps around her, blocking her view of what's behind him. Sam tips her head to the side with annoyance.

"If I would have wanted you to tag along, I would've asked. Get it? I don't want you here. Now go back and leave me alone!"

He looks stunned by her directive. And a little dejected.

"I absolutely will not," he returns after he composes himself.

"Then stand way over there," Sam says, pointing toward a clearing. "I don't want you near me. Way, way, way over there."

"What? That's…"

"Go! I mean it, Simon. If I would've known you'd be here today, I wouldn't have come. I don't want to be around you anymore."

"That's rather rude," he comments as if offended.

She sighs and says to him as patiently as possible, "Simon, we are not friends anymore. You hurt me." This causes him to flinch, but Sam just keeps going. "I don't want to be around you. This won't happen again. Trust me, this is my last trip over here when you're home."

"Sam!" he says as if he can't believe her.

She sees that her words have assaulted his feelings, but he hadn't given any particular amount of care to hers when he'd rejected her so callously knowing full well that she was in love with him. Every time she is around Simon, it is like a kick in the pants reminder of that day. She has been spending a lot of time with Henry and her new friend, Courtney. She likes them both very well, and they have a lot of fun together. They play cards with Courtney's love interest. At first, Sam hadn't understood the rules to some of the games, but she has come to enjoy their time together in the evenings. It passes the loneliest hours of the day, something she needed in order to help her grow stronger.

"Hey, guys!" Gretchen calls to them and waves as she comes into view behind Simon.

"Hi, G," Sam greets her, trying to offer a smile, even though she'd like to punch Simon.

330

"Let's go swimming," she says as she puffs on a cigarette. "Grandpa said we could. Derek even said that Henry and his friends could join us and he'd keep an eye on the place for a short bit while we cool off."

"Why are you smoking?" Simon asks with judgment in his voice. "Where'd you get that?"

"I grew and harvested my own tobacco plants, nerd boy," G says.

This 'nerd boy' thing must be new. Sam smiles. Good. He deserves someone to give him a hard time.

"Don't be obtuse, G," he scolds. "Put that out right now."

"I will. Right before I jump in the lake!" she replies with an ornery attitude.

Her hair has grown out just a bit, but Sam knows she'll probably want it lobbed right back off. She is wearing her signature black skinny jeans, combat boots, and what looks like one of her brother's t-shirts because it is way too big for her.

"The lake's probably not even warm enough for swimming yet, Gretchen," Simon states. "It's only May."

"So? I'm sweating to death. Susan said it'll be warm enough. We're all hot and miserable."

"Sure," Sam says just to irritate Simon. "I'll go."

"You'll both get sick."

G rolls her eyes and says, "It's like eighty-five degrees. We're hardly gonna die. Besides, according to your motherly nagging about my smoking all the time, I'll probably die from emphysema first."

"I only lecture you for your own good."

"Look around, dude. In case you missed it, the world's kind of a real shit storm now. I'm more at risk of catching a bullet than lung cancer."

"I doubt your actual mother would like you smoking. Or your brother."

"Gosh, you're a grump today. Someone piss in your Cheerios this morning?"

Sam bursts out laughing at G's garish reference. Simon scowls hard at her.

"Hey, that's an inappropriate thing for a young lady to say," he reprimands. "Watch your language."

G shakes her hands in front of her and says, "Oooh, I'm so scared."

"You will be if I report this to your brother."

Sam is enjoying their interaction. She didn't know G was such a thorn in Simon's side.

"Blah, blah, blah. What are you gonna do? Tattletale on me? Don't be such a bore, Simon," G comes back on him. "Come swimming with us. It'll help lighten your mood, nerd boy."

Sam can see him clenching his jaw tightly.

"No, thank you," he finally utters angrily.

"You never do anything fun. I'd bet you've never done a bad thing in your life. You're such a square."

"At least I won't be catching pneumonia today."

"All right, then you can sit on the shore and watch us have fun!"

"This is a ridiculous idea," Simon tells them both.

Sam loops her arm through G's and begins walking. They stride with confidence right past Simon, and Sam feels a tad bit of a gloat coming on. Although it is hot out, Sam doesn't particularly feel the need for a swim. But if it is going to annoy Simon, then she's up for a nice, long swim in the lake, however cold the water might be.

Simon follows after them all the way to the house where he then attempts to convince Derek that the water is too cold for swimming. Derek just laughs and tells him to get in and check it out for himself. Henry and his friend Jerome are going to swim with them, but the other two have opted out and will stay by the house with Derek. Sam runs upstairs to her old room and pulls a swimsuit out of Paige's drawer since she won't have need of it today. It may be slightly too snug because her friend is thinner and taller. She meets G in the downstairs hallway along with Ari, Huntley, Justin and Reagan.

"Swimming with us, Reagan?" Sam asks her mentor.

"Hell, yes. If I get any bigger, I'll be mistaken for a whale, and you all will be trying to push me back into the water."

"No swearing in the house!" Hannah calls from the kitchen. Reagan just rolls her lovely eyes and laughs bawdily.

"Be back in an hour or so for dinner," Sue instructs them as they file through the kitchen with towels in hand.

"Yes, ma'am," Huntley answers for them.

Henry and his friend are waiting in the back yard and are both borrowing cut-off blue-jean shorts for swim trunks, which is what most of the guys on the farm wear since they never really have found a lot in the way of swimwear on runs. When the fall happened, it wasn't even April yet, so stores hadn't stocked their shelves and racks with swimming apparel. They were fortunate enough that the McClane sisters already had swimsuits on the farm. One time at a surplus sporting goods store in Nashville, John found a few women's swimsuits but still nothing in the men's department for them.

"Too bad Cory's not here," Ari says, pining as usual for him. "He loves swimming with us."

"Yeah, too bad," Sam agrees and looks at Reagan with knowing eyes. Reagan shakes her head and chuckles. Poor Ari. She's still in love with him. Cory is her hero, right behind her dad, of course.

They walk to the lake, and before they even get to it, the kids take off on a foot race to see who can be the first to cannonball in. Huntley wins, of course, being the oldest, but he is just lucky that Ari didn't trip him.

Simon meets up with Reagan and Sam on the path, and Henry and his friends are a few paces ahead of them.

"Reagan, be careful in the lake," Simon warns with genuine concern.

"I will," she answers. "It's a rare day. I don't feel like throwing up for a change, and I actually have a tiny amount of spare energy."

"You won't once you get done swimming," Sam remarks with a smile.

"Right, so don't overtire yourself," Simon reminds her.

"No kidding," she says. "You guys might have to carry my big butt back to the house."

"No, it's almost dinner time," Simon hints. "You'll probably run us down to get to the table."

Reagan slaps his arm, to which he chuckles. Sam even smiles. Henry and his friends jump in from the dock while Reagan and Sam take their time and use the ladder. The water isn't cold at all, but it does feel refreshing. At least it washes away some of the humidity that was clinging to her skin from the oppressive heat. Grandpa said he thinks it's going to be a really hot summer. He estimates with the mild winter, they will probably suffer a miserable, stifling summer. The men are concerned about a drought. They haven't had this problem yet, but Sam is quite sure they will know how to handle it.

Huntley and G take turns doing back flips off of the dock while Sam swims out farther into the deeper area. Grandpa's lake is nearly five acres in size, so she won't attempt an English Channel swim of it. Reagan stays near the dock floating on her back, her tummy bump sticking up above the water.

"Hey, getting kind of far from the dock, aren't you?" Henry asks as he swims up to her.

Sam stops paddling out and treads water beside him. "No, I'm a good swimmer."

"I can see that," he praises. "The water feels great."

"Yes, it does," she says, wishing he'd swim away. She can see Simon "standing guard" on the dock. Although his ball cap is pulled down low on his forehead, she can tell he is mostly staring her down, so Sam looks away.

"So were you in the same group with Dave's men in the Army?" she asks, curious as to how they know each other.

"No, ma'am," he answers. "I was in the Marines. Dave's a G.I. Joe. Army. I was a gunner in the Marines. That's why they call me Gunny."

"Then how did you know each other before? I mean, you were friends, right?"

"Yes, I knew Dave from way back," he answers. "We were in a situation over in Somalia once. His unit was called in to help us. We ended up working together for about three months that time. Another time we ran into each other stateside at a benefit dinner for some friends of mine who were killed during a practice run."

"What's that mean, stateside?"

"Oh, it just means here, in the states, not overseas or deployed or anything like that. We just became friends. He even came down to the farm once and met my folks, stayed for a weekend while he was on leave."

"That's cool," she says, marveling at how small the world seems sometimes. He reaches toward her, and Sam jerks back. It is an innocent, instinctive reaction. She doesn't particularly like being this close to men, even though she trusts Henry. That doesn't mean she wants him reaching for her.

"Sorry, ma'am," he says and points instead. "You've got a twig in your hair.

"Oh," Sam says and feels around until she finds it. The twig is more like a small stick, and it is tangled and stuck and won't budge. She tugs and can see it out of the corner of her eye. It's more like a twig from a bush with barbs, and the barbs are what's holding it in place. She pulls harder. "Ouch! Stupid stick!"

"May I?" Henry asks this time and swims closer.

Soon they are doggy paddling and laughing as he works for nearly two full minutes trying to dislodge the twig without ripping out a big chunk of her hair.

"Thanks!" she finally says as he holds up the eight-inch long, mangled branch. "Gosh, that was in there good."

"Must've picked it up in the water," he acknowledges and flings it far away.

Sam laughs and teases, "I was trying to go for a swamp monster kinda' look today. Now you've ruined it."

Henry laughs and says, "I think you'd have to try harder to be unattractive than just a stick in your hair."

His brown eyes have taken on a softness, and she knows he is flirting with her. Sam swallows hard and looks away.

"Race ya' back!" she blurts and starts without waiting. She's not above cheating.

After thirty yards or so, Henry grabs her foot, pulling her under. Sam comes up spurting and laughing. Then she hefts herself onto his shoulders and shoves him under and takes off again. It goes this way until they reach the dock, and she's pretty sure he lets her win.

"You, Miss Samantha Patterson, are a cheat!" he exclaims with a laugh as he catches up.

Huntley calls to them from the dock where he is lounging on a towel and soaking up the sun. He gets even darker in the summer, his skin a beautiful bronze. "Derek called down. Dinner's almost ready!"

Sam sends him a wave and approaches the ladder. Reagan is already out and drying off. As Sam is climbing the ladder, her foot slips on the wet wood, and she nearly falls. Henry is there to help her, though, by grasping her around the waist and holding her steady.

"Careful there!" he says and releases her again.

"Thanks," she mumbles and then laughs. "Slippery steps are not ideal for the uncoordinated."

"No problem, Sam," Henry says with a smile.

Sam climbs the rest of the way by herself and takes a towel from Huntley's outstretched hand. He regards her with a curious expression. When she looks at Simon, he is looking at Henry with a less curious but more deadly expression on his face. Sam notices his finger methodically tapping the trigger guard on his rifle. His ball cap is pulled low, his left eyebrow arched, his back slightly curved like a cat's before it pounces. Sam ignores him and turns to Henry and Jerome.

"Tonight we're having Italian!" Sam announces and hands them both a towel to use. Jerome's dark skin is glinting in the late day sunshine. He's always kind and appreciative and takes the towel with a smile that nearly glows his teeth are so white. Her friend, Courtney,

336

looks up to him like a father figure. She is also an orphan like his young grandchildren. Sam has watched him around her new friend and believes Jerome's feelings are reciprocal. He seems to have taken an interest in her friend's safety and happiness. He's great with his grandchildren, but always makes time for Courtney, as well. He is a good man in Sam's estimation.

"Oh, that's not necessary," Henry is fast to say. "We brought some apples and jerky, ma'am."

"Sam!" she corrects him about her name again. "And you have to stay for dinner. Sue and Hannah knew you guys would be joining us. It'd be an insult not to eat what they've prepared."

"No, it wouldn't," Simon says and steps out of the shadow of the weeping willow tree near the dock.

Reagan whips around and smacks Simon on the back of his hard head. "Don't be a dick. These are our guests, and they're helping you and Derek keep the place safe tonight while the men are gone. They help us. We feed them."

Sam's mouth falls open. Reagan loves Simon; everyone knows this about her. Sam can't believe she was just mean to him.

"Yes, ma'am," Simon retorts through gritted teeth.

"Now, Huntley, run along with these men and show them where they can get cleaned up for dinner," Reagan says.

"Yes, ma'am," Huntley says and bolts with the kids and Henry and Jerome with fear of Reagan in his hazel eyes. Arianna immediately starts jawing the ears off of Henry and his friend.

Reagan turns and says to Sam and Simon, "You two, collect the towels and come up in a few minutes."

"All right," Sam says with leery speculation.

Reagan looks at Simon and says, "Work out whatever issues you have and get it done before you come up to the house. But don't bring your attitude to dinner and ruin it for Hannah and Sue."

"Yes, ma'am," he says, although he looks as though he'd enjoy drowning Reagan right now.

"I don't need to talk to Simon. I'm fine. I'm coming with you," Sam says, ignoring him and poking her nose in the air.

"Yes, you do," Reagan says and turns to leave. She doesn't look back but marches away from them and up the hill toward the house. From behind, she doesn't even look pregnant. She's as petite as ever.

Sam picks up the three damp towels from the dock and hangs them over her arm. She avoids Simon and starts walking past him. He snatches her by the upper arm, stopping her.

"What do you think you're doing?" he asks, unhidden anger in his tone.

"Going up to dinner." She isn't about to be lectured by him. Again. "Let me go."

Simon doesn't release her but steps in front of Sam, blocking her escape.

"Bullcrap. What's going on with you and Henry?"

Sam scoffs in his face and rages, "None of your business. Leave me alone. Get out of my way."

"Not until you tell me what's going on. I told you I don't like him."

Sam laughs haughtily and states, "As if I would take relationship advice from the likes of you. Get real, Simon. And as for a judge of someone's character, I'll take Dave's opinion over yours. Your opinions mean nothing to me anymore."

"Is that why you came here today? To rub it in my face that you're with someone I clearly don't approve of?"

Sam groans and says, "No, I didn't do any such thing. Why would it be rubbing it in your face? You didn't want me!"

Simon flinches and says, "It doesn't..."

She ignores him and keeps going, "As a matter of fact, I only came to the farm today because I thought you wouldn't be here. Why do you think I don't come to clinic days? Because I don't want to help people? Of course not! I have no desire to see you, be around you, or even talk to you, Simon."

Simon swallows hard. She has to get around him and up to the house before her anger turns into tears. Her statements are untruths, but she can't allow them to be. She has been practicing

338

these hateful mantras in her head for weeks hoping they'd stick. Just seeing him, his auburn hair glinting in the sunshine, his stupid ball cap in place to hide the red of his hair, his eye glasses, and his hands stuffed deep in his pants pockets make her heart jolt to a sudden stop. It's always like this when she has to see Simon. It just hurts her and creates new scars. This is the real reason she doesn't want to be around him. However, he is making her truly mad with his managing attitude.

"That's very immature, Samantha," he says.

Irritating, judgmental, managing attitude.

"Who cares what you think?" she asks and steps back, thinking she'll fool him. He just advances.

"You should care what I think. I only have your best interests at heart."

"Lie."

"Not a lie. I care about you. So, are you with him now? Is that it? Are you…involved?"

Sam tries to go around him, but Simon steps in front of her again. "I don't owe you an explanation. Henry is a good person. He's the right-hand man of Dave, so, of course, he's a good man."

"He had his hands all over you, Samantha. He's a lecherous person. I can tell."

Sam attempts to sidestep him again, but he's too fast. It's starting to piss her off. He's acting like an annoying bully.

"Move!"

"Explain!" he demands as if he's her personal guardian and has the right to do so.

"Damn it, Simon! Stay out of my life," she retorts with mounting anger and resentment and eyes filled with unshed tears. "Listen to me. I told you before. We aren't friends. I don't like you anymore. As a matter of fact, I don't owe you a damn thing! You're just the bastard that hurt my feelings and made me so miserable I had to leave my home and start over elsewhere. I hate your damn guts!"

"Stop swearing!" Simon mandates. "It sounds ridiculous and lewd on you. And stop acting like a child. Swearing is for adults, which you obviously have not yet become. Or is this swearing phase something you're learning from your new boyfriend?"

"Maybe he's teaching me more than that!" she suggests on a hiss of fury. Of course, it's a lie, and she knows it, but Simon is pushing her too far. Sam steps past him only to have him grab her arm again. She screeches at him this time. "Stop it! Let me go, you jerk!"

Sam wrenches her arm free, but it causes Simon to lose his balance. He teeters, flails his arms and a second later falls into the water making a big splash. Sam's eyes about pop out of her head. His rifle is with him. He's going to be so angry! Simon is not the sort of person to laugh about such an accident on a good day, let alone when he is in such a bad mood. There is no way she's sticking around to find out. Sam sprints for the house, carrying the towels and leaving her borrowed flip-flops. When she gets to the horse pasture, she just climbs over the fence instead of opening the gate. She runs as if the devil himself is on her heels. She knows that using logic and explaining to him that it was his fault, not hers, isn't going to work in this situation. She risks a glance over her shoulder and sees that he is hot on her trail, although he is walking with methodical single-minded determination and not running for dear life like her. Unfortunately for Simon, she beats him to the back porch and into the house. Simon comes in only mere seconds later.

"Oh, Simon!" Sue says. "I see you decided to go swimming, after all."

He isn't carrying his rifle, and he looks fit to be tied.

"Off you go, you two kids," Hannah says with less patience. "Go on now and get ready for dinner. Nobody wants to eat cold pasta."

Simon looks from Sam to Hannah and back again.

"I'm not hungry," he snaps.

Then he flees to the basement in a huff of unrequited rage and resentment. Sue chuckles, looks with accusation at Sam, who shrugs, and goes back to her work at the stove. Sam runs upstairs and changes back into her dry clothing, including a sweatshirt to chase

340

away the chill of the lake. She brushes out her hair and braids it, leaving it damp. Then she looks in the mirror and sighs. It's going to be a long twenty-four hours before she gets to depart the farm again. Then she heads downstairs to help the family with final preparations for dinner. All the while she works in the kitchen with her sisters, Sam looks over her shoulder, keeping an eye on those basement stairs lest he come up them in a fit of anger. From time to time, Sue chuckles. Sam wishes she could find the situation humorous, but she's never seen Simon so angry. She is relieved when he doesn't take his usual seat at the table. Henry unknowingly sits in Simon's assigned place.

Chapter Twenty-two
Cory

They've been watching the country club for nearly three hours, and the sun is getting low in the sky. John and his brother even took a break and went raiding for more supplies and came back. There is near constant movement on the overgrown grounds of the club. They've been to this place before, raiding it for supplies, but didn't find much. They certainly never found people living there. It would seem that there is an established community complete with armed guards and a large garden already planted and flourishing, much like their gardens at the farm. The question is whether or not these people are the highwaymen, potentially new allies, or future enemies.

"It's getting late," John says. "Why don't you two head to the cabin? We'll go there tonight instead of the hotel up by Fort Campbell."

"We're good. We can stay here while you guys go to the cabin," Cory says in return.

"Paige needs to rest," Kelly corrects him. "Go to the cabin. John and I will stay here and continue surveillance."

"Yes, sir," he answers his brother. "Don't do anything I wouldn't do."

"You mean kill all of them?" Kelly jokes and punches his shoulder.

Cory just laughs. "That's always plan B."

"Kind of hard to make new friends when they're all dead, little brother."

"Your call," he jokes, making John laugh. "Ready, beanpole?"

Paige shoots him a snarky look.

"Sure, Neanderthal," she replies and gets a laugh from Kelly and John.

"We'll come by at oh-four-hundred hours, Cor," John says. "We'll keep an eye on this place and see if anything turns up."

"Got it," Cory answers and bumps his fist against John's.

He takes Paige down the small incline to their hidden four-wheeler and maneuvers them safely back out of the city. Cory drives them to the cabin in the woods, the one they stayed at a while back with Simon and Sam. The foliage of the warm season has covered in their path well and has even concealed part of the cabin. They already unloaded all of their loot into the back of the truck, so now all they have to transport are the packs on their backs.

"Doesn't seem like we'll need a fire," Paige says, fanning her face with her hand. "It's so hot."

"As hot as Arizona?" he teases as he parks the ATV behind the cabin.

Paige chuckles and gets off. "No, not quite that hot. But it's still pretty warm. Looks like it's going to rain, too. I hope the guys don't stay out if it rains."

"Why? Are they gonna melt?"

She lightly backhands him, connecting with his stomach. He just laughs at her.

"Let's get inside and eat some dinner before that storm hits," he suggests as he opens the back door to the cabin.

He watched for signs of intruders as he drove slowly up the path to the cabin and again when he veered off the path around the purposely felled tree across it. There were no footprints or tire tracks, and also no smashed down grasses or broken twigs and branches. The cabin doesn't show any evidence of anyone having visited it recently, human or animal. The dummy security system of string across the inside of the front door is still intact, too. They are safe.

343

"I'll get the food set out if you need to use the facilities," Cory offers.

"Great, thanks," Paige says.

"If you want a hot bath, I'll start getting the water ready," he suggests.

"Yeah, maybe."

She leaves for the small bathroom, and Cory digs out their food from the saddle bag that he had draped in front of him on the four-wheeler. He places everything on the small table near the window. He takes cut firewood from the bin near the cook-stove and ignites a fire inside of it. Then he pumps water from the sink into the large, metal bucket and places it on the stove to warm it. Paige emerges from the bathroom and joins him at the table.

"Who do you think those people are at the golf course?" she asks as they eat their dinner of cold potato salad, slices of cured ham, and a dish that he doesn't know how they make but he likes it just the same which contains cold kidney beans, chunks of tomato, corn kernels, onions, a variety of different peppers, cucumber, and spices from the garden mixed with vinegar and some kind of oil. It's one of his favorite summertime dishes. "I'm so glad they made the bean salad. This is the best vegetarian dish I've ever eaten. I love it when Sue and Hannah make this."

Cory hides his smile and says, "I have a feeling the people on the golf course are innocent enough. I don't think we have anything to worry about from them."

"They were armed. They had guards and a lot of people."

"So does our town now," he reminds her.

Paige nods as she takes a dinner roll from the plate. "True. I guess we can't judge people for doing what we do, too."

"Right, and they didn't look like they had captive people or like they were doing anything to hurt people. I'm not exactly sure if we want to approach them or not. I'll leave that decision up to John and Kel."

"Would you have approached them back when you were on your own?" she asks, her gray eyes searching his.

344

Cory shakes his head. "Nah, probably not. I would've done the same thing we're doing. Observing, moving on if they aren't a threat to myself or others."

"It sounds like you were doing a lot of vigilante justice stuff when you were out there on the road."

Again she is trying to read him. Cory doesn't really want to hide things from her, but he also doesn't want her to be disgusted by him or find him abhorrent.

"Some," he answers as honestly as he can.

"I wish you'd been around when my friends and I had trouble with people," she reveals.

Cory rises and dumps the hot water into the tub and fills the bucket again. He returns to the table to continue their meal.

"So do I, Red," he agrees. Cory is so thankful that she had sufficient survival skills those three years on the road to stay alive. He watches as she takes a jam-filled danish from the bag. Apparently, she's going for dessert. Her cheeks are flushed with high color, her nose sprinkled with newly sprouted freckles from the early summer sun. Paige looks fresh and young, carefree even.

"What?" she asks, catching him staring.

"You just look so pretty," he compliments.

"Hardly," she criticizes. "I'm covered in dirt and grime from the day."

He dumps her water into the tub again and refills the bucket. Cory is hoping to fill the tub rapidly so that he can extinguish the fire in the stove. It's already hot enough without adding more heat to the small cabin. When he returns, she has put away the remainder of the food and is still eating her sweet roll. Cory walks to her and takes the danish out of her hand. A low grumble of thunder rolls over the hills in the distance.

"Hey! What are you doing?" she asks as he tugs her upward to stand in front of him.

"I have a different dessert in mind," he says and kisses Paige ardently. She tastes like strawberry jam. After a moment, she returns his attentions and pulls him closer. He leans back and says, "I'm also proving to you how lovely you look. I can't have you insulting my favorite vegan redhead."

She laughs, tossing her head back and exposing her long, thin neck, which Cory immediately kisses.

"You don't even know any other vegan redheads," she tells him.

He is glad when she leans into him instead of pulling away. "I know some blondes, but compared to my feisty redhead, they're kinda' dull."

"I'm not *your* redhead," she corrects.

"Let me prove it to you that you are," Cory offers and swings her into his arms.

He gently places Paige on the bed and removes most of his clothing. Then he takes his time and removes hers.

"Your brother and John…"

"Won't be here till four in the morning," he informs her. It is exactly the reason he isn't waiting until later to initiate this.

Then Cory makes her forget all other silly notions of stopping him. He makes love to her in a leisurely fashion, slowly, controlled, and patient. She pants, and he touches her more deeply. He groans, and she cries out with tiny sounds of her own in his ear. Cory wrings everything out of her that she has to give and more. They are both spent, high on passion, and breathing hard when it is over. Afterward, he holds her in the crook of his arm, hands clasped with hers across his bare stomach, her right leg draped carefree over his. He's pretty sure she's asleep. Cory slips out of bed and goes back to his task of filling the tub for her. He lets Paige sleep while he prepares her bath. Then he leans down and kisses her neck to awaken her.

"Time for your bath, milady," he teases and gets a groan.

The sun is long since gone from the sky, and the cabin is illuminated only by the dying glow of the cook-stove, lightning flickering across the sky, and the single lantern he has lit. The thunderstorm outside has picked up with intensity, and the wind occasionally rattles the single pane windows.

346

Paige pulls on his t-shirt and her hair back into a ponytail. Then she twirls it around and around and around and secures it into a knot on the top of her head. Cory is fascinated by her feminine rituals. He's never been around women in this capacity, not since he lived back home with his mom and Em. He certainly never paid attention back then. Paige has never looked more alluring to him, and he also has no idea how she just did that with her hair. Women have some strange and unusual talents for odd things. Cory's small ponytail, not more than three inches most of the time is a pain in the ass. Sometimes he thinks he'd like to go with a high and tight like Derek. Of course, lately, Derek doesn't even shave. Cory fears that John's brother is sinking deeper into a depression with each passing day that he can't walk without the use of the walker- or the wheelchair when he can't take the pain anymore. He knows that John has noticed it, too.

"Take your time," he says as he places the lantern on the floor of the bathroom for her.

"I'll probably fall asleep in here," she says, looking at the steaming bath water.

"No worries," he says. "I'll rescue you before you die of hypothermia."

"Good to know," she says and actually raises on her toes to kiss his cheek before swiftly turning away.

It makes Cory smile ear to ear as he turns to leave, closing the door behind him to offer her privacy. She's coming around. Or at least he hopes she is. He'd like to announce their relationship to the family and let the chips fall where they may. She is so much more easy-going when they are away from the farm, but Cory would eventually like to see their relationship get to this point back on the farm, too.

He cleans up after them and even makes their bed again in case John and his brother come back earlier than four a.m. He also packs their bags so that they'll be ready to go when the guys do get to the cabin. He's thankful that they aren't staying in the cabin in Nashville. It holds too many bad memories. He loved his little sister, but he doesn't want to relive the night he lost her over and over again. That already plays out in his memories and bad dreams more nights than not.

Cory closes the door on the cook-stove as the last embers die. He's glad to be done with that. No sense in tossing and turning later in a ball of his own sweat. He decided, after watching her fall asleep so quickly after sex, that he will relieve his brother and John at the golf course without Paige. He doesn't need her just for a simple surveillance job. Hopefully, he wore her out enough that she won't put up an argument and want to join him for a night of spying. He wishes he could just send a text to his brother and inquire about the status of the people at the country club. It was so much easier four years ago to communicate with people. Of course, if the world hadn't fallen apart, then he wouldn't be surveilling the inhabitants of a golf course. He would likely be overseas killing people of extreme religious views who wanted to destroy America and all of her citizens.

He hits the button on his watch, illuminating the numbers. Almost midnight. Four hours until his brother returns. Cory slings his rifle and goes to the bathroom door.

"Gonna go out on a perimeter check, Paige," he says through the door to her.

"'Kay, I'm finishing up here," she calls back.

He can hear water splashing.

"Need any help?"

"No!" she exclaims and then laughs softly.

"Be back in ten."

He takes a ball cap out of his pack to cover his head from the rain and goes out the front door. He climbs to the left of the cabin up into the woods until he is at the top of the hill where he can see for a long distance. He rests against a thick oak tree while taking shelter under its massive branches and fully bloomed leaves. The creatures of the night are alive and conversing, those brave enough to confront the storm. The birds have burrowed down somewhere and are likely hiding from their predatory counterparts, but he can still

348

hear the occasional hooting of an owl and the scurrying of tiny feet along the forest floor. Cory walks in the general direction of the road, which is still a good two miles away. If the city were still functioning, he'd probably be able to see lights or at least a glow from where he is, but not anymore. There is nothing left to see in any city, and it makes him question again why Robert McClane is so hell-bent on taking over the eastern half of the country. He'd like to be rid of him as they rid themselves of Gram's brother and his band of merry marauders. The only good thing that came of that situation was Huntley, Simon and Sam. The irony of inheriting Gretchen and her brother Lucas in the same manner is not lost on him.

Suddenly, the dim flicker of headlights in the distance bouncing along the rutted path toward their cabin alerts him and draws Cory's attention. He picks up his radio.

"You're kinda' early," he says to his approaching brother. He can tell the vehicle is the family truck by the space between the headlights. Soon it will stop at their downed tree, and they will hike the rest of the way. "Get hungry for your wife's cooking, huh?"

There is a long, pregnant pause and then static before John says, "Come again?"

"Why are you back so soon? I thought we were rendezvousing at oh-four-hundred?"

"What?" John asks. "We're still at the club. Come again?"

"You aren't here?" Cory asks, his voice filled with dread.

"No, man," John says with confusion still in his tone. "Is someone there, Cor?"

"Shit!" he curses and sprints down the hill, nearly stumbling twice. "Damn it."

"Cor?" the radio bleeps again. "Repeat sit rep, over."

John's tone is serious now as he must realize what is going on.

"Someone's here. I've gotta get Paige and get the hell outta' here."

"We're on our way," John says. "Get outta' there!"

"It looks like a truck approaching. I'll keep you posted."

John says, "Let us know if you will need to engage."

"Not with Paige," he says to his friend.

There's no way in hell he's bringing her into a firefight if it should come to that. He'd rather do that with Kelly and John. He has to get her moved to safety because the cabin is small and not well-built. Bullets from a high-power rifle could go straight through the walls. He gets one last look at the truck, which was stopped a moment ago, presumably at the fallen tree. It is moving again. Whoever is driving the vehicle has enough people with him that they have moved the tree. They are slowly making progress toward the cabin and are about a mile out. He has to get her away from here.

"Let us know where to meet you when you get it figured out."

"Breaking radio contact," Cory tells them. "I'll call you when I can. Over and out."

He turns the volume down to zero as he leaps onto the front porch, forgoing the stairs altogether. Cory blasts through the door, startling the hell out of Paige who is standing there in nothing but a towel.

"Get dressed!" he shouts. "We've got to get outta here. Someone's coming in a vehicle."

"Shit!" she blurts and flies into a flurry of movement. "What about the tree? They'll have to stop…"

"They moved it, Paige," he says and spins. He can hear her cry of fear.

Cory grabs their packs and tries to erase all signs of them having been here. It's not going to work. He doesn't have enough time to cover their tracks completely. The wood floor has wet footprints on it, and the bathroom probably does, too. The fire in the cookstove is out, but any idiot will be able to tell it is still hot.

"Hurry!" he urges when he turns back to her to find Paige pulling on her jeans.

"I am," she says with panic. "How many are there?"

Cory slings her rifle and extinguishes the oil lamp on the table where she must've placed it. He slips it under the table toward the back wall.

"Not sure. Truck. Enough men to move our log," he tells her honestly so that she can properly assess and realize the danger they could be in. It's enough to spur her into even faster motion. She has her shoes on in two seconds flat and her pistol belt strapped around her waist in three more. The front of her long-sleeved tee looks wet in places. Obviously, she hadn't even dried off when he'd come in. It doesn't matter; she is about to get a whole lot more drenched outside.

"Take your bag," he orders and leads her from the cabin. He passes Paige her rifle, too. His adrenaline is pumping, but he's not afraid. He only wants to get her to safety, and Cory doesn't care if he has to go through those people and kill all of them to do it.

They go out the back door and close it. Paige runs to the ATV.

"No," he commands and walks around it. She follows.

"Why? We can't outrun them if they're in a truck and we're on foot," she complains. He knows she's scared.

"Because there's only one way in. There aren't any other cleared paths but the one to get here. We're land-locked. We've got to get out of here on foot. Hurry."

He leads her back up the same hill but much further past the cabin. He still wants to see who they are up against. This could be the highwaymen or the ones who ran over Derek. He was hit by an SUV, but they also took Henry's truck. Dave's men think they found the abandoned SUV, but Henry's truck has yet to be recovered. He needs intel. Without it, they are simply running from an unknown threat.

"You ok?" he asks as he climbs the steep hill in front of her.

"Fine. Go faster. Let's get out of here," she says.

Cory frowns. "Don't panic. We're fine. I just want to put some distance between them and us and check them out."

He glances over his shoulder and sees the truck pulling slowly to a stop near the cabin. The people in it are obviously using caution, as well.

"Hold up," he says and pulls out his binoculars.

Paige is panting and leans over to rest her hands on her knees. It pisses him off. He knew she wasn't ready for this yet. Or ever if he had any say in the matter, which he obviously did not. She's as stubborn as her brother.

Cory spies the truck as six men jump out of the bed, and four more exit from the extended cab. He can't tell if it is Henry's truck or not because it is too dark, but the vehicle is definitely an extended cab like his.

"How many?" she asks in a whisper.

"At least ten," he answers, not sure of the exact numbers yet.

"Shit," she swears. "That's too many. We need to go."

Cory squats down, tugging her arm to follow him. He's fairly confident that the men can't see them from their low-lying position, but he doesn't want to take a chance. They are waving their flashlights around, searching the grounds around the cabin. One of them goes inside. He runs out again only a moment later and starts shouting to his comrades. Then the men tear off in different directions, some into the woods. They know that someone just left the cabin. The wet bathtub, the damp spots on the rustic wood floor, the warmth from the recently extinguished fire are all clues.

"Time to move," he says to Paige and pulls her to her feet.

"Are they coming after us?" she asks with fear in her voice.

Cory doesn't want to lie. She needs to know that they are in danger. "Yes. They know we're still here. We need to get to safety."

He leads her farther into the woods intent on making it to the grade school he knows sits just south of them where a local rec center is also located. Getting to the spot may not be difficult if they can remain hidden, but crossing the open fields when they get there and leaving the cover of the forest may be impossible. They need his brother and John to pick them up.

352

He speaks into the radio as they nearly run, "We're gonna need an evac stat. Do not approach the cabin. I repeat, do not go to the cabin."

"Sit rep," his brother asks.

"At least ten men. Armed. Cabin is overtaken. We're on foot."

Kelly says a moment later, "Grid cords for evac."

"The school," Cory says plainly. They don't have a normal rendezvous spot for this area because the cabin is supposed to be their safe haven. Now it has been invaded, and Cory isn't sure if they mean them harm or if they are not a threat at all. He knows those men have never stayed there; nobody has. But they are actively searching for him and Paige. That can't be a good sign

"Give us fifteen minutes," Kelly says.

"We'll need at least thirty, over," Cory tells them and cuts the transmission.

He knows they will have to move much faster in order to make the location for the evacuation. Unfortunately, he has to do this tactfully and without getting both of them killed. He'd gladly give his life for Paige's, but he wouldn't want to leave her behind. They could catch her, kill her, take her, torture her to find out more about her home base.

"Stop, Cory," she says, panting hard. "I've gotta stop."

Cory waits with her as she catches her breath. Paige is pressing her back against a tree. He watches their surroundings. "I'm using our night-vision goggles, Paige. You do the same."

They pull out their night-vision gear, something he thought they wouldn't need this trip. This will help them get around without running into anything or being sneaked up on. He can see better now and scans the area. The rain isn't helping, but he knows it also provides more cover. However, the ground is fully saturated, which means they are leaving muddy footprints and slides in the soft, wet earth. If any of those men can track, they'll be easy prey to find. Cory could track a chipmunk in these conditions. Off in the distance, but not far enough, he can just make out the foggy tint of hazy white light from a flashlight.

"I'm ready again," she tells him.

He takes her hand and pulls Paige along after him. A shot rings out in the night. It isn't from him. This isn't deer season. This isn't friendly fire or an accidental discharge. They are now shooting at them, taking a shot and trying to make a round stick.

"Fuck," he states in anger.

"Assholes! Why are they shooting at us?"

"Not friendlies," Cory says.

"How can they even see us?" she whispers to herself.

Cory doesn't answer but stops with her. He presses her up against a wide tree trunk and a mangle of fallen trees. It could be an animal den, so he hopes nothing comes out of it. For now, it's the safest place for her.

"Behind here. Stay low."

He pulls his rifle up to his shoulder and scans the perimeter through the scope. Another shot rings out, this time closer, ricocheting off of a tree near them. The sound is piercing in the quiet of the night. It pisses Cory off. He takes aim at the shadowy figure of a man running through the woods. Cory can see that the other person also has on night-vision gear. He doesn't pull the trigger because the man is concealed the next moment by a tree, and he doesn't have a clear shot. He doesn't want to draw attention to them without at least making one kill.

"Stay here," he says to Paige and touches her arm. She is shaking. "I'll let you know it's me when I return. If I don't give you the signal, shoot whoever comes over here."

He sprints to the north a few yards, hoping to outsmart the man, who seems to be heading in that direction. Cory hides behind a tree and removes his dagger from its sheath on his hip. He waits patiently, listening to the sound of the man's footsteps drawing closer, slapping in sloshy, shallow puddles. He allows the man to take two steps past him before pouncing on him from behind. His opponent is not small, but Cory is still able to overpower and kill him

354

with one stab into the side of the man's neck. He lays him down quietly, wipes his dagger on the man's shirt, and notices that his opponent has on a Kevlar vest and is wearing night-vision. His gun looks like a military or police issue rifle.

As he is standing again, a shot is fired and hits the tree near Cory's head. The second round wings him in the right leg. It feels like a hornet's sting slicing through his outer thigh. He drops to his stomach and crawls to the cover of a dense copse of trees. The shot came from behind him, so Cory shimmies his way around a particularly thick tree and rises to one knee. He doesn't see the person who shot at him. He scans along the edge of the trees, watching, waiting patiently. Nothing. He doesn't see movement, but he does hear shouting, and it sounds like it is close. He has to get Paige out of here.

Another shot rings out behind him, and the unmistakable cry of a man being clipped by a rifle's bullet rings true in the darkness of the overcast night. He spies through his scope but doesn't see anything.

Cory limp-sprints back to her, splashing mud all over his boots and pants and emits the sound of a bird as quietly as he can so that she doesn't shoot him.

"Let's go," he says with new urgency.

"I shot that man," she fervently whispers. "I took my time and shot him like Simon taught me."

"The dude over there where I went?"

"Yes," she says breathlessly. "I saw him trying to track you down, and I saw him take a shot at you."

"Apparently your brother isn't the only sniper in the family, Red." He omits the fact that their opponent connected with his own shot, too.

She gives an awkward smile. They take off, Cory stumbles a few times.

"Are you all right?" she frets.

"We gotta get to the school. They're catching up to us," he urges and presses on.

He knows his wound needs a tourniquet, but there's no time. It'll have to wait, and he just hopes he doesn't lose enough blood in the meantime that he passes out. Paige stumbles, but Cory helps her back upright. It feels as if they are moving at a snail's pace, although he is thankful that she isn't ready for an hour long sprint since he's not in top form at the moment. He skids a few feet down a short incline and grits his teeth at the pain in his outer thigh.

"You've been shot," she hisses with new fear.

"I'm fine," he says. "Keep moving."

Another shot rings out, this time to their south, which is where he needs to go with her. Whoever it is shooting at them this time is almost parallel with them in the woods as if they were trying to flank. He refuses to be outmaneuvered. Cory will need to take care of it in order to go down the hill that will lead them to the school. He also doesn't want to lead his brother and John straight into an ambush.

Paige cries out with a high-pitched yelp at the loud crack of another shot and ducks instinctively. They both stop simultaneously and get low.

A few seconds later, she says, "Oh, shoot. Cory, you're bleeding pretty badly."

Her fingertips touch the forest floor and come away with sticky, red blood on them, his blood.

"I said I'm fine. We just need to get to the school."

Paige brings her pack around front and pulls out gauze from the side pocket.

"Dammit, I'm fine," he whispers. "I need to take care of whoever's below us."

"And I need to take care of you," she corrects him vehemently.

Cory can still hear shouting far away. Some of these men seem to have experience, but others are behaving in a loud and boisterous manner. He wonders if they are doing it to intimidate them or if they are just idiots without training and experience.

He winces as she tightens the gauze strip around his upper thigh, stemming the blood flow. A loud grunt below them somewhere sounds as if the man who'd just shot at them has fallen or tripped. They need to move. If Cory can hear the man grunt, then he's too close to them. The school is only a half mile from their location, which means they will have to make a run for it.

"Wait here," she says and runs in a hunched over squat to peer down over the hill before he can stop her.

"Damn it," he whispers and rises, only to wince and stumble.

She runs back and says, "I don't see him. Let's make a run for it."

She is mimicking his unspoken directive. This is a decision that he should be making, but he's in no position to argue. They get to the crest of the incline when more shooting at their backs surprises Cory.

"I got this, brother," John says through their radio.

Cory frowns with confusion.

"Keep your heads down a minute," John commands.

A moment later, a shot rings out. It is coming from a makeshift path along the long, narrow ridge of the hill. Another shot. Then another followed by silence. A few seconds later, John jogs up to them.

"Ready, girls?" he asks with a cocky smile.

"Someone's down that hill," Paige tells John.

"Yeah, we already met," John says, still smiling.

"Good," Cory says, knowing his friend has killed the man.

"Cory's shot," Paige blurts quietly.

"I figured something was up," John says. "Too many creeps still alive up here. Let's roll. Dave's waiting for us a few miles from here to make sure we get out."

"Yes, sir," Cory says.

John punches his shoulder and says, "Unless you need me to carry you, pretty boy."

"No, thanks," Cory remarks. "You'd just fall in love with me, and where would that get us?"

"I did like that perfume…"

"Guys! Stop. We have to get out of here," Paige hisses with irritation and fear.

"Paige, you help Cory. I'll watch our backs and get us outta here. Kel's just at the bottom of the hill with the truck."

"Got it," Paige says with relief.

They move down the hill as fast as possible with him and Paige leading and John walking backward covering them. John shoots again. And again, another cry of pain from on top of the hill can be heard even over the sound of the thunderstorm. It's the last fool who messes with them. His friend is a deadly man, he's learned. When John pulls the trigger, people die. There's no in-between, no gray area, no missed shots. A few minutes later, they make it to the truck, which his brother has idling near the back of a soccer field. Cory is glad they don't have to run across the open field. They get in, all three riding in the bed of the truck as Kelly speeds away from their cabin, their former safe haven.

Chapter Twenty-three
Simon

Once he has his rifle disassembled and the pieces laid out on the table in the shed, he begins the laborious task of drying and re-oiling all of the intricate parts. The barrel, precision trigger, and action are the last parts to be oiled. This is a highly, fine-tuned rifle for which there can be no mistakes. His Remington 700 BDL is his trusted friend. The Schmidt and Bender scope has him worried. Without it, he'd have to remove the scope and go with iron sights like he used to. The scope was found for him by Kelly three years ago in the back of a pawn shop. He doesn't know why nobody looted the entire store, which they had, and left such a valuable tool, but they did. He sighs with irritation and wipes down the ebony forend tip. He can't believe Sam caused this. She knows how much this rifle means to him. It feels like his right arm has been severed off. He feels the same way about her move to Henry's farm.

He uses Doc's tools and begins the slow process of reassembling his rifle. The work is precise and intricate. If just one screw is slightly off, it will throw his shot. It could be the difference between life and death, maybe even for someone he cares about in the McClane family. Just the other day he took his rifle to the back of the property and did some practicing with Cory. He missed a shot. That never happens. Cory had teased him, which Simon hadn't found humorous. Lately, he's had a hard time concentrating. He and Cory have been working out a lot more than usual, too, which normally helps him clear his head. Simon also goes on long runs by himself just to occupy his brain for an hour. He can tell he is gaining bulk muscle because his t-shirts are becoming too tight. It's worth it.

The rain is hitting the roof of the shed, clinking and tinkling against the metal. Lightning flashes across the sky, brightly lighting up the armory for just a brief second as he slides the barrel into place. He is so angry with her he could spit.

Having changed into dry clothing, Simon is dressed in clean jeans and a short-sleeved white t-shirt. The rain is only making the air muggy. When he is finished, he stands his rifle in the open case with others and takes an older rifle, a Mannlicher-Schonauer. It's an antique rifle, but one with which he is familiar and finds reliable. For watch duty tonight, he'll have his night-vision gear along with the rifle and sidearm. Hours have gone by since he fell into the lake. The sun has set, taking its rays with her but leaving behind the heat.

Simon locks up the armory and heads for the house, hoping to scavenge for food. He is met in the kitchen by Reagan, who is sitting at the island making notes from a medical book on a yellow legal pad.

"Get it dried out?" she asks without looking up.

Her hair is pulled up into a messy bun on top of her head, and she's sipping a hot beverage with steam rising out of the mug.

"Yes," he answers and leans his borrowed rifle in a corner.

"Good," she answers and looks at him with a grin. "You weren't getting mine."

"I have no doubt," he answers without smiling.

"Sue left you a plate in the oven," she tells him, going back to her work. "She was pissed you weren't at the dinner table."

"Had to get the water out of my rifle," he tells her what she already knows.

"It could've waited," she argues softly.

Simon ignores her and removes the hot, metal plate from the oven with a towel. He joins Reagan at the island, pouring himself a glass of milk.

"Want some?" he offers.

"Sticking with this nasty tasting tea shit," she says.

"Still sick?" Simon asks as he tears into his chicken parm. Sue can do wondrous things in the greenhouse with plants and herbs. She can do even more miraculous things with Italian dishes. He suspects she made this meal for her husband, who loves her Italian food. Derek is not doing so well. He has discussed his friend's case with Reagan and Doc quite thoroughly. They both hypothesize that the damage to Derek's leg was even worse than they'd hoped. Even though the cast is off, he would still need reconstructive surgery to be able to overcome the extensive disabilities that the vehicular assault caused.

"Not as bad," she answers.

"That's good," Simon admits with a nod, thankful he's not a woman.

Reagan shakes her head and says, "It'll be good when it gets out. This cohabitation thing is fucking irritating."

"You're swearing about your baby? That just seems wrong," he jokes with a grin. Reagan can always make him laugh, even if she isn't necessarily trying to.

"Yeah? Well, wait till you see how many times I spank this brat for making me sick all the time."

Simon chuckles quietly. The house is quiet, which means the kids have all gone to bed for the night.

"I'll have to call Child Protective Services on you."

"Who's that? Grandpa?"

He smiles. "Or Hannie. Not sure who would be worse."

"I'm still spanking this little shit for all the trouble it's causing."

"Sure, sure. You never spank Jacob," he points out.

She looks at him with the utmost seriousness and says, "That's because Jake's a little angel. This one's not."

Simon smiles. Reagan will likely never discipline either of her children, and John's certainly never going to. Jake is a cute little dude, who shadows his father all over the farm and talks constantly about being a soldier when he grows up. Simon hopes he chooses a different path in life. He also prays that there will be other choices available for the next generation instead of just survival and killing and death and diseases that the world conquered a hundred years ago.

"Probably no more than what you deserve. I hope it's a girl who drives you nuts. It'll be the biggest case of karma ever."

"Oh, Jesus," Reagan swears and looks like she just took a drink of sour milk. Simon smiles wider.

"What're you studying?" he asks as he enjoys the last chunk of perfectly crusted chicken.

"Smallpox," she answers and tips the book toward him.

"Do you think we should try to make a vaccine? I know you prick the skin with the virus and a blister forms and falls off a few weeks later," he tells her as Sam walks into the kitchen. She is wearing navy blue sweatpants and a long-sleeved black tee that blends in with her dark hair which is wavy from being wet earlier. The sleeves hang almost to her fingertips, and the hem almost to her knees. It swallows her petite frame.

She barges right into their conversation. "Right, a bifurcated needle that has been dipped into the solution containing the virus would be scraped across skin to pass the virus."

Simon takes his plate and silverware to the sink and washes them, then places them in the strainer to dry. When he turns back, Sam has claimed his chair at the island, so he stands. He stays near the sink so that he doesn't have to be too close to her.

"I don't know if we have the ability to stabilize a vaccine," Reagan admits. "We don't have phenic acid or formaldehyde. Plus, we'd need some sort of suspension liquid like glycerol."

"Why couldn't it work like chickenpox? Expose the patient to it, let them fight it off on their own and get over it," Sam suggests, twirling her long hair through her fingertips.

Reagan shakes her head and says, "It's not quite going to work like that. Smallpox is much more severe and debilitating than chickenpox. There are different strains of smallpox, too. Some are deadly like hemorrhagic."

"Gross," Sam says.

Reagan says, "Yeah, well one of the things that was a major concern for our government was biological weapons that our enemies could use against us. Supposedly there were enough vaccines at the CDC that they could inoculate every man, woman and child in this country for smallpox."

Sam asks, "Why don't we go to the CDC and find out? We could do it. We could travel there and take everything we can get our hands on. Heck, maybe there might still be doctors there, too. Maybe they'd like to come here and live where it's safe."

"We've talked about that before," Reagan says. "Grandpa and I aren't even sure what's still going to be there or if workers just abandoned the place."

"What about your father?" Simon proposes, catching a look of utter loathing from Reagan. "He said they had CDC doctors and scientists at the bunker facility in Colorado. Perhaps some of them will come to Fort Knox."

"Supposedly, according to John, there are already some doctors there who came. Maybe. If they are total buffoons, they might have followed my father."

Sam laughs. Simon just frowns.

He suggests, "But we could learn from them. If they have experience with infectious disease, it might be a good idea to establish a research facility somewhere, maybe Fort Knox."

"This is why I'm studying pediatrics with my uncle," Sam says. "I don't want to study infectious diseases and disgusting stuff. Little kids are more interesting than most adults anyway."

"You're studying with your uncle?" Simon asks. "You never mentioned that."

She shoots him a look that clearly lets him know that he is not in her inner circle anymore.

"That's a great idea, Sam," Reagan says.

"He said he'll teach me everything he knows so that I can specialize in peds like him."

"Good, with the current baby boom, we're going to need more pediatricians around here," Reagan remarks.

Simon adds, "I still think we should look into working with your father's doctors."

"Perhaps," Reagan says begrudgingly. "I'm off to bed, kiddos. Try not to get into any trouble."

"That won't be hard," Sam volunteers. "I'm going out to the barn to check on the horses."

Reagan touches Sam's shoulder and says, "Simon, you should stay with her. Make sure she gets back in safely."

"I don't need a babysitter," Sam disagrees.

"Just do it for me, 'kay?" Reagan pleads. "I'm just a little jumpy with the guys being gone and all this highwaymen shit happening all the time."

"But Henry and his friends are out there, too," Sam reminds her.

Simon grits his teeth to prevent himself from saying anything.

"Stop being so stubborn, Sam," Reagan says and leaves without another word.

"I don't need you to walk me out to the barn," she says the second Reagan is out of the room and levels him with a glare.

"Do you really think I'm stupid enough to argue with Reagan in the state she's in?" he asks.

Sam doesn't smile like she used to when he joked with her. She simply squints her eyes at him, grabs and umbrella, and leaves the house. Simon is left trailing after her to the horse barn. He spies Henry and two of his men laughing about something farther away near the end of the cow barn. Simon narrows his gaze at the man, although he knows Henry cannot see him in the dark.

Sam turns on the switch in the barn that will only illuminate the center aisle. They try to conserve electricity, especially in the barns.

"What did you want to check? Is one of them concerning you?" he asks, deferring to her judgement on the matter of horses.

"The gelding Reagan brought in yesterday. She's concerned he has a cough. It could be hay dust, but it could be stable cough. The first is ok, but the latter could mean trouble."

"Don't they get stable cough when there are a bunch of horses locked in all the time in the same barn?" he asks.

"Yes, and he was shut in for about a week and a half, Reagan said," Sam explains.

"Right, we thought he could have a pulled ligament. He was the one limping for a few days there."

She looks at him before entering the horse's stall. Her expression is one of leery caution, caution of him. She is guarded around him, has been all day.

"She checked him for strangles, too," she says and goes in with the gelding, who immediately blows hard through his nose and then settles into a series of low, rumbling nickers for her attention. He is glad to see her, of course. Simon knows the feeling. It just isn't being reciprocated lately.

"Is that worse?" he asks.

"Haven't you read this stuff? I thought Grandpa had you studying animal care, too."

"Yeah, but I'm in the middle of crash course med school. It's kind of difficult to study both. They have me focusing more on the cows. We need them for food."

"We might someday need the horses just as much. Transportation may one day come to a screeching halt if there isn't any more gas."

"We've got the natural gas vehicles now, so we're good," he says.

"Don't be too sure. That's how this all came to be in the first place. Overly optimistic world leaders who were living with their collective heads in the sand."

"That's awfully cynical. At least it is for you, Sam," he says, concerned that she is changing, and not for the better.

She ignores him and says, "Strangles would present with signs of mucus in the nostrils, fevers, enlarged lymph nodes, stuff like that. Stable cough probably isn't the problem, either."

"What do you think it is?" he asks, genuinely wanting her expert opinion.

"Could be a virus or just an allergy to something. Normally, it's just hay dust, but Reagan said she took him off the hay for a few days and he was still doing it. I told her to put him in the stallion's pen for a few days and see if it clears up. It might be something he's getting into in the pasture. Grandpa said he agreed."

"He's not doing it now," Simon observes.

"Right, so it's probably something he's exposing himself to in the field. Horses aren't exactly geniuses. They do stupid things. They get into stuff they shouldn't. They will eat things that will literally kill them."

"I know that firsthand," he says as Sam picks up a handful of bedding and sifts through it. "The other day, Reagan's gelding Harry was chewing on the side of the cow barn. It's metal."

"Yep, they aren't the brightest," she says, then rubs the horse's muzzle. "But we love you anyways."

Her tone has softened, her demeanor gentler when she talks to the horse.

"I saw you outside earlier standing and looking down at the lake. What were you doing?"

"Just watching the sun set before the rain started," she explains patiently. "I like watching it set over the lake, how the water reflects the colors."

"That's because you're an artist," he reminds her. "Everything with color attracts you."

"Or maybe because I'm a romantic," she tells him. "I like sunsets."

"Probably," he says with scorn. It bothers Simon that she finds anything romantic because the world has no place for such pretenses anymore. She needs to let all of her girlhood fantasies go

366

and face reality. Pretty sunsets, perfect romantic evenings, and finding her soulmate are just a waste of time.

She ignores him and coos to the horse again before saying, "I don't see any mold or anything in this bedding. That would definitely make them cough."

"You should go in and get some rest now," he tells her.

"Maybe I'm not ready," she back-talks.

Simon rolls his eyes. "Come on. I'll walk you back."

"No," she says defiantly and exits the stall, latching it closed. "You can go back without me. I'm staying out here for a while. I want to observe the horses in the sick bays and the two mares that are pregnant. I don't need you for that."

"Right, you've got your new boyfriend for that, don't you?"

"Sure, Simon," she says, looking up at him.

He'd like to yell at her, tell her what he thinks of her new relationship.

"I can do all those things for you and look after the horses," he offers, trying a nice-guy approach.

"You really don't think much of me, do you?" Sam asks, shocking him.

"What do you mean? I don't understand," he asks, confused as usual about women.

"Just a few short months ago, I told you that I wanted to be with you..."

"That was more than a few months. It's been nearly five," he corrects her.

"Right. Whatever," she says in a flippant tone. "So you believe that I already found someone? That I moved to Dave's camp and immediately started seeing Henry? Or one of the other men over there?"

"I don't..."

"You think I just throw my feelings after the next fish swimming by hoping to hook it? How low your opinion of me must be to presume such a thing, Simon Murphy."

She is getting this all confused. "No, I didn't..."

"As much as you like to deny them, my feelings for you were real. And now you think I've just gone and found someone else so quickly? That's saying a lot about what you think of me."

"I don't mean that at all," he inserts before she can continue disparaging him. "I don't think about you like that. You're not the kind of person to do that."

"But you keep accusing me of being with Henry now."

Her eyes are searching his with arrogant accusations behind them. She is pinning him to an answer he doesn't want to admit, and she knows it. He also feels perplexed because she made it seem as if she was seeing Henry or that they were in a relationship. Why would Sam let him think that?

"He would certainly like it if you were," Simon informs her. Perhaps she doesn't understand or see the desire in Henry's eyes. Maybe she's the one who is confused.

"So? I know that. Doesn't mean I feel the same. Or maybe I do. Who knows what the future will hold? But I'm not going to spend my life pining away after someone who doesn't want me."

"Don't say that."

"It's the truth. I'll say what I like."

She walks away, angering Simon anew. He's still mad about her pushing him into the lake and potentially damaging his best rifle. He's tired and stressed out about his sister being away from the farm. They haven't called in yet, either, which is heightening his anxiety. Samantha is pushing all of his buttons, and she needs to stop. First, she tells him that she isn't with Henry. Now she is insinuating that perhaps she is interested in him. His brain is fried tonight from stress and misunderstanding.

"Stop being so bratty," he scolds, hoping it will settle her down. Of course, since he has little to no insight into the female brain, it fails.

She spins around and points her finger at him. "Simon, you need to stop thinking you can still control me. You can't. I'll say what I please, do what I want, and be with whatever man I choose. You can just stay out of it. As a matter of fact, my uncle was just saying the other day what a nice man Henry is, especially to us for letting us stay on his farm and not in the town over there."

"Great!" he nearly shouts, then regains his composure. "Why don't we just throw a parade in his honor? We can call it Henry Day, and everyone can come over and lay alms at his altar."

"Sounds like a good plan," she says with a flash of her blue eyes. "My uncle will approve."

"Don't be asinine," he lectures and tightens his grip on the leather strap of his rifle sling. It is worn and smooth under his hand. He'd like to remove it and use it on Samantha's behind.

"Nobody's gonna lay alms at *your* feet. You're a royal jerk."

"Stop behaving childishly," he scolds, hoping she'll calm down. This usually works on Ari. Sometimes. Not the majority of the time actually. Women must become irrational, emotional creatures at an early age.

"The only nice thing about you is your sister," she continues right on as if she has suddenly become deaf and didn't hear his dictate.

She is pushing her luck. First the shove into the lake. Then the attitude. Now the insults. Simon seethes, blowing harder through his nose than the horse had a few minutes ago.

"You're so blind, Simon," she says, stepping away from him and going down the aisle.

He follows, in a hurry to receive his next insult apparently. He steps directly in front of her so that she cannot go into the mare's stall. "Oh, yeah? How am I blind, Sam?"

"Because," she explains and hops around him and keeps going down the aisle. She is not deterred. Simon presses his lips tightly together and trails after her again as they close in on the mare at the end of the barn where it is slightly darker. "You had a chance at happiness. Not a lot of people have that option anymore. But you threw it away. You threw me away. I just wanted us to be happy."

She reaches for the sliding lock mechanism, so Simon clasps his hand over hers to stop her. He forgot how small her hands are.

"I didn't throw you away," he says, guilt filing away at the serrated edges of his anger. "I just wanted you to have a good life. I can't give that to you, and we both know it."

"You didn't even try," she says. "That makes you a coward."

It takes a moment for her words to register. Swearing at him was one thing. Pushing him in the lake was another. Calling him cowardly is going too damn far.

"What did you just call me?" he asks in a deadly quiet tone.

Sam swallows hard and juts out her chin. She won't answer.

"Did you just call me a coward?" he repeats.

She must be registering the intensity of his malevolent stare because she tries to back up. Simon holds fast to her hand to prevent her from leaving and slings his rifle to the ground where he rests it against the stall door.

"A coward, huh?" he repeats and gets no answer again. "You think I'm a coward?"

Her eyes narrow, she yanks her hand free, and raises her chin another quarter inch in defiance.

"Want me to prove I'm not? I could go out there and snipe your new boyfriend," he suggests and adds, "And all of his friends. Even with this antique."

He indicates the rifle.

"Hm, where's your rifle, Simon? Take it with you when you went for a dip?" she taunts.

"Stop. You're playing a dangerous game, little girl," he warns.

"I'm not afraid of you."

She arches her back to appear taller, which doesn't work. She only manages to press her chest out farther, and Simon needs no help in staring there. He thinks about this particular part of her body quite often, usually at night when he's lying in his bed in the cabin staring at the ceiling wishing he had an Ambien or six.

"Go back to the house. Now."

She just smirks cockily and raises her left eyebrow in defiance.

370

"You're not a coward in the way you think I mean," she corrects.

"What way? What way, Samantha, am I a coward?" he asks and looms over her. She may be small, but she is irritating him as much as a horde of rabid bees.

"You're a coward with your feelings," she says. "You are so afraid of feeling what I know you feel for me that you tossed me away like a piece of garbage."

"Nobody tossed you away," he counters. "Stop being melodramatic. I wanted you to find someone else. I wanted you to be happy."

Revealing his true feelings and the reasons he can never allow himself to be with her would kill Simon. She can never know.

"I am happy. You're not. You're a miserable, nasty person who is stupid and irrational and blind and who will end up alone someday because you can't move past something that happened almost four years ago. Not me! I'm moving on without you, and you can't stand it. You're pissed that I might be happy without you being involved in my life. You're pissed that I might be having a fruitful and promising relationship with someone. For all you know, I could be having a relationship with more than one man. I don't know. You already see me as soiled goods, obviously. Maybe I'll just sew my wild oats all over the county!"

Something in what she just said is bugging him, but Simon can only focus on the last thought she verbalized.

"I wanted you to be happy. I didn't reject you to make you act like this. You obviously need to be kept on a tighter leash. I didn't intend for you to bed hop like a common trollop with everyone in Dave's compound."

She sharply inhales a gasp of shock a split second before she lands a solid slap across his cheek. The sound reverberates off the tall ceilings in the barn. Simon is stunned and stands there in mid-sentence staring at her. It takes a few seconds to register that she has slapped him. He doesn't think anyone has ever slapped him in his entire life. Her fists are balled at her sides. Her cheeks are colored brightly but not from the muggy heat of the evening. Her eyes are positively burning blue flames of anger and outrage and unshed tears.

Simon turns to leave, too livid to deal with her.

"Coward," she whispers hoarsely.

That's it. She has pushed him too far. Simon spins back, grasps her shoulders and wrenches her forward. The defiance leaves her eyes right before he plants his lips on hers. Then he exacts punishment on Sam in the form of a searing kiss. His mouth moves roughly over hers. Sam is not yielding like she normally does. She is standing stiff as a board in his hands. She even attempts to shove him away by placing her hands on his chest. This isn't a good idea on her part. Having her hands on him anywhere is only worsening an already bad situation. He doesn't want to hurt her by bruising her shoulders, so he allows his hands to slide down her back. Now he can pull her more snugly against him, molding her soft form against his. Every rational, moral thought in his brain is gone, dissipated like the fragmented memories of his former life before the fall. He can feel himself slipping, his self-control vanishing into another dimension.

His sense of awareness is being flooded by the feel of her in his arms again, the swish of her long hair against his bare arms, her curves pressing against his hard angles. Lately, it has seemed like years ago that they were in her parents' home where he almost made love to her. Now it feels like it was just last night. Those pent up emotions have re-opened fresh, and so has his lust for Sam.

Simon senses a slight yielding in her and pounces. He pulls back and looks down at her, waiting for her eyes to pop open. When they do, Simon feels as if he is drowning in two, vibrantly blue orbs of hope and joy and sadness.

"Simon," she cries softly. "Don't do this."

Her advice is good, solid, reasonable. He does the opposite and moves his hands to cup her soft face, his thumbs stroking her cheeks. Then he leans down and this time gently brushes his mouth against hers. He pulls back again and gazes down at her lovely, delicate face, still stroking softly with his calloused thumbs. Simon feels as if his head has been filled with helium and he's floating up above himself watching this play out.

Instead of letting her go, he allows his right hand to slide down and cup her bottom. Her chest rises and falls at a faster rate, but she does not shove him away. Her lips part, and her left eyebrow raises. Simon goes in for another sampling of nectar and touches his lips to hers. He hears himself groan and can feel himself doing it inside her mouth but doesn't recognize the place from whence it came. It sounds guttural and untethered. Sam cries out softly against him and yields as if communicating with the animalistic sounds coming from him. Her hands slide up his chest and bury in his thick hair, sending his ball cap to the dirt floor of the barn aisle. She smells fresh and clean like the rain that is falling outside. Perhaps she can cleanse his tainted spirit with her purity and goodness.

Simon lifts her against him, letting her slide languidly down his front until she has her feet on the floor again. Sam whimpers against his mouth. His resistance breaks down a little more with every small sound she makes, every soft sigh. She is shaking under his fingertips. He is tired of fighting his feelings for her. Their pasts be damned. He will never deserve her, but he can't seem to stay away.

"Sam!" Henry calls loudly near the other end of the barn. "Sam, are you in here?"

Simon ignores her new beau and continues his onslaught.

"Sam!" he yells again.

She pulls free and jumps back, her eyes meeting his. Sam steps farther away as Henry approaches them. Simon isn't sure if Henry saw them or not, but he sure hopes his nemesis did. Maybe it will make the other man back off.

"Yes, Henry?" she asks, her voice sounding strange and high-pitched. "What is it?"

"Your grandfather and Derek sent me out to get you," he explains and looks at Simon. "And you, too, Simon."

"Why?" he asks, stepping forward.

"Your neighbor's wife is in labor," he tells them.

"Talia?" Sam asks.

"Yes, ma'am," he answers.

Sam looks at Simon, and he nods with grave intent. They no longer have the time or luxury to finish what they started. Their medical training has to come first, so they jog to the house together in the rain. He holds her umbrella over her head for her. He doesn't want her to get sick.

"Reagan will be staying here," Doc tells them in the kitchen. "I have not and will not awaken her to go with us."

"Why?" Simon asks. "She's a great OB."

Doc hits him with an intense expression and answers, "Because if this goes in the wrong direction like Mia's birth, I don't want her there for it. We'll let her rest. With the three of us going, we don't need her."

"Yes, sir," Simon answers and looks at Sam. She seems nervous. Their last birth went badly, and they are raising an orphaned boy because of it.

"We'll be fine," Doc answers their unspoken fears. "I checked her just last week. Everything's going to go like clockwork. I'll meet you out back in five minutes. Wayne's coming over to pick us up."

"Yes, sir," Simon says with a nod and heads to the mudroom to wash up and change. He is in the middle of pulling a clean t-shirt over his head when Sam comes in. She has also changed but into green scrubs and has pulled her damp hair back into a tight bun. He'll take his scrubs with him over to the Reynolds farm and change there.

As promised, Chet's brother Wayne picks them up ten minutes later. Doc and Sam are riding in the cab with Wayne, which leaves Simon in the bed of the truck. He holds an umbrella over his head. Unfortunately, Henry has come along as extra security detail while they are attending Talia. He isn't happy about his rival being with them, not that he's really a rival because Simon should never allow himself to make a bid for Sam's attention. Plus, if Henry continues pecking around where he doesn't belong, Simon will have to kill him.

They check Talia, who is heaving and panting in her bedroom. Doc declares that she is six centimeters. This could be a long night.

Simon says to Chet and Wayne, "We're going to need a lot of hot water, clean, sterile towels for packing later, and some boiling water to sterilize equipment and instruments."

"I've already got a steel pot of boiling water on the back burner for Dr. McClane's tools," Bertie says.

"Great," Simon says with appreciation.

"Right," Wayne remarks and turns to his brother who is as nervous as one man could be. "Come on, bro. Let's get some buckets and pans from the basement. Bertie, we'll be right back."

His wife nods and smiles and says, "I'll get the towels and linens."

"Thanks, Bertie," Sam says to her before Bertie leaves.

Sam opens Herb's doctor bag and begins removing surgical instruments and other tools they'll need for the labor and delivery like scissors, clamps, a ventouse, forceps, and suction bulbs. She also removes a package of previously sterilized surgical instruments and a breathing apparatus in case of an emergency. Simon takes the stainless steel tools and drops them gently into the boiling water. Doc will want a full, rolling boil on them for a while before taking them into the other room on a sterile tray, which they brought with them.

"Nervous?" Sam asks him.

"This is my sister's friend," he tells her what she already knows. Bertie rushes in with a bundle of towels and leaves again.

"And?" Sam prompts.

"Yeah, I'm a little nervous, I guess," Simon admits, although he normally wouldn't do so with any other person, especially not Herb or Reagan. He knows they want him to appear confident and sure of himself, most importantly in front of their patients. Sam already knows that he is nervous. It's why she is bringing it up at all. There isn't much she can't figure out about him.

"You'll be fine," Sam says. "Grandpa said he'll assist and you'll take lead."

"Great, if I wasn't nervous before, I am now," he says with a grin and pushes his glasses higher up onto his nose.

She rests her hand on his arm and says, "Don't worry. I'll be there, too. Grandpa said if I keep up my OB studies that he thinks I'll know enough to start delivering babies over in the new practice. My uncle's been studying that with me, too."

His smile slides south into a frown as her face lights up with an expressive smile of her own. Simon doesn't like to think of her staying on Henry's farm. He wants her to come back, but his reasons are purely selfish. What she and her uncle are doing is a good thing, generous and charitable and giving, everything that Sam has always been.

Chet and Wayne come up the basement stairs and place two large cook pots in the sink.

"I'm going to fill these at the pump outside," Wayne tells them, holding two more. "It'll go faster that way."

"I'll help," Chet says.

Simon offers, "I'll get these two pans filled here in the sink."

"Thanks, man," Chet says with fearful eyes that speak to his panic over his wife before leaving with his brother.

Sam just keeps going, telling him about her uncle, "He knows everything there is to know about pediatrics, but he needs to study obstetrics and adult care more thoroughly. We're learning together."

"That's great," he praises with little to no genuineness, which sounds obvious to his ears. She hears it, too, because her smile disappears. She shakes her head with disappointment and goes back to unpacking their equipment. Since they are alone, Simon feels that the coast is clear to speak with her about what just happened in the barn. He places the full pot of water on the stove and lights the burner. Then he walks slowly with great apprehension to her where

376

she is folding towels and small linens into neatly divided piles at the table.

"Sam," he says, touching her arm to gain her attention. She looks up at him with softly pleading eyes. "We should talk. I just…"

Herb comes into the room and announces, "She's moving more precipitously than I thought she would. Seven."

"That's good news," Sam says. "No sense in dragging out her misery."

"Exactly, Miss Samantha," Herb says. "Ready, Dr. Murphy?"

Herb is speaking to him, but Simon still doesn't like it when he calls him doctor. He certainly doesn't deserve the title yet. He turned twenty-one almost six months ago in December, but he hardly feels like an adult most of the time. It doesn't help when Reagan and some of the other family members call him and the others "kids." He figures after a person kills as many people as he's killed, they are no longer kids. But he doesn't usually feel like an adult and definitely not a doctor. He's at best a twenty-one-year-old med student sniper.

Simon remembers his friends from school back in Arizona and how much they couldn't wait to turn twenty-one so they could go out drinking legally in bars and pick up chicks. He was never in any hurry for that. He definitely wouldn't have been in the picking up of hot chicks category, either. He probably would've been studying for finals or taking summer classes at this time of year and not partying.

A little after midnight Talia delivers a healthy baby boy who screams his outrage at being brought into this world and taken from the warmth of his mother's womb. Simon feels the full weight of the privilege of delivering her baby safely. She is not embarrassed or ashamed and lies restfully on a pile of pillows as he and Doc attend to her after she passes the placenta. Sam is a great midwife and helped them, as well as encouraged Talia throughout the process. Doc thoroughly examines Talia and the baby and declares them healthy and safe and strong.

"What are you naming this little angel?" Sam asks as she touches the baby's fuzzy, tiny forehead.

Talia takes Sam's hand and replies, "Elijah after my grandfather."

Chet smiles down at his wife and then kisses her forehead and then the baby's.

"A good name, Mrs. Reynolds," Doc says as he makes notes on her chart. "A very important prophet in the Bible."

"Yes, sir," Talia says. "He was. And my grandfather would love it, too."

"I'm sure he's looking down and smiling right now, honey," Doc says and smooths the hair on her forehead.

They leave the Reynolds farm a short time later, exhausted but euphoric at the same time. Being present for the birth of a child is something to be proud of, an honor, and he is thankful for the opportunity to study medicine from Reagan and her grandfather. Even Chet and Wayne were high on happiness and joy.

When they get back to the farm, everyone cleans up and starts the process of re-sanitizing the medical instruments, although Bertie already dropped everything into boiling water again. Doc is a stickler for sanitary medical conditions. They send Herb to bed and finish without him. Unfortunately, Henry hangs out in the kitchen with them and helps. Simon would like to kick him out so that he can talk with her alone. When their task is complete, Sam immediately goes to bed without saying anything to Simon, leaving him to wonder at her mood. Derek tells him to crash for a few hours instead of doing his night watch shift. Simon doesn't even put up an argument. He's exhausted and feeling the full brunt of the stressful situation of childbirth through a doctor's eyes. He makes the long trek through the rain to the cabin for some shut-eye before he must rise at six a.m. for watch duty, which he'll share with Henry and Huntley.

He doesn't fall to sleep immediately, although he thought he would have given the long and eventful day. Instead, he lies awake in his bed with Cory's hairy mutt lying on the floor next to him. He cannot sleep because of what happened with Samantha in the barn.

378

What is it about her? Why can't he just leave her alone? He can't put his finger on it. He doesn't understand his lust for her. He tells himself sometimes that it is because of their shared traumatic journey to the farm and the horrible situations and conditions they were subjected to that brought them closer together, but Simon sees her as more than just a fellow victim of abuse. He knows that she said she loves him, but he didn't believe her, still doesn't really. Sam is trying to pin some label of superhero on him that he just doesn't deserve, and it always strikes the wrong chord with Simon. If he were a superhero, the sort he idolized growing up reading comic books, then he would've saved her from the bad-guy that took her innocence, physically and mentally battered her, and the others in his aunt's group who were so cruel. He wasn't that man. He was a failure, and it is something for which he'll never forgive himself. He doesn't deserve forgiveness. There will never be an absolution for this, never freedom from the horrendous guilt he carries like a millstone around his neck, never liberty from the chains that bind him to her through the course of their tragic pasts.

Every time he thinks he can resist her, he ends up falling right back down into that same rabbit hole of desire. Sam has the ability to transport him to another place, a better and more hopeful place where he is deluded into thinking he has the power to protect her, to take care of her, to be with her in every way. These ridiculous fantasies usually get replaced by a healthy dose of reality. Not tonight. He'd allowed himself a blessed respite from the guilt and torment he usually feels around her. It was simple and stupid weakness on his part to allow it to happen. She'd provoked him, angered him to the point of losing his self-control. This is a trait he normally prides himself on having around Samantha. He wonders if she did it on purpose. She has been behaving very different lately, more independent and also mouthy. Obviously, it isn't enough to stop him from still wanting her.

Why does she hold this power over him? How will he ever rid himself of his desire for Samantha once and for all? Perhaps Cory was right when he suggested that he should start dating women in town. He can't imagine that working out, either, when all he wants is Sam. He could never succeed in deserving her. He doesn't even care to try. It would simply be setting himself up for more failure where she is concerned. Simon has a stomach full of failure and disappointment and doesn't require any more.

He falls asleep playing on repeat the memory of her in his arms, his mouth touching hers, his hands on her body, her cheeks flushed and pink, and her eyes filled with desire for him, the same desire he felt for her.

Chapter Twenty-four
Paige

They take shelter in a warehouse with Dave and his men to wait out the storm and tend to Cory's injury. Paige wishes that she would've stayed at the farm and allowed Simon to go instead of her, which was supposed to be the plan until she got involved. Her brother would know exactly how to treat Cory's wound. Dave's medic is one of the men with them, so she hopes the man knows enough about bullet wounds to help Cory.

She holds the flashlight while he works on Cory's leg. It is very bloody. It seems like it is a serious wound to her, but the medic said that it is mostly superficial and that the bullet passed through his outer thigh muscle. He will still need stitches.

"We should call this off and go home," Kelly says, hovering over his little brother.

"No way," Cory argues. "I'm fine. Let's just stitch this bitch up and get back out there."

"You're not going back out anywhere!" Paige says loudly, earning a surprised look from Kelly. "He's…he's in no shape to be running around the countryside looking for the rest of those men. I know that's what he's thinking."

"Damn right," Cory agrees.

John steps forward, "She's right, Cor. You're in no shape to go back out with us."

"Wait, you're going?" Paige asks. She doesn't want any of them tracking those men at the cabin.

"Maybe," he admits. "We'll see. It's getting late."

"We should go home," she reiterates.

"No, not home," Cory pleads. "It's hard enough finding the time to get out on supply runs and look for the highwaymen. We need to stay out, follow through with the plan. I'm fine. Right, Doc?"

The medic looks at Cory and chuckles, "I'm no doctor. The only doctors we've got are back on both our compounds."

"Can you stitch that up, Sonny?" Dave asks of his man.

"Yeah, Sarge, no problem with the stitching, but he should have a round of antibiotics, which I don't have."

"No need," Cory says, waving his hand away from his body as if he is invincible.

She knows he is not invincible. Nobody is anymore. Six inches to the left and his femoral artery could've been pierced. He likely would've bled out before they even got him back to the farm. Currently, he is sitting on a stainless steel table that they sanitized by wiping down with their bottles of water and a rag from John's pack. Not very sanitary at all but the best they could do. They removed his pants carefully and laid them to the side. He still wears his boxer briefs and the same t-shirt from earlier. It has blood on the lower right side from the spray of his leg wound.

"You can start a round when we get back to the farm," Kelly tells him.

"Whatever. It'll be ok one way or the other," Cory says.

John adds, "We'll leave that decision to the docs."

"When we go back tomorrow night," Cory makes sure to put in.

"We'll see," Kelly says.

"No, man," Cory argues. "We need to check out Fort Campbell. We haven't been there for a long time. If the highwaymen are up there, then we've gotta check it out in the morning."

There is a long pause as John stares at Kelly. Then they take Dave and his men to another room to discuss it. The warehouse used

382

to house party and events rentals. There are tents, tables and chairs, and just about anything someone would need to host everything from a small baby shower to a grand, outdoor wedding including canopies, arches, and even a plastic swan paddle boat in the corner. It comes off as eerie to Paige, that swan boat with the big, round lifeless eye staring back at her from the dark corner of the abandoned warehouse. They are deep in the back of the building, and Dave has two men on the roof, keeping watch on the neighborhood and canvassing it for highwaymen.

"Gauze, please," Dave's medic, Sonny, says to her.

Paige hands it to him.

"Keep the flashlight in real tight now. I've administered some xylocaine into the wound site, so I'm ready to irrigate and apply the stitches. Sorry, Cory, this might still hurt."

"No problem, man," Cory says as if he isn't affected in the least bit by the fact that he has a small hole in the fleshy part of his thigh muscle.

Blood is dripping onto the ground. She knows nearly nothing about blood loss, so Paige wonders how much a person would be able to lose without needing a transfusion. She knows she was given more than one transfusion of blood, care of her local librarian, when she was unconscious. She's glad she was comatose for it. That would've been disgusting.

The medic uses a small bottle of clear fluid, which could be water for all she knows, and squirts it in a steady stream into the wound. She chances a peek at Cory. He doesn't seem to notice. She knows he has scars on his body from being wounded when he was on his own. He always tries to play them off as nothing, no big deal, but she can't imagine having to apply her own stitches or irrigate a wound. She and her group performed minor medical procedures on one another, but that was luckily all they had to do. It was mostly taking care of one another if someone got sick on the road. She helps Simon sometimes at the clinic, but it usually turns her stomach. Gore is not her specialty. It's probably the root of the reason for her affinity to fleeing dangerous situations instead of fighting it out.

When the stitches begin, Paige curls her toes in her leather boots. It is a gruesome process, made even more so since it is Cory the one on the receiving end. She looks at his face, sees that he has his eyes closed but notices that his teeth are clenched, and there is a bead of sweat rolling down his forehead.

"Sorry, man," the medic apologizes.

"It's cool, bro. Just do it fast. I ain't entering any beauty contests anytime soon."

She smiles, and so does Sonny. It's funny that she finds Cory so handsome, although four or five years ago if she'd met him on the street somewhere, Paige highly doubts he would've turned her head. He is rugged and wild looking with his longish dark hair, usually unkempt, his facial hair, for which he seems to have a preference, and his brooding looks. Now Cory would and does turn her head. She doesn't like all the blood coming out of his leg, though. That she could live without.

A moment later, the men return and announce that they'll continue on with their plan of going to Fort Campbell tomorrow. Dave is taking three of his men tonight, along with John, to look for the men at the cabin. This plan makes her even more nauseous. It is entirely too hot in the warehouse.

"Irrigate this for me, please, ma'am," the medic says, indicating toward the little bottle of fluid.

"Oh, um...sure," she says as Kelly holds the flashlight this time. Paige picks up the bottle and squeezes the fluid over Cory's partially stitched wound. Blood literally spurts from the other end of the unstitched hole. She's not Sam. She has no desire to be a field nurse, doctor, helper, wound cleaner or anything else that involves this process. The room starts going black. "This is...um..."

There are stars zooming at her like in the opening credits of that old movie, Star Wars. Only these ones are colorful like a rainbow of brightly spotted dots in a deep, black void of space. Kelly is talking to her. Then John. Falling asleep on the job is never going to get her a position in Doc's practice. Where did everyone go? More importantly, where is she? Maybe she died. She's not sure. Maybe the

384

highwaymen broke into the warehouse and shot her in the head sniper style. She can't see anyone, but Paige can hear them calling to her. This is like some sort of trippy dream.

"Paige, kiddo, it's ok," Kelly says gently. "Open your eyes, darling."

"Is she ok? What the fuck?" Cory is yelling angrily.

Her eyelids flutter a few times, the stars dissolve into the darkness, and a foggy lens is now covering her eyes.

"There ya' go, kiddo," Kelly is saying to her. "Easy, slow, deep breaths. There you are."

"Is she ok?" Cory yells again, this time with less patience.

"Yeah, she's cool, Cor," John answers.

Her perspective is off. For some reason, she can see the ceiling and the steel rafters of the building and John's boots. Where did Cory go? Her vision clears further, and she can see Kelly's sweet face leaning in close to hers.

"What... what happened?" she asks, fear edging into her voice.

"You just passed out, Red," John explains off to her left. Paige looks that way but mostly sees his knees. Then he squats down. She's on the floor. "Kelly caught you. Lucky catch, bro."

"Well, it was the least I could do. She did catch a bullet for me."

"Yeah, that's pretty much the same," John says with a gentle laugh.

"I passed out?" she asks, and a tear rolls down the side of her face. She suddenly feels overwhelmed with emotion and fear.

"It would seem so," Dave says off to her right behind Kelly. "Do you do this often? I'm just askin' so that I can bring my catcher's mitt on our missions."

She smiles as a few more tears run down her face and disappear into her hairline.

"Ready to get up?" Kelly asks.

Paige nods and wipes her face. Passing out and crying? Wow, they must be so impressed.

"Easy," Kelly orders. "Let me help."

Her legs feel weak and shaky. He holds on to her waist with one arm and her elbow with the other hand. His strength feels solid, reliable, safe.

"Don't like the sight of blood?" the medic asks. He is still stitching Cory, who looks utterly freaked out.

She shakes her head and scoffs, "Guess not."

"No more clinic days for you," Kelly tells her.

"I was fine. Then it got really hot in here. Then I was rinsing Cory's leg. I thought it was gross. Then..."

She pauses for a few seconds.

"Kaboom," John says.

"Yeah, I guess so. I thought I was dead. I saw stars and stuff."

"That's normal," Dave says. "We've all been there a time or two."

"You have?"

"Sure. Mostly bar fights on leave," Dave says, joking and lightening up the mood.

Paige feels like a complete and total wimp.

John adds, "Or concussion grenades. Those are always fun for getting your bell rung."

"Or Kelly's fist," Dave points out. He bumps fists with John, and they laugh heartily.

"Are you all right?" Cory asks, his face a tormented mask of frustration and helplessness as he sits on the table still.

"Yeah, I'm fine."

"Why don't you lie down for a little bit?" he suggests.

John steps forward and says, "Yes, that's a good idea, Cory. Even for you."

Cory shoots him a look of irritation.

"There were some rollaway cots back in the one corner," John says.

"I'll help," Dave tells John, and they leave.

"Thanks, Kelly," she says, looking up into his soft, brown eyes that are so much like Cory's. Kelly's eyes have a tenderness in them, whereas Cory's are much harder. Sometimes, when his guard is down around her, usually when they are in a sexual situation of some kind or another, she sees this in him, too. It doesn't happen often.

Sonny finishes Cory's stitches, cleans the wound site one last time, and applies a fresh bandage and tape to hold it all together.

"Right as the rain," he announces.

Cory does the unthinkable and immediately springs off of the table, winces from the pain, and comes to her. Heedless of their need to keep their relationship private, he touches her arm in front of everyone, then her face, tipping her chin back. Kelly still has a hold on her.

"You sure you're all right? We can go back to the farm tonight. We don't have to stay."

She smiles. "That's a change of tune from twenty minutes ago- wait, how long was I out?"

"'Bout ten seconds," Kelly answers as he looks queerly at Cory. There is suspicion in his direct stare.

"Really?" she asks. "Whoa. I thought I was gone for like twenty minutes or something. Seemed like it."

"I know. That's what it's like," Kelly explains.

"Oh, yeah," Sonny says. "I used to fight MMA when I got out of the Army. I got my bell rung a lot. It's always like that. You forget time and space and go on a little trip."

Paige looks at him, and he winks playfully at her. She smiles feebly, feeling like a weak-kneed loser.

"Cots are ready," Dave announces a minute later.

"Cory, why don't you and Paige crash for the night?" Kelly suggests, helping her along.

"Right," John says more warily. "Paige needs to lie down and rest."

"And Cory should, too," Kelly says to his best friend.

"Uh huh, as long as he lets her rest," John states.

Kelly laughs, but Paige isn't sure of the meaning behind John's tone. It sounded cryptic. Perhaps it is from the passing out episode.

"Plus, he can keep an eye on her while we're working," Kelly further explains. "We have a lot to go over tonight before you guys head out."

"Good idea," Dave says and leaves them.

Kelly helps her all the way to the cot, which is probably unnecessary but still appreciated. Cory walks gingerly to his own cot where John and Dave have even placed their bags for them and a single lantern.

"Need any more help?" Kelly asks.

"Nah, we've got this. I need to change anyway," Cory says to his big brother. "Don't want to do it in front of you, old man. You'll get body envy and start binging and purging."

"Envious of what? The hole in your leg, dumbass?" Kelly points out teasingly.

"Burn," Paige adds to it.

"No sympathy from you two, I see," Cory says with a grin.

"Radio if you need me," Kelly says and bumps his fist against Cory's before leaving.

Paige sits, unsure of herself at the moment. That was weird, and she hopes it never happens again. She would not recommend passing out to anyone. She offers to help Cory change but gets rejected. He sits on the bed and pulls on new pants and socks. It looks painful when he has to bend his leg. He locks his jaw tightly, and she knows it must hurt terribly. When he is done dressing, Cory pushes his cot right up lengthwise against Paige's. She isn't going to argue. The warehouse is dark and spooky, and she's even more uneasy after her blackout moment. The shadowy corners could be concealing someone, although she knows the men thoroughly inspected every nook and cranny to ascertain the building for safety before entering.

"Lie down," he orders. "Rest."

"I'm fine now."

"Doesn't matter. Tonight was stressful."

"What are you talking about?" she asks. "The whole day was stressful."

Cory just sends her a slight grin. He probably isn't stressed at all.

"You're bad luck," he states and proceeds to wipe down his rifle with an oiled rag.

"What's that supposed to mean?"

"The last time I took you with me, we ran into trouble."

"So? Pretty much every day on the road was the same as this for me and my friends."

"There's something I don't want to think about," he admits with a heavy scowl.

"In case you didn't notice," she points out, "I'm good at running away and staying alive another day."

"True, but if you'd just stay on the farm, you wouldn't have to worry about all this. You wouldn't have ended your day on the dirty concrete floor of an old warehouse."

"Stop hovering. I just passed out. Not a big deal."

"Have you ever done that before?" he asks and looks at her with concern.

"No, not that I know of," she answers truthfully. "I felt woozy a couple times at the clinic when I was helping Simon with gross stuff, but I never actually blacked out. That was…just strange."

"Maybe you're more delicate than you think," he adds and takes her rifle from the floor and begins wiping it down, too.

"Maybe I'm less delicate than you think of me," she counters.

He smirks, smiling with his brown eyes at her and says, "Doubt it. That would require me to be wrong, and we both know that's no possible."

She giggles at his stupid comment and then smiles. He is so handsome when he smiles, which isn't often. He does so more than her little brother, though, which worries her. Simon has spiraled into a dark place full of regret and blame, and she'd like his old self to reappear again. And now Derek seems to be falling apart. She worries about them both.

"Cory," she says to gain his attention. He immediately stops wiping down her gun and looks up. His hair has mostly come out of the tie that was holding it back, and some has fallen across his face.

"Yeah?"

"Do you think Derek will ever walk again?"

He sighs and says, "He went through Special Forces training. He served two tours. He's a hardcore mother."

"That doesn't answer my question."

"I don't know, sweetie," he answers, surprising her by the endearment. He never calls her anything but Beanpole or Red. It twists her insides just a little.

"I hope he does. I don't want him to be permanently disabled. He seems depressed already."

"John will get him through it," he says with a confidence she doesn't feel.

Paige nods and finally lies down. She leaves her boots on and tucks her jacket under her head for a pillow.

"Are you in a lot of pain?" she asks

"Nah, not really. He numbed it for the stitches."

"What did you do when you were gone on your own and had to give yourself stitches? Did you have numbing shots or anything?"

He just gives her a tell-tale look that lets her know that he just suffered through it.

"That only happened once, so it wasn't a big deal," he says.

Paige frowns, "It would be a big deal if you were in pain. Sticking a needle in your own skin over and over again isn't something that doesn't involve pain, Superman."

"Mind over matter," he replies and reaches over Paige to lay her rifle on her cot with her. "If you don't mind, it don't matter."

She chuckles, "You're so annoying."

"Yeah, but you love me anyway," he teases.

Paige doesn't like the sound of that word on his lips. She doesn't want that sort of relationship with him.

"Not even close, Neanderthal," she replies and adds a snort.

"Maybe not, but I'm workin' on it," he says and reclines back tenderly, trying not to disturb his leg. He rolls to his side so that he is facing her. "First I wore you down and got you into bed with me. Then I forced you to like me and not want to kill me all the time…"

"Not all the time. I still want to murder you most of the time," she jokes and grins because she can't help it. There is a devilish look in his dark eyes. She pushes a lock of his hair back from his forehead. So hopeless.

Cory just keeps going as if she hasn't disputed his claim, "And now I'm working on wearing you down so that we can stop sneaking around…"

"Also not happening."

"Happening. Then we can get married, of course, and have a bunch of baby Reds and Neanderthals."

"Cory, that's not happening ever. I mean, like never ever."

"Sure," he says so smugly she'd like to knock him over the head with something.

She lowers her tone to a whisper and says, "Sex. That's all this is. Got it?"

"What?"

"I said sex. That's all…"

"Huh? You'll have to speak up. I was shot today, ya' know."

She groans and rolls her eyes at him. He is the most annoying person she's ever known. Of course, she won't speak up, and he knows it. The others could hear. That's why he's taunting her and pretending not to be able to hear her.

"You are getting on my last nerve," she warns.

"Go to sleep, Red," he commands. "Get some rest. We can talk about our love life tomorrow."

"No, we won't."

"As you can see, I don't really need you to participate in the conversation. I'm totally ok with it being one-sided."

She fumes and glares at him as he extinguishes the lantern and lies back again. The lightning outside temporarily illuminates the room. Somewhere on the other side of the warehouse, the men must still be awake because there is a warm glow from their lantern just barely reaching her and Cory. She can hear the low murmur of muffled conversation taking place.

"Feeling all right?" he asks and searches and finds her hand, and clasps and links their fingers.

"Yes, fine. You?"

"Better now," he says and kisses her fingers.

Within two minutes flat, Cory is out. He needs his rest more than she does. He was seriously injured tonight, not that he would show it. He's tougher than she thought. She worries that he will get an infection in the wound or that it will open again.

She lies awake for a long time just thinking about Cory and his promise to win her love. There's no way she can allow that. She'll never marry, nor will she ever bring children into this messed up world. She doesn't dislike Cory. As a matter of fact, she has come to like him very well, but loving him is out of the question. She'll never surrender to that sort of love. The only person she'll ever love that deeply is her brother. Losing him would kill her. Losing someone else, too, would end her.

The sound of the rain increases until it becomes loud, louder, and finally an intermittent pounding. It doesn't sound right, so she rises and walks to the nearest, cloudy window and looks out. The sky has opened up just slightly, the clouds moving on to torment others with their endless precipitation, and Paige can see a nearly full moon glowing up there in that dark vastness. There are golf ball sized hail balls laying on the streets and abandoned cars. The hail ends as suddenly as it began. What a dismal night.

Paige walks back to her cot, hears the men still talking a short distance away and removes her canteen from her bag. She's parched and takes a long swig. Cory is still dead asleep, which leaves her to wonder if their medic gave him more than a numbing shot. She lies down on her cot again staring up at the ceiling, studying the trusses and structure itself. A train in the distance makes that familiar rumbling, reminding her of her apartment in Georgia where she was going to school. There was a scheduled stop in her area somewhere every night near midnight, so she got used to hearing it, which was much different than where she grew up in Arizona where the most common noise at night was the occasional coyote's howl.

She blinks, blinks again and sits straight up in bed.

"Cory! Wake up!" she yells, startling the hell out of him. His hand instantly grips his rifle, and he springs to his feet. Then he winces and grabs his leg.

"What the hell's going on?" he asks in a hoarse whisper.

Kelly comes sprinting to them a second later.

"Tornado!" he yells and is followed by Dave's men, who are all shouting orders and commands. John runs around the corner the next instant with Dave and his other three men.

"Everyone, take cover!" John screams. "Let's go!"

The train is getting louder, but she knows this is not a train at all. The rumbling wasn't the familiar sound of a locomotive running on its tracks, the big engines pumping full bore. She knew something wasn't right. Her instincts had kicked in. Trains don't run anymore, neither do planes or any other form of public transportation. She'd always read that tornadoes sound like a train, but she'd never experienced one herself, only watched coverage on the news of them like most people. Then she thought perhaps it was a large truck like Dave's deuce and a half. That thing's loud, too, but not this loud. The noise she'd mistaken for a train or a loud truck for just that split second is a tornado.

She huddles in the corner with the rest of the men under the heavy duty metal staircase that leads upstairs to the small second floor, likely where office space once was located. The rest of the building is open rafters and roof, which may fall in on them. Paige begins vigorously praying for her brother to be kept safe as Cory covers her head and upper body with his own. Then she hears glass breaking.

Chapter Twenty-five
Sam

"Sam, wake up," Huntley says in her dream. Then he says it again. She's not sure why he's even in this dream. She's having a dream about competing in a jumping competition up in Lexington and her parents are in the stands clapping for her zero faults round on her favorite mare. Her brother is even there. He's clapping, too, but he looks older than when they last saw each other.

"Sam!" Huntley says again.

Her eyes pop open, and she startles to find Huntley hovering above her in her bedroom.

"Get up," he says.

"What's wrong? Is something wrong? Are we under attack again?" she asks in rapid fire words that slur. Her brain is still riding that victory round waving to the crowd.

"Something's wrong," he says. "Get up, shadi. Hurry."

"What is it, Huntley?" she asks and swings her legs over. She's wearing nothing but a t-shirt and sweatpants that have seen better days. She never sleeps in a bra, but she's comfortable enough around her adopted little brother not to be embarrassed.

"My mother just came to me," he explains.

He is bare-chested but wearing jeans and loafers. Hannah would not be happy if she saw him wearing his shoes in the upstairs where the carpets are a lot lighter in color.

"What? What do you mean? Did you have a bad dream?" she asks as she pulls on a zip up sweater with deep pockets that she stole from Derek last year. He never wears things like this. He's more of a flannel shirt kind of guy.

Huntley probably needs to talk. They used to do this, bounce their bad dreams off of each other. Sometimes, most of the time, she only shared her really bad ones with Simon.

"No, something's wrong. She came to me in a dream and told me we're in danger. Come. We must wake everyone."

"What?" she asks, surprised and kind of freaked out at the same time. "We can't just get everyone out of bed at…" she consults the clock on the nightstand, "three-thirty in the morning, Hunt. Just go back to bed."

"You come with me right now, shadi," he demands and stands to his full height which is nearly six foot.

He is holding a lantern and hasn't turned on her bedroom light. For the first time, she realizes that he's carrying his bow and has a shotgun slung on his other shoulder.

"I need to get to the little kids. I just left them in the basement. We have to wake the adults. Something bad's about to happen."

"Oh…ok, Hunt. I'm coming," she agrees, this time reading the true fear in his light eyes. He's not the kind of kid prone to exaggerations and lies, so she knows he's serious. If it were just a bad dream, he's old enough to tell the difference.

"Don't tell anyone how I knew. Promise," he demands before they leave her room.

"Yeah, sure. I promise. I'd never," she says and touches his arm. He nods and leads her upstairs to awaken Reagan.

This goes less smoothly. She's pregnant, sleeping soundly, and is usually a tad on the scary side on a good day. Jacob is sleeping with her since John is gone. Their little boy always sleeps with her when his dad isn't home, and Sam thinks he has taken on the responsibility of his mother and her safety. He's a little Ranger in the making.

"What the hell?" Reagan asks, her voice even scratchier than usual. Her curls are a messy halo around her head, but she still looks beautiful.

Huntley explains that they are in danger, and Reagan instantly wakes and then wakes Jacob. She grabs her son into her arms and her rifle and sidearm in her other. Huntley takes Jacob from her.

"We must warn the others," he says and leads them to Gretchen and Lucas's shared room down the hall from Sam's. Luke reacts like Reagan and is immediately ready for a fight.

The rain has grown loud on the roof, but the lightning has stopped. Good. If they have to fight people, it'll be easier to see if the thunderstorm goes away.

"Good grief," G announces at the sound of the rain hitting the roof as she pulls on a hoodie over her pajamas.

"That sounds like hail," Luke states and pulls his sister from the room.

They go as a group to the first floor where they find two of Dave's men in the kitchen having a midnight snack. They are supposed to be relieved by Simon and Henry soon. Sam takes it upon herself to get Hannah and baby Daniel, while Reagan gets Sue, Derek and Grandpa. By the time they reconvene in the kitchen a few minutes later, Sam's heart is racing.

"The kids," she says. "Where's Huntley?"

"Went out to get Simon. He's out in the cabin alone," Reagan explains.

"What's going on exactly?" Derek asks.

"Something's going to happen," Sam explains. "I don't know how to explain it, but Huntley and I both got a bad feeling at the same time."

Nobody laughs at her. They are used to listening to that inner voice of instinct warning them of danger. It happens often, and they've learned to heed the warning and not mock each other when it does. It hadn't actually happened to her, but she didn't want to expose Huntley's secret. Outside the kitchen window, she can see the beam of a flashlight bouncing along the path back to the house. A

396

minute later, Huntley and Simon are inside. Henry's friend has roused him from his slumber in the spare bedroom in the basement.

"Man, that hail's huge," Simon says as he enters the kitchen. "Size of baseballs, I think. I could hear it hitting the barn roofs and the cars that are outside."

"Gonna need to file an insurance claim," Henry jokes, to which some give a chuckle.

Sam appreciates that he's trying to lighten the mood. Everyone is on edge.

"Should I take watch, sir?" one of his friends asks.

"What kind of danger are we in?" Derek asks Huntley, who squirms.

"I don't know, sir," he answers honestly. "Just…"

"Just a bad feeling, right? Like the same one I had?" Sam covers for him, to which he nods.

"We need to get the kids," Huntley says with urgency. "They're all still asleep."

"Are you sure?" Sue asks, her eyes heavy and drowsy.

She's probably envisioning having to get the kids back to sleep after a false alarm.

"Positive, Sue," Huntley answers.

Sam isn't sure about what he's seen, but she is sure of her friend's sense of foreboding. If he believes something is going to happen, then so does she. His conviction is good enough for Sam.

"I'll get them," Sue says and leaves the room.

"I'll help," G offers and runs after her.

A few minutes later, they have the kids gathered with them in the kitchen. Their little faces are puffy and soft from sleep, but they aren't complaining. Every one of them understands danger all too well, unfortunately.

"The hail's stopped," Derek says.

They are all standing in the kitchen and hallway with just the single lantern still lit. They can't afford to light up the whole house in case they are about to be attacked.

"Should I go outside and check it out, sir?" Simon asks Derek, who squints his eyes in thought.

"We were just out there," Henry's friend says. "We just did a wide perimeter check not ten minutes before we came in for some food."

"Right," the other one says. "There's nothing out there. Other than the rain, it's been quiet."

"That storm has stopped," Henry says.

Then a sound in the distance alerts them all in the silence of the room where nobody dares to make a peep.

"What's that?" Ari is the first to ask.

"Noise from an engine," Jerome remarks and goes to the window in the music room to check on it.

"Sounds like a jetliner," one of Henry's friends says.

"John and the others coming back?" Reagan questions.

"No, he would've called when they were in range," Derek corrects.

The sound grows louder, rumbling the floor under Sam's feet with the vibration it makes.

"Dear God," Grandpa says as a loud crashing sound in the barnyard occurs. He rushes to the children and begins ushering them, "Get to the basement. Hurry, little ones."

"Twister!" Henry yells and grabs Sue's son, Isaac, in one arm and Ari in the other.

He doesn't wait for anyone but takes off with the kids for the old part of the basement.

"That's a twister as sure as I know it," Henry yells again. "Get to the basement!"

Everyone jumps into motion. Jerome and Simon help Derek to the stairs.

"No, I go last," he yells. "Get the rest of the family down there first."

"Yes, sir," Simon answers tightly.

She knows this is going to be a hard order for Simon to obey, but he does it anyways.

"Get Hannah," Derek commands.

Sam takes Hannah's hand and baby Daniel in her other arm and leads Hannah down the stairs, letting her use the railing.

"I'm fine," Hannah argues. "Help the children."

And she is fine because she breaks away from Sam and goes faster on her own. One of Henry's friends takes baby Daniel and sprints down the steps after Hannah. Sam sees him catch up to her and grasp her elbow. Lucas grabs his sister's hand and takes Justin's hand, too, even though he is hardly a little kid anymore. It's not about being an adult now, and everyone knows it. It's about being accounted for. Once they have Reagan and the rest of the children down the steps, Henry's men go down, followed by Jerome and Henry who has come back to help with Derek. They get him down the stairs, too, and Sam can hear him frantically speaking into the radio to reach their neighbors and their town officials and John.

"Sam," Simon says softly, touching her arm.

She looks up to find him pointing. He's indicating toward Grandpa, who is standing near the back door transfixed. She can hear him mumbling words quietly. The words he speaks break her heart. She can't let him stand there in the doorway, though.

"Grandpa!" Sam calls and runs to him. "Come! We have to get downstairs!"

"My farm," he says, his eyes transfixed in a far off stare.

"Come on, sir," Simon orders gently. "Come on. Everything will be fine. Let's get Sam downstairs."

"Right, right, Samantha," he says, snapping out of it and moving with them at the thought of her needing his help.

When they get to the stairs with him, Henry is there again waiting. He is looking at her with a soft expression. A scratching sound draws her attention away.

"Help Grandpa!" she says with fervor and turns. "Help him get downstairs, Henry!"

He does as she says and takes her grandfather by the arm, making sure he doesn't trip in the dark.

"Shadow!" Simon yells and opens the back door. It slams against the wall from the high winds. "Get in here, girl."

Cory's dog rushes in and stands next to Simon.

"Thank God. We almost forgot her outside," Simon says.

Their other dog usually spends more time over at Chet's, which suited them just fine since it gave little Maddie a pet of her own, but Sam still hopes the dog will be safe.

Simon manages to shut and lock the kitchen door again, although it is no easy task. Sam runs to the fridge and grabs a glass container of fresh water in case they are buried in rubble for days on end. They used to talk about situations like this in her health classes in school. It was part of disaster preparedness week. The children will need something to drink. Then she also takes Daniel's bottle and stuffs it into her pocket.

A roaring at the door captures her attention, and she spins to answer it, this Grim Reaper that has come a-knocking. Her heart is pounding in her chest so hard from fear and adrenaline that it might burst. She can see it, the tornado. The roof is peeling off of the cow barn like an orange rind. The fence posts in the paddock around the barn lifting right out of the ground as if they are not made of heavy gauge steel wire and wood and each post buried three feet deep, but merely tiny needles and thread in the playground of some supernatural predator and being plucked by said creature of the night. She can hear the cows mooing loudly and the horses screaming with the same terror she feels. Then she cannot hear them anymore at all because the howling of the Devil himself is pounding her eardrums and blocking out all other sound.

She turns in slow motion to see Simon running at her.

"Come on, Sam," Simon says, although she can barely hear him. He yanks her with him, taking her hand firmly in his. Shadow follows them.

This is where she belongs, and they both know it. There is nobody else with whom she would want to spend her last minutes on earth if this is going to be that precious combination of seconds. They close the door to the basement and lock it from the inside.

Simon makes her go ahead of him, and she hurries down the steps. They gather with the rest of the family as Henry and his men try in vain to clear away as many items as they can so that nobody is injured by flying debris. Some of the littler children are crying. Sam can barely hear them. The roar of the beast outside is deafening. Sue and Reagan huddle together with Hannah, surrounding her, protecting her, and holding each other. Grandpa is sitting with the children on stacks of pillows and blankets the men must've gathered. He is speaking in a soothing manner to them. Most of their daddies are absent, so they must see Grandpa as their stand-in for emergency situations. Gretchen is clinging on to her brother, who looks scared but brave at the same time as if he'd like to run outside and sacrifice himself for his little sister. They have found a chair for Derek to sit on, and he is holding his rifle out in front of him as if he will shoot and kill their enemy. These men, these battle-hardened old soldiers, don't understand an enemy they can't conquer. This is how they deal with things that threaten their families.

Sam gets down on her knees next to Huntley and places the water jug and baby bottle under a built-in wooden shelving unit. If she is killed, maybe others will survive and can at least feed baby Daniel until help comes. Although she isn't sure who would help them since there isn't a National Guard or fire department any longer. They are on their own. Everyone is now.

When Simon is finished helping Henry and his men, he joins her on the floor and takes her hand again. He doesn't even look at her. She knows he is afraid, too, because of the way he keeps flexing his jaw. He does this when something has him upset.

Henry and his men stand in front of Grandpa and the little ones as if they will stop whatever malevolent force might come down the cellar stairs.

Grandpa begins saying the Lord's Prayer, and everyone soon joins him as the roaring outside reaches new heights.

"Everything's going to be ok," Derek assures them all. "This old house has been here a long time. It's not going anywhere."

Arianna goes to her father and sits on his lap.

"I'm scared, Daddy," she cries.

"It's ok, baby," he coos and holds her close. "Daddy's got you."

"Where's Uncle John?" she cries loudly.

Sam can see the fear in his eyes. She's never seen this in him before, which makes her scared anew. He also seems angry.

"He's fine, baby. He's safe," Derek lies.

Sam looks at Reagan in time to see her green eyes light up with fresh tears. But she doesn't let them fall. Instead, she tightens her arm around Hannah. Kelly is also still out there somewhere, and she knows it.

Sam then squeezes Simon's hand, but he releases her. Sam's eyes meet his with uncertainty. He instead wraps an arm around her back and pulls her closer. Relief floods her. She wasn't sure if he was going to get up and leave her or move away or just drop her hand so no one saw. Apparently, he doesn't care tonight.

"It'll pass soon," he reassures her.

It doesn't seem like it's going to. The noise and the winds seem to go on forever. Upstairs she can hear the windows rattling and the doors banging as if it is trying to force entry. Will their home be lifted in the wind and taken away, them with it? She knows that some tornadoes have leveled entire towns. She read in her health book about one in Xenia, Ohio, that very nearly did just that many decades ago. She just never thought she'd be living in the same scenario. Meteorologists were more accurate with predicting the weather patterns and could send out alerts so that fire stations, radio and television could sound the alarms and post alerts when bad weather approached. Today the only predictor is to look up in the sky. Or have Huntley's dead mother as a protector. There are still a lot of things in life that she'd like to experience. This just isn't one of them.

The lantern blows out, causing the kids to cry harder.

"It's ok, guys," Derek yells. "Stay calm. Stay where you are. Don't get up and walk around. Stay down!"

The one child she doesn't hear is baby Daniel, who seems to be sleeping through the entire event. The kid wakes up at all hours of the night with a soiled diaper or for his bottle but is sleeping through a tornado so massive that it took the roof off the barn.

She can hear even more destruction going on outside. Simon pulls her closer and kisses the top of her head.

"I'm so scared," she confesses.

"It's ok. I'm here," he says and then kisses her forehead.

"Don't let me go, Simon," she makes him swear.

"Never," he promises and kisses her softly on the mouth in the dark, damp and chilly basement.

The kiss is sweet, gentle, so much like Simon and not the aggressive, angry encounter in the barn. He pulls back, and she hugs her arm around his waist and rests her head on his chest. This isn't the worst place to die. She's also worried about his sister and wonders if they are in the path of this destructive machine. She prays they are not. Sam dares not say her name right now. She knows how much he must be worrying about Paige's well-being.

Simon rocks her gently in his arms and kisses her hand or her fingertips or her forehead from time to time. Jerome lights the lantern again, which erases a little bit of the fear.

"No matter what, don't let me go," she says.

"I won't," he swears again as the roaring become ear-splitting. "I'm with you, Samantha. I'm here. I'm not going anywhere. You're gonna be ok. I promise."

The love she feels for Simon has never been greater than in this one moment, and she knows he is meant for her as sure as Grandpa knew about Grams so many years ago. Even if they never do come together, she will find some way to content herself with just knowing it.

She tries not to notice Shadow trying to dig her way out of the basement by clawing frantically at the concrete floor. Jerome goes to her, kneels and takes her by the collar, settling her down so that she doesn't frighten the children even more with her erratic behavior.

Sam is reminded of Grandpa in the kitchen standing at the door worried about his farm and family. She heard his words loud and clear even if nobody else could. Initially, he was praying to God. Then his words changed.

Grandpa said, "Watch over them, Mary. Don't let anything happen to our family."

Chapter Twenty-six
Reagan

It is nearly dawn by the time they come out of the basement. Henry and Simon went up to check it out, made sure it was safe. The first gray streaks of sunlight are starting to chase away the shadows of the night's events. Reagan holds her son's hand as she climbs the stairs behind Grandpa.

It doesn't take long to see the damage left behind by the storm, either. There are broken dishes on the floor in the kitchen, and a cupboard hangs crookedly on the wall. The plates must've come out of the same cupboard since the doors are open. Dirt and leaves cover the kitchen floor and entryway. The back door to the outside is standing wide open. They all make their way slowly outside onto the porch, which is intact.

"Careful, anyone who doesn't have on shoes. Be careful, especially you little ones," Grandpa warns the children. "There is debris everywhere that will cut you."

Reagan would like to remind him that his cotton, canvas slip-ons hardly count as shoes. She's wearing tall rubber boots, but Jacob is barefoot, so she carries him. Derek goes down the porch stairs ahead of her, Simon at the side of his walker. Sue is on his other side just in case.

"Hannah, stay on the porch," she tells her sister, who nods and sways Daniel from side to side in her arms.

"Mary, stay up here with Momma," Hannah orders her frightened daughter, who immediately grabs a handful of Hannah's dress.

A damn tornado and Hannah is still clean and fresh and pretty as ever. Reagan kisses her sister's cheek.

"How bad is it?" Hannah asks because she cannot see the damage for herself.

Reagan touches her forearm and says, "Not too bad. We'll have to walk around and take a look. Stay here. Some of the kitchen took a hit, so don't go in there."

"No word yet from Kelly?" Hannah asks, although she already knows the answer.

"Be patient, sis," Reagan tells her. "He'll be here. They may not even know about this yet. It might have missed their area. Not like they saw the news footage. But you know they always check in every the morning. They'll call."

Hannah nods, and Reagan is positive that her sister can tell she isn't confident in what she is saying. They could be dead for all she knows. John included.

Reagan swallows hard and goes down the steps with Sam beside her. The men are already talking.

"Check on my chickens," Hannah calls out.

"Got it," G returns and heads in that direction.

From what Reagan can see, it doesn't look good. She hadn't wanted to tell her sister this. As a matter of fact, she doesn't even see the coop. Livestock is pretty much scattered everywhere, hiding under the big branches of trees, walking around outside of the fence, one cow is clearly dead laying near the barn. A few chickens are, as well. She hopes the horses are alive. They need them now more than ever.

She turns and gets a look at the house. It doesn't look too bad for all that it sounded like a few hours ago. She was sure they were all dead. The wind had shaken the old mansion on its foundation, but it put up a hell of a fight and stood its ground. It's a fighter just like they are. She is quick to send up a prayer of gratitude.

A window upstairs looks broken, the roof has some missing shingles here and there, and the front porch has some damage on the roof, as well, but all in all, it's still standing.

Scratching on the radio sounds off, and Derek answers the call.

"How are you over there McClanes?" Wayne Reynolds asks.

Reagan tries not to be disappointed that it isn't John.

"Alive. Can't say the same for some of the barns," Derek answers. "You?"

"Yeah, took the roof off the hog barn. Other than that, we're good. Johnson's lost a shed and some windows in the house. They're all fine, too."

"Good," Derek says. "Talia ok?"

He is asking about her since she just gave birth less than eight hours ago. When she came down to get a glass of water, Reagan found Grandpa in the kitchen going over the notes of the event she missed. She was not pleased. It had stung a little knowing she was left behind, but now it hardly seems to matter at all.

"Yes, shook up but fine," Wayne says. "Baby's fine, too."

There is a tree down near the side yard of the house. It looks like it was split in two with a giant axe the size Paul Bunyan would've used. Part of the roof on the cattle barn is…just gone. There is a mangled chunk of metal the size of a mini-van in the field, leaving Reagan to wonder if that was once the roof. The tornado scrunched it up like a ball of used tin foil. The horse barn seems fine other than some missing boards on the outside walls. The roof is still there. They'll learn more about structural integrity soon enough. When she rounds the corner, she sees that their SUV is turned on its side. The windshield is also broken.

"Radio if you need us," Derek tells Wayne.

"You, as well, brother. You might need our help with your barn."

It seems as if they are all just thankful to be alive. She is, too, but she'd rather spend the rest of her life with John instead of without him, especially with a baby on the way. Not hearing from him is making her crazy. Jacob has asked about his father's whereabouts twice already.

The lake where they all swam and had so much fun yesterday has debris floating in it. A tree has fallen on the west side and is now laying in the water. Leaves and branches galore also clutter up the water's smooth surface. It will all need to be dredged from the lake so as not to cause disturbances with the fish life. She'd seen Sam standing there in the side yard yesterday looking down at the lake and watching the sun set. Reagan likes to do the same. Sometimes she takes Jake up the hill near the cow barn to do just that. He loves the colors in the sky when it sets over the water and reflects so brilliantly. Reagan had assumed that her little friend was remembering Simon falling in, which Reagan is sure he did since he came up to the house mad as hell and soaked.

"Doctor Death or the Hulk call in yet?" Wayne asks over the radio.

"Not yet," Derek answers. He is trying to be calm, but Reagan can read his frustration.

"Let me know when they do. We'll give them a few hours. If we don't hear from them by then, Chet and I will go find them."

"Thanks, man," Derek says and cuts the transmission.

Reagan knows how helpless he feels not being able to go on his own and get them back. John is his brother, Kelly and Cory his friends. He probably feels like it's his job to rescue them if they need it. Reagan just hopes they don't need it and aren't even aware of what happened last night. This feeling of impotence is not going to sit well with her brother-in-law.

Tornadoes are hit and miss; they recycle and reappear miles away from where they start; they bounce around on the tops of hills and sometimes miss valleys below. She hopes all of these theories applied last night to wherever John and the rest of them were staying in Clarksville.

"Chet and Talia's baby was born on the day of a tornado," Sam remarks as she and Simon walk by.

"Maybe that's a sign of good luck," Sue says.

"Seriously?" Reagan asks. "I don't know if you could have worse luck."

"I don't know about that," Sue adds as if she disagrees with Reagan.

Sam says, "Well, I don't know if it's good or bad luck, but it's a strange fact. The baby will have stories to tell someday about it."

"I wouldn't know," Reagan states. "I wasn't there for the birth."

Sue wraps an arm around her shoulders and says, "Good. You needed your sleep. You've been running on less than a quarter tank around here, Reagan."

"Half tank," she comes back and causes Sue to smile. They touch their heads together. Sue kisses her cheek and goes to relieve G, who is holding Isaac. Reagan is so thankful that last night didn't go any worse than it had. They can fix the barns and buildings and even rebuild an entire house if they have to. But she could never replace her family.

Derek's radio sounds off, "Baby Bird to Papa Bird, come in," Kelly's voice comes over.

"We've gotcha," Derek answers as fast as he can.

"We're comin' in," Kelly says. "Be home in five."

They all sigh with relief. Reagan has to wipe away a tear before anyone sees how badly she has been affected by the uncertainty of not knowing whether or not John was still alive.

A few minutes later, Kelly pulls the truck, trailer and only one ATV down the lane. Reagan rushes to their truck, as does everyone. The second John is out of the truck, he has her in his arms. Jacob is hugging him so tightly around his neck. She can see Hannah and Mary doing the same to Kelly.

"I was so worried about you, boss," John states and buries his face in her hair.

She is too overcome with emotion to even verbalize, so she nods against him instead.

"It came through here, too, I see," he says as he pulls back.

Reagan swallows the hard lump of sentiment in her throat and says, "Yes, but we made it. We're all fine. We weren't sure if you guys were hit in Clarksville."

"Not this bad. We were in a warehouse. Buildings took a beating, I see," John observes and wraps an arm around her waist. Then he presses his large palm against her stomach. "Everything ok?"

"Yes, we're fine. All of us," she answers with a smile and pats his hand.

"Thank God," he says. "How'd you guys know it was coming? Did someone see it and wake everyone? Most of our group was still up when it went through."

"Huntley and Sam said they had a bad feeling. I don't know. They just woke everyone up and said something bad was going to happen."

"Lucky they're such weirdo clairvoyants," John teases with his usual humor, but his grin is lopsided and nearly a frown. He must've been just as stressed out about her and Jacob. Reagan just nods and touches his cheek. "The buildings we can fix," he notes. "I'm just glad everyone's safe and unharmed."

"Why is Cory limping?" she asks, noticing him walking unsteadily across the yard toward Simon and Sam where Paige is hugging her brother.

"Long story," he says. "Lots to go over."

Reagan looks around at the damage and feels an overwhelmingly huge burden resting on her shoulders. How will they ever clean all of this and rebuild? It seems insurmountable.

"Don't worry, babe," John says and squeezes her shoulders gently, tugging her closer. "We'll handle this. Just like combat engineers. It got blown up, and now we need to put it back together."

She smiles and sighs. They join the others in the backyard and greet one another. Everyone just seems relieved to be alive and have their loved ones safe and sound and home again.

"Oh, we forgot," Kelly says, now holding Mary with one arm. "Dave called in when we were almost home. He headed back to your compound, Henry. Guess the clinic you guys were working on building for Dr. Scott got leveled."

"What?" Sam asks on a gasp and covers her mouth with both hands.

Henry says with a look of disgust, "Are you serious?"

"Yeah, the house you all were going to use for the medical clinic is just gone, man. Sorry," Kelly repeats.

"No worries," John says. "You can always relocate the clinic to another house."

"Sure, right," Henry says with a nod of agreement. "Did he say if anything else was damaged?"

"Kind of like here," Kelly informs him. "Just some building damage. Not much. They were going to head into Hendersonville and check it out."

"Good," Henry says with appreciation.

Reagan feels bad for Sam and her uncle because she knows how hard they were working on it. They expected to be ready to open it soon.

"What about our people?" Jerome asks next.

"He said a few got banged up 'cuz they were in the barn when it happened or something, but all just worse for the wear," John explains.

Cory is standing next to Simon and Simon's sister, who looks exhausted. This was not the best time for her to have taken a supply run in light of current events. She's only just healed. Reagan can also better see Cory's leg. It is wrapped tightly in white gauze that has a small spot of blood on it. This has her concerned. Huntley pulls Simon away to help him.

Jerome and Henry look at one another before Henry announces, "We need to get home."

"Right, we understand," Grandpa says and shakes his hand. "Thank you for everything you've done for us, Henry."

"Yes, sir," Henry says with a nod. "Let's get ready."

His men move into action and go to the house and barns to gather their things.

"Sam, will you stay here or go back with them?" Paige asks.

Suddenly, everyone is staring at Sam and waiting for her answer; she looks uncomfortable at being put on the spot and as if she'd like to be anywhere else. Her blue eyes slide to Simon, who is helping Huntley lift a piece of wood off of the demolished chicken coop.

"I should go," she says.

"No!" Paige cries and steps forward to take Sam's hands in hers. "Stay a few days. I didn't even get to see you."

"I need to go," Sam reiterates and hugs Paige. "If anyone is injured, my uncle will need my help."

Paige nods and backs away again. Reagan feels bad for her because she knows how close the two girls are.

Grandpa walks over and hugs Sam before saying, "That's a very mature and responsible decision, Samantha. I'm so proud of you, honey."

She nods, fights back tears at Grandpa's praise, and says to Paige, "Oh, hey, Talia had her baby last night."

"Good grief!" Paige exclaims. "I miss everything."

Everyone laughs. It feels good to laugh for just a second standing amidst the rubble of their farm, and Reagan suspects she threw her wit into the ring to lighten the mood.

"Then stay home from now on," Cory puts in unexpectedly.

"Shut it, Neanderthal," she responds, making Reagan grin.

"We need to get to work, people," Derek remarks, stopping the teasing and conversation.

"And have a meeting later," Kelly says.

"Right," Derek agrees.

Kelly pats his daughter on the back and scans the crowd of family members before saying in a serious tone, "There's a lot to go

412

over. We had problems last night. We may have found our highwaymen, and we also found a new settlement that has popped up since we last went to Clarksville."

"Yeah, Kel? Is that so?" Reagan asks with sarcasm. "Well, we had stuff happen here, too."

Kelly chuckles and rubs the top of her head. Then he wraps an arm around her and hugs Reagan. She doesn't pull back right away. She loves Kelly and is glad he made it safely home along with her husband. She doesn't think she could ever watch Hannie go through another devastating loss. Losing Kelly would be her sister's demise.

A short time later, everyone says their goodbyes to Sam and Henry's group. There are tears of joy and sadness. Huntley clings on to her for a long time, whispering in her ear. Reagan knows how close they are, but she doesn't see Simon anywhere. It bothers her that he is obviously avoiding sending her off. She's not sure why, but Reagan plans on finding out. Last night in the basement, he wouldn't let her go. He'd held her so tightly to him that Reagan was concerned about her breathing abilities.

They work for hours, but Reagan knows repairs will keep them busy for days, maybe weeks or even months. Grandpa and John walk the fields and declare that the harvest has not been disturbed much, only one small section of the planted corn field in the top pasture. There are many downed trees that will need cut up, some resting on sections of fence in their final repose. Sue's greenhouse was heavily damaged, the roof in some areas collapsed. The plants inside did not fare well, either. Many of them lay on the floor of the greenhouse, mutilated and dead. The barn siding on many of the buildings will need to be replaced in some areas. The men are already on the roof of the house replacing missing shingles in case it rains again. The sky is bright and blue and cloudless today, but that doesn't mean it can't change in an instant. The storm brought with it a cold front, and the temperature is hovering in the high fifties according to the outdoor thermometer nailed to the wall near the entry door to the kitchen.

Some of the animals are slowly returning, scared and timid and shaken up just as badly as their human counterparts. She even manages to catch a few of the horses and lead them back to their pastures. Simon, Huntley, Justin and even Cory, who she knows now was shot last night after she questioned him, have been working all day on repairing the fences so that the animals can be contained within them again. Reagan is going to insist on examining Cory's wound later today. He shouldn't really even be around all the dirt and debris, but he wouldn't listen.

She and Grandpa lectured everyone about the importance of handling metal carefully. They do not have vaccinations for tetanus bacteria, and the sickness can be deadly. Anyone touching pieces of metal are to be wearing leather gloves. Also, everyone is wearing their best work boots to prevent their feet from being cut by the chunks and slivers of metal laying around the yard and fields.

Condo Paul and K-Dog called in for a sit rep on the farm and reported that their tiny community is fine and was not affected by the twister. She is relieved and happy for them. She knows their condos do not have basements. It might be time for them to build a storm shelter underground.

Their sheriff in town also radioed to inform them that the town was hit but not severely. They had many windows broken and trees knocked down, but the wall is still erect except in a few small sections, which the men are already working on.

Dave called over again to report three deaths and two missing people in their town of Hendersonville. Many homes were damaged, some destroyed altogether. Their town seems to have been hit harder than everywhere else so far. Reagan wonders if her father's base was struck down, too. They have no way of knowing the scale and scope of the storm. They are too far away and the communications not capable of reaching the base to find out from him on their status. He sent one of his men last week to report in that another two hundred people have shown up at the base and that everything was progressing well up there. Reagan is curious if he could still report the same after the storm. Hopefully, they were far enough north out of the path of its destruction.

The men have been talking all day while working, speculating on the size of the twister. John and Kelly think it could've been an F3 rating, while Derek and Grandpa peg it more for an F4. She's going to take her grandfather's word for it since she knows from Simon that Grandpa saw it firsthand while standing in the kitchen looking out the window.

She goes inside after helping put away a few more animals that she can actually manage to catch and finds Hannah and Sue in the kitchen trying to make some order of the place.

"Your bedroom window is broken, Reagan," Sue tells her.

"Free air-conditioning," she remarks with sarcastic humor, to which Sue smiles.

"That's one way of looking at it," Hannah says as she stirs a mixture of something in a big soup pot. It smells good, whatever it is.

Reagan washes her hands at the kitchen sink and watches out the window as G and Lucas carry lumber across the yard toward the coop. She's not sure if it is part of the previous coop or if it is new wood to make repairs.

Sue adds, "Derek said they'll have to make a run to a building supply center and see about some materials we don't have here."

"Like what?" Reagan asks. They keep so much of those articles in the barns and storage sheds just in case. Of course, their supplies may be in the next county over now.

"Nails, tar paper…"

"I know we have tar paper in the top of the horse barn in storage," Reagan interrupts.

"They've used all of it already," Sue tells her.

"Oh, wow," Reagan says with surprise.

Sue shakes her head and says, "They just got back. I hate for them to leave again."

"If everyone was hit like this," Reagan starts, "then the home improvement stores will be busy like it's a Memorial Day home reno sale at the Lowe's."

"True," Sue says. "That's why I don't want them to go."

"But we need to repair the buildings," Hannah reminds them gently. "Huntley said they found some of the chickens."

"Yeah," Reagan says. "I saw a few hiding up in the trees."

She doesn't tell her little sister that some are also dead and some are just piles of feathers.

"See?" Hannah teases. "They aren't stupid like you call them all the time. They know how to get out of danger."

"Right," Reagan jokes. "Fly up into a tree during a tornado. That's genius."

Hannah chuckles and holds out her hand to find Reagan. She obliges and touches her sister's arm. Hannah pulls her closer and hugs her.

"I'm just glad our family's safe," Hannie says.

"Yeah, me too," Reagan acknowledges. She spares Hannah from the news that Dave called in about Hendersonville and the people who were killed there. Reagan secretly wonders if there are now orphaned children because of the tornado strike in Hendersonville. She covers her stomach with her hand as a cramp hits.

"Everything ok?" Hannah asks, although Reagan can't fathom how her sister knows.

"What?" Reagan feigns. "Yeah, everything's fine."

It isn't, but she is not going to tell them that. She has been having cramps all afternoon. She just hopes they are Braxton Hicks contractions and not full-blown labor contractions. This is too early. The baby would only be at thirty-one weeks if she has calculated correctly.

Sue touches her back and says, "Why don't you go lie down, Reagan? We've got this."

"I might head back out soon," she tells her sister.

"I could use some help with Daniel," Hannah says. "He's almost ready for his bottle if you could give him one."

"Oh, um…" Reagan stammers. "Sure."

416

They pass his bottle to her, and Reagan goes to the music room to find him still asleep in his bassinet, leaving her to wonder if she just got manipulated by her sisters. The kid is out and clearly not ready for his bottle. The little monster slept through the whole storm. Now he's sleeping again as if nothing at all happened last night. For all he knows, nothing did happen. He got his bottles on schedule and his diapers changed according to plan, his plan.

The second she sits down, Daniel starts fussing. Babies are so selfish and annoying sometimes. Reagan rolls her eyes and gets back up. She takes a seat in the rocking chair and feeds Daniel, all the while wishing she could be outside. Everyone is working and contributing, and she's parenting. Kids are such a bother. Holding him makes her realize just how helpless these children of the apocalypse are. He could've been killed last night, so could have the other kids on the farm. It turns her stomach to think of them being so dependent on everyone. They don't even realize the dangers around them.

Someone outside yelling draws her attention. Cory is waving at the kitchen window calling Hannah's name and holding another chicken he must've found. He's got a huge, bright white smile plastered to his face.

"What a moron," Paige says behind her, startling Reagan.

"Yep, that's Cory," Reagan agrees with a laugh. "What are you doing inside?"

"Said moron sent me in," she tells Reagan as she sits on the cushioned window seat.

"How come? I thought you were helping in the greenhouse," Reagan asks.

"I passed out last night, so he's freaking out. Now he's got John and Derek freaking out about it, too, and they all ganged up on me till I came inside."

"Passed out? Blacked out, lost consciousness?"

"Yeah, I guess," she answers. "I don't remember much other than the colorful stars."

"Had you not eaten? Were you dehydrated?" Reagan asks with growing concern. She places Daniel on her shoulder and pats his back. Why had nobody ever invented a baby-burper? That would've been convenient.

"Yes, I ate. I felt fine. I wasn't dehydrated. I was just overwhelmed looking at Cory's gory leg. And he got shot, right? I'm the one who has to come in and take a break, but he was shot last night and gets to keep working."

She groans, causing Reagan to smile.

Then she remembers, "Paige, you never passed out at the clinic when you were helping us. Has this ever happened to you before? I mean, before you came here."

"Nah, I'm fine. It was just hot."

Reagan regards her, studying Paige through doctor's eyes. She seems healthy, strong even. She ate, wasn't dehydrated, doesn't have a history of passing out. Puzzling.

She decides to let it pass for the time being but does tease her with a chuckle, "Maybe you're pregnant."

Paige's gray eyes meet hers and then she laughs. Reagan laughs, too. Paige's laugh came later than Reagan would've expected.

"Immaculate conception?" Reagan asks, more serious this time.

"Right," her friend says with a half-grin.

"Are you withholding information from your doctor?" Reagan inquires, laying Daniel down in her arms again to finish drinking his bottle. High maintenance pains in the butt, babies are.

"What?" Paige asks with surprise. "No, nothing to report."

"Hm," Reagan says with speculation as she regards Paige through critical eyes. She's acting strangely. "Seeing someone in town?"

"What? No," Paige repeats. "There's nothing to tell. Why? What have you heard?"

"Nothing. You're acting awfully guilty about something, though. What do you want to confess?"

Paige laughs nervously, "Nothing. Stop it!"

Her friend is squirming and trying to joke. Reagan smiles and lets her off the hook but finds herself more curious than she was only a moment before. She wishes Hannah were here for this conversation. She'd sniff out a ruse if there is one.

"All right," Reagan says and drops it. "But I want to check your blood pressure later this evening after dinner. Be careful getting a shower, too. Have one of us girls sit in there with you."

"What? No, I'll be fine."

"I'm serious," Reagan warns. "If your blood pressure is bottoming out, it could happen again. You had very low blood pressure for about two months after the shooting. I want to check you out thoroughly tonight. Doctor's orders."

"You are the bossiest doctor I've ever known," Paige teases and looks out the window. Something has her full attention, but Reagan can't see what it is from her seat.

"Incorrect, I just have stubborn patients," Reagan responds.

"I'm going to help the girls with dinner," Paige says and leaves before Reagan can ask any further questions.

As the sun sets on their first day after the tornado, the family eventually joins together for dinner, although the men want to continue working. Hannah will not take no for an answer and insists they all sit down for a good meal.

"We salvaged some of the vegetables from the greenhouse and made a nice venison stew," Sue says as they all take a seat at the dinner table.

"Was everything in the greenhouse destroyed?" Grandpa asks.

"No, not everything," Sue answers. "Just beat up pretty badly. I think we can transplant for new starts. Gretchen helped me earlier with some. I'll try to finish tomorrow."

"Good," Grandpa says.

"Mm, smells wonderful, darling," Derek praises, earning a smile and a kiss from his wife.

"Yeah, this looks great," Reagan says as she takes her bowl back from Kelly who is serving from the soup tureen. It is a white, stoneware antique, passed down from Gram's mother, and Reagan was told by Grams that it was a piece from Ireland. She's thankful that it wasn't destroyed last night in the storm or much else in the house for that matter. As wonderful as the stew smells, she is going to be cautious about eating too much in case she is in labor and not just having false contractions.

The children are eating in the other room and being supervised by Huntley and G and her brother while the rest of them eat in the dining room. They keep the conversation light until dinner is nearly over.

"We'll work on getting the rest of the animals rounded up when we're done with dinner, sir," John says to Grandpa between mouthfuls of stew. "Huntley's going out on horseback to see if he can find the five horses that are missing."

Her husband seems ravenous. None of them stopped to eat breakfast or to grab food at all today. They came straight home without sleep and began working on putting their precious farm back together.

"You guys need to get some rest," Sue tells them.

"We're going back out," Kelly says. "We have to. There's just too much to do still tonight. The kids are gonna need to be in charge of feeding the animals and handling normal chores without us while we finish up on the roof. If it storms again, water will come in."

"Yeah, I don't want to wake up in the middle of the night wishing I had a pontoon boat instead of a bed," John remarks lightly.

"Wish I could help more," Derek laments quietly.

John places his hand on his brother's shoulder and says, "You are, bro. Staying on the ground is actually helping a lot. You can send Luke and Justin for tools and nails and supplies and stuff. It's actually going faster having you on the ground acting as the liaison."

John goes right back to his meal without missing a beat. Reagan knows he is trying to act nonchalant so that attention doesn't focus on Derek's new disability. Her husband must feel so helpless about his brother's condition. Reagan feels the same. She and

420

Grandpa have had many late night meetings about what they could do for Derek. Neither of them has come up with a solution yet.

The men have second helpings, but Reagan passes. The cramping has let up, but she wants to do some tests later in the shed to make sure she's not in labor. The med shed, thankfully, went unscathed. She's not sure what they would do without that small building.

"Are you guys going on a supply run?" Hannah asks with trepidation.

"Yeah, Hannie," Cory answers. "We have to. We're gonna need some metal roofing for the barn. Or, heck, I guess whatever we can find. We'll try not to mess up the aesthetic of your farm, Herb, and make it look like a patchwork quilt."

"I understand," Hannah says.

"I appreciate that, Cory," Grandpa jests with a smile. "I'm just glad it's still here to patch together at all, son."

"Amen to that," Kelly says.

"When will you go?" Hannah asks with pleading eyes.

"Soon, probably tomorrow, baby," Kelly answers her.

She looks down at her bowl of soup and doesn't look back up. Sue does the same. Reagan knows her sisters are displeased, but the men are right.

"The cabins are both fine," Simon tells everyone. "I went out earlier with Huntley to check on them. I didn't see any damage at your house, Derek, or ours."

"Great," Sue says with genuine feeling.

Derek just offers a grim expression of gratitude. None of them are sure if his family will ever be able to live out there again so far from the main house.

"Thanks for checking it out, Simon," Derek says.

"Well, boys," Kelly says and stands, "Let's get back to it."

"Hooah," John says as he also stands.

Cory jams a piece of bread into his mouth and follows, snatching another piece from the basket as he goes. Simon dabs at his mouth with a linen napkin, praises the meal to the girls, and takes his empty bowl to the kitchen. Those two could not possibly be more different, but Reagan loves them both. Without the younger men on the farm, they'd be in trouble. It takes every member of the family to keep the farm operating correctly. She still can't believe she didn't want John and Kelly to be allowed to stay on their farm when they first came to it.

"Give us a few hours," Derek says to them as John helps him to his crutches. "We'll come back in and have a meeting at twenty-two hundred hours."

"Ten? Can't you just say ten?" Reagan razzes him and gets a broad smile.

"Ten, little Doc," he returns.

The kids clean up after dinner as she takes the littler ones to the upstairs bathroom to help them get ready for bed. It's always a long process, but one that she usually enjoys. Tonight is just difficult because she doesn't feel so great, and the kids are filthy from helping as best as they could outside today. They wanted to be helpful, too, so the men gave them small tasks, all of which were apparently dirty jobs.

An hour later, she has Jacob, Isaac, Ari, and Mary tucked into their bunks in the basement. She has to reassure them many times that they are safe and that another tornado isn't coming tonight. Kissing their downy soft foreheads and then a few cheeks is the best part of her day so far. G and Justin are still upstairs doing their own nightly rituals, but Lucas is outside helping the men and was glad to do so according to what John told her earlier. Her new brother has been an asset to the family dynamic, especially since Derek is down. Once she makes sure Hannah has everything she needs, Reagan takes Paige to the med shed to check her out against her will and with many protests.

"Your pressure's up," Reagan says when she removes the cuff. "I thought it might be low, so it's definitely not that. Heck, all of us probably has overly high blood pressure right now, but yours is fine. Right in the normal range."

422

A cramping in her stomach causes her to touch it, wince, and turn away.

"Hey, what the hell? Are you ok?" Paige asks.

"Fine. Just a lot of activity tonight," Reagan fabricates and checks the glands in Paige's neck. Grandpa comes in a moment later.

"I just heard you got a little light-headed last night, young lady," he remarks and pulls on gloves.

Paige groans, "No, I'm just fine, Dr. McClane. I just got too hot, and there was a lot of blood and… ugh."

He chuckles and looks at the notations Reagan has made on a notepad.

"BP looks good. Color is good," he remarks. He then puts Paige through a thorough examination and has Reagan write down more notes. "Pupil dilation is normal. We can do a blood count tomorrow again, but I don't see any atypical signs of a problem there anymore. Everything seems fine. Pulse is a little high, but nothing to worry about."

"I agree," Reagan states. "Like I said, be careful, take precautions, don't be overly confident."

"Got it," Paige answers with a salute and hops down from the exam table.

"Hey, can you get Cory for us?" Reagan requests.

"Isn't he on the roof?" Paige asks.

"No, I think I saw them coming down a little bit ago. He's probably out by the barns now," Reagan says. "Some of them were headed that way."

The second Paige is gone, Grandpa touches her arm.

"What's going on, honey?" he asks.

"What do you mean?"

He just tilts his head to the side and gives her a knowing look. She's never been good at hiding anything from her grandfather.

"Nothing. Just some contractions or cramps or something."

"Are you spotting?"

"No, nothing that serious. Like I said, just false labor. Probably."

"You should let me check you," he says.

Reagan snorts. "No, thanks."

"Reagan!" he scolds softly. "Who do you think is going to deliver this baby?"

"Me?"

He chuckles, removes his gloves, and pushes his hands into his trouser pockets.

"Symptoms, Dr. McClane?" he requests.

"Tired. Irritable. Tornado hit our farm last night," she jokes.

He nods and smiles, "This could be stress. I have seen this with patients quite a bit in my lifetime as a doctor, especially pregnant patients. It's not good for women to get overly stressed during pregnancy."

"Well, we almost died last night, so..." she lets hang.

He smiles again and says, "Yes, but you need to slow down. I don't want you laboring on the clean-up detail around here. Let the others handle that. Stay inside and take care of the children. Help your sisters. Put your feet up for a few days."

"Like that's gonna happen," she argues softly.

"It is," he says firmly, drawing Reagan's attention. "Don't make me get John involved."

She sneers at her grandfather. "That was dirty."

"I've still got a few tricks up these old sleeves," he says with a smile. "Let me at least get a listen."

Reagan sits on the exam table while her grandfather listens to the baby's heartbeat and then hers. He makes her lie back and listens again. Reagan does the same. He smiles at her when she also presses her stethoscope to her stomach. It seems strange to hear her own heart and another in the same body beating so much faster.

"Fast and strong. This little guy might come out ready for airborne school," he says.

"Or a scientist," she corrects.

"Maybe both like our Simon," he suggests.

"Good Lord, let's hope not," Reagan jokes as he presses his hands to her stomach, moving them all around and examining it thoroughly. "We don't need another eighty-year-old young person around here."

"He is an old soul, isn't he?" Grandpa asks rhetorically.

"Pain in the ass sometimes, too," she tells him. "Thank God G came to live here. She's giving him a hard time a lot lately, I've noticed."

"I would expect no less from one of my granddaughters," he teases with a smile.

"Hey," she says softly and grins.

He says and helps her sit upright again, "I wouldn't have it any other way. My girls are perfect just the way they are."

Then he hugs her. Reagan hugs him back. She knows how stressful the past twenty-four hours have been for him, too, and that he could use a shoulder to lean on. Grams is gone. He doesn't have that companionship anymore. He feels a lot of responsibility for the future of his family and knows their desperate need of this farm.

"Love you, little honey."

"I love you, too, Grandpa."

Cory walks in a second later with Paige. It's good. It gives Reagan something to do other than getting overly emotional. She starts griping at Cory instead. First, she lectures him because two of his stitches have pulled. His leg is bleeding pretty steadily in a thin trickle and is completely filthy. The bandage Dave's medic used has turned brown with dirt, and the wound is covered in it, as well. Grandpa assists and twenty minutes later, they have him patched back up. Paige even sticks around to help, although Reagan advises her to leave lest she hit the deck again. She stays anyways.

"Might wanna' keep all that out," Cory says with a smartass smirk and points to their tray of instruments. "I'll probably need it again tomorrow."

"Idiot," Reagan says and hits the back of his head the way Grams used to do to people. That woman was a genius because it does actually make Reagan feel a little better.

He laughs and leaves the shed with Paige. He may be a cocky man, but he is limping a little more now. He's going to be sore as hell tomorrow.

The family reconvenes at the dining table for a meeting with the men and Paige. Hannah and Sue have set out cold milk and scones they must've made while everyone finished working throughout the evening. It is late, but the men attack the sweets as if they haven't eaten in days. Her sisters must've pulled frozen blueberries out of the freezer in the basement and used them in the recipe. There is even a drizzle of icing on the tops. Reagan helps herself to one to cease her growling stomach. If this kid thinks she's gaining forty pounds to please him, he's got another thing coming. He'll get the rations he's given and be happy about it.

"So you were saying earlier, John, that you think you found the highwaymen?" Simon is the first to ask.

"Yeah, I think they attacked Cory and Paige last night," her husband answers.

"When he was shot?" Reagan asks.

John nods and says with a frown, "Yes, they were at the cabin alone when they received unexpected company."

"Where were you?" Simon asks, a nervous edge to his voice.

Reagan's not sure why he seems to have a problem with this. It's normal for teams to split up on a run. What's not normal is for strangers to find the family's safe sanctuaries that they thought were hidden so well.

"Doing surveillance on a golf course over there," Kelly answers.

"What was going on at the golf course?" Sue asks.

"A lot actually," Kelly says.

John gives a more in depth answer for them, "There is a fairly large community established there now that wasn't the last time we went to Clarksville."

"That was fast. Were they a threat?" Derek asks.

"Not sure," her husband says. Reagan takes his hand under the table. He squeezes tightly. "We watched for hours but didn't see

426

anything that could be considered trouble. Then we were interrupted when Cory needed us."

"They could be trouble," Cory adds. "We aren't sure. They had armed guards and a lot of people."

"Women and children, too?" Hannah asks.

"We eventually saw women but not kids," Kelly answers her.

"Did they seem dangerous?" Hannah further questions, her pale brow wrinkling.

Kelly encompasses her frail hand and says, "I don't know yet, baby. Dave watched them with us for a while, too."

"Are they the highwaymen?" Grandpa asks.

"Don't think so," John answers before taking a drink of his milk. "I didn't see any of them with weapons like I took off of the ones up in the woods who were shooting at Cory and Paige. Like I said, we could be wrong. I don't know if the golf course people are or aren't the highwaymen. We were pulled away from our observation."

"We never saw a dark pick-up truck leave the golf course compound, though," Kelly says.

"How did they find the cabin, the ones who shot at Cory and Paige?" Reagan asks, concerned about their small sanctuary that provided a temporary respite from the stresses of going on a run.

"Not sure," John tells her. "Could've tracked Cory and Paige, but I don't see how."

"Those men that shot Cory and attacked the cabin, they got away?" Grandpa inquires.

He's taking notes. This doesn't surprise Reagan. The only thing missing is a mug of coffee in front of him and his pipe.

John answers again, "We were able to deal with some of them, but quite a few got away. I even grabbed one of their guns and a set of their night-vision gear. The one I...saw on the ground had on a bulletproof vest, too."

She's quite sure how the man got on the ground if John was in the vicinity. Her husband probably killed him.

"What evidence do we have that these men could be the highwaymen?" Grandpa asks.

"They had a truck that could've been Henry's, the one that was stolen when Derek was hit," Kelly says. "Cory got a look at it. With the rain and the dark, it was hard to see it clearly. Kind of hard to confirm it, but it did have an extended cab. It was also dark blue or black paint like Henry's."

"Interesting," Grandpa remarks. "And their weaponry, John?"

"The pistol I took was the same as what we'd call standard issue 9 mill. The vest was military grade Kevlar. But the people at the golf course weren't carrying anything like we used to carry in the Army. They mostly had shotguns and pistols, wood grips and stocks, that kind of thing. Nothing tactical, no military or police gear or weapons."

Reagan interrupts to make a point, "The men that attacked the cabin could've looted a military base, though. Or they could've killed a group of military men like Dave's or…you guys and took their weapons."

It is hard to say that their men could've been killed by anyone. It makes her anxious just thinking about such a sickening scenario.

"Possible," Derek says. "What else?"

"They seemed more organized than the others we've come up against," Kelly tells them. "They outflanked Cory in the woods. I mean, seriously. Cory got outflanked? *Cory?* That ain't right."

Reagan can tell that he holds his little brother's experience at being more lethal and stealthier than their enemy at fairly high standards of measure. She agrees wholeheartedly. The kid survived for nearly a year by himself, unless she counts his horse and dog, who were both glad to see him today.

"I was slowing him down, though," Paige puts in, defending her mortal enemy.

"No, you weren't," Cory counters. "Not really, Red."

"This could be a potential problem," Derek notes with concern.

"It was raining, so I couldn't see well enough to know if they were wearing headsets and mics or were using hand signals or anything," John says. "We were just trying to get out of there, especially with Paige being with us. She's just now better. Don't want her to get any more bullet holes in her just yet. The librarian's only got so much blood to give."

Everyone chuckles, Paige included. She also nods with good humor. Reagan notices that Cory does not. Neither does her brother. They are both sullen, and Simon actually looks offended by the joke. If John notices, he does nothing to acknowledge it. Simon already wasn't happy about her going.

"We aren't sure yet how many we're going up against," Kelly says.

"And now the hunt needs to stop," Derek explains. "We've got to put this place back together first. Then our town. There are bound to be people in town who can't take care of their own property damage, older people or single moms. They're going to need our help."

"Agreed," Grandpa says. "It's the right thing to do."

Derek continues, "If the people in Dave's town need our help, we should assist Dave, as well. He'd do it for us. They do a lot for us."

Sue observes, "Traveling to get supplies all the time during the next few weeks then is going to become very dangerous. We aren't going to be the only people who need things."

"True enough, Sue," John agrees. "But we need supplies. I'm sure we'll be making a hodge-podge patchwork job of it, but we can't manufacture our own metal and nails and things like that. The barn siding we can rip on the portable mill out of the lumber we already have, but the other stuff will have to come from a supply yard or stores."

"Simon and I can take Huntley and go first thing," Cory volunteers and gets a nod from Simon.

429

"Agreed," Simon states emphatically. "I'd be happy to go."

"Sounds good, guys," John says. "I'll see if any of the neighbors want to go along with you. I'm sure they're going to need things, too. I could stay here with Kelly and Luke and start working on the buildings. We've got a lot of repairs that need done, and this isn't going to be a quick job."

"Right," Cory says.

"I could go and help, too," Paige volunteers.

Derek stops her, "No, we'll need you here. If a structural issue comes up, I'd like to be able to consult with you on it. Plus, with me not able to do much, you could help John and Kelly."

"Great. Sounds great to me," she agrees.

"And Luke could go, too, for added security," John suggests.

"Yes, sir," Lucas is quick to say. "I'd be happy to go. I used to do it with my father."

Reagan finds this curious. She didn't know her father and brother were going on runs, and it makes her wonder if it was when they were at the bunker or alone out in the woods at her father's hidden cabin in Portland. A lock of her brother's dark brown hair has fallen over his forehead, and he pushes it back. Normally, he is impeccably neat and put together like Robert, but tonight he looks disheveled and dirty like the rest of the men.

"The barn spigot broke in the milk house," Kelly tells them. "Piece of four by four lumber hit it during the storm. I patched it to get the water to stop flooding into the loafing shed, but it'll need to be dealt with first thing."

"Yeah, the floor's nice and clean now," Cory says.

Lucas, in an unusual move, jokes, "I wish I would've known that was going to happen. I wouldn't have wasted my time shoveling manure the other day."

"Just needed a flood," Kelly says and slaps him on the back. Luke smiles.

John joins in, of course, "Don't worry, buddy. There'll be more to shovel by the end of next week."

Everyone chuckles. Reagan yawns and stretches her tired back. The meeting ends a few minutes later, and she joins her husband upstairs where they share a fast shower together. When she finally hits the sack for the night, her muscles are sore, achy and her body is physically spent as if she's run a marathon. She understands that most of her fatigue is from stress. The rest is from the alien invader.

John snuggles up to her, spooning her from behind. He rests his palm flat against her distended abdomen like he does most nights. Then he nuzzles into her neck.

"I'm so glad you weren't hurt, babe," he says with a frown she doesn't need to see to know is there.

"Ditto," Reagan says, not as capable of expressing her inner feelings as her husband.

"Don't know what I'd do without my boss," he says and kisses her neck.

"Probably get into more trouble than you should," she informs him.

John smiles against her cheek where he then kisses. He is dead asleep in the next instant, his face buried in her hair, his hand expertly trained to lie protectively over her stomach. Reagan doesn't fall asleep so fast. She stays awake for a while thinking about what she'd do if she lost John. The results and scenarios she plays through her mind all have disastrous outcomes. She could never bear to lose him. John is her whole world. They have become two halves of a whole, and he's probably the better half if she's being honest with herself. Her heart begins to pound harder as she imagines him not having returned to her this morning but having instead been killed by the storm. And now they are bringing another life into an even bigger storm, the new America, one filled with danger and disaster and unhappy endings at every turn.

The baby kicks harder as if picking up on her anxiety, and Reagan is forced to calm down. Bringing this child into the world may just be the dumbest thing she's ever done. She just hopes she can hold onto this pregnancy long enough to give the kid a fighting chance.

Epilogue
Herb

A knock at his office door draws his attention away from the notations he was making about Talia's new baby, and Herb calls for the person to enter. The meeting with the men ended almost an hour ago, but he couldn't sleep.

"Hey," Gretchen says softly as she enters his den.

"Couldn't sleep, honey?" he asks, knowing full well that she must not be able to or she wouldn't still be awake at this late hour.

"No, I'm a night owl anyways," she replies.

He indicates the comfortable leather sofa and takes a seat across from her on the other one, which is usually his bed.

"And what has you awake this fine evening?" he asks.

She shrugs, but Herb can tell she has a lot on her young mind, probably too much.

He tries a different angle, "Have you ever been in a storm like that before?"

Her eyes widen. He's hit a tender spot.

"No, way. That was...holy cow."

"Don't get a whole lot of tornadoes in the Northwest, I suppose," he says with a nod.

"None that I know of," she remarks. "Not where we lived."

His granddaughter is fighting with every ounce of herself to suppress all feminine traits she might have. She's mostly failing, but he'll let her work this out on her own. Her rebellion is written all over her appearance, and Herb assumes it is to lash out at Robert. It likely works, too, because his son would not like his daughter to have a short, cropped, tomboyish hairstyle; short, dark fingernails; oversized, disheveled clothing; black lug sole, combat-style boots; and multiple earrings in both ears. He can only imagine Robert's fits of temper over his daughter's grungy, unruly look.

"No, I don't suppose you would have storms like the one we had last night. Heck, we don't usually have storms like that, either," he says. "A lot of rain where you lived, though, I presume."

"Yeah, that got old sometimes," she admits. "I like the weather here a lot better."

"Good, I'm glad," he says and takes a sip of his hot tea. Then he offers a drink to her. She declines.

"I used to live on caffeine," she confesses.

"I wonder where you got that trait," he teases. "Chip off the old block, your grandpa's block, that is."

"Yeah, probably. Mom would drink tea sometimes but not coffee. Dad, well, you know Dad. He didn't believe in vice, so no caffeine or coffee for him."

"Where'd you get such a nasty habit?" he asks with a smile.

"I used to get up late for school all the time, and Dad would get pissed," she swears, then blushes. Herb just urges her to continue. "So, I learned to hit the soda machine in our school to get my caffeine fix. That did the trick. I drank soda every day. That was my breakfast. I'd buy coffee and espressos in coffee shops. They were on every corner up there."

"Probably why you're so lean," he comments on her figure. "A young lady needs more than sugar and caffeine to grow bigger."

She grins crookedly, and something in her smile reminds him of his Mary. He wishes his wife could've met Gretchen and her brother. She would've loved them.

"I had some major bad withdrawal headaches when I couldn't get any more," she says.

"Yes, you and I both, my dear."

"Luke never drank soda or coffee," she tells him. "He was too square for that."

"Square?"

"Straight-laced, a real dork," she says.

She may be admonishing her brother, but Herb has watched them together. Gretchen rarely leaves his side for more than a few minutes, and when she does, Lucas's eyes monitor her every move.

"Would that we could all be so disciplined," he joins in with a patient smile.

"He never did anything bad. I was always the one getting reamed by Dad."

"Perhaps he just cares too much," he says, trying to soften her severe opinion of his son. "Sometimes parents push hard because they care too much."

She snorts.

"Do you miss them, Gretchen?" he asks, noting how her eyes flash for just a moment.

She doesn't answer but, instead, hits him with a surprise question, shocking Herb to his core.

"Can I stay here, Grandpa?"

He frowns. "What do you mean, honey? You are here."

"No, I mean if my dad wants us to come up there and live, can I just stay here? I don't wanna' go up there. I don't wanna' live on some military base and start over again. I don't know anyone there. Me and Luke will just be ignored all the time again. Dad'll only want Luke when he needs his help with something stupid that he can't handle himself."

Herb was actually afraid of this happening. He's watched Gretchen very closely every day on his farm, observing her habits, seeing who she has been interacting with, and what she does with her time. She fits in with the girls, seems to enjoy the companionship of the men, as well, and never complains.

"I don't know if that will be up to me, honey," he answers what he's been thinking.

"Why not?" she asks, all bright eyes and hopefulness.

Gretchen has her legs tucked under her on the sofa, and she looks like a little girl not more than Ari's age. Beneath her surly exterior, this false appearance that she wants everyone to believe, there is a little girl that's scared and lost and who's seen more than she ever should have if Herb were to guess.

"Your mother and father are your guardians."

"Would you...let me stay if they say I can?"

The timidity in her tiny voice breaks his heart. She is so used to rejection- the rejection of her father which makes it even harder for Herb to swallow- that she is afraid to make eye contact.

"Oh, sweetheart, of course, I would," he says and crosses to sit next to her. There are unshed tears in her hazel brown eyes. "You and Lucas are family now. You belong here. You're my blood. You never have to leave unless your mother and father won't allow you to stay."

"But I don't want to live up there on that stupid base with them," she says. "Grandpa, I want to stay here with you. I like it here. I feel safe. I have friends finally."

This makes him sad and also a little protective of his young granddaughter. He doesn't want to come to verbal blows with Robert on the matter someday.

"I'll see what I can do, all right?" he says, to which she nods and offers a sad little smile. "Now, why don't you tell me what it was like where you grew up? Tell me about your schooling."

She rolls her eyes and talks for the next hour about herself and her brother, and even occasionally about her mother. She never once mentions Robert, which provides Herb with just a little further insight into their dysfunctional relationship. She asks about his life, and Herb shares with her what it was like growing up on this farm and then leaving it for med school when he was so young just like Reagan. She tells him about her life in her private school, where it doesn't sound like she had many friends. Then she talks extensively about life in the bunker. She didn't have a whole lot more friends there. No wonder she is anxious about leaving the farm. He doesn't want that for her and her brother, either.

After a few quiet minutes without her chatter, Herb realizes that she's fallen asleep against his shoulder where she'd slowly but surely started to droop. He lies her gently down on the sofa and props her head with a throw pillow. Then he pulls down the worn, soft, patchwork quilt that Mary stitched years ago when they were first married. Smoothing her short hair back from her face, Herb looks down at his granddaughter and smiles. She's a joy to have around, much like the rest of his granddaughters. He's also looking forward to getting to know her brother better, although he seems a bit more standoffish than Gretchen. He wonders if Lucas will share her sentiment of wanting to remain on the farm or if he'll insist on going to live at Fort Knox with his father. His grandson seems a lot more loyal to Robert than Gretchen. Only time will tell, but he's not sure where he stands on the issue of them remaining on the farm if Robert wants them with him. His loyalty to his son should take precedence in this matter, but he has come to love Gretchen.

He leaves his office, turning off all but the low wattage lamp on his desk and meanders down the hall to the kitchen. Reagan is seated at the island.

"Everything all right, dear?" he asks, worried about her pregnancy. Last night was a lot of stress for a pregnant woman, even one like Reagan.

"Yeah, just hungry and couldn't sleep," she tells him.

It's after midnight, but he'll refrain from pointing out the possibility of acid reflux. She could use the extra calories.

"Want some?" she asks, pointing to her bowl.

The smells are appealing. "What are you having?"

"Leftover pasta," she answers. "Don't care if it gives me heartburn. I'm hungry. The kid's asleep for now and not making me puke. So I'm eating."

He chuckles and says, "I'll stick with my tea. And maybe a muffin."

He reaches for the sweets under the glass dome.

"Hannah's gonna kick your butt. Those are for breakfast."

"I'll take my chances," he says. "I thought I smelled something baking earlier this evening."

"What kind did they make?"

Herb takes a bite and answers, "It would appear to be chocolate chip."

"Oh, man," Reagan laments. "Damn it! If I'd known that, I would've had one of those instead. I thought they were blueberry. The guys must've found chocolate chips. Damn, why can't we grow cocoa beans on the farm?"

He chuckles and nods in agreement. "And coffee beans while we're at it."

"Right," she complains as she twirls more pasta onto her fork. "Screw this fixing up cars and CNG gas crap."

"And corn and wheat," he adds playfully.

She smiles and returns to her midnight meal.

"Huntley found three sheep out behind the barns," she tells him.

"Sheep, huh?" Herb says. "Wonder where they came from?"

"Not sure," she replies. "The tornado must've sent a lot of animals scattering. I told him we should fence them in with the goats and keep them."

"Yes, we should," Herb agrees. "If the neighbors hear of anyone missing them, we'll at least have kept them safe from predators until then."

"Or mutton stew is always an option in the fall if they go unclaimed," she quips on a deviant grin.

He smiles and touches her soft cheek, the one with the faded, white scar. It does nothing to detract from her beauty, nothing could.

"We still lost a mare and two cows," she says sadly. "And three horses are still missing."

"That's a shame," he says.

"Yeah, John and Cory used the tractors to haul them away and bury them."

"Too bad we didn't know about it in advance," he says. "Could've butchered them. Such a waste."

438

"And thirteen chickens," she tells him. "We didn't tell Hannah yet."

'Probably a good idea."

"Some of them are just missing," she says. "I guess they were blown away or something."

"I'm sure there is more damage yet to be discovered," he comments.

Reagan lays her hand across his and nods. "We'll get it all figured out, Grandpa. Don't worry."

He attempts a smile but is sure it doesn't come off as much of one. Reagan rises and places her plate in the sink. She stands there for a long time just looking down at the ledge of the sink where her hands are placed. Then she turns to face him.

"Grandpa, we have to tell Derek," she says quietly.

Herb nods with acknowledgment. "I know."

"John doesn't want us to, but Derek is starting to figure it out. He's asked me more than once about his leg, the condition, whether it's going to get better than this. It's not, but I can't tell him that. John swore us to secrecy. And I don't feel right by lying and avoiding his questions all the time. It's not right."

"I know," he repeats. "I'll speak with John soon. Derek has a right to know."

"'Kay," she says, her brow wrinkling.

"You, go on up to bed now, honey," he orders softly. "You need your rest."

She kisses his unshaven cheek and remarks, "Cory's not the only one around here who is resembling a caveman lately."

This time he does smile. Leave it to his Reagan to point out his unkempt appearance.

"G'night, Grandpa," she says and touches his shoulder gently.

"Get some rest, honey," he says and pats her hand before she leaves.

Herb goes to the back porch and sips his hot tea in the dark while sitting on the glider rocker he used to share so often with his beloved wife. He can just make out Cory and Simon down by the horse barn. Cory laughs at something his friend says. Then they split up and go their own ways on watch duty.

He's thankful for the men on this farm because he's not getting any younger, and the farm needs protected and now rebuilt. They are lucky they weren't all killed last night. The home his ancestors built so many generations ago still stands, which makes him proud of it in some ways. It has stood the test of time literally against weather, people who would destroy it, and hardship. It has seen family come and go and return again. It has seen the loss of its people and the birth of a new generation. This farm is so ingrained in his veins that he could never lose it. It's a part of him, a part of his children and grandchildren and adopted children. There is something about this place, the land, the valley in which it is nestled that calls to each and every one of them. It belongs to all of them and has become their ancestral homeland.

Herb rocks gently back and forth on the bench and takes a sip of his tea as he ponders his farm. He can almost feel his Mary sitting with him talking about the kids and the farm. These phantasmal hallucinations are the useless longings of an old man who has lost his mate, but he's accepted them, nonetheless.

As long as the family living on this farm continues to thrive and hold it all together, it'll make it. He just worries that something or someone will intervene and change the path they are all on and destroy their home and them. They must not allow that to happen. They must, at all costs, hold on to the farm and each other. This land is an integral part of who they all are now. Whether or not they were born of others, the McClane farm is theirs. They cannot ever allow it to be taken or destroyed because they are all McClanes.